THE OUTSIDER

BY PENELOPE WILLIAMSON

The Outsider

Heart of the West

Once in a Blue Moon

Keeper of the Dream

A Wild Yearning

Hearts Beguiled

Beloved Rogue

Wings of Desire
(as Elizabeth Lambert)

THE OUTSIDER

PENELOPE WILLIAMSON

POCKET BOOKS
New York London Toronto Sydney New Delhi

Pocket Books
A Division of Simon & Schuster, Inc.
1230 Avenue of the Americas
New York, NY 10020

First Pocket Books paperback edition July 2014

Interior design by Leydiana Rodríguez-Ovalles
Cover design by Min Choi
Cover illustration by Anna Kmet

Manufactured in the United States of America

10 9 8 7 6 5 4 3 2 1

ISBN 978-1-4767-3101-8
ISBN 978-1-4767-4007-2 (ebook)

For Derek.

Because, still, after twenty-five years . . .

1

HE CAME INTO THEIR lives during the last ragged days of a Montana winter.

It was the time of year when the country got to looking bleak and tired from the cold. The snow lay in yellowed clumps like old candle wax, the cottonwoods cracked and popped in the raw air, and spring was still more a memory than a promise.

That Sunday morning, the day he came, Rachel Yoder hadn't wanted to get out of bed. She lay beneath the heavy quilt, her gaze on the window that framed a gray sky. She listened to the creak of the wind-battered walls and felt bruised with a weariness that had settled and gone bone deep.

She lay there and listened to Benjo stoking up the fire in the kitchen: the clatter of a stove lid, the rattle of kindling in the woodbox, the scrape of the ash shovel. Then the house fell quiet and she knew he was staring at her closed door, wondering why she wasn't up yet, fretting about it.

She swung her legs onto the floor, shuddering at the cold blast of air that billowed up under her nightrail from the bare pine boards. She dressed without bothering to light the lamp. As she did every morning, she put on a plain dark brown bodice and skirts and a plain black apron. Over her shoulders she draped a black triangular shawl, whose two long ends crossed over her breasts and pinned around her waist. Her fingers were clumsy with the cold, and she had a hard time pushing the thick blanket pins through the stiff wool. Yet it was the Plain and narrow way to use no hooks and eyes or buttons. The women of the Plain People had always fastened their clothes with pins and they always would.

She did her hair last. It was thick and long, curling down to her hips, and it had the color of polished mahogany. Or so the only man who'd ever seen it let down had once told her. A soft smile touched her lips at the memory. Polished mahogany, he had said. And this from the mouth of a man who'd been born into the Plain life and known no other, and surely never looked upon mahogany, polished or dull, in all of his days. *Oh, Ben.*

He'd always loved her hair and so she had to be careful not to let it be her vanity. Pulling it back, she twisted it into a knot, then covered it completely with her *Kapp,* a starched white cambric prayer cap. She had to feel with her fingers for the cap's stiff middle pleat to be sure it was centered on her head. They'd never had any mirrors, not in this house or the house she'd grown up in.

The warmth of the kitchen beckoned, yet she paused in the cold and murky light of the dawn to stare out the curtainless window. A stand of jack pines along the hill in back of the river had died during the winter and was now the color of old rust. Clouds draped over the shoulders of the buttes, leaden with the threat of more snow. "Come on, spring," she whispered. "Please hurry."

She lowered her head, laying it against the cold glass pane. Here she was wishing for spring, but with spring came the lambing time and more than a month's worth of worry and toil.

And this spring she'd have to live it on her own.

"Oh, Ben," she said again, this time aloud.

She pressed her lips together against her weakness. Her husband knew a better life now, the eternal life, warm and safe in God's bosom and the glory of heaven. It was selfish of her to miss him. If only for the sake of their son, she had to find the courage to surrender to God's will.

She pushed away from the window and made herself smile as she pulled open her bedroom door and stepped into the warmth and yellow light of the kitchen.

Benjo stood at the table, pouring coffee beans into the mill. At the click of the latch his hand jerked, and beans scattered across the brown oilcloth. His eyes, too bright, fastened hard on her face.

"Mem? Why are you up suh—suh—so late? Are you fuh—fuh—fuh . . ." He clenched his teeth together as his throat worked to expel the word that was stuck somewhere between his head and his tongue.

Doc Henry said that if her boy was ever going to get over his stuttering, she had to quit finishing his sentences for him and let him do his own battling with the words. But she did ache to watch him struggle like this, so much that sometimes she couldn't bear it.

She shook her head as she came up to him, saying, "I'm only feeling a little lazy is all." Gently she brushed the hair out of his eyes. She hardly had to reach down to do so anymore, he was getting that big. He would be ten years old come summer. Before long he would be growing past her.

The days, how they could flow one into the other without your noticing. Somehow winter, no matter what, turned into spring, and the lambs came and the hay was cut and the wool was sheared and the ewes were mated and then the lambs came again. You got up in the morning and put on the clothes of your grandmother, you went to the preaching and sang the hymns your grandfather once sang, and your faith was their faith and would be the faith of your children's children. It was this—the way the days flowed like a river into the ocean of years—that she'd always loved about the Plain life. Time's passing became a comfort. The sweet sameness of it, the slow and steady sureness of time passing.

"I expect we got ourselves a bunch of hungry woollies out there," she said, her throat tight with a wistful sadness. "Why, folk can likely hear their bleating clear over in the next country. You'd best get started with hitching up the hay sled, while I see to our own empty bellies. We're going to be late for the preaching as 'tis." She ruffled his hair again. "And I'm feeling fine, our Benjo. Truly, I am."

Her heart ached in a sweet way this time as she watched the relief ease his face. His step was light as he went to the door, snatching up his gum boots from in front of the stove and his coat and hat from off the wall spike. His father had been a big, strapping man with black eyes and hair and a thick, chest-slapping beard. Benjo took after her: small-boned and slender even for his years, gray eyes. Mahogany hair.

He had left the door open behind him, and winter came into the kitchen on a gust of stale wind. "Mem?" he called out from the porch stoop, where he'd sat down to pull on his boots. He craned his head around to look at her, his eyes happy. "Why is it shuh—shuh—sheep're always eating?"

This time she had no trouble smiling. Benjo and his impossible questions. "I couldn't say for sure, but I suppose it takes a powerful lot of grass and hay to make all that wool."

"And all that shuh—sheep p-poop." He hooted a laugh as he jumped up, stomping his heels down into the boots.

He pumped his arms and leaped off the step into the yard, splattering icy mud all over her porch.

His shrill whistle cut through the air. MacDuff, their brown and white herding collie, burst out of the willow brakes that lined the creek. The dog made a beeline for Benjo, jumping onto his chest and nearly knocking him down. Rachel shut the door on the sound of the boy's shrieking laughter and MacDuff's barking. She smiled as she leaned against the door a moment, her head back and her shoulders flat against the rough-hewn pine.

The burp of the coffeepot sent her flying to the stove. Judas, she'd have to hurry with breakfast if they were going to make it to the preaching without being unforgivably late. They met for worship every other Sunday, all the Plain People who homesteaded this high mountain valley. Short of mortal sickness no one ever missed a preaching.

The hot lard sputtered and popped as she laid a thick slab of cornmeal mush into the fry pan. She cracked the window open a bit to fan out the smoke. The mush sizzled, the wind moaned along the sill, and from out in the pasture she heard the sheepherder's traditional call: "O-vee! O-vee!"

She glanced out the window. Benjo was having trouble coaxing the band of pregnant ewes out from beneath the shelter of the cottonwoods and into the feeding paddock. The silly animals milled in a stubborn bunch. With their long bony noses and wide eyes staring out of ruffs of gray wool, they looked from this distance like a bevy of spooked owls.

Just then Benjo stopped flapping his arms at the sheep and stood still. His head was up and slightly tilted, his gaze focused on the distance, and something about him in that moment pierced Rachel's heart. Poised still and alert beneath the cottonwoods, he suddenly seemed his father in every way.

She stepped up to the window, the pan of sizzling mush forgotten in her hand. Her breath fogged the glass and she had to wipe it clear. That was when she saw him, too, the stranger walking across their wild hay meadow. An outsider, wearing a long black duster and a black hat. Headed toward them.

There wasn't anything particularly threatening about him, yet her fingers gripped tight the handle of the fry pan. A gust of wind rattled the windowpanes, and she shivered.

HE WALKED IN A lolling, floppy kind of way, like a whiskified man whose legs were no longer on speaking terms with his head. No one ever walked in these parts. It was too empty a place for a body to go anywhere without a buggy or a horse. And a man on foot, so most of the outsiders believed, was no man at all.

Rachel left the warmth of the house and met Benjo in the yard. They both watched the stranger come, making his slow, staggering way right at them. "Maybe he's a drummer whose wagon has broken down," she said. MacDuff, still guarding the sheep beneath the cottonwoods, stood stiff-legged, a growl rumbling deep in his throat. "Or maybe he's a cowhand whose pony's pulled up lame."

The snow in the meadow had been blown into waves by the winter wind and frozen over and over by winter days and nights. Although the wind was blowing shrill now, she could hear the crunch of his boots as they broke through the ice crust.

He stumbled onto one knee. The wind caught his black duster, making it billow so that he looked like a crow, wings spread for flight, silhouetted against a pewter sky. He lurched to his feet again, and left a streak of bright wet red on the waxy yellow of the old snow.

"He's huh—huh—huh—!" Benjo cried, but Rachel had already lifted her skirts and was running.

The stranger's foot caught in a crest of ice and he went sprawling, and this time he didn't get back up. Rachel fell to her knees beside him so abruptly that Benjo, following at her heels, almost ran into her. Blood seeped into the snow in a spreading circle around them.

She laid a hand on the stranger's shoulder. The man recoiled at her touch, rearing onto his knees and flinging up his head. She saw utter terror well in his eyes before they fluttered closed and he slid again to the ground in a heap of black cloth and red blood.

The pool of blood had grown larger. The whole lower half of his black linen duster was wet and shiny with it. Bright red footprints led from the meadow back into the stand of pines from where he had come.

"Benjo," she said, her voice croaking. The boy jerked and took a step back. "Benjo, you must ride into town and fetch Doctor Henry."

"Nuh—nuh—nuh—!"

She turned on her knees and reached up to grasp the boy by the shoulders. "Benjo . . ."

His eyes were wild, and he swung his head back and forth, hard. "Cuh—cuh—cuh—"

She gave him a little shake. "Yes, you can. He knows you, so you won't need to talk. You can write it down for him."

Benjo's wide gray eyes stared back at her, his face skewed up with fear. It was always an ordeal for a boy with his Plain dress and his Plain ways to go into town, to go among the outsiders. Most often they merely stared and whispered behind their hands, but sometimes they were cruel. To a skinny Plain boy who choked on his words, they were almost always cruel.

She gripped him by the neck, nearly knocking off his hat. "Benjo, you *must.* The man is dying." She spun him around and pushed him toward the yard. "Go on, now. Go!"

The man *was* dying. She couldn't imagine why he wasn't already dead, with the blood he had lost, was still losing. She needed to get him into the house. Out of the cold wind and off the icy ground where he would die surely, and soon.

She tried to lift him and couldn't. She grasped him by the arms and dragged him, then saw the river of fresh red blood pour out from beneath him, and stopped.

She heard the suck and plop of hooves in mud and looked over her shoulder. Benjo had just come out of the barn, riding their old draft horse bareback. He stared at her a moment, then nudged the mare's rounded sides with his heels and slapped her on the rump with his hat. The horse snorted and broke into a trot, clattering over the corduroy bridge that spanned the creek and heading up the road to town, following the wagon wheel tracks left in the snow.

Rachel scooped up a handful of snow and rubbed it in the stranger's still, white face. He groaned and stirred. She slapped him on the cheek hard, then slapped him again harder. "Wake up, you. Wake up!"

He woke up, partly. Enough to push himself half onto his knees again. She saw that his right arm was broken, and bound up roughly in a sling made from a man's black silk neckcloth.

She laid his other arm over her shoulder and grasped him around the waist, and somehow got him onto his feet. "We're going to walk to the house now," she said, though she doubted he heard her. The wind blew hard, buffeting them. His breath came in ragged gasps.

They crunched through the crusty snow, wrapped up arm in arm, so close his beard-roughened cheek scraped hers and his hair whipped at her eyes. The butt of the rifle he carried in a saddle scabbard over his shoulder kept banging her on the head. The revolver holstered at his hip gouged her in the side. Her nostrils were choked with the smell of him, the smell of his blood.

SHE MANAGED TO JERK the quilt off her bed before they fell into it, still locked together in their strange embrace. She stiffened, rigid beneath his weight, terrified that he had just died on her, that she was lying beneath a dead man. She bucked and heaved against his chest, and flung him onto his back. A bright red stain had already begun to spread on her muslin sheets.

If he was still bleeding so, he wasn't dead yet. His face was a gravestone white, though, his eyes closed and sunk deep in their sockets. Livid welts marked his cheek where she had slapped him.

He lay awkwardly on the rifle scabbard, and she had to struggle against his weight to pull it out from beneath him. She spread open his blood-wet duster. His worldly clothes, once dandy fine, were now so blood-soaked she had to spend precious seconds trying to discover where he was hurt. She ripped open his bloody vest and shirt.

He had a bullet hole in his left side.

The hole was small and black and pulsed blood with his breathing. She made a thick pad out of a huck towel and pressed it to the wound, leaning against it hard with the heels of her hands. She did this until her arms began to tremble with exhaustion. But when she lifted the pad she saw that, while the bleeding might have slowed some, it hadn't stopped.

She ran from the room, banged out the door and into the yard. The wind whipped her skirts and slapped the strings of her prayer cap against her neck. She frightened the chickens that scratched in the straw by the barn, scattering them in a squawking cloud of flapping wings and molting feathers. She pulled open the barn door and was struck in the face with the pungent smells of cow and chicken and sheep, sheep, sheep. Smells that were so much a part of her life that she seldom noticed them. But this time nausea rose in her throat and she coughed, retching.

It was the blood. He'd been covered with so much blood. She squeezed her eyes shut and all she saw was blood.

She gathered up all the cobwebs she could find, thinking that if Ben were alive there wouldn't have been so many. She wanted Ben alive, to take care of the man who was dying in their bed.

She brought the sticky cobwebs back to the house cradled in her apron where the wind couldn't snatch them away. She was almost afraid to go into the bedroom, sure that he'd have died while she was gone. But he hadn't. He lay in a dreadful stillness, though, and his blood now dripped onto the bare pine floor.

She poured turpentine into the bullet hole. He jerked at the sting of it, the skin of his belly shuddering, but he didn't waken. She laid the webs over the wound and packed it with a clean compress, then backed away from the bed, and kept backing away until her legs nudged the seat of her rocking chair. She sat down slowly, her blood-stained hands lying palms-up in her lap. She shut her eyes, saw blood, and wrenched them open.

She lifted her head and for the first time really looked at the face of the outsider who lay on her bed.

He was young, no older than twenty-five, surely. His hair was the brown-black of fresh plowed earth, his skin milk pale, although that could have been from the loss of so much blood. He had arresting looks: high sculptured cheekbones, long narrow nose, wide-spaced eyes with thick, long lashes. She couldn't remember the color of those eyes, only the pure and utter terror that had flooded them when she first touched him.

It was *Mutter* Anna Mary who had the healing touch. From her father's grandmother Rachel had learned the healing lore, but the touch—that was a gift from God and so far He had not seen fit to give it to her. Her great-grandmother said the healing touch came simply of faith. Of opening one's soul to the power of faith the way a sunflower unfurls its petals to the warmth and the light.

Rachel stood slowly and went back to the bed. She laid her hands on him the way she'd so often seen her great-grandmother do. She closed her eyes and imagined her soul opening like a flower, petals unfolding one by one, reaching, reaching, reaching for the sun.

His chest moved beneath her hands, a ragged rise and fall. She thought she could hear the rush and suck of his heart beating. Beating and beating, louder and louder, and she tried to imagine the life passing from her fingers, like a river pouring into the ocean, until she became part of the rush and suck of his heart.

But when she opened her eyes and looked down at his face, she saw the blue lips and pinched skin of coming death.

"COME ALONG THERE, YOU. Open up."

Rachel pushed the rubber nipple between the outsider's lips and tilted the kidney-shaped nursing bottle so that the milk would flow more easily down the feeding tube and into his mouth. "That's it, that's it," she crooned. "Suckle now, suckle it all down like a good little *Bobbli*—"

She looked over her shoulder as if she'd just been caught doing something foolish. Judas, what was she thinking of, to speak such outlandish words, and to an outsider, no less? And she couldn't imagine what had prompted her to do such a thing anyway, to try to feed him from a pap bottle as if he were a bum lamb.

Only it seemed she would have to do something to replace all the blood he'd lost or he would surely die. And she'd saved many an orphaned lamb in just this way, by feeding it a mixture of milk, water, and molasses from a nursing bottle.

She was having as little success getting the outsider to cooperate, though, as she sometimes did with the bum lambs. Most of the milk leaked out the corners of his mouth and dribbled down his chin.

She was sitting beside him on her big white iron bed. She swung her legs up and leaned against the acorn-spooled rails of the headboard. Struggling against the dead weight of him, she rolled and lifted him up against her, then cradled his head to her chest. She felt him stir a little beneath her hands. And when she rubbed his throat like she did to the lambs, to get them to suckle, she felt him groan. When she put the rubber nipple to his mouth, he drank from it hungrily.

She laid her hand against his cheek, pressing him even closer to her, and lowered her head, resting her own cheek against the softness of his hair.

SHE WAS OUT IN the yard, waiting, when Benjo came back with the doctor.

The phaeton lurched over the frozen ruts in the road, swaying on its high wheels. It pulled abreast of her, and she caught her image mirrored in the shiny black lacquer. She was startled to see her prayer cap askew and straggles of loose hair flying about in the wind. A streak of dried blood slashed across her cheek like Indian war paint.

"Whoa, now!" Doctor Lucas Henry called out, pulling on the reins. He gripped the crown of his beaver bowler, and his tawny mustache curled around a lopsided smile. As usual, the whiskey shine was bright on his face.

"How there, Mrs. Yoder." He slurred the words, but then she'd always thought he enjoyed for pure mischief's sake putting on a show of wicked drunkenness, especially before someone who was Plain. "It sure is blowing something fierce this morning," he said. "A body needs two hands and a pot of glue to hold down the hair on his head."

Benjo rode up alongside the buggy. She searched his face. He was pale and a faint line creased his forehead, but his eyes shone more with excitement now than with fear. It was at him that she smiled, so he would know how pleased with him she was, though she said only: "Those poor woollies still haven't been fed yet."

The boy's wide-eyed gaze jerked to the house, then back to her. When she said nothing more, he pulled the mare's head around and headed for the barn.

The doctor swept his hat off his head and bent over at the waist in an exaggerated bow. "And a pleasure it is to exchange a howdy with you, too, Mrs. Yoder."

His words and actions flustered her. It wasn't the Plain

way to speak empty phrases on coming and going, and she never knew quite what to do when an outsider chose to practice such manners on her. She settled for nodding her head at him.

The doctor sat in the buggy, looking like a gaudy bird in his green and blue plaid woolen greatcoat, his lean face ruddy from the wind, his eyes laughing at her. "You keep on chattering like a demented magpie," he said, "and you're liable to wear out my ears."

He stared down at her a moment longer, then heaved a deep sigh. He wrapped the reins around the brake handle, picked up his black bag, and swung out of the buggy. With one foot still on the booster and one on the ground, he wobbled and almost fell.

Beneath the drooping curve of his mustache, the doctor's mouth pulled into another crooked smile, this one with a touch of meanness in it. "Well, hellfire and brimstone. There's no call to go looking down that disapproving nose at me." He tapped her nose with his finger. "Because while I'm hardly what you would call church-sober, neither am I gutter-drunk. What you could say I am is somewhat pleasantly skunked. Or rather you would say it, if you ever found the proper use for that tongue your Lord gave you. Well, my dear Plain Rachel? What do you think God gave you a tongue for if it wasn't to use it?"

She wasn't sure quite what he meant by most of the blasphemous nonsense he was always spewing. Like his smile it wasn't a kindness, though, she was sure of that much. And she met his outsider's animosity in the way the Plain People always did: by turning silently away from it. She started for the house, leaving him to follow.

"Your boy," he said, falling into step beside her, his stride long-legged and only a little wavery now, "managed to communicate to me in his unique way that you've had trouble come a-calling in the form of a devil, a demon, a prince of darkness . . . an incubus, perhaps?" He tried to wiggle his brows at her. "Dressed all in black and leaving bloody footprints in the snow."

"He's not a devil, he's one of you outsiders, and he's been gunshot—"

"Hallelujah, she speaks!" he exclaimed, flinging out his arms with such exuberance that he staggered. He smiled at her, but she didn't smile back. He shrugged. "So, how bad off is he?"

"He'll die of it, I should think. I bathed the wound with turpentine and packed it with cobwebs. And I fed him from a pap bottle, the same as I do my bum lambs, to make up for all the blood he's lost."

She held the door open for the doctor. He paused next to her on the threshold, tall and slender, and so close she could have counted the fine lines that cracked the glazed skin of his face. The smell of whiskey oozed from him, sour as old sweat.

His eyes were golden-brown and full of mockery. "What a wonder you are, Plain Rachel. The very soul of ingenuity and efficiency and so much charity you have, too, for a dying sinner. Indeed, it's a wonder you didn't manage to resurrect the poor bastard all by your lonesome."

She spoke the truth that was in her heart, because that was the only way she knew how to be. "I did try to heal him," she said. "I laid my hands on him and I reached out to the Lord. But the Lord didn't answer because my faith wasn't strong enough."

His gaze fell away from hers, and his mustache pulled down at one corner. His voice was serious for once. "No? But then whose faith ever is?"

As they stepped into the kitchen, the hot air from the cookstove and the smells of fried mush and blood hit them in the face. She waited while the doctor shrugged out of his greatcoat and then his frock coat and hung them both on the spike by the cookstove, along with his hat. She was relieved to see that his movements had sharpened. Perhaps he wasn't as inebriated with the Devil's brew as he had seemed.

He unfastened the pearl and gold links from his cuffs, slipped them into the pocket of his maroon brocade vest, and began to roll up his shirtsleeves. His dress was always flashy as a strutting gamecock, but today his high stiff wing collar was yellowed at the edges with dried sweat, and his gray silk tie hung loose about his neck. His fair hair, which he usually wore parted in the middle and slicked down with pomade, looked as if he'd been thrusting his fingers through it again and again.

He washed his hands at the slop stone and then went without asking into her bedroom. He knew where to go because he had been there once before, on the day he had brought home Ben's lifeless body.

There hadn't been anything he could do on that day, though, for a man the outsiders had hanged.

"I DON'T KNOW HOW he still lives," Rachel said.

The doctor had removed the compress and was studying the wound. The hole in the stranger's side continued to seep blood. Lampshine glinted off the blood and off the pale hair on the doctor's bare forearms.

"During the Sioux wars I saw men punctured with more holes than a pie safe," he said. He'd taken an instrument from his black bag and was probing the wound. "Yet they clung to life. One wonders why, in defiance of sense and science and damn good manners, they bothered. . . . The bullet's bounced off a rib and lodged in his spleen. I'll need hot water and more light."

She hurried to fetch the water from the cookstove reservoir. She came back to find Doc Henry standing at the dying man's bedside with his head thrown back, a silver flask to his lips, his gullet rippling with his hearty swallows.

He lowered the flask, wiped his mouth with his wrist, and saw her. He flushed just like Benjo did when she caught him with his fingers in the sugar tin.

She set the water pail and an enamel basin on the floor with a loud clatter and a splash, then left. This time when she came back with the peg lamp, he was making a production out of laying his surgical instruments on the bedside table. But his eyes, when they looked up at her, were too bright and his hands trembled.

She stuck the peg lamp in a candle socket above the headboard. She adjusted the screw and turned back to the bed just as Doc Henry dropped the stranger's leather cartridge belt and holster into her arms. His words came at her on a gust of whiskey breath: "You'd better put this up where—"

The weight of the belt surprised her. She juggled it in her hands, and the revolver slid out of its greasy holster and hit the floor. Something smacked into the wall, spitting splinters. The air itself seemed to explode with smoke and flame, and Rachel screamed.

She looked down at the floor as if hell itself had opened up beneath her feet. In truth, she could smell the sulfur smoke of hell, and the roar of its terrible fires smothered her ears.

Cursing under his breath, Doc Henry stooped over and picked up the pistol. She watched, stiff with fear, her ears still ringing, while he emptied it of its remaining cartridges.

He held the gun out to her, and he was actually laughing. “I was going to tell you to put the damn thing up where we won’t trip over it and shoot ourselves stone dead.”

She stared down at the revolver. So black and cold it was, like some terrible dead thing. She couldn’t bring herself to touch it. He huffed an impatient grunt and took the gunbelt back from her. He looked around the room, his gaze falling on the wardrobe of rough unpainted knotty pine. Ben had built it for her with his own hands the first year they were married—even though it was breaking the rules for a man’s wife to have such a thing when it was the Plain way to hang your clothes on wall hooks instead.

“An oiled holster and a doctored trigger,” the doctor was saying, as he turned the revolver over and over in his hands. Rachel stepped back, afraid it would somehow fire again, even without bullets. “What a dangerous hombre you’ve brought into your saintly home, Mrs. Yoder.” He gestured at the wardrobe as if to say: “May I?” She nodded.

Her finger shook as she pointed to the corner behind her spindle-backed rocker, where she had set the stranger’s rifle scabbard. “There’s another,” she said.

He put both firearms into the wardrobe. But when he went back to the bed, she saw that there was still another, a small one tucked into a shoulder holster that hung beneath the stranger’s left armpit. The doctor seemed pleased to tell her it was a belly gun. Further exploration showed the man had tucked into a sheath in his boot a bowie knife, which Doc Henry called an Arkansas toothpick.

“Yup, this bum lamb of yours is sure enough a real desperado,” he drawled, putting these weapons with the others. The latch to the wardrobe door made a startlingly loud click in the quiet room as he shut it. “He’s packing enough hardware to outfit Custer's army." He glanced sideways at her, mocking laughter in his eyes. She wasn't sure if the laughter was meant for her or the dangerous desperado.

They undressed him then together, she and Doctor Henry. They undressed him down to the skin. He was built lean and strong, with long shanks and a deep muscled chest, a taut flat belly, and the maleness of him lying heavy against the dark hair between his legs.

She glanced up to catch the doctor's eyes watching her, laughing at her again. And though it wasn't like her at all, she blushed.

One of the doctor's pale eyebrows lifted and his mouth curled slightly. "There's nothing wrong in admiring God's handiwork, *Plain* Rachel."

He was still wearing that faint smile as he took a pair of spectacles from his vest pocket. He polished the lenses with a white handkerchief, over and over, then hooked the temples one at a time behind his ears. He seemed to be moving so slowly suddenly, like a man swimming under water. In the tense quiet Rachel could hear the moan of the wind, the tick of the tin-cased clock in the kitchen. The ragged breathing of the man in the bed.

Doc Henry's long fingers slipped into the pocket of his striped pants and curled around the neck of the silver flask. She caught his wrist before he could lift the flask to his mouth.

The sinews and flesh beneath her fingers tightened. "Getting that bullet out is going to be trickier than braiding a mule's tail," he said. "I'll need just a little nip or two to settle my nerves—"

"You've already had enough nips to settle your nerves into a stupor."

He stared at her with bleary eyes a moment longer, then

pulled his wrist from her grasp. But he slid the flask back in his pocket. "I believe I liked you better, Rachel my dear, when you were the tongueless wonder." He sighed deeply, looking down at the wounded man. "Pity I haven't chloroform along with me to settle *him* into a stupor. But then he's already so far under, just the shock of cutting into him is liable to kill him anyway."

The doctor's hand shook only a little as he picked up a scalpel from the bedside table and pressed the blade of it against the stranger's pale skin. Blood welled and the flesh gaped, and it was Rachel who had to look away.

She heard the soft clinks of metal on wood as the doctor laid down the knife and picked up another of his gruesome instruments. She could hear his breathing and her own, and the clock ticking and the wind blowing.

The stranger groaned, and to Rachel's shock the doctor actually huffed a soft laugh. "Feel that, do you, dear heart?" he crooned. "That's good, that's good—as long as you're suffering, you're still living." The gunshot man groaned again and jerked violently. "Dammit, don't stand there like a fence post, woman. Hold him down."

Rachel leaned over the bed and gripped the stranger's shoulders. His flesh was cold and hard and slick beneath her hands. The doctor probed and dug at the bloody wound. Rachel drew in a deep breath and swallowed. A bead of sweat trickled down from beneath her prayer cap and ran along her neck.

The doctor pushed out a grunt between his pursed lips. He straightened and held the bullet, pinched between a pair of long silver tweezers, up to the light. "A forty-four-forty," he said. "Probably fired from a Winchester. See where it's slightly flattened at one end—that's where it struck the rib."

He dropped the bullet into the basin of bloody water. "You're looking kind of peckish there, Plain Rachel. I expect you could be using some of the Devil's brew now yourself, huh? Well, to serve you right I'm not giving you any. And don't you go fainting on me just yet either. We've work still to do."

He had her help him sew up the hole in the man's flesh, made by a bullet and enlarged by his doctor's knife. "Suturing" he called it, which he did with a curved silver needle that wasn't unlike the carpet needle *Mutter* Anna Mary used. Once, Rachel had helped her great-grandmother stitch up her brother Levi after he'd sliced open his calf with a sickle during the haying. She hadn't been at all queasy then, but now the sweat clung cold to the roots of her hair beneath her prayer cap. Her stomach felt like a knotted fist.

Doc Henry dressed the wound and then took a look at the man's broken arm. The doctor's hands no longer trembled. Maybe he was feeling surer of himself, she thought, and no longer needing the whiskey.

He made a clucking noise with his tongue and shook his head. "An oblique compound fracture of the radius, and it looks as if the blamed fool tried to set it himself. Your bum lamb sure does fancy himself a tough one."

Rachel thought that surely it would take a lot of courage to set your own broken arm. She wondered if it had happened before or after he'd been shot, and who had shot him, and why, and what had been behind that wild terror she'd seen in his eyes. But then, she had so many wonderings about him, this outsider who had come staggering across her hay meadow and leaving his bloody footprints in the snow.

ALL THE WAY THROUGH the clay-chinked cottonwood logs of her house Rachel could hear the terrible gagging, choking sounds that came from the yard. Doctor Lucas Henry throwing up the whiskey that had soured in his belly, and trying to throw off the fear that made his hands shake and his smile a little mean at times.

She sat in her spindle-backed rocker, her own hands folded in her lap and her gaze on the young man in her white iron bed. They had bound up his broken arm in a sheet of surgeon's plaster, cleaned the blood off him, and dressed him in one of Ben's old nightshirts. She thought his eyes no longer looked so sunken into the bones of his face. A tiny blush of color touched his lips.

She heard the squeal of the yard pump handle and then the gushing splash of water. Doc Henry cleaning himself up now.

The man on the bed lay in utter stillness, but she thought she could see the throb of the pulse in his throat. She thought that if she listened hard enough she would be able to hear the rush and suck of his heart.

A sound at the door made her look up. Doc Henry leaned against the jamb, his worldly elegance decayed, his clothes stained and water dripping from the ends of his mussed hair. A cigarette drooped from one corner of his mouth. The cigarette and his mustache lifted together with his lopsided smile. "Well, and aren't you just a-sitting there looking as pleased with yourself as a pig in pokeweed."

She was so pleased she beamed a smile back at him. "He's going to live," she said.

The doctor raised one shoulder in a careless shrug. "For today." He drew deeply on the cigarette, squinting at her through a haze of smoke. "Wild boys like him don't make old bones. That last bullet gets them all in the end."

He didn't sound as if he cared much that a "last bullet" would get his patient in the end. He was a strange man, was Doctor Lucas Henry. She supposed she knew him better than she'd ever known an outsider, and yet of course she really knew him not at all. One afternoon last spring she had sat in this very chair, beside this bed, holding the hand of her dead husband, and Doc Henry had stayed with her for a time, talking to her. He had stayed because he'd sensed somehow that she—she who had always so loved silence and being alone—could no longer bear either.

Most of what he'd said that day had been merely words to fill the empty corners of the room, but some of it she'd heard and remembered. He'd been born the same year and month and very day as she, to her a wondrous happenstance that made her feel strangely linked with him, as if two souls who'd begun the journey of life together ought to have a special care for one another along the way. And which made him thirty-four. Everyone in Montana had left a home behind somewhere, and his had been in Virginia. She could often hear the echoes of that place in his speech. For a time he'd done his doctoring in the U.S. Cavalry.

Those things he had told her about himself, and one other thing she'd only felt. He was a man apart from the world, but not out of choice as she was. Rather it was as if the world had locked him out, or shunned him, or he believed that it had. His was a bleak and lonely soul.

She watched him now as he pulled the silver flask from his pocket and drank deeply. "Strictly for medicinal purposes," he said, mocking himself this time. "Merely replacing some of the vital fluids I just lost." He gestured at the bed with the flask. "The very thing that must be done with our desperado here. The nursing bottle was a fine idea—see if you can get him to take it again, along with as much beef broth as you can force down him. And after a couple of days, when he's stronger, give him some of that god-awful sweet rhubarb wine you Plain People make."

She nodded, and then the full sense of what he'd said struck her. "But I thought you would be taking him back into town with you?"

"Not unless you want to undo all our good work."

She crossed her arms, gripping her elbows. "But . . ."

"Change the dressing often—I'll leave you plenty of alum. And for mercy's sake, don't clean the wound with turpentine again. He doesn't need blistering on top of everything else. I'll give you some carbolic acid instead. And make him stay quiet. He can't afford to start bleeding again."

The doctor pushed himself off the doorjamb. He held all of himself gingerly, but especially his head, as if he feared it might fall off if he moved too abruptly. He went to the bed and picked up the stranger's wrist to feel his pulse. The stranger's hand, Rachel saw, was long and fine-boned, with fingers so slender they looked almost as delicate as a girl's.

But then the doctor's own long fingers slid down to grip the man's hand, and he turned it over almost roughly. "Have a good look at that, Plain Rachel. All pretty and smooth on the outside and a pure mess on the inside. Somebody's worked this boy brutally hard for a time in his life. And look at this finger. It takes hours of shooting practice to put a callus like that on your trigger finger."

He laid the scarred and callused hand on the bed, gentle now, brushing the back of it with his fingers. "He's got shackle scars on his ankles, and someone's taken a whip to his back—those are the sort of marks a spell in prison leaves on a man. He probably killed his first man about the time he was weaned and he's been riding the owl-hoot trail ever since."

His touch again oddly gentle, he smoothed the dark hair off the stranger's pale forehead. "So will he thank you for saving him, I wonder? And I wonder why you even bothered, for he's already caught fast in the Devil's clutches. Isn't that what you believe?" His gaze lifted to hers. His face was stark with something, some inner torment she couldn't begin to fathom. "You people who are so sure that only you are saved, for you alone are the chosen of God?"

She shook her head at him. Strangely, she wanted to brush the dripping wet hair back out of his eyes, to touch him with that same soothing gentleness with which he'd touched the wounded man. "No one can be sure of salvation. We can only yield to God's eternal will and hope things turn out for the best."

He stared at her hard with a frown between his eyes, as if she were a puzzle he was trying to piece together. She had always thought that he was one of the few outsiders who looked at the Plain People and saw beyond their long beards and prayer caps and clothes that belonged to the last century. What he saw was the peace in their hearts, she supposed, and it both frightened and drew him.

He made a sudden jerking motion now with his shoulders, as if throwing off the weight of his thoughts, and he laughed. "Knowing how rarely things ever turn out for the best, I reckon hell's got to be a mighty jumping place, then."

He moved abruptly away from the bed and began to pack up his instruments. Except to tell her that he would be back in a day or two to check on his patient, he said nothing more. Rachel too was silent. She no longer looked at the outsider sleeping in her bed, the man who had a callus on his trigger finger and whip marks on his back.

She went with Doctor Henry out into the yard. The wind, raw and cold, twisted her skirts around her legs and snapped at the long tails of his greatcoat. She was surprised to see Benjo still on the hay sled, feeding the ewes, for it seemed that hours surely must have passed.

At his buggy Doctor Henry turned and looked back to the house. Lampshine spilled from her bedroom window in a soft yellow pool on the mud-splattered snow.

"That boy in there . . ." he said. "He might be handsome as a July morning, but he's also probably mean enough to whip his weight in wildcats when he's not half dead." He brushed the backs of his fingers against her cheek, touching her gently in the way that he had touched the stranger. "Have a care, Plain Rachel. The powers of darkness really *do* sometimes prevail."

2

THERE WAS NOTHING QUITE so eye-watering as the sour stink of sheep. Even with the wind blowing hard enough to take the bark off the trees, Rachel Yoder could still smell the woolly monsters. They crowded around the sled, bleating and bumping their bony faces against the slats, while she stood on the deck and heaved pitchforkfuls of hay out beyond their wriggling backs.

She braced her legs apart as Benjo drove the sled lurching over the frozen ruts in the pasture. The muscles in her shoulders and arms ached as she bent to lift the damp hay, but it was a pleasant ache. She'd always loved working in the open air, much more than she did the cooking and washing and keeping up of the house, the woman's work. The drudge work, she thought, and then almost as a matter of habit she sent up an apology to the Lord for her willful ways.

Benjo hauled up on the reins and the sled squeaked to a stop. Rachel thrust the pitchfork into a loose bale and jumped to the ground. She pulled off a glove and swiped the prickly hay dust off her forehead with the back of her hand.

"Muh—Mem?"

She turned slowly, careful to keep her face calm, for even with the gusting wind she'd caught the thread of fear in her son's voice.

Benjo stood at the head of the draft horse, one hand wrapped around a hame on the harness collar as if he needed its weight to anchor him to the ground. Next to the mare's shaggy bulk, he looked so frail. His bony wrists, chapped red from the cold, stuck out from the ends of his coat sleeves.

"Mem, thuh—thuh—that outsider . . . is he an outlaw?"

She came up to him, her gaze moving gently over his pale face. "I don't know," she said. "Perhaps."

"Will he shuh—shuh—shuh . . . ?" His tongue pushed so hard against his teeth that his head jerked, and the muscles of his throat clenched around the word that wouldn't come.

She put her hands on his shoulders, stilling him. "Sssh, now, and listen to me." She spread her fingers up over his collar into the ragged strands of his hair. She could feel a fine trembling going on inside him. "The outsider has no reason to shoot us. We mean him no harm."

He tilted his head back to stare up at her, his eyes as leaden as the clouds overhead. She saw the question in those eyes and the unspoken truth. The outsiders had been given no reason to hang his father, but Benjamin Yoder had died that way nonetheless, choking at the end of a rope.

It was hard, so hard sometimes to accept God's will.

The boy's mouth tightened and spasmed once, and then the words burst out of him fierce and whole. "I won't let him hurt you, Mem!"

Rachel dug her fingers into his shoulders as she pulled him against her. She knew she ought to tell him that he mustn't resist whatever happened, for it would be the will of God. But this time it was her own throat that closed up tight around the words and kept them from coming.

THE EWE BUTTED HER black face against Rachel's thigh, making a *buuuuhh* sound deep in her throat. "It's the hay you're supposed to be eating, you silly old thing, not me," Rachel said, laughing as she thrust her fingers through the sheep's rich oily fleece.

This ewe was an old one, and her mouth was so broken she could barely chew even the softest grass. She should have been culled from the band last mating season, but she'd always been such a sweet, gentle mother, producing strong and healthy babies year after year. Rachel just hadn't the heart to ship her off for slaughter where she'd wind up as someone's mutton stew.

The ewe stretched out her neck now, lifting her head, and looked calmly up at Rachel through big round dark eyes. Rachel had always imagined she could see wisdom in their gentle depths, as if they possessed not only all the world's secrets, but heaven's as well. She'd said as much to Ben once and he'd laughed at her, for in truth sheep were probably among the stupidest of God's creatures.

"But there's something you know that you're not telling us, isn't there, dear old thing?" Rachel said, rubbing her knuckles along the length of the ewe's bony face.

While the sheep fed off the scattered hay and Benjo led the draft horse and sled back to the barn, Rachel and MacDuff walked among the herd, checking on all the ewes whose woolly bellies were round and heavy with lambs. But it would be another month at least before they started dropping.

Rachel sure hoped it would warm up a bit before then. She let her head fall back to stare up into the shifting, boiling sky. From the looks of those clouds they were in for more bad weather.

The wind gusted through the cottonwoods and flapped her skirts like sheets on a line. She felt so strange inside herself. Sad and lonely and missing Ben so much. And yet all trembly and shaky, too, as if she'd been sipping on Doc Henry's whiskey. She stood in the feeding paddock among the sheep, buffeted by the wind, her face lifted toward the drooping clouds, and it was as if a part of her had been blown loose and up into that sky and was flying around up there, wild and lonesome and scared.

A horse's whinny floated to her on the wind, followed by the rattle of wheels over the log bridge.

To the outsiders, all the Plain People looked alike, with their austere conveyances and their drab old-fashioned clothes. But as soon as the light spring wagon with its faded brown canvas top turned into the yard, Rachel knew who it was. Although her neighbors and family would all have been worried when they didn't see her at the preaching this morning, she had known Noah Weaver would be the one to come.

Yet something held her back, so that it was Benjo who came flying out of the barn to meet him. She could tell from the way her son was waving his arms and pointing to the house that Noah was now getting an earful about the trouble that had come a-calling in the form of an outsider dressed all in black and with a bullet hole in his side.

It had started to sleet. The boy led Noah's horse, still hitched to the wagon, into the big barn. Rachel snapped her fingers at MacDuff and they left the paddock together. MacDuff took off after the boy in a mud-splattering gallop, barking joyfully. Rachel sometimes thought that dog was better at herding Benjo than he was the sheep.

She walked through the slushy snow and mud in the yard with her back straight, her head lowered against the stinging ice pellets. Noah Weaver waited for her with his hands hooked on his hips, the wind tugging at his long beard. She stopped before him, and their gazes met and held. Their breath entwined like white ribbons in the cold air.

He looked down at her with brown eyes that were warm and concerned. His craggy face, with its bumpy nose and thick ginger beard that lay on his chest like a forkful of hay, was so dearly familiar to her that she wanted to laugh and throw her arms around him in a big welcoming hug.

Instead she stood before him with her hands linked behind her back, and she was smiling, but only inside herself.

White air puffed from his mouth. "*Vell,* our Rachel?"

"I've some fried mush left over from breakfast, should you want it."

He smiled at her, openly, and so she let her own smile come out in a quick curve of her lips and a little downward tuck of her chin.

They turned together toward the house and the wind drove the sleet right at them, stinging their faces. The lampshine from the kitchen window was a beacon, Rachel thought, pointing the way home. Standing out there in the paddock, beneath the big sky and the wild wind, she had felt lost and alone. But she was herself again now, and this was Noah walking beside her, and the hearth that beckoned was hers.

The wind slammed against them. Noah's hand flashed to his head, barely snatching his hat before it went sailing. "It's warming up some," he said, and Rachel laughed. Only Noah Weaver could find the good in Montana weather.

He heard her laugh and another smile wreathed his face. "What I meant to say was, it could be worse. It could be snowing."

"It could be blowing up a blizzard, too. And likely will be again before spring gets here."

"Now, don't you go hexing the weather like that—hold on a moment." He stopped to lean against the porch rail and bent over, tugging at the laces of his thick-soled cowhide brogans. "I've the barn all over my shoes."

He must have hurried right over after the preaching, then, as soon as he'd finished his evening chores. At least as much as he was capable of hurrying. Noah Weaver was a slow moving man, slow in thought, word, and deed. He took his own good time arriving at a place within himself, but once he got there not even a barrel of gunpowder could budge him loose.

He padded into her kitchen, cumbersome and big-footed as a bear. He looked so *right* standing there, in his Plain clothes of brown sack coat and broadfall trousers and big-brimmed felt hat, with his face framed by his long shaggy hair and full, manly beard. His big toe was poking through a hole in his stocking, and it gave her a pang to see it. He needed a wife to care for him.

His gaze roamed slowly from the slop stone to the cookstove to the bathing screen, looking for the outsider, she supposed. As if he expected the man to be sitting at her table eating Sunday supper. "So, where is he then—this *Englischer?*" he said, his lip curling around the word as if it tasted foul.

They were speaking *Deitsch,* the old peasant German of their roots, for the Plain didn't use the *Englische* talk except around outsiders. And only then when they chose to be friendly. Still, Rachel had to stop herself from putting her finger to her lips, as if the outsider could hear and understand Noah's strong words.

She led the way in silence to the bedroom. The outsider slept in utter stillness, that long fine-boned hand with its scarred palm and callused finger lying lax on the sheet. As it did every time her gaze fell on him, her breath caught at the arresting quality of his face. It wasn't the Plain way to attach importance to physical beauty, but she couldn't help noticing his.

She felt Noah stiffen beside her and knew that he, at least, saw only an outsider who had come unwelcomed and unwanted into their Plain and separate lives. He said nothing, though, until they were back in the kitchen, facing each other as they had out in the yard. Only this time neither of them was smiling.

His head jerked up and around as if he was pointing with his beard. "In your bed, Rachel?"

"He was gunshot and bleeding to death. What else was I to do with him? Dump him in the corner like a bundle of old gunnysacks?"

"Did I say such a thing?"

The gentle reproach in his eyes stung. "I'm sorry, Noah. I guess I'm just . . ."

Weary and lonely and scared. She felt as if she were back out in the paddock again, being buffeted by the wind and getting lost up in the sky.

Noah shrugged out of his sack coat and hooked it on the wall spike. He took off his hat and reached to hang it there as well, but he paused, facing the wall, with his hand resting on the crown of the hat, as if he had to collect his thoughts and carefully choose his words. When he turned back to her, he was very much the church deacon, with his eyes all solemn, his mouth stern. As Deacon Weaver, it was his duty to be sure everyone followed the straight and narrow way and conformed to the understanding of what it was to be Plain.

"That *Englischer* in there . . ." Again he pointed with his chin, as if the man didn't warrant more than the crudest of gestures. "He's tainted. What he's seen, done . . . He reeks of the world and the evil that's in it."

"You don't know him."

"And what do you know of him?"

Rachel had nothing she could say to that. What little she did know of the outsider—the callus on his trigger finger, the shackle scars, the whip marks on his back, the bullet hole in his side—was all wickedness. It spoke of the hurt he had done unto others, as much as the hurt that had been done upon him.

Noah stared at her, his face settling into deep lines, and Rachel stared back, her head held high, erect. A silence drew out between them, underscored by the drumroll of the sleet hitting the tin roof above their heads.

She turned away from him and went to the stove. She forked a slab of the cold fried mush onto a plate and poured sorghum syrup over it, then brought it and a tin mug to the table. She stopped there, her hand that held the plate suspended in air. She felt a bittersweet ache in her chest at what she was thinking, what she was about to do. Yet she did it anyway: she deliberately set the plate down in Ben's place at the head of the table.

She felt Noah move and she looked up to catch his gaze on her, questioning. She quickly averted her face and went to the stove for the coffeepot.

When she came back to him, he was seated, his head bent in silent prayer. She thought of the many times she had stood like this beside the table, looking down at Ben's black head. Noah had shoulders broad and blocky as anvils, straining the seams of his hickory shirt and filling her kitchen. His hair wasn't dark, though, but rather the rusty brown color of baked apples.

They had all been the best of friends when they were children, she and Ben and Noah. It seemed strange only now, looking back on it, that a couple of rowdy boys would welcome a shy, skinny girl three years younger into their games. Maybe she had been as sinew is to bone and muscle, holding them together. For even as boys they'd been very different—Noah slow and steady, and maybe just a little stiff in his ways, Ben so quick to laugh and quick to anger, reckless and a little wild.

She poured coffee into Noah's cup from a battered blue speckled pot. He ate in silence, as was the Plain way, his gaze on the painted clay plates that lined the shelf along the far wall. They were like having a rainbow in the room, those plates. Rachel had painted them herself, copying the wildflowers that burst upon the valley in the spring. She had meant to do a dozen, but she'd stopped at five, when Noah showed her how she was taking too much sinful pride and worldly pleasure in what she was creating. Painted clay wasn't nearly as useful as tin, he had said. To have painted plates was not to follow the straight and narrow way.

Yet Ben had been so angry with him that day, for shaming her into quitting her painting. "And did even God not make some things just for pretty?" he'd shouted at Noah, so loud the plates had rattled.

Noah's fork made a soft clink in the quiet as he laid it on the plate that wasn't painted clay but made of tin. "The boy said you had that doctor out here to care for the outsider."

"He did have a bullet in him that needed getting out."

Noah picked up his coffee, then set it down again. "Having that doctor out here, though, and not a year hardly passed since that . . . that other happened—"

"Ben's dying."

"*Ja,* that. Next thing you know you'll have him caught up in your lives, in yours and the boy's, and that can't be good."

"Well, he's not likely to start paying us social calls." She sighed, impatient suddenly with Noah's stiff ways. "Lucas Henry's not a bad man. Not really. He pretends to laugh at sacred things, but only because it hurts him to think of them."

"'Ye cannot drink the cup of the Lord, and the cup of devils: ye cannot be partakers of the Lord's table, and of the table of devils.'"

Rachel swallowed another sigh. For Deacon Weaver to be quoting Scripture at her, he truly must have reached the end of his tether.

He pointed his finger at her now, as if she were a child that needed scolding. "You'll go too far one of these days, Rachel. And you'll suffer then, for your proud and willful ways."

She lowered her head. She understood the warning he was giving her. He'd soon have her on her knees confessing her sins before the entire congregation if she didn't mend her ways. And perhaps deep in her heart she wasn't sure she could bring herself to do such a thing, not even for the sake of her immortal soul.

"Ben was always doing that," Noah went on, "always going toe to toe with the rules. Seeing how far he could push things. For the sake of his own soul that was bad enough, but he shouldn't have encouraged you to—"

Her head snapped up. "Ben was a God-loving and a God-*fearing* man."

For a moment Noah said nothing, and his mouth kept that tight, stern look. Then he sighed, pulling at his beard. "Aw, I was only saying about that doctor, that he can never be a true friend to you."

"He isn't. He's only what he is. I couldn't heal a gunshot wound, and so he came for that reason and no other. He's not my friend."

Yet as soon as the words were out of her mouth she felt guilty for uttering them. Though not a lie, they were certainly a denial of the truth. "That doctor" had cut down Ben's hanging body and brought him home to her. He had filled the empty room with his comforting words. He had taken her in his arms, and she had pressed her face into the expensive watered silk of his flashy waistcoat and she had stained it with her tears. She and Doctor Lucas Henry . . . perhaps they weren't friends, but they were something to each other.

She heard Noah pull in a deep breath. His gaze was now focused hard on the lard pot and salt bowl that sat in the middle of the table. He leaned both elbows beside his empty plate.

"Rachel." He lifted the plate, cradling it in his two big hands. He turned his head and captured her gaze, held it as surely as if it too were caught fast in his hands. "You set this food that was meant for me at Ben's place. I got to believe that—"

"I did it without thought," she said quickly, before he could go on, for words once spoken couldn't be taken back.

And her own words just spoken were an outright lie, may God forgive her. By inviting him to take her husband's place at her table, she'd all but told Noah Weaver she was willing to make a place for him in her heart and bed as well. Oh, yes, she had thought of it, and then she had acted on that thought, and now she wanted it all undone.

Noah set the plate down and reached for her hand. "I know what you're thinking, but it's no disloyalty to him, what you did. He's nearly a whole year gone now. And the boy needs the firmness of a father's hand to guide him."

And the church frowned on a woman who went her own way, without a husband to guide her, for the Bible said: "The head of the woman is the man." Those were all good reasons why she should become Noah Weaver's wife.

It had seemed when they were young, she and Noah and Ben, that the three of them would always be together and with all of life to share. It was because of the changeless way time passed in the Plain life, she supposed. Without seam or nub or end. But then there had come that day, the day Noah Weaver had first kissed her, and Rachel had realized they wouldn't always be able to share everything.

On that day Noah had been up in the mow of his papa's barn, forking hay into a wagon bed. She'd tried to sneak up on him and give him a shove from behind, only he'd caught her at the last instant. Caught at her apron strings, too, so that she'd gone flying with him down into the bed of hay. One moment she'd been lying in the hay, laughing, her arms and legs spread wide like a snow angel, straw tickling her nose and the sun dazzling her eyes. And then his head was blocking out the sky and his lips were pressing down hard on hers.

She could still remember the way that kiss had made her feel, all trembly inside, scared and excited, and filled with strange wantings to have him kiss her again. And a wanting for Ben to do it to her as well, so that she could see if it would feel the same.

So she'd gone looking for Ben later and she'd found him at their fishing hole, stealing a nap when he should have been at his chores. He lay flat on his belly on the grassy bank, his head cradled in his arms. It was a hot day and his sweat-damp shirt clung to his back. She could see the bulge of muscle in his shoulders, and the way the curve of his ribs met his spine, the way the small of his back flared up like the smooth inside of a bowl into the taut hard roundness of his bottom. He had the legs of his broadfalls rolled up to his knees, and she saw that his calves were hard and curved like the yoke of a plow and covered with fine dark hair. She couldn't remember ever noticing these things about him before.

She sat down next to him and looked at him for the longest time. Slowly she reached out and touched his black hair where it curled over his collar.

He opened his eyes and smiled at her.

"Noah kissed me on the mouth," she blurted.

His smile deepened, putting a crease in his cheek. He sat up in one quick, graceful movement that was the way of him. He studied her, his head cocked slightly. "I'll allow that," he finally said. "I suppose. As long as you go no further with it, and as long as you don't forget I'm the one you're going to marry."

She made a face at him. "Hunh. Don't you think I might have something to say to that, Benjamin Yoder?"

He leaned into her until it seemed their faces were but a breath apart. That if she did so much as breathe their lips would be touching.

She felt the heat of his own breath as he spoke. "*Ja, Mee-*

del, I reckon you will be having something to say to that. On the grand day I do my asking, you'll be saying, 'Yes.'"

Somehow his hands were on her arms and he was pulling her even closer. Her lips seemed to pucker of their own accord. She heard a strange moaning, like the sound the wind made blowing through the rafters of a barn, and then she realized it was coming from her.

He let her go so abruptly she fell back in a sprawl on her elbows. He'd let her go without kissing her at all. She watched him gather up his pole and wicker creel and saunter away while she lay there, with her mouth burning and feeling naked, thinking that maybe she hated him and knowing already that he was the one she loved best.

And Noah, dear Noah, had always known it, too. She looked at Noah Weaver now, so many years and memories later, and his dark brown eyes stared back at her, searching her face, trying to see into her heart.

She had seen those eyes looking back at her so often over the years. Seen them bleak with hopeless yearning on the day she had stood up before God and taken another man as her husband. Seen them hollow with anguish the night his own wife had died in childbirth. Seen them dark with despair that summer most of his sheep had eaten the camas plant and died. Seen them countless times shining with the rapture of prayer.

And now because of this simple, foolish thing that she had done she saw those eyes glowing bright as Christmas candles with hope.

Oh, she could imagine herself making a life with him, imagine him sitting at her table like this of an evening while they talked over the day and planned the morrow. She could imagine kneeling with him in the straw, laughing together, as they watched the miracle of a lamb being born into the world. She could imagine catching his eye during the preaching and sharing a smile—well, maybe not that, for as deacon it wouldn't do to have his attention go wandering during the worship service.

But when she tried to imagine going into the bedroom with him and undressing for him and feeling his weight settle on her and hearing his groans as he . . .

She had to take a deep breath to ease the pressure growing in her chest. She pulled her hand from his and reached for his empty plate, but he caught at her wrist.

"Rachel—"

"Noah, don't say anything more, please. I'm just not ready to listen to anything more."

He let her go, stretching to his feet. His face was flat and empty as he put on his hat and coat. But he paused at the door, his hand on the latch, and when he turned she could see he was all set to play the part of the deacon and lecture her again and she didn't want to hear it. She turned her back on him, taking the plate and cup to the slop stone.

"*Ach, vell,* our Rachel," he said. She said nothing. "I know," he went on, "how you'll say that if the *Englischer* showed up here as he did, gunshot and bleeding, then it could never have been God's will for you to leave him to die. And you're right in that. . . . There, you see," he added, a teasing in his voice now because her shoulders had jerked at his words, "I'm even allowing as how you can be right on occasion."

She heard him take a step toward her. She stiffened, keeping her back to him. "But it's not for nothing that we Plain People have kept ourselves separate from those things that can corrupt the soul. I know it was Ben's belief that we shouldn't always be blind to change, that we shouldn't always turn our back on the world and those who dwell in it, but he was wrong in that, and now he's got you thinking you can—"

She tossed the tin plate into the slop stone with a loud clatter and swung around on him so fast her cap strings flared. "You stop blaming me on Ben!"

She surprised him so, his face flushed red above his beard. He looked at her now as if he'd never seen her before, as if she wasn't the Rachel he had known all his life.

She reached up and felt that a swatch of hair had indeed slid loose from beneath her prayer cap. She thrust it impatiently back up under the stiffly starched white cambric. The gesture, one she had made a thousand times over the years, brought a reluctant smile to Noah's mouth.

"Aw, Rachel." He sighed a ragged laugh, shaking his head and studying the toe that poked through his stocking. "You never change. Not even Ben could really change you, for good or for ill."

He half turned to the door, then swung back. "I saw when I drove up that you're getting low on wood. I'll send my boy on over in a day or two with his ax."

The smile she gave him came a little shakily. "That would be kind. That is, if Mose won't mind the extra work."

"That boy'll do what I tell him," Noah said, suddenly all stern and stiff again.

He waited, but there was nothing more she had to say to him, or at least she hadn't within her the words he wanted to hear. The silence fell heavy between them, thick and cold, and after a moment too long of it, he turned and left.

As soon as the door shut behind his broad shoulders, she went to the window. The sleet lay on the slushy yard like a cloak of ice; the wind blew wild. She watched him lead his horse and wagon from the barn and climb aboard, but he didn't drive off right away. He sat there, his shoulders hunched against the weather, one hand clutching at his hat.

She wanted to go to him and take the hurt away, to go to him and say: "I will marry you, my Noah. Then you can have what you've always wanted, and I can have . . . if I can't have Ben, I can at least have a husband who is dear to me, a friend."

She wanted to run out into the yard and say all those things to him. But though she watched until his wagon disappeared over the rise, still she stayed where she was. The house was silent, except for the sleet raking at the window and the moaning sound the walls made as they trembled beneath the onslaught of the wind.

SLEET STILL PECKED AT the window and pattered on the tin roof, and the wind whined in the stovepipe late that night as Rachel took off her brown shawl and apron, storing their pins in the wide apron belt. She removed the top pin from her bodice as well, and untied the stiff strings of her prayer cap. She twisted her head from side to side, stretching the ache of a long day out of her neck.

She took off her cap and put it in its place on the shelf beneath the window. When she looked up she caught her reflection in the night-blackened glass. The woman who stared back at her was not herself at all, but a stranger with a wild tangle of hair falling over her shoulders.

She sat in her spindle-backed rocker, its rush seat squeaking softly as it took her weight. The outsider lay in her bed, a silent collection of lumps and hollows beneath the quilt. The pattern of the quilt was an enormous white star with diamond rays spread out across a field of midnight blue. In the murky light of the coal oil lamp, the star looked jagged and broken as if it had fallen from the sky and shattered.

The oil in the lamp gurgled softly, a homey, comforting sound. In a moment she would join Benjo, although she'd probably have to shoo off that bed-hog of a dog to make room for herself. Her head itched as it often did after a day of wearing the starchy cap. She thrust her fingers through her hair, rubbing her scalp, indulging herself with a frenzy of scratching. She would go. In a moment. The breath eased out of her in a soft sigh. Her head fell back. . . .

And she let the music come.

The drumbeat of the rain on the tin roof joined in syncopation with the beat of her heart. The wind whistled like a pipe, blowing shrill. The log walls moaned, resonating her bones with their deep bass sound.

The music became wilder. Jagged clarions of trumpets joined with bright cymbals crashing through her blood. She shook with the force of the thundering chords, shocked at their violence. Streaking ribbons of light flashed behind her closed eyes, pulsing and throbbing in cadence with the pounding notes. Never had the music been so awesome, so wild. So forbidden.

No music was allowed in the Plain life, save for the chanting of the hymnsongs on worship Sunday. Yet it seemed that all her life the music had been with her, as elemental as breathing.

She had no notion of why it came, only from where. It came from nature's songs—from the violin scrape of a cricket's wing, the clap of a thundercloud, the pop of the cottonwoods freezing, a cat's raspy purr. She'd heard the outsiders playing on their worldly instruments, of course. Walking down the main street of Miawa City, she couldn't help but hear the tinny honky-tonk tunes coming out of the saloons. But those were nothing like the delicate, joyful melodies and the symphonic furies that could sometimes flood over her, through her, whenever she shut her eyes and opened her heart to the earthsong.

No one knew about her music; not even Ben had known. If the church ever came to hear of it, she was sure they'd make her give it up. She would have to confess it as a sin, bowed on her knees before the congregation, and promise never to allow it to happen again.

Yet the music was her way of praying. Words were difficult for her. They seemed such hollow things, all noise and air. She couldn't use mere words to speak of what was truly in her soul. But the music—it did more than speak. It rejoiced and pleaded, it praised, and wailed sometimes, and shrieked in anger, too. It worshiped. When the music came, the Lord was somehow there as well. She could *feel* Him then in the same way she felt the music, and she knew He heard and understood the thoughts the music spoke. Many were the nights she had sat in this rocker, alone with the Lord and her thoughts and the wild chords and gentle melodies. And time passing at its slowest and sweetest.

In those first months after Ben's death, she had lost the music. There had been only emptiness then, as hard as a cold stone inside her, and silent, so silent. She'd moved through the days staggered with grief and crushing loneliness, able to summon only a pale shadow of the faith that had always steadied and comforted her. For how could a loving God allow a boy's father, a woman's husband, to be so unjustly hanged at the end of a rope?

Yet the music found a way to be heard, just as God always found a way. It came back to her at first in sweet bits and snatches, like the whispered perfume of apple blossoms on a windy spring day. Then one night she had shut her eyes and opened her heart to the wind howling and moaning through the cottonwoods. And the wind became a chariot of wondrous, booming chords, carrying her higher and higher, home to God. The music brought Rachel Yoder back to her faith again.

And so when the music came to her on this night, Rachel opened her heart. It wasn't sweet or gentle, not on this night. It was all violence and fury, fiery bursts of notes that exploded in a black sky, sudden and shattering as the sound of a bullet slamming into a wall.

As always the music ended abruptly, falling into a hollow, echoing silence. Slowly, she opened her eyes.

The room wavered before her, hazy from the lamp smoke. The outsider still lay in utter quiet on her bed. A gleam of sweat ran down his cheek and jaw and settled into the hollow of his collarbone. Lampshine reflected off the sheen of his eyes.

He was awake.

Her breath caught, first in surprise and then in fear. The way he was just lying there, staring at her with that taut silence . . . No, she was being foolish. He was only bewildered, and perhaps frightened himself, to come awake in a strange place.

She rose and went to him. She thought she'd gotten used to him, somewhat. Hours, after all, had passed since he'd come staggering across her hay meadow. She had held him and fed him with a pap bottle, she had bathed his naked body. But she had never understood until that moment, until she looked down into his face, why the eyes were called windows into the soul. In the gloomy light his eyes glittered up at her, fierce and wild, and haunted with old and terrible fears.

She didn't realize she'd taken a step back until his hand grabbed her arm. His fingers dug painfully into her flesh, surprisingly strong. His ragged breathing sawed across her own gasp.

"Where's my gun?"

She opened her mouth, but the words wouldn't come until she had sucked in a deep hitching breath. "We put it up. In the wardrobe."

"Get it." His fingers, so long and slender, whitened with the force of his grip. His strength seemed unnatural, unholy.

"You'll shoot me."

"I'll shoot you if you don't get it." His eyes, glowing wild, locked with hers. "Get me the goddamned gun."

She believed him, and it didn't matter that he was lying there gunshot and with a broken arm. Looking into those eyes, she believed him capable of anything. "I will, then. As soon as you let go of me."

She pulled against him but he didn't let go. And then he did, so that she lost her balance and stumbled.

The door to the wardrobe groaned as she opened it. She knelt and retrieved the leather cartridge belt from the back corner where Doctor Henry had put it. Even though she'd watched the doctor empty the gun of its bullets, she was still afraid of it. It slipped easily and quickly out of the oiled holster, surprising her anew with its weight. Its wooden grip had the smooth worn feel of an old ax handle.

She thought the stranger had fallen back into sleep, for he lay utterly still again, eyes closed. Yet as she held the revolver out to him, his fingers wrapped around it with that unnatural strength. She felt the breath leave him then, on a sigh of relief.

She stared mesmerized at the hand that held the gun. She hadn't cleaned that part of him very well. Dried blood stained the creases of his fingers, and lay crusted beneath his nails.

She prayed he was too far out of his head to notice the missing cartridges.

His fingers tightened on the gun's grip. Her gaze jerked up to his face. He was staring at her, his eyes wide open, unblinking.

She didn't realize she was holding her breath until he relaxed his hold on her by looking away. His gaze roamed ove. the bare walls, decorated only with knotholes, to the curtainless window that showed only an infinity of black sky. In his eyes was the same wealth of fear she'd seen in the meadow when she had first touched him.

"Where am I?"

"You're safe," she said softly. She leaned over him as if she would lay her hand on his forehead, the way she did with Benjo when he awakened from a bad dream and needed comforting. But in the end she did not. "You can go back to sleep now. You're safe."

He closed his eyes. When he opened them again they were flat, empty but for her own reflection. His mouth pulled up at one corner, but it wasn't a smile. His gaze went back to the black, empty window. "There's no such place."

She did touch him then, on the cheek with the tips of her fingers. "Hush now, and sleep," she said. "There's nothing out there but the night and the dark."

As she bent down to lower the wick in the lamp, her loose hair brushed over his chest and face. She felt a tug on her hair and she saw that he had tangled his fingers in a thick hank of it. In his eyes was a look of surprised bewilderment, but then his heavy eyelids closed as if against his will. He slid into sleep again, but not before letting go of her hair and wrapping his hand once more around the grip of his gun.

She turned off the lamp. The expiring flame leaped and

fell, and darkness swallowed up the room. She paused in the doorway to look back at him. But the bed was only a black shadow now, joined with the phantoms of the night.

She turned away, leaving him to the dark and the night. His eyes, she now knew, were blue.

3

IT WAS BARELY NOON and Rachel was already a day's worth behind in her chores. She had cream souring in a bucket that needed churning, an apple duff that needed boiling, the bed linens yet to soak. And the floor had been begging for a good scrubbing ever since that last sleet storm had muddied things up so.

But first the outsider's wound needed tending.

Rachel stuffed a wad of fresh bandages under her arm. She filled an enameled basin with vinegar water and headed for her bedroom. The water slopped over the edges, leaving splatters in her wake and filling the air with its pungent smell.

Doctor Henry had ordered him seen to three times a day. She was to cleanse the bullet hole with carbolic acid and sponge him down all over with the vinegar water. He'd been in a terrible feverish state since that first night. He didn't toss about and rave, though, as one might expect. Most of the time he just lay there and sweated. Except for twice, when he'd been startled awake, all wild-eyed and pointing his six-shooter at some unseen menace.

Since she'd put it in his hand, he hadn't once let go of his precious gun. But Doc Henry said that because the wicked thing appeared to bring him comfort, she wasn't to take it away. Do this, don't do that, and all easy for that doctor to say when he'd been out here himself only once since the first day. That doctor, she thought with a harried grumble, could be as free with his commands as a new bishop.

Skirts swishing, Rachel entered her bedroom just as, out in the yard, MacDuff let go with an ear-busting *woof.* The man in the bed exploded into a blur of motion. Rachel staggered to a stop, her wide-open eyes staring down the black muzzle of his Colt.

She screamed and flung the basin up in front of her face, dousing herself with the vinegar water. She squeezed her eyes shut and hunched her shoulders as if she could make all of her small enough to fit behind her puny shield. The air grew thick and still, except for the *drip-drip* of the water.

She lowered the basin slowly, peering over its chipped rim.

He still held the six-shooter trained right on the bridge of her nose. She tried to assure herself that with her own eyes she'd seen Doc Henry take out the bullets, but she didn't completely trust any outsider, let alone their violent and unpredictable weapons.

MacDuff barked again, and the outsider's whole body drew taut. The gun barrel didn't waver, but she could have sworn his finger tightened around the trigger, a trigger that had been doctored to go off at the slightest touch. She stared into eyes that were wild and savage.

"*Lieber Gott.* Don't shoot me. Please."

"That dog—" His voice was savage like his eyes, and shaking. "What's it barking at?"

She was holding her head so stiffly it seemed to creak as

she turned to look out the window. MacDuff was loping in and out of the willow brakes and cottonwoods that lined the creek. A dirty gray fluff of tail flashed ahead of him, disappearing into a burrow pit.

"It's only our herding collie, chasing a jackrabbit." She creaked her head back around to the man in the bed. She tried to make her voice sound matter-of-fact, as if she conversed daily with strangers who held guns pointed between her eyes. "MacDuff's got a running feud going with every rabbit in God's creation."

The barrel of the gun jerked upward. His thumb flashed and there was a loud metallic click, and Rachel nearly jumped out of her skin again. He sagged down into the pillows. Sweat gleamed on his face. His hand that held the gun trembled briefly, then stilled.

She stared at him. Her heart was pounding like an Indian war drum and he was the cause of it, he and his six-shooter.

His gaze suddenly snapped back to the window, focusing on the running figure of her son outside. MacDuff's barking must have drawn Benjo away from his chores in the barn. The foolish rabbit, out of its burrow again, was now making a dash for the wild plum thickets that grew between the creek and the lambing sheds. The boy was going after the rabbit with his sling, whirling the rawhide cords over his head like a lasso.

"Who's that?" said the man in the bed, the man with a gun in his hand.

Rachel thought she might be sick. "M-my son. Don't . . ." The words faded as her throat constricted. "Don't hurt him."

Out by the wild plum thickets Benjo released one of the sling's rawhide cords, and the rabbit dropped like a stone.

The man turned his eyes back to her and stared with a concentration that was frightening and tangible. Unexpectedly, he smiled. "Looks like you'll be having rabbit stew for supper."

His words and his smile disconcerted her. His eyes remained terrifying.

Her gaze dropped to the floor, where the vinegar water had made a dark wet stain, almost like blood. *Lieber Gott, lieber Gott.* If it had been Benjo to come through the door instead of her . . .

"What kind of crazy person are you?" she shouted, advancing on the bed. "*Englischer, litterlich und schrecklich!* Waving that wicked thing around like a crazed fool, pointing it at innocent folk. I've already one bullet hole in my wall and I'll not have another. Not in my wall, not in my son, nor my own person, for that matter. Why, I've a good mind to . . ." She trailed off as she heard the echo of her own shrieking voice.

The brackets around his mouth deepened ever so slightly, and his eyes tightened at the corners. "You're gonna do what, lady—take a switch to my sorry ass?"

Flustered, she jerked her gaze away from his. "Hunh. I ought to."

She saw that she still held the basin hanging empty in her hand and she slammed it down on the floor with a clank. She had dropped the roll of bandages back by the door. She went and got it and slapped it on the nightstand next to her black calfskin Bible and the bottles of carbolic acid and alum Doc Henry had left with her. She jerked the bedclothes down to his waist and tugged up Ben's nightshirt.

"What the hell . . ." He reached for the sheet, but she batted his hand away.

"Whatever you've got, mister—I've already seen plenty of it."

Blood had seeped in a starburst pattern through the

white linen bandage. She leaned over him, reaching for the knot where the bandage ends wrapped and fastened around his middle. Her arm pressed against the hard sinewy muscle that encased his ribcage. He was still feverish, his skin sweaty and hot to the touch.

His chest heaved beneath her arm as he drew a ragged breath. She glanced up, her fingers abandoning their battle with the knot. He was studying her, his gaze moving slowly over her prayer cap, her brown Plain clothing, then back up to her starched white cap again.

"What are you?" he said. "Some sort of nun?"

"What a notion. I'm a daughter of the Plain People."

His eyes were certainly blue, cold and sharp like broken shards of river ice reflecting a winter sky. And he was staring at her as if he were trying to crawl inside her skin.

"I don't know as I've ever heard of such a thing," he said. He flashed a bright smile that showed off his even white teeth. "You sure don't look plain to me. A bit starchy maybe, and undoubtedly a holy-howler. But definitely not plain."

It occurred to her that he was trying to be friendly. As if he could wave a six-shooter in her face one minute and expect to make it up with a smile in the next. His was a charming rascal's smile, and she trusted it for about as long as it took to blink.

He gave an exaggerated sigh. "I guess I should know by the scowl I'm getting that you are definitely a holy-howler of the serious sort."

"I don't know what you mean by holy-howler. There's nothing special about us, except that we raise sheep, so I suppose if you're a cowman you might call that an aggravation. We follow the straight and narrow way, working and praying together and trusting in the mercy of the good Lord to take care of us."

"And does He? Does your good Lord take care of you?"

It was a question only an outsider would ask. A Plain man was born knowing the answer. She felt no need to reply.

A ragged silence fell between them, and his gaze went back to the window. She busied herself with unfolding the clean bandages, though she hadn't finished removing the soiled one. "You aren't from these parts, are you?" she said.

"No."

"Were you just passing through, then?"

He made a sound that could have meant anything.

"I only ask because if you got folk expecting you somewhere they've likely worried themselves sick by now, and I could send them word if I knew . . ." She let the end of her thought dangle open for him to finish off. He didn't even bother to grunt a response. Rachel was beginning to have some sympathy with the outsiders, who became so frustrated with the Plain People when their questions were met with silence and single syllables.

She slid another glance at him. He was looking her bedroom over now; he seemed to be analyzing and cataloguing it the way he'd done with her.

Her house was like most every other Plain farm in the valley, a simple structure made of cottonwood logs and a tin roof. Three simply furnished rooms: a *Küch*, or kitchen, and two bedrooms opening off the back of it. No curtains on the windows, no rugs on the floors, no pictures on the walls. Just a Plain house. But then he wouldn't know that, so doubtless it seemed some strange to him.

She had been looking around the room as he was, but now her gaze came back to him. His face revealed nothing of what he was truly made of, whether good or evil.

As they stared at each other, the air seemed to acquire a

thickness and a weight. She had no idea how to be with him. She knew she could never manage a smile, but she thought she could try a bit of friendliness herself. He was after all a guest in her house, and they didn't even know each other's names.

She wiped her hand on her apron and held it out to him, as was the Plain way. "It seems a bit late for a proper meeting, being as how you've already cursed me, like to have shot me, and bled buckets all over my best muslin sheets. But I'm Rachel Yoder. Mrs. Yoder."

He lay there looking up at her with his eyes so cold they burned. Yet the hand still wrapped around the gun held it gently now, his thumb caressing the butt, slowly, slowly. The silence dragged out and her own hand hung in the air between them until it trembled and started to fall.

And then he let go of his gun and took her hand in his. "You have my gratitude, ma'am. And my apology."

They remained that way for only the briefest moment, touching palm to palm; she was the one to pull away. "Your gratitude and apology are both accepted," she said. "While you're at it, do you have a name you'd care to give me? If only so's Benjo and I can have a handle to put on you when we speculate about you behind your back."

She had thought to show her willingness to be friendly by doing a bit of teasing, and then making a little joke at her own expense. But that was a Plain way of going about it; obviously it made no impression on him. He let her wait so long for an answer, she didn't think she was going to get one.

"You can call me Cain," he said finally.

She nearly gasped aloud. *And now art thou cursed from the earth, which hath opened her mouth to receive thy brother's blood from thy hand. . . .*

Surely no one could be born with such a name. He must have taken it on as some sort of cruel and bitter joke. She thought of the callus on his trigger finger. Cain. The name he killed under.

She knew her thoughts showed on her face. His mouth twisted. "If you don't like it," he said, "pick something else. I'll answer to most anything that ain't an insult. Is this Benjo your husband?"

"My—" Her voice cracked and she had to start over. "My son."

He stared at her in that intense way of his, and she could feel the color building in her cheeks.

"So, you're a widow, are you?"

She opened her mouth to lie; but a lifetime of believing it a sin stopped her. "Yes. My husband died last year."

He didn't say he was sorry for her loss, as most outsiders would have done. He said nothing at all. His gaze had wandered to the window again; he seemed to have forgotten her. Beyond the weathered gray fence of the feeding paddock, beyond the black cottonwoods that lined the creek, beyond the snow-clotted meadows and rocky buttes and weed-choked coulees, the mountains beckoned. Surging up against the harsh blue of a wind-tossed sky, they looked splendid, and lonely.

A stillness had come over him. The silence in the room took on a prickly tension, like a strand of barbed wire pulled tight between two fence posts.

"You still haven't told me where you call home," she said. She felt a need to put him in some familiar place. Not that she could imagine him walking behind a plow or tossing hay to a band of ewes. She couldn't even imagine him roping a cow or clinging to the pitching back of a wild mustang.

He pulled his attention from the great outdoors and looked at her. "I don't call anywhere home."

He seemed about to say more, but he was interrupted by the rattle of wagon wheels over the log bridge. He swung his gun up and pointed it at the door in a movement so quick she didn't even realize it had happened until it was over.

His jumping like that set her own heart to clamoring again, and it was pounding still as she stepped up to the window to see more of the road. The Weaver spring wagon rolled into the yard with Noah's son at the reins.

She turned back to the outsider. He could barely hold up his six-shooter, it was trembling so hard in his outstretched hand. His chest jerked with his rough breathing, fever-sweat sheened his face, his eyes glowed wild. Strangely, he reminded her of an etching in the *Martyrs Mirror* of a true believer being burned at the stake, his clasped hands raised to heaven in rapturous prayer as the bright and terrible flames consumed him.

She walked to him and put her hand against his chest, pressing him down into the bed. Ben's muslin nightshirt was slick beneath her palm; he'd sweated through it. She could feel him shuddering. "It's only Mose," she said. "My neighbor's boy, come to chop up some wood for me."

His harsh breathing made his words come out as a gasp. "This neighbor and his boy, do they know about me?"

"The whole valley can't help but know about you by now, the way rumor flies and grows with each telling. If a body coughs on Sunday, he'll hear about his own funeral come Tuesday."

"What are they saying?"

Through the window she watched Mose set the brake, tie the reins around its handle, and jump to the ground. He slapped the hat off his head, wiped his coat sleeve across his mouth, then smoothed back his light brown hair. He rolled his broadening shoulders like a horse with an itch. At seventeen he showed the sure promise of someday being as big and sturdy as his father.

"If they're Plain, they're saying you're a fool *Englischer* who went and got himself shot almost dead, and it's only by God's bountiful grace that you're not—dead, that is—although it would probably be no more than you deserve for your wicked ways. Nevertheless we all pray you will eventually arrive at the Truth and the Light. As for what the outsiders are saying—you could probably imagine that better than I could. Now, if you think you can be still for longer than a tick at a time, I'll tend to your hurt. The day's waning and I've got chores forming up a line for me to do."

He looked up at her, his eyes bright and slightly unfocused with the fever. "You are an oddity," he said. His gaze went slowly around the room again. "This whole place is an oddity."

"I'm Plain, and this is a Plain house. Our ways are the true ways, and they're not an oddity to God. Lie quiet now."

She used a pair of scissors to cut through his soiled bandage, since the knots were hopeless. She'd lied to him that first night, she thought. Lied without meaning to. He wasn't safe here. There was no place safe for a man like him this side of heaven, and he'd likely never be going *there* this side of eternity.

The flesh around the wound was raw and black and puckered at the edges; fresh blood seeped from all the jerking and jumping he'd been doing. Flesh. It could be sliced with a knife, smashed and torn by a bullet, whipped and burned, chained and degraded—how easily could the flesh be hurt. How frightening that flesh was so vulnerable when it was the vessel of life, the temple of the soul. It was solely by God's grace, surely, that this man still lived. He lived because God had sent him staggering across her wild hay meadow.

And then it occurred to her, with a sudden horror that almost made her heart stop, that if he wasn't safe, then neither were she and Benjo. That on taking him in, his enemies had become their enemies.

Slowly she looked up. He had a way of making all the life go out of his face, of making his eyes go flat and empty so that it was as if she looked through two holes into a husk of a man.

"The one who did this to you," she said, "is he going to be coming after you here?"

Nothing stirred behind his eyes. Nothing.

And then she realized the truth. He'd killed him. He had killed the man who had shot him; she had no doubt of it.

A terrible feeling came over her, a feeling she struggled to disown, for it was not the Plain way to seek redress against one's enemies, but rather to yield absolutely to God's will and trust in His ultimate mercy. *Not my will but thine be done.* But the feeling was there, nonetheless. She felt *relief.* Relief that she and Benjo would be safe because this man had killed.

She ripped off a piece of clean bandage and dabbed at the seeping blood. "You don't need to be pointing that gun of yours at every little noise or visitor. No outsider will be having a reason to come here." She dabbed at the wound, and dabbed and dabbed. "As for us, we Plain People bring suffering to no one, least of all the helpless and the sick."

"You're bringing suffering to me now, lady, the way you're prodding at me like I was a cow in a bog hole."

He'd put on his charming rascal's smile again, but this time it didn't quite work. This time his mouth betrayed the wildness in him, revealing the potential for meanness.

"The Bible says, Mr. Cain, that a man's sins do find him out." And Rachel tipped the bottle of carbolic acid over the raw hole in his side.

He made no sound, but his belly shuddered hard. She knew she'd hurt him and she felt mean now herself for having done it. It was what Noah meant about the taint of worldly corruption, she supposed. Already she was doing and saying things that weren't Rachel Yoder at all.

She finished putting on the fresh dressing, saying nothing more, not meeting his eyes. She was about to leave him when she saw that his gaze had fallen on the bullet he'd brought with him into her house, buried in his flesh. It sat there on the nightstand, next to her Bible. Small and round and bronze, and flattened a bit at one end where Doc Henry said it had struck a rib bone.

"The doctor dug that out of your spleen," she said.

He actually let go of his precious gun to pick up the bullet. He held it up to the shaft of sunlight pouring through the window, examining it almost with awe, as if it were a gold nugget. But then his fingers curled around it, making a fist.

She followed his gaze from the bullet in his fist to the wardrobe. The door was half open, although it should not have been. The wardrobe where Doc Henry had put the outsider's guns—and his cartridge belt with the extra bullets.

Rachel gasped, and her own gaze flew to the gun lying at his side, and then back up to his face.

Blue eyes, dead of all feeling, looked into hers. "The last bullet, almost."

MOSES WEAVER SCUFFED HIS feet along the rough boards of the Yoder front porch, scraping the worst of the sheep manure off his tooled leather high-heeled boots. He lifted his derby to slick back his pomaded hair, gave his checked trousers a hitch, and raised his arm to knock.

The door opened before his fist could fall. Mrs. Yoder gave him a slow look-over, pressing her fingers to her lips and making her eyes go round as shoe buttons. "Why, if it isn't our Mose. And don't you look flashy in those clothes, like a tin roof on a hot summer's day?"

His fist fell to his side and his cheeks caught fire. "Uh, I've come to chop up that wood for you, ma'am."

"I figured as much, and it sure is good of you. Especially when I know how your da has got you working over at your place from can't see to can't see." Her eyes squinted up at him, as if with silent laughter. "My, but you do look handsome, though."

He craned his head to see around her into the kitchen, but she shifted her weight to lean against the jamb. "So, did you get those fancy new clothes of yours out of a mail-order wishbook?"

"Yes, ma'am. I sent off for 'em with last summer's wool money." He stretched out his neck to see over her. He got a glimpse of a milk bucket and strainer sitting in the middle of the floor, a flour tin and a string of dried apples waiting on the table. With all the talk he'd been hearing, he almost expected to see the outsider lurking in there, wearing a black duster, armed with a pair of pearl-handled six-shooters, and leaking blood from a bullet hole in his side.

Mrs. Yoder stepped across the threshold onto the porch, pulling the door half shut behind her. The smell of vinegar wafted off her, pinching Mose's nose. She must be pickling, he thought, though it was the wrong time of year for it.

And he hadn't gotten so much as a whiff of the stranger. Folk said the man was a desperado, an outlaw whose face looked out of wanted posters that offered a thousand dollars in pure gold for his capture dead or alive. But the only reward, so it was also said, that anyone had collected thus far was hot lead from the end of the desperado's blazing six-shooters. Mose sure wished he could've gotten a look at those six-shooters. It was just the sort of wild tale to give the shivers to his girl, Gracie. Sometimes if he got Gracie worked up enough, she'd let him put his arms around her and hold her close.

Mose suddenly realized that Mrs. Yoder was still standing there smiling at him, and probably wondering why he didn't get on with it. He stuffed his hands in his pockets and backed up, and stumbled when his boot heel caught on a warped board. "I'll just be at that wood, then."

He got halfway to the chopping block before she called after him. "Mose? Why don't you knock on the door after you're done and I'll give you some dried apple duff to take home with you."

Mose spun around, grinning broadly, and touched the curled brim of his new black derby in a cocky salute. She hadn't actually invited him inside, but maybe he could get a gander at the desperado after all, might even get a chance to exchange a howdy with the man. Wouldn't Gracie be impressed when she heard about that, he thought, although his father would likely have a conniption. Old Deacon Noah was of the mind that all a Plain boy had to do was get within hailing distance of the world outside, with all its evil and corrupting influences, and he would be damned. As if the purity of a body's soul could be corroded by exposure to the world, the way a rake got rusty if it was left out too long in the rain.

Mose looked back at the house, shading his eyes from the dazzle of the sun striking off the tin roof, but Mrs. Yoder had gone inside. He looked flashy, she'd said, flashy as a tin roof in his new clothes. He grinned to himself at the thought of it.

There'd been a lot of talk lately about his father and Mrs. Yoder marrying. It wasn't any secret the old man had been hankering after her for years. It didn't appear like she was going to have him, though, not even with Mr. Yoder dead and buried nigh on a year. Mose didn't really like to think of how beaten down and sad his father had been looking lately.

Mose wished it would happen—them two getting married. He liked Mrs. Yoder a lot. She had a nice way of smiling and touching him in little ways, like patting him on the shoulder and brushing the hair back out of his eyes, and she was always asking him whether his coat was warm enough and giving him food, like the offer of dried apple duff. He'd often imagined that if his own mother had lived she'd be like Mrs. Yoder. But his mother had died having another baby when he was only a year old. His aunt Fannie had moved in after that, to keep house for him and Da, and if she'd ever spared so much as a smile for either one of them, he sure couldn't remember it.

Even with the sun shining, the wind still had winter's bite to it, and Mose shivered as he shrugged out of his four-button cutaway. He didn't want to sweat stains into his new coat before Gracie got a look at it. She probably wouldn't recognize him in it, she was so used to seeing him in that ugly brown sack coat that all the other Plain boys wore.

He ran his finger over the skin beneath his nose to see if anything had started sprouting there yet, but he didn't feel so much as the prickle of a single whisker. He'd bought a tonic at the drugstore in Miawa City that guaranteed to grow hair on a man's bald head, but it seemed to work squat-all when it came to mustaches. He wanted to grow one of those mustaches that curled up on the ends. He'd really look flashy then.

And old Deacon Noah would have himself another conniption.

As it was, his father's lips puckered up as if he'd been sucking on a lemon every time Mose stepped out of the house wearing his mail-order clothes with all their forbidden buttons and pockets and fancy stitching. But it wasn't really against the rules for Mose to dress worldly because he hadn't been baptized into the church yet. Once he took his vows, once he promised to walk the straight and narrow way—well, then he'd have to dress Plain, to grow a beard but not a mustache, and quit parting his hair for the rest of his life. So the way he saw it, there was no sense to doing all that before time.

Mose carefully hung his new coat on the low branch of a nearby yellow pine. He gave the satin-piped collar a caressing stroke. All his life he'd been taught not to love the world, nor the things of the world, but he loved that coat. Every time he put it on, every time he so much as looked at it, he felt a forbidden exhilaration. Sort of like what he felt when he dove into Blackie's Pond. There was that first sudden, exciting shock of it when his head would break through the water. Then the excitement would start to edge over into fear as he'd be sucked down into the pond, down, down into the cold black depths. And just when the fear would be about to take hold, he'd touch bottom and shoot back to the surface, back to the warmth and light again.

He thought about that, about the heady and scary temptations of the world, as he laid a thick piece of cedar trunk on the chopping block. He raised the ax above his head and brought it down. The ax split the wood with a solid *whunk!* and a ring of its steel blade. Chips spun off into the dirt, and the spicy scent of cedar floated on the wind.

His body settled into the rhythm of the swinging ax—arms stretching above his head, shoulders bunching as he brought the ax down, and the hard shudder of the blow through his body as the blade bit the wood. Chopping firewood was hard work, but Mose liked it. It helped to calm some of the wild and edgy feelings that had been churning in his guts all winter. "Work sure will keep a boy from getting the bighead," old Deacon Noah was fond of saying. "Hard work is the answer. The bad thoughts and feelings—they come out with the sweat." Except they didn't all come out, Mose thought, not completely.

The ax blade caught in a knot, and Mose jerked hard on the helve. He winced as the sudden movement pulled at the bruises and welts on his back. He was still some sore from the thrashing his father had given him for what he'd done in Miawa City last Saturday afternoon. He thought he was getting too big to be whipped, but the trouble was he wasn't so big yet that he could stop his father from doing it.

Ach, vell, he did know of one way. He could renounce the evil world, marry Gracie, and settle down into the Plain life forever after. If he did all that, he would make things right again between him and his father. But every time he thought of it he got this suffocating, choking feeling in his chest, as if he'd somehow gotten nailed up in a coffin alive.

Mose tossed a piece of the fresh-cut wood onto the stack and was reaching for another when a stone whizzed past his head and smacked into a burl on the trunk of the pine tree that held his coat.

"Hey!" he shouted and whirled, a scowl pulling at his face.

Benjo Yoder trotted up, his herding collie loping at his heels. Both boy and dog must have just come from the creek. The dog gave himself an allover shake, misting the air. The boy's broadfalls were wet to the knees, his coat matted with last summer's thistles. A braided rawhide sling dangled from his left hand.

Mose jammed his fists on his hips and pointed to the sling with his chin. "I 'spect you fancy yourself David the giant killer with that thing."

"I kuh—kuh—killed me a m-muskrat." Benjo raised his arm to show off what he had in his other hand. He held the animal up by its webbed hind feet. Its long flat tail curled around its glossy brown fur. Its crushed head dripped blood into the dirt.

"Pee-uw!" Mose said, rearing back a step as the muskrat's powerful stink slapped him in the face. He looked the trophy over, his lips curling into a sneer. "Come see me when you bag yourself a grizzly bear, Benjo Yoder, and then maybe I'll be impressed."

Hurt crumbled the boy's bright-eyed grin, and Mose had to look away. Just because he was feeling aggravated with his own life, Mose thought, that was no reason to take it out on poor Benjo.

"Hey," he said, punching the boy lightly on the arm. "You gonna serve up that ol' muskrat for supper?"

Benjo snorted a laugh. He hauled back and flung the wet carcass into the air. They both watched until it landed in a wild plum thicket with a soggy *splat*. MacDuff barked and took off after it, only to get sidetracked by a rabbit that darted out of the thicket and led him on a chase behind the barn.

"So how come you're out hunting muskrats, instead of being in school?" Mose said.

"It's an outsider huh—holiday."

"Hunh. It's no outsider holiday. But I bet your mem don't know that."

Poor Benjo was one of the few Plain kids whose folk actually made him go to the *Englische* school. Most of the Plain didn't hold with book learning, figuring it a waste of time for a boy who was only going to grow up to be a farmer. Schooling wasn't forbidden by the church, though. It was one of the few things that weren't forbidden, Mose thought sourly.

At the mention of school, Benjo had suddenly turned deaf, busying himself with looping up his sling and tucking it into the waistband of his broadfalls. Mose hefted another piece of the cedar onto the chopping block. He wiped the wood dust off his ax blade, spat into his palms, gripped the helve and settled his shoulders for the first upward swing. He looked up in time to catch Benjo casting a worried glance back at the house.

"What's he like?"

The boy jumped like a cricket, then lifted his shoulders in an exaggerated shrug. There'd been no need for Mose to specify who *he* was. The whole valley had been talking about *him* for three days now. "Mem says I'm to stuh—stuh—stay away from him," Benjo said. "He's juh—juh . . . jumpy."

"Yeah?" Mose cocked a grin at the boy. "No more than you are, I reckon."

Benjo jutted out his chin. "I'm not scuh—scared of him."

It was on the tip of Mose's tongue to ask the boy if he intended to take on the desperado's six-shooters with his puny sling, but this time he held back. He didn't want to hurt the boy. Because he was built small and stuttered, a lot of people, especially outsiders, thought Benjo Yoder was weak and maybe a little stupid, and they picked on him because of it. Mose himself was sometimes mean to the kid, though he was always sorry for it afterward. He supposed he'd always been a little jealous of Benjo because he had Rachel Yoder for a mother.

With the mean words he'd been about to say drying up in his mouth, Mose found himself out of conversation. He bent over the chopping block again, rubbed his hands across the seat of his trousers and wrapped them around the ax helve.

"Muh—Mose?"

Mose glanced up, waiting while the muscles in Benjo's throat strained and his lips pulled back from his teeth.

"Duh—duh—duh—duh . . ."

Mose huffed an impatient sigh. "*Ja, vell?* Spit it out or swallow it."

Benjo pursed his lips and bulged his cheeks, and the stubborn word indeed shot out on a spray of spittle. "D-did you really go into the G-gilded Cage last suh—suh—Saturday and buy yourself a g-glass of the Devil's b-brew?"

Mose straightened with a snap, bringing the ax with him. He flushed, glancing around guiltily as if he expected his father to come popping up out of the buffalo grass and give him what-for again. "So what if I did?" he said.

"So d-did you drink it . . . the Devil's brew?"

"I said I drank it, didn't I?"

Mose wedged the ax back into the chopping block and wiped his mouth with his sleeve to hide his smile as Benjo launched into the first round of his many whats, whys, and how comes, barely slowed by his stutter. The truth was Mose relished the opportunity to tell someone about his adventure in Miawa City's grandest honky-tonk. The good Lord knew his father and his aunt Fannie sure hadn't wanted to hear a word of it.

Just talking about it brought back to Mose all the flavors of that day. There'd been the first panicky excitement that had dried his mouth as he pushed open the door of the Gilded Cage, his eyes blinking against the sting of thick cigar smoke. The place had been rank with the smell of tobacco slop, spilled beer, and woolen union suits that hadn't been washed in weeks, maybe never.

The floor had been sprinkled with sawdust, and in the sudden quiet that marked his entrance, it ground under the heels of Mose's new boots as he walked up to the bar. Shyness kept his eyes on his boots, and he became sort of mesmerized by the way their pointy toes could cut such a dashing swath. When he glanced up, he was startled to see himself reflected in a huge gold-framed mirror. He thought he looked flashy in his new mail-order suit and derby, and not at all like a Plain boy. Until he heard somebody snicker.

Besides himself, the mirror had shown Mose a half dozen watermarked wooden tables that were ringed by spindly chairs. The walls were decorated with deer antlers and one moth-eaten moose head. A man plucked halfheartedly at the yellow keys of a piano. A brassy-haired woman leaned over the piano player's shoulder, and Mose barely kept his mouth from falling open at the sight of all that naked skin she was displaying. Four other men lounged on their tailbones on chairs drawn up to a potbellied stove, cradling tin pails of beer in their laps. They were gawking at Mose as if he'd suddenly started sprouting a set of horns to rival the moose head's.

Mose looked away from the reflection in the mirror, his gaze moving over the shelves of decanters, cigar vases, and jars of brandied fruit, finally settling on a man polishing the bar with a wet rag.

The man gave him a slit-eyed once-over, then let loose a long splatter of tobacco juice out the corner of his mouth. It hit the side of a brass cuspidor with a loud *ping*. "How there, Plain boy," he said. He had thick purple lips, hanging jowls, and wispy white hair that sat on his head like a dandelion puff. "Who let you outta the zoo?"

"I'd like a glass of your finest whiskey, please."

The barkeep hawked a deep laugh, along with another glob of tobacco juice. " 'A glass of your finest whiskey, puleeze,' " he mocked. But then he stretched his thick lips into a long flat line that curved up on one end like a fishhook. Mose hoped it was meant to be a smile. "You got two bits?"

Mose braced his foot on the bar's brass rail while he dug the coin out of the fob pocket of his flashy new vest.

The barkeep sat a bottle and a glass in front of Mose and gave him another one of those fishhook grins. "This here is the best damn tarantula juice this side of hell. One slug is guaranteed to cure whatever ails ya," he said, and filled the glass to the brim with what to Mose's eyes looked like swamp water. Mose carefully lifted the glass, drew a deep breath, and prepared to join hands with the Devil.

He coughed and sputtered and shuddered with the first fiery swallow, but the next one went down a little easier. The barkeep watched Mose for a moment longer and then went back to his polishing.

The men around the stove also went back to what they were doing, which appeared to consist of smoking, chewing, spitting, and blaspheming. Mose had been just starting to think that sinning wasn't all it was cracked up to be, when the woman with all that naked skin sidled up to him and asked him if he wanted to buy a dance.

"The way it works," Mose told Benjo, unable even now to keep the wonder of it out of his voice, "is you pay another two bits to the barkeep for a piece of red tin called a token. Then you give the token to the lady and she tucks it in her, uh . . . she puts it away, and then you dance." Actually what Mose had mostly done was stumble and trip across that sawdusted floor. But, oh my, she'd felt as soft and fluffy in his arms as a goose-down pillow.

"Those dancing ladies, they fly fast as silk flags in a high wind," he said with a wink and a grin. He doubted, though, that Benjo knew what the word "fast" meant when applied to a lady. Mose wasn't quite sure himself about all the nuances of the word.

Benjo was looking up at him in wide-eyed wonder, and Mose felt a bright glow. "So, how'd you know about me paying a visit to the Gilded Cage anyway?"

"I . . . I h-heard your da talking to Mem about it. He said you're buh—buh—breaking his heart."

All the brightness left Mose, like clouds swallowing up the sun. *Breaking his heart.* Put like that, it suddenly didn't seem enough that he'd paid for his grand adventure with the lick of the old man's razor strop across his back.

"Aw, old Deacon Noah's just afraid I'm going to stroll into some honky-tonk one day and come out an *Englischer.*" He snorted as if such a thing was beyond belief, but this niggling doubt tickled at him, like an ant crawling up his ankle. Just that one little jaunt into the Gilded Cage had shown him that seeing certain things made you want other things that maybe you shouldn't want.

"Wh-what does it t-taste like?"

"Huh? What? The whiskey?" Mose cuffed his mouth, his lips pulling back from his teeth as if he were just now taking his first big swallow of what the barkeep had told him was the best damn tarantula juice this side of hell. "It's like swallowing fire. And it makes your belly buzz and tingle, when it hits bottom."

"Wh-what does it smell like?"

"Huh? I don't know. It smells like whiskey."

Benjo nodded seriously, as if this bit of knowledge only confirmed his own vast experience, and Mose hid a smile.

"What about that f-fast lady you duh—duh—danced with? Wh-what did she smell like?"

"Criminy!" Mose swiveled his head around as if looking for eavesdroppers. He leaned on the ax helve, bringing him eye to eye with the younger boy, and he lowered his voice to a harsh whisper. "There's a question you shouldn't be asking."

"Wh-why not?"

Because she'd smelled of sweat and old talcum powder, and he didn't like tarnishing his adventure by exposing it to the light of too much truth. "Because you're a pesky, wet-behind-the-ears, snot-nose kid, that's why not."

"Yeah? W-well, your da told Mem that you had *your* nose buried in her b-bosom and it was nuh—naked."

"Criminy!" Mose snatched up his ax with such force the boy jumped. "I don't know why I bother with you anyway, Benjo Yoder. And if you don't quit pestering me, it'll be the Fourth of July before I'm done chopping this wood."

"I w-w-was only wuh—wuh—wondering whuh—whuh—what she smelled like," Benjo said, stuttering so badly Mose barely understood him. He had decided to ignore the pesky kid anyway.

Benjo took out his sling and dug a stone out of the ground with the toe of his brogan. He cast Mose a look, but Mose was still ignoring him. He fitted the stone into the sling's leather socket, held the two ends of the rawhide cords in his left hand, and whirled it above his head. He let go of one cord sharply and the stone whizzed through the air, hitting the pine burl bull's-eye. But Mose ignored that as well.

Benjo released a tiny sigh, turned, and shuffled away.

Mose waited until the boy was almost at the house before he looked up. He thought maybe Benjo would glance back to see if he was watching, but he didn't.

Mose snatched off his hat and slapped himself on the thigh with it hard enough to sting. "Gol-blimey, Mose Weaver. You've got straw for brains!"

He'd been so busy answering Benjo's questions that he'd let slip by the opportunity to ask a few of his own. Benjo probably knew all sorts of interesting things about the outsider, like what he was wanted for and how much lead he was packing and how many people he'd killed. Above all, Mose wanted to know exactly what sort of flashy duds the desperado had been wearing when he was shot.

THAT NIGHT THE OUTSIDER'S fever settled into his chest, and Rachel knew he wouldn't live to see the sun rise.

He breathed as if he were drowning inside his own body. It was horrible to hear him, the way the air gurgled in his lungs and rasped wetly out his throat. And she found herself waiting, with her own breath suspended, to see if each strangled gasp would be followed by another, or if it would be his last.

She refused to let him go easily. In the early hours, while he could still swallow, she dosed him with onion syrup. She stripped the sweat-soaked nightshirt off him and bathed his naked body. And while the vinegar water rose off his burning flesh in a steam that enveloped the bed, she prayed for him. She prayed not that God would save his life, for his life already rested in God's loving hands. She prayed only that He would have mercy on the outsider's soul. For she had learned long ago that not all the bum lambs could be saved.

Once, deep in the night, she thought he came awake. He struggled to sit up, and she leaned close in to him and laid her arm across his chest to calm him, while taking care not to jostle his gunshot wound or his broken arm. His breathing was coming in such hard shocks now that she wondered how his ribs didn't crack from the strain. Long ago he'd ruptured his sutures again; the bandage shone wet-black with blood in the flickering lantern light. And she supposed it was a testament to how close to death he was that he'd finally let go of his gun.

Suddenly his hand lashed out, his fingers spanning her neck as if he would strangle her, pushing her chin up.

He held her suspended with his strong and violent hand. She stared down into his face and she was lost for an instant in the compelling facets of his eyes—eyes that turned black and wild as his grip on her throat tightened.

"Bastard," he said, the words torn raw from his throat. "I'll fucking kill you, you goddamned bastard."

His fingers clenched, hurting her. She clawed at his wrist. She brought her knee up against the side of the bed to use as leverage to pull against him. His grip tightened and tightened, choking off her air now. Rachel's chest burned, her ears roared with surging blood. The lantern-lit room began to blacken at the edges.

Then he let her go, so abruptly that she collapsed in a

sprawl on top of his chest. Air flooded into her starved lungs on a rush of pain. A small, startled cry escaped her bruised throat. Frantic still with fear, she pushed herself off him and staggered away from the bed.

He had fallen back into a deep faint, although his chest still strained for every breath. She stared at him, her hand to her throbbing throat, her own chest heaving. The agony of pity and horror that she felt was nearly as paralyzing as his fingers had been. It wasn't the foul words he'd spoken; she'd heard such words before, although never from the mouth of a Plain man. But that look in his eyes. She couldn't imagine the rupture of spirit it would take to so fill a man with such black and bottomless hate.

She wasn't sure how long she'd stood there before she realized that his fevered body was now racked with chills. She covered him up with the sheet and her star-patterned quilt, and then another quilt, and still he shuddered and shook so hard the iron bedstead rattled. Finally she took off her half boots and crawled into the bed with him, fully clothed from her shawl to her prayer cap, to warm him with her own body's heat.

She had held only one naked man in her arms before this, and that was her husband. She'd always been intrigued by how different Ben's body was from hers. The weight and size of him that could seem so overwhelming and yet so comforting. The pelt of hair on his chest and legs that gave him a warm fuzziness to snuggle up to. The way a man's back felt beneath a woman's hands, taut and smooth and powerful beneath her touch. It was wondrous to think how a man's skin could feel so soft, and yet underneath there was all muscle and sinew, hardness and strength.

The memory of Ben, of holding Ben like this, tore at her, sharp and raw and nearly unbearable.

A man such as this one killed my husband, she thought, hanged him with a rope and laughed while he was doing it. My Ben, to have died in such a way, and all because of outsiders like this man. This man who calls himself Cain.

No, no, those were the Devil's whisperings, coming as they often did at night when the will was weak and tired. This outsider had done no evil to her and he shouldn't have to suffer for the evil that had been done unto her by others. She couldn't blame him for what happened to Ben, or she would become like him. The rage and hate that lived in him would become a part of her.

Later, during the gray hour that harbingered the dawn, while she held his chill-racked body tight to her breast and her face lay close to his, his bruised and weighted eyelids lifted a little.

"Don't leave me," he rasped. And all the world's sorrow, all the world's loss, was in those blue eyes.

HE DIDN'T DIE THAT NIGHT, or the night after that. During the second day Doc Henry came out to the farm. He listened to the outsider's chest with an instrument he called a trumpet stethoscope. He frowned, shook his head, and said, "Whoever claimed only the good die young never lived in Montana."

And then, before he left, the doctor gave her laudanum to "help ease your bum lamb's passing, because once he gets where he's going he's sure to know suffering enough."

Sometime during the third night Rachel fell asleep on her knees beside the bed where she had been praying. When she awoke just after dawn, she was lying half across the bed, and she was holding his hand. Groggy, disoriented, she knew only that something was different, and then she realized what it was. The room was quiet. The outsider's choking, stertorous gasps had subsided to the slow, even breathing of a deep sleep.

White winter sunwash flooded through the window, limning the hard planes and angles of his body like the silver edging on a cloud. It made him seem not a real man at all but a thing made of stone. A statue, perhaps, that a pagan might worship.

A pagan statue, indeed. The thought made her smile, for he was lying on a very ordinary old sheet that was gray and thin from many boilings and washings, and stained now with his own fever sweat. She supposed if she was looking at him and smiling then she must have lost some of her fear of him. Some, not all.

She pushed herself to her feet, aching, feeling battered. She looked down at his face, quiet now in his deep sleep. It seemed strange that a face could be so familiar to her eyes, and yet not be dear to her heart.

His fever had broken, and he slept. She thought she ought to see to her hungry sheep and get Benjo off to school, yet she felt reluctant to leave him. She took a jar of glycerin from the nightstand and rubbed it over his fever-cracked lips. Strangely, the intimacy of what she was doing struck her in a way that holding his naked body had not.

She felt an odd affinity for him. Not one of friendship and caring, for he was an outsider. Not even one of liking, for she didn't know him. Yet she wondered . . . no, it was more than a wondering, it was almost a conviction: that he had been sent to her for a purpose.

But that was vanity, surely. She had saved his life twice and now she was thinking she had some claim on him, when he belonged only to God. Or, more likely, to the Devil. For he was a man who lived surrounded by the weapons of death, and he carried the damning sin of hate in his heart. In truth, although she didn't know them, she thought his sins must be too numerous and too terrible even to be named.

And yet, and yet, if God was the Creator of all things, then surely He wouldn't create a soul that was completely unredeemable.

RACHEL ANCHORED HER CHIN into the teetering pile of kindling in her arms and nudged the door open with her hip. She was almost safely to the woodbox with her precarious load when she heard a deep, death-rattling moan.

The wood fell from her arms to the kitchen floor with a clatter. She ran into the bedroom with a prayer on her lips. She couldn't nurse him through another bout of fever, Judas, she just couldn't.

He wasn't dying again. If anything looked close to expiring it was MacDuff, who lay sprawled alongside the outsider on the bed, getting his belly scratched by that long, dangerous hand. And getting muddy paw prints and dog drool all over her best quilt.

Rachel headed right at him, her arms waving, her temper flying, and her tongue letting loose in *Deitsch*. *"Geh naus! Geh veck!"*

MacDuff leaped into the air, scrambling off the bed. He came slinking to meet her with his tail tucked deep between his legs. She felt mean for having yelled at him, and bent to push her fingers through the collie's thick pelt.

The outsider was regarding her with inquiring eyes, his head slightly tilted. The man seemed to have all his senses back for the first time since the fever had felled him again three nights ago. Shooing the dog out of the room, she raised her gaze from the sun-speckled floorboards to the man's face. "*Guten Morgen.* . . . Good morning."

He stared at her for what seemed like forever. Then came one of those unexpected and dazzling smiles. "Mornin'."

"I'm sorry MacDuff woke you like that." At his slightly puzzled look she added, "MacDuff's that pest of a dog."

His mouth deepened at the corners. It wasn't quite a smile this time, yet he seemed amused. "Who would think to stick a poor dog with a name like MacDuff?"

"That was what he was called when we got him off a Scottish sheep farmer in the next valley. Later, Doc Henry told us the name came from a play about a king who was foully slain. A terrible thing. But it was too late by then, because MacDuff already thought of himself as MacDuff."

He laughed, a soft laugh that turned into a cough. And then he looked surprised, as if he didn't really laugh all that often. It surprised her, as well, to hear him laugh, so that she blushed.

He made her uncomfortable, she decided, because she had no idea how to be with him. She had little acquaintance with outsiders, with their peculiar ways and outlandish thoughts. Yet there was that strange affinity she felt for this particular outsider, because of what they'd been through, she supposed. You couldn't hold a man close to your heart while he was naked and dying and come away from the experience without feeling you knew him, even when you really knew him not at all.

She struggled to find words to fill the silence and break the uneasiness that lay between them. He was lying propped up slightly on the pillows, as if he'd tried to push himself upright earlier and found he hadn't the strength.

"How are you feeling, Mr. . . . Cain?" she said. Judas, it was hard to call the man by such a name. But then perhaps, like MacDuff the dog, it was all what you became used to.

His mouth had tightened in that strange almost-smile. "I feel weak and sore enough to figure out that I should be offering you my gratitude again. How long was I sick for this time?"

"Two days and three nights. And you should be offering your thanks to God, for truly it is by His miracle that you still live."

"I guess a holy-howler like you ought to know. For a while there that first morning you looked like you were trying to decide between heaving that basin at my head and damning me to hell, or falling on your knees and praying for deliverance."

He nearly surprised a smile out of her, the way he talked. Judas, she didn't know what to make of one such as he. And she was having a hard time meeting his eyes, the way he stared at her. But then she knew he found her a curiosity, with her prayer cap and all.

"So, how are you now, truly?" she said. "I mean, can I be getting you anything?"

"Well," he answered, drawing out the word long and slow. "I woke up with such a dry throat, it would've taken me three days just to work up a whistle. But then I found a pitcher of water miraculously sitting right handy next to the bed. Thank you . . . God." He cast a droll glance heavenward. "And now," he went on, and this time his smile had a rascal's tilt, "I'm feeling so hungry I could eat a grizzly but for the claws. Do you think the good Lord might be cooking up another miracle in the kitchen?"

She covered her mouth with her hand, her eyes widening with a shock of near laughter. She shook her head, backing up a step, then fled the room.

And it was like running out of a dream, only to awaken

in a place she'd never seen before. She stood in the middle of her kitchen, in a house she'd lived in for years, and looked around her as if in a daze. She brought her shaking hand up to her forehead. I'm tired, she thought. And still scared of him.

She'd never thought of herself as timid around outsiders before. Careful, yes. Or resigned and accepting of God's will when they could be mean. But she'd never really been fearful, the way she was with him. And it had nothing to do with what had happened to Ben. She had already decided to forgive this outsider for being like the men of violence who had hanged her husband. No, this fear went deeper. As if he threatened her very essence.

Impatiently she shrugged away such strange thoughts. The man had said he was hungry, and for that, at least, she knew what to do.

She made up a bowl of stewed crackers and took it in to him. He had pushed himself further upright against the pillows while she was gone, and the effort had cost him. He was breathing heavily and sweating, his face was pale, the skin around his mouth taut.

She said nothing as she pulled the rocking chair up to the bed. She untied her stiff cap strings and tossed them over her shoulders. But then she waited a moment, the bowl of stewed crackers cradled in her hands in case he prayed silently before eating, as the Plain did.

He didn't pray. He looked down at the saltines soaked in hot milk and made such a face he reminded her of Benjo. She could feel a smile trying to come, teasing at her mouth. She tightened her lips.

"My mouth," he said, "kinda had its heart set on something it had to chew."

"I doubt your stomach could handle anything your mouth had to chew."

"Lady, my stomach is so starved that my bellybutton is shaking hands with my backbone."

She almost laughed again, and she didn't like herself for it, for responding to his calculated charm. He obviously had a whole repertoire of smiles and his own reasons for these friendly, teasing ways of his. Still, she supposed she ought to be thanking the good Lord he was aiming smiles and jokes at her now, instead of that six-shooter of his.

She dug the spoon into the bowl and brought it, dripping milk, up to his mouth.

He curled his fingers around hers, which were in turn curled around the spoon's handle. "I can manage," he said. A trace of color rose under his fair skin. "I can manage, if you'll hold the bowl. Please."

She slid her fingers from beneath his, allowing him his pride.

She held the bowl for him and watched him eat. She watched his hand, the subtle flex of bone and tendon, and she thought of how that hand had felt wrapped around her throat, the cruel strength of it. She watched his mouth, his lips as they closed over the bowl of the spoon, and she thought how the very set of that mouth betrayed the wildness in him. She watched his slightly lowered face and thought how his eyelashes were so long and thick they cast shadows on his cheekbones, and she thought how surely she'd never seen such eyelashes on anyone, man or woman.

And she thought of the Scripture Noah had quoted, of how you couldn't drink both of the Lord's cup and of the Devil's.

SHE WAS OUT ON THE sled feeding the sheep, a bare hour later, when she heard Benjo's scream.

Her son banged out the door of the house, with MacDuff at his heels. The boy was running so hard he lost his hat, and his brogans kicked up big splatters of mud. Rachel stabbed the pitchfork into a hay bale, jumped off the sled, and took off running herself.

They were nearly to the creek before she caught up with him. She snagged his arm and swung him around. He looked frightened, but he also looked guilty.

"Benjo—" She had to stop and take a deep breath after the scare he'd given her and then running like that. "Benjo, what happened?"

"Nuh . . . nuh . . . thing!"

He tried to pull away, but she gripped his shoulders. Her gaze darted over him, searching. "Was it the outsider? Did he hurt you? If he's touched you in any way—"

"Nuh!" Benjo shook his head hard. "He d-didn't!"

He twisted out of her grasp and ran off, MacDuff barking at his heels, thinking it a game of chase. This time Rachel let her boy go. He'd been frightened apparently, but not hurt, and she wasn't likely to get anything more out of him. Benjo had never been one for confiding his troubles.

She crossed the yard and entered the house. She didn't even take the time to wipe her boots on the burlap bag she kept on the porch to save tracking mud onto her kitchen floor.

It seemed she crossed that kitchen floor in three strides, such was her anger with him. When she entered the bedroom, though, she was stopped by the bemused expression on the outsider's face. During the long hours of nursing him, she had hung one of her soiled prayer caps on a bedpost, to be tossed into the washtub later, and then forgotten about it. He had it now in his hand, holding it up to the light. He seemed to be looking at his own fingers through the sheerness of the cap, and his skin was nearly as pale as the white cambric.

"What did you do to my son?" she demanded.

His gaze flashed from the prayer cap to her face. "How come he acts like he's got a frog stuck in his craw?"

She brought herself right up to the bed so that she could stand over him. "What did you do to frighten my son?"

He laid the prayer cap in his lap, trailing his fingers along one of the ribbons. But his eyes stayed on her face. "If anyone ought to be frightened, it's me. I woke up and there he was staring down at me, nose to nose, hacking and spouting like a geyser at me. All I did was point my finger at him. . . ." His mouth curled up slow at the edges. "Well, I might've said, 'Bang.'"

Rachel gripped her elbows, hugging herself to stifle a sudden chill. That had been mean, what he'd done.

His gaze held her quiet and still and frightened. The way he could go from that lazy smile of a moment ago to the way he was now, his eyes all flat and cold, his face hard.

But then he looked away from her, down to the prayer cap in his lap. He ran his finger along the edge of the stiff middle pleat. "I don't like surprises, Mrs. Yoder. I thought your boy should know that."

The strange note of weariness in his voice touched her heart with pity. How terrible, she thought, to have always to be living life on the wary edge. To never be able to let yourself feel safe anywhere, with anybody.

"The trouble is, Mr. Cain, that you seem to be dealing frights out to us here quicker than we can duck."

"I want your boy to be careful of me," he said slowly. He lifted his gaze back to her face. "But not scared. And I don't want you scared either."

She watched, mesmerized, as his hand let go of her

prayer cap and came up, and she thought for a moment he was going to touch her, but what he did was even more shocking. He laid his palm on her Bible, which she kept on the table by her bed.

"I swear to you, Mrs. Yoder, on this book you set such store by, that—"

"No, you mustn't do that!" She reacted without thought, covering his mouth with her fingers to stop his words. She got a spark from touching him, like you could get sometimes pressing your fingertips to the windowpane during a summer lightning storm. "You mustn't swear to me on the Bible like that. Oaths are serious things. To be made only to God and they are binding for life."

She had taken her fingers off his lips the instant she had touched him, but the spark had given her a strange feeling inside, like a tickle. She curled her hand into a fist and wrapped it up in her apron.

He stared at her a moment in that intense way of his, with his hand still on her Bible. Then he brought his hand back to his lap, his fingers lightly, lightly brushing over her prayer cap. "How about a simple promise, then?" he said. "If I tell you I'll not harm you or your boy, will you take my word on it?"

"Why shouldn't I take your word?" she said, surprised by the question.

"What if I was a gambler, a thief, a shootist of some repute, and a liar of considerable practice?"

"I think you've probably been all those things at one time in your life."

He laughed, shaking his head. "Lady, you have sure got me pegged."

She stared at him, trying to understand him. He seemed

unable to imagine anyone trusting in him, because he trusted in no one himself.

"If *you* believe you won't harm us, Mr. Cain," she said, "then we believe you."

SHE WENT BACK OUT to the sled and took up the pitchfork and began to feed the hungry woollies again, her head full of strange thoughts and feelings that flickered and were gone like moths darting at a lamp.

Later, when she was on her knees scrubbing up the mud she'd tracked onto her kitchen floor, she thought about what the outsider had done to Benjo, pointing his finger and saying "bang" like that, scaring him so.

She worried about him, her Benjo. She knew his heart was sore and lonely, but she couldn't find a way to ease it, not when she couldn't even get him to talk to her. Much of his unhappiness was a grieving for his father, she knew. But she didn't know how she was going to get him to understand, to accept, the will of God when her own heart and mind balked at understanding.

And there were other things troubling the boy, she thought, things that had to do with his edging up to being a man. He'd taken to disobeying her lately, doing things he'd never have dared to try to get away with around his father. Like he should have been at school today. . . . *Ach, vell,* the Plain didn't set much store by book learning, and so she'd tended since Ben was gone to let the *Englische* school slide.

But now this outsider had come into their lives to add to her boy's troubles, and she didn't know how to say to him that he should not be afraid. Not when her own mind and heart knew such fear.

She wished she could share with Ben the story about their boy getting scared with a "bang." Knowing Ben, though, he probably would have laughed to hear it. He was such a man for that, for appreciating how life had a funny way of twisting itself all inside out and backward. *Bang!* It made her smile to think of how Ben would have laughed.

Her hands stilled in their scrubbing, and she shut her eyes. A single tear fell onto the wet pine board, followed by another and another, and then she had to press her hands hard to her face to stifle the sounds of her weeping.

RACHEL SUPPOSED, WITH SUCH a day as she was having, it was inevitable that she would get a visit from Jakob Fischer.

She'd had a goodly number of visitors over the last three days, neighbors who had come calling with pots of mulligan stew or offers to do chores for her—like young Mose, who'd chopped up enough wood to see her through another six months of winter. And all of them, of course, harboring a hope of glimpsing her notorious houseguest.

But Jakob Fischer was the worst snoop among their people. Indeed, he'd been sticking his meddlesome and inquisitive nose into others' affairs for so long that the Plain had started calling him Big Nose Jakob to his face. He didn't seem to mind, but then he did have a big nose, red and ripe as a late summer tomato, and Rachel wondered sometimes if he just didn't get the joke.

She was putting a snitz pie in the oven when the door cracked open and Jakob Fischer's nose came right on in, along with the rest of him. "I'm here to see this outsider you've got for yourself," he said, as if it were a new prize ram she'd just acquired. And without waiting to be announced he headed straight for her bedroom.

No sooner did he poke his nose around the jamb than he let out a thunderbuster bellow that shook the air. He flew out of the house, his nose leading the way. He was screaming at the top of his lungs, something about the Devil having fangs on him that were as big and shiny as carving knives.

It had all happened so fast that Rachel was still standing by the stove. She sighed, wiped her hands on her apron, and went in to see what the outsider had done now.

The man called Cain lay propped against the pillows, holding a long, flat metal tube up to his mouth. She could see where Big Nose Jakob might think he was seeing a devil with fangs, especially with the setting sun pouring fiery red light in through the window and making the room glow like a cauldron in hell.

The whole thing suddenly struck Rachel as funny. She covered her mouth with her hand, but the laughter came out of her anyway, in startled, bright little gasps.

The outsider took the metal tube out of his mouth. He gave her one of those wide-eyed, butter-wouldn't-melt looks her son got whenever she caught him smack in the middle of some mischief. "What did I do?" he said.

She looked away from him so that she would quit laughing. "That Jakob Fischer," she said, when she finally caught her breath. "I expect he came here thinking to see horns and cloven hooves on you, and he saw fangs instead. He thinks he's somebody, does Jakob Fischer."

"He isn't somebody?"

That nearly set her off laughing again. She took a deep breath to stop it and almost snorted instead. "A person who's proud, who shows off and is pushy, we Plain say that he 'thinks he's somebody.'"

They said it, too, about someone who broke the rules, but she didn't tell him that, for she doubted he would understand. A man like him, who probably lived by no rules at all.

He was studying her as if he didn't quite know what to make of her, but he seemed to be looking at her in a friendly way this time.

"Where did that come from?" she asked, indicating the metal tube.

"My duster pocket."

His duster. She'd hung it from a hook on the opposite wall, and he could never have reached it from the bed. His strength of will was a frightening thing.

"You shouldn't have gotten up like that," she said. Her gaze went to his gun—his *loaded* gun, she had no doubt—which lay now on the table by the bed. "Again. I don't much fancy having to nurse you through another bout of wound fever."

He smiled at her scolding, turning the metal tube over in his hand.

"What is it, anyway?" she asked, curious in spite of herself.

He held it up for her inspection. "You've never seen a harmonica before? I won it in a monte game a while back."

She had no idea what a harmonica was. Or a monte game, for that matter, although that she could at least guess at.

"I thought one wagered money at games of chance," she said. She hoped this harmonica-thing wasn't another instrument of death and wickedness, like his knife and guns.

"The fellow I was playing with ran out of money. This was all he had left."

"It was that poor man's last possession and you took it?"

"It would've been an insult to him not to."

She was trying to puzzle out this quirk of outsider logic,

when he put the tube thing in his mouth and blew on it. Out of it came a wonderful wailing noise, like an elk bugling for a mate. It raised the hair on her arms and made her tremble.

"Oh! It makes music!"

He lifted his shoulders in a little shrug. "Well, it's supposed to. I only know the one tune, 'Oh Susanna!,' and I ain't much good at that one."

"Will you play it for me?" She was so excited, she forgot herself and smiled at him. "I should like to hear it just the once, if you wouldn't mind."

She sat down in her rocking chair, with her shoulders rolled forward and her hands tucked between her knees, full of anticipation like a child. He watched her through half-open eyes.

"This is liable to hurt your ears some, but here goes. . . ." And he brought the metal tube back up to his mouth and blew on it, and that wonderful wailing filled the room.

Rachel closed her eyes and let the sound fill her. It was like the music the wind made. It yowled and roared. It shrieked to the heavens with joy. And when it ended, it trailed off with an eerie veil of sad moaning.

She breathed out a long, slow sigh. "Oh, that was such a wonderment."

She opened her eyes to find him staring at her. "I only know that one tune," he said, the words strangled and rough, as if he'd blown out all of his air through the harmonica. "But I could teach you to play it if you'd like."

She straightened up with a start. "No, you mustn't. Music played on worldly instruments such as your harmonica-thing—it isn't allowed in the Plain and narrow life. It was very wicked of me to ask you to play it in the first place, and now I must ask you never to do so again. Not in my house. It's against the rules."

"What rules?"

"The rules we live by."

He considered her words a moment, then he smiled his naughty-boy smile. "And I don't suppose you'd want that fellow who goes around thinking he's somebody to catch you breaking the rules."

She shook her head, although she had to struggle hard to keep her face set serious.

She scooted forward in the rocker, with her fingers curled around the edge of the rush seat, beside her thighs. But she didn't stand up. He was looking down at the harmonica in his hand. His hair was mussed from the pillows and there was the lingering flush of fever on his cheeks. He looked roguish and rowdy, and a little lonely.

Slowly he lifted his head. He seemed to be searching for something to say to her, as if he was the one this time who felt the need to break the silence that kept falling between them.

"What's that delicious baking smell?" he finally asked.

"A snitz pie. Do you like it?"

"I might if I knew what it was."

"It's a pie made of dried apples and spices. I'm baking it for my Benjo, to make up to him for the way you scared him this morning. He ran off like he does sometimes, when he's troubled, but he'll come back when he's good and hungry, and then I'll have a snitz pie fresh out of the oven for him."

"It's a wonder to me where you found the time to bake a pie. Just lying in here and listening to you work through this day has got me plumb exhausted. I've never known a woman for going from one chore to another like you do."

"Hunh. Obviously you've never been married, Mr. Cain.

Otherwise you'd know that every woman's day is pretty much as busy as mine."

She'd never seen a person's face change so fast. She thought she caught a flash of something in his eyes, the echoes of a bleak sadness long ago put away, then there was nothing.

Now she was the one struggling to fill the silence. "Besides," she said, "idleness is the cause for all sorts of wickedness in this world. Satan has great power over the idle to lead them into many sins. King David, for example, was lying idle on his rooftop, when he fell into adultery."

Perhaps that had not been quite the thing to say. But the bleakness had left his face; he seemed amused with her again.

"Do you never sin, Mrs. Yoder?"

"Of course not." She felt herself flush a little. "Well, I don't go out of my way to do it."

"I do."

"You do?" she asked, astonished.

"Uh huh. I go far, far out of my way to sin. So far I can practically smell the hellfires burning."

He was teasing, surely. She had discovered that he enjoyed teasing. He was like Ben in that. He—

Thin wisps of black smoke trailed like mourning ribbons through the air.

"Judas Iscariot! My pie!" she shouted, pushing so hard to her feet that the back of the rocker smacked against the wall.

As she ran from the room she heard him laughing.

5

THE OUTSIDER STOOD ON Rachel Yoder's porch with one leg bent, the sole of his boot propped on the wall, and one thumb hooked in the leather cartridge belt that hung heavily from his hips. His hat cast his face in shadow, and his whole body looked relaxed and lazy. Yet there was a crackling anticipation to the air around him, like on a hot summer's afternoon just before a lightning storm.

At the sight of him on her porch, Rachel's steps faltered. She was already out of breath from chasing the ewes from the feeding paddock back into the pasture. Now, suddenly seeing him standing there, dressed and wearing his gun, she felt her heartbeat give a hitch.

She crossed the yard toward him, passing through the deep shadow cast by the barn. The morning frost crackled beneath her shoes. At the bottom of the steps she stopped and looked up at him. His hat brim hid his eyes, and his mouth was set hard. She mounted the first step, but couldn't manage the next.

"Lady, them sheep 'pear to have got you running every which way out there," he said, and he smiled.

She blew out a startled breath. She wasn't sure what she'd expected—that because he'd suddenly willed himself well enough to get out of bed, he'd be coming after her now with his six-shooter blazing? And after all the work he'd done to charm her, too. Why, if the man knew it, he'd probably be disappointed in himself.

She climbed the rest of the way onto the porch. "Sometimes I think it would be easier to get that creek to go where I want it than those confounded woolly monsters. I should've brought along a tin dog."

He thumbed his hat back. "A tin dog? What's wrong with the dog you got? Beyond his propensity for rabbit chasing, that is."

She lifted a strip of baling wire, which was hung with a half dozen empty milk cans, from where it dangled over the porch rail. "A tin dog," she said, and she gave the noisemaker a vigorous shake. The sheep, which were bunched up against the pasture gate, whirled and took off as fast as they could for the safety of the cottonwoods.

The outsider laughed, a sound rich and thick.

For a moment Rachel stared at him in wonder. There he stood, a bullet wound in his side, his arm all bound up in a sling and a Colt revolver hanging deadly off his hips, a hard-jawed man, laughing at a bunch of witless sheep. He made Rachel feel a dizziness in the pit of her belly just to look at him, the kind of feeling she'd get as a little girl when she'd hang upside down by her knees from a tree limb.

"You shouldn't be out of bed, Mr. Cain," she said.

"Another day spent lyin' on my back countin' the knotholes in the rafters and I'll end up crazier than the bedbugs."

"There are no bugs in my bed!"

He scraped a hand over his beard-roughened jaw. The way his eyes crinkled at the corners, she suspected he was hiding a grin. "Show me who's been sayin' there is, and I'll call him a pernicious liar. No, ma'am, that bed in there is sure enough clean, and it's soft, too. But it's lonesome, real lonesome."

She had to tangle her hands up in her apron to keep from pressing them to her hot cheeks. *Lonesome.* It was indecent, what he'd said, and wicked.

But then she wondered if maybe the wickedness wasn't all in her own head, if maybe she'd added a meaning to his words that wasn't there. She rarely sensed anything heartfelt behind what he said or did, only a detached calculation. She wondered what he saw when he looked at her, wondered what he thought of her. And surely it was wicked to have such thoughts. Rachel Yoder thinking she was somebody.

He pushed himself upright, his boot hitting the floor with a soft thud. He stepped further out onto the porch, until he was standing almost on top of her. He was taller than she'd thought him to be. Taller and with a look of elegance about him, with his fine gabardine trousers tucked into glossy black leather boots, his black Stetson hat and bottle green vest and . . . Ben's shirt. He was wearing Ben's shirt.

He noticed what she was looking at. "I found everything but my shirt, so I helped myself to one of your husband's. If it hurts you to see me in it . . ."

She came to herself with a start and shook her head hard. "No, no. As if such a thing would matter. It was stained and torn beyond salvation—your own shirt, I mean." Torn by a bullet, stained by his blood. His shirt had little tucks and pearled buttons set in the bosom, and a choker collar. The shirt he had on now was collarless and buttonless and tuckless. "I'm afraid you'll have to dress partly Plain for the time being, Mr. Cain."

"Well now, I'm not sure as how my reputation can stand that," he said, drawling the words. "I'm pretty much known far and wide as a man with a certain *tawdry* appeal."

She felt a smile pull at her mouth and fought it back.

He turned, a bit unsteady, so that he had to fling out

his good arm for balance. "Would it inconvenience you if I brought a chair out here? I thought to take a little sun, but I don't reckon after all that I can do it on my feet."

Earlier this morning, when she'd changed the dressing, his wound had still looked angry and sore. And after all, he'd been two weeks in bed, consumed with fever a good part of the time. She wasn't surprised he was feeling unsteady.

"You shouldn't be up at all," she said. "What Doc Henry will think, I can't begin to imagine." Yet even as she was protesting, she was passing through the open door into her kitchen, fetching one of her spindle chairs for him. She thought if he was going to be inflicting his disturbing presence on the world, she'd rather have him doing it out here than in her house.

As she came back out onto the porch, he took the chair from her hands and put it flush up against the wall. He lurched again when he went to sit in it, so that she had to help him, and for a moment they were side by side, her arm around his waist. But then he was in the chair and she had taken a step back from him.

He leaned his shoulders against the unpeeled cottonwood logs of the house and lifted his face up to the sun. The wind caught at her skirt, dark and heavy with frost, slapping it against his shiny black boot. He looked so worldly sitting there, so different from what she was used to. It was too bad he'd ruined his shirt. Ben's shirt stood out on him the way a wild thistle would stick out in a tulip bed.

She wondered if his soul had also been torn and stained beyond salvation.

RACHEL'S SKIRTS SWAYED as she whipped the lather brush around and around the shaving mug, working up a thick foam. From his position in the chair on her porch, the outsider was casting a concerned look up at the whirling white bristles. "Are you riled at me, Mrs. Yoder?"

Rachel whipped the lather brush even harder. "Ought I to be, Mr. Cain?"

"Heck, I don't know. A man never knows. And now that I've had a chance to think some more on your kind offer to give me a shave . . ." He stretched out his neck and rubbed his hand over the scruffy beard under his chin. "Well, the regrettable fact is, ma'am, that in my experience it ain't wise to allow a riled woman to get paired up with anything pointed or sharp." He gave her his teasing smile. "You know what they say about the snakebit man being scared of a rope."

"Myself, I haven't had all that much experience with snakes, Mr. Cain." Rachel wrung out a huck towel she'd had soaking in a basin of steaming water. "But the more regrettable fact—regrettable to you, of course—is that riled or not I am already paired . . ." She unrolled the towel with a snap of her wrists. ". . . up with a warranted Perfection razor that is sharp enough to split the hair on a frog."

With that she slapped the hot cloth down over his face, smothering his startled yelp.

Truth be told, she was more than a little nervous to be doing this, even though she'd had some practice. Although Plain men grew thick, flowing beards on their chins, they still had to shave their cheekbones, upper lips, and necks. One winter, Ben had been felled by a grippe that left him too weak to do the chore himself, so Rachel had done his shaving for him, to keep him pure in the sight of God.

This morning, as the outsider was taking the sun on her porch, she'd noticed how he kept scratching at the sprouting hair on his face. The next thing she knew she'd been offering to scrape it off for him. She'd figured that even if she loaned him her husband's shaving things, with his right arm bound up the way it was, he'd never manage them on his own.

His gaze was riveted to her every move as she spread open Ben's warranted Perfection razor and stropped the blade, moving it back and forth over the smooth leather. She tested its sharpness with the pad of her thumb, deliberately giving herself a little nick. She pulled a face and sucked on the wound. He swallowed hard.

She removed the towel and began to brush the lather over his thick dark beard. She knew the badger bristles were as soft as a baby's hair. The soap smelled sweetly of spring laurel, and steam floated through the air, warm and moist. She waited until his eyes had drifted closed before she said it:

"I reckon when I see the blood start to spurt a geyser, I'll know I've scraped off too much."

His eyes flew open wide, and Rachel laughed. Once started she couldn't stop. She laughed so hard, she buckled at the waist, and it felt good, so good. She hadn't laughed like this since Ben died.

When her laughter quieted she looked at him. He was trying to act insulted, but his mouth gave him away.

"You done making a fool of me?" he said.

She nodded solemnly.

"Let me see you hold that razor, then. I want to know if your hand shakes."

She picked up the razor, deliberately jiggling her hand so that the blade flashed in the sun. It made her laugh again, and him as well. But the quiet that followed brought an odd uneasiness with it, as if they both were wary of the intimacy their shared laughter had stirred.

The razor made a soft snicking sound as it cut through

his beard. She enjoyed watching the lean ridges and smooth skin of his face become bared by the blade. She had forgotten how young she'd first thought him. There were hard edges to him, a toughness, that made him seem older, as if he'd been through more of life than his face could ever show. She had asked him once how old he was. He said he didn't know. As if you wouldn't know something like that about yourself.

She leaned closer to him, to get at the whiskers along the far line of his jaw, and her belly pressed against his shoulder. She jerked back, her startled gaze sweeping over his face. But his eyes were focused not on her but on something beyond. Or perhaps something deep within.

She had just shaved off the last of the beard beneath his chin and was wiping the razor clean when she felt him stir. She looked down and saw that he had her pincushion again, and again he was squeezing it over and over.

Yesterday, when she'd sat down in her rocker for a minute to darn a sock of Benjo's, he'd noticed the pincushion. Made of red velvet, it was the size and shape of a small crabapple—a bit of frivolity she probably shouldn't have allowed in her Plain life. He'd asked her if she would loan him the use of it for a time. She couldn't imagine what he wanted with it. Not even when he took out all her pins and needles and began squeezing the cushion with his right hand, the hand of his broken arm, did she understand. He just kept squeezing, again and again, although she could see from the taut set of his mouth that it was paining him.

"Why?" she'd asked.

He hadn't answered her. When it came to answering questions about himself, he was like the sheep, who might spook and run off at the slightest movement toward them. But she'd seen his gaze go to the bullet that still sat on her nightstand next to her Bible. What he had called "the last bullet, almost." He'd looked at that bullet and all the while his hand had been squeezing and squeezing her crabapple pincushion.

Squeezing and squeezing, like he was doing now. Her gaze was drawn by the way his fingers gripped the red velvet so tightly his knuckles went white, and the fine bones of his wrist and hand pressed out against the skin and receded, pressed and receded. The mystery of him fascinated her, the complexity of him. There were so many things she wondered about him, the loneliness and the restlessness she saw in him, and the sin.

She washed off his face with a clean hot towel. "There you are now, Mr. Cain," she said. "No, wait." She leaned over him, using a corner of the towel to wipe one last bit of foamy soap off his earlobe.

He reached up and curled one of her prayer cap strings around his finger and gave it a little tug. "What do you wear this thing all the time for?"

"We've always done so. It's part of the *Attnung*, the rules of living. The prayer cap is a symbol, a reminder that we must always submit ourselves to God, and to men. The Bible says, 'For if the woman be not covered, let her also be shorn.' So we wear our prayer caps during the day, and we've other caps for night as well."

She had not, however, always worn her night cap, not when Ben was alive. He had so loved the feel of her hair, the way it wrapped around them when they came together in the dark. Sometimes he would leave the lamp lit, just so he could see it. *Polished mahogany.* She had thought it only a small breaking of the rules, not to wear her cap in bed with Ben.

But the way the outsider was staring at her now made

her wonder suddenly if he didn't know somehow about all those times she had not worn her night cap, and why.

"You ever seen a prairie fire?" he said. "The way the flames light up the bellies of the clouds from underneath, turning them all scarlet and wine-red? I opened my eyes that first night I was here, lying in your bed, and I thought I was looking at a fire-lit cloud. I thought it was a dream, but it was you. Only your hair was down. Why should God or any man breathing want to hide something so pretty?"

She felt a little flutter of pleasure in her chest from what he'd said; he'd called her hair pretty.

But it was sinful to have such feelings, vain as well as foolish. Rachel Yoder thinking she was somebody again. She began to gather up Ben's shaving things. "Listen to you talk," she said. "I suspect the Devil used similar such blather on Eve to persuade her to taste of the forbidden fruit."

His mouth curved into an unholy smile. "Yeah, I 'spect he did." Capturing her gaze, he transferred her pincushion over to his good hand and held it up, as though offering the apple to her.

"But I also reckon she liked the taste of that apple so much, the ol' Devil didn't have to do any persuading at all to get her to take a second bite."

RACHEL SAT ON THE porch steps, her arms wrapped around her bent legs, her head tilted back. The sun was a pulsing red ball behind her closed eyelids. The wind had the barest thread of warmth to it. It smelled of the thawing earth, of spring.

She opened her eyes and was sucked up, up, up into the sky. A sky that was a vast and empty blue.

She stretched her legs out flat, leaned back on her elbows, and turned to look at the outsider. The man sat with the chair braced up against the wall of her house and his long legs sprawled over the warped boards of her porch. He sat so still she thought about getting up and going over to him to see if he was breathing.

She ought to get up in any case. She had bread to bake, clothes to wash, and a million and one other things that needed to be done. She knew it was slothful just to be sitting there; she didn't have the excuse of a bullet hole in her side.

Benjo would be done with school soon, too, and she wasn't sure she wanted the outsider on the porch when her son came home. Ever since he'd been scared off with a "bang," Benjo had stayed clear of the man. Rachel felt easier inside herself because of it, although she wasn't quite sure why anymore. She wanted to believe the outsider's promise that he would bring them no harm.

They hadn't spoken in a long while, she reflected. It shouldn't bother her. She was used to spirits that were silent and at peace, because the Plain believed that needless words were a displeasure to God. Only she didn't think the silence in the outsider's spirit came from peace, but rather a hard and brutal emptiness.

In the pasture, a couple of ewes suddenly jumped up and started butting heads and doing a lot of blatting. The outsider's hat brim lifted slightly as he watched them.

"We've hardly lost any of the woollies this winter," she said. It was strange, but she, who had never minded silences, kept feeling this need to talk to him. To fill up his emptiness, perhaps. "That big snow a few weeks back was the only real bad one we had. Not like other winters when the skins can pile up to the rafters in the barn. It's the blizzards, mostly, that kill sheep. They huddle up so close together, they smother to death."

He didn't say anything, but she sensed that he was listening.

"Except for the blizzards," she went on, "sheep really like winter. They're all snug in their wool coats, they've no flies to pester them, and some two-legged creature comes out twice a day no matter what the weather and feeds them forkfuls of hay." She drew her knees back up and cupped them with her hands. She rounded her shoulders, pressing her mouth to her knuckles, smiling to herself at her thought before she voiced it aloud. "Winter is a good time to be a sheep." As she spoke she turned her head to look at him.

The creases around his mouth deepened for a moment. She was coming to believe that when his smile was real, when it came from his heart, it was nothing more than a quick tightening of his mouth and a crinkling of the sun-creases around the eyes. "They do seem to be having themselves a time," he said.

"They do," she agreed, and then her heart was suddenly too full for words as she let her gaze roam lovingly over the farm: over the haystacks built tall and square, the neat lambing sheds, the lofty barn. It was a good home for sheep, their farm. Plentiful grass. A creek that ran almost the year round. And a wide belt of cottonwoods and willows to give shade in summer and break the wind in winter.

The ewes had quit their fighting and gone back to eating. Rachel had always enjoyed just sitting and watching the sheep. They slowly munched and dozed their way around the pasture, passing the time in the way they loved best, all the while quietly growing their wool and the lambs in their bellies. That old gappy-mouthed ewe did know a secret after all, she thought. She knew the comfort of time passing gentle and sweet.

As she sat there on the steps of her porch, hugging her knees, the barn and the haystacks and the sheep all shimmered before Rachel's eyes in a white light, and the light exploded into a soaring, tumultuous melody. For no more than a heartbeat the music seized her. Then it let her go, leaving her with a breath-held feeling of utter joy—a joy so intense it spilled out of her.

"A day like this is so *good,* don't you find it so, Mr. Cain? It makes you want to praise God, and thank Him for giving you the life to enjoy it."

Her words fell into an empty silence. She turned her head and saw his eyes lift quickly to the mountains, as if he didn't want to be caught looking at her. Something cold seemed to shiver across his face. She had the notion that he'd just seen something, or thought something, that hurt him terribly. She wanted to go to him and touch him, just touch him. Just lay her hand against his cheek.

Instead she gripped her knees tighter and held her breath.

"What made y'all settle away out here, anyway?" he said, a strange roughness in his voice.

"The Lord." She drew out the words with the slow easing of her pent-up breath. "It's all part of the wondrous and mysterious ways of the Lord, how that came about. We began as a larger community of Plain People that farmed the Sugarcreek Valley in Ohio. But there was a division of thought, I suppose you would call it, among the members. Some of us felt that the others were becoming tainted by the world. Taking up modern things, like lightning rods and whip sockets on their carriages. And doing prideful things, like posing for photographs and wearing buttons and suspenders. Why, some of the men even took to wearing neckcloths!"

He made a snorting sound. "Heaven forfend. I've known many a man to be led down the merry path of sin by his neckcloth."

"You ought not to laugh at things you don't understand."

His face sobered, but she sensed he was still laughing inside.

"Well," she went on, a bit tentatively, "what happened was, my *Vater,* my father, he had a powerful awakening. A revelation from God."

She paused to see if he was going to laugh again, but he just sat there looking at the sheep.

"Da saw this very valley in a dream and he led us here. Those of us who were determined to keep to tradition, to follow the straight and narrow way. And during our first worship service in this place, when the lottery chose my *Vater* to be our bishop, we knew it was a sign from God that his awakening had guided us true. But then the land turned out to be too dry for farming."

"This country's too high to grow much of anything but hay."

His comment surprised her. She tried to imagine him walking over a furrowed field behind a mule-drawn plow, and she just couldn't. "Are you a farmer, Mr. Cain?"

"God, no. Never again as long as I draw breath."

She waited to see if he would say more. She thought he probably hadn't meant to reveal even that much about himself. She tried to imagine him standing spread-legged on a sled, forking hay over the wriggling backs of a bunch of hungry ewes. But the image that came to her mind was of Ben.

"It was Ben's, my husband's, idea to try sheep. But even though the Bible speaks often of shepherding and flocks, and of Adam's son Abel being a keeper of sheep—still, it took my *Vater,* as bishop and leader of our Church, many days of prayer to come around to the idea of it. We'd always been farmers, you see. To put up the plow and raise sheep instead, it was such a drastic change from what we'd known.

It wasn't a thing that could be done lightly. It took a lot of contemplating and praying on my da's part."

"It don't sound like he bends much, your old man."

"It isn't our way to bend. There is one Plain way of doing things, and no other. Ben, though, he always used to say God wouldn't have given us a brain if it wasn't to think with. He had a way of looking at things from the other side, Ben did." She waved her hand at the wall behind them. "It's like that window over there, you always look through it from the kitchen out into the yard. But one day you're out here on the porch and you walk by that window and you look through and you're surprised to see the kitchen. It's the same sheet of glass, but you're looking through it from the other side. Ben was always doing that, looking through windows the wrong way. Our people thought him a bit wild at times—"

A sadness welled up inside her, choking off the words. She shut her eyes and pressed her fingers to her lips. She didn't want to grieve for Ben in front of this man. Ben was . . . hers.

She swallowed and drew in a deep breath. "Oh, listen to me rattle on. I don't know what's wrong with me. A moment ago I was feeling so happy, and now . . ." She thought she wasn't going to cry after all, and in the next instant scalding tears pushed against her eyes.

"You miss him." He said the words simply, his voice low and flat.

"I do miss him. So much that at times I . . ." She shrugged, pressing her lips together.

He kept his gaze on the sheep, as if watching them eat were the most fascinating thing in the world. But then he said, in a voice that hurt her with its gentleness, "How did he die?"

She covered her face with her hands, but for just a moment. Then she let them fall to her lap, where they made a single, gripping fist. She'd never spoken aloud of the hanging, not with her *Vater* or Mem, not with any of her brothers. Not even with Noah. The Lord had taken Ben home, they all acknowledged. No one ever spoke of how.

"Look, forget I asked," he said. "It ain't none of my—"

"They hung him is what they did. The outsiders hung my husband for a cattle thief."

She looked at him, daring him to say he was sorry. Instead he said, "Was he?"

"Ben would sooner cut off his hands than allow them to take up a thing that wasn't his!"

Her words had come out harsh, but it was an old and festering anger that she felt. "The outsiders in this valley, most of them don't like us much because our ways are different and we keep ourselves apart. So they're mean to us at times, in little ways, like tossing firecrackers in our wagons when we drive through town, or hooking their spurs into our skirts when we walk down the boardwalk. They laugh at us and call us names sometimes, but mostly they never do us any real hurt. Except there's this cattleman, a Scotsman by the name of Fergus Hunter. He owns a big spread on the other side of those hills over yonder."

She looked hard at the rock- and pine-studded buttes, as if she could see through them to the big white house with its gables and spooled-railed galleries, to the acres of corrals and miles of fences, to the big cedar-shingled stables, to the thousands of cattle that needed so much land to roam in.

"At one time this whole valley was all open range, and Mr. Hunter got used to grazing his herds wherever he pleased. He got to be what the newspapers and such call a cattle baron. And he got so puffed up in his pride he even allowed some folk to call him that, to call him Baron. Like some king had come along and knighted him, or something."

"I knew a horse, once, named Baron."

They looked at each other, sharing a mutual thought, that life really does have a way of twisting itself all inside out and backward.

"Mr. Hunter sure wouldn't like knowing he'd been named for a horse," she said. "And he sure didn't like us Plain People coming here to homestead on what he'd come to think of as his land. He liked it even less when we started raising sheep. In those early years, he tried to drive us out by setting fire to our barns and tearing down our fences, poisoning our watering holes and pastures with saltpeter. But when he saw that we weren't to be driven out, he eased up some on his cruel ways. After a time we thought he'd come to see the light of Our Lord, and had chosen to live with us in peace."

Her gaze fell to her lap. She put a pleat in her apron with her fingers, then smoothed it out with her palm. "But then a year or so ago, he went and made up this boundary to go down the middle of the valley, like some sort of line you'd draw on a map, that he called a deadline, and he said to us: 'If you cross it, bring your coffin along.'"

The outsider made a small sighing sound, as if he'd heard this story before. "But you didn't believe him."

"Oh, no, we believed him. But we were not leaving here, no matter how many lines Mr. Hunter drew. It's not our way to seek confrontation with outsiders who wish to do us harm. But we can't always avoid suffering for our faith in a hostile, sinful world. It has always been so with us."

"'Yea, for Thy sake are we killed all the day long; we are counted as sheep for the slaughter.'"

"Why, you know the Bible, Mr. Cain!" she exclaimed. She was so pleased to discover this about him that she nearly smiled despite all the memories of Ben that were pressing like a pile of stones on her chest.

The outsider was gazing on the far mountains again, and his face had taken on his flat look. "A man can come to know the smell of a sweetgrass meadow," he said. "He can know the feel of a prime horse between his legs, and the taste of a beautiful woman. He can come to know them, without ever once understanding them."

She felt deflated. There was surely no knowing or understanding *him*. She thought that he probably really didn't care much at all about how a Plain sheep farmer came to die. He was only listening to her out of politeness. Because if he wanted to take the sun on her porch, he figured he had to take her prattling, too. But she wasn't going to betray Ben by leaving his story unfinished.

"About the time Mr. Hunter marked off those deadlines, he hired on this man he said was a stock inspector. He said his calves were disappearing quicker than he could slap a brand on them, and this inspector, he was to put a stop to it." She tried for a scornful laugh, but what came out was a strangled sound. "Maybe that inspector should've had a talk with those Hunter cows, because they were always wandering uninvited onto our hay meadows. One morning last spring we woke up to find a bunch of them grazing right alongside our woollies. Ben rounded them up to drive them back home."

It was her last memory of him, sitting astride their old draft horse, yipping and waving a lariat at the milling cattle that were churning up the mud in their yard. She'd teased him, told him he made a dashing cowboy. But he'd barely managed a smile for her. He'd been that aggravated over those Hunter cows.

"He was always quick to anger, was Ben, and just as quick to get over it. I suppose he did leave here that morning with the intention of giving Mr. Hunter a piece of his mind for allowing those strays to wander all over wherever they felt like. And Ben was always hard to talk with when he had himself a mad on."

She closed her eyes, but there weren't any more tears inside her that she had to work to keep down. Only an emptiness that burned.

She was seeing her other memory of him, a remembrance of a Ben she'd never seen but only imagined over and over—a Ben who swung from a cottonwood tree, his big hands hanging limply at his sides, his long legs twisting slowly, the rawhide rope around his neck creaking as it bit into the wooden branch above his head. It had been April then. The branch would have just been sprouting the red buds of new leaves.

She opened her eyes and looked at the ragged pine-studded buttes that shielded the Hunter ranch, and a cottonwood tree she'd never seen except in her memories. "Doc Henry brought him back to me that afternoon. He was dead. They'd hung him for rustling those silly strays."

"And may God be with him," the outsider said, so softly she wondered if it was more his thought than his voice she'd heard. Maybe she'd only hoped he would say it.

She nodded and tried to swallow, but couldn't. Her eyes were now so dry it hurt to blink. The emptiness inside her burned and burned.

She'd been looking at the buttes, but now she swung hard around to face him. "You know what Mr. Hunter said? That he was sorry. *Sorry.* He came with the sheriff out to the farm. First the sheriff explained how the mistake had happened, how a man's got a right to try and protect his cows if he thinks they're being rustled. Then Mr. Hunter said it was a terrible tragedy, and how sorry he was for it."

"You don't sound like you believe much of his explanation, or his apology."

"Ben is still gone to me."

The outsider was looking at his hand, where it rested on his thigh, looking at it hard as if he could see through flesh and skin all the way to the bones. "I reckon you're right in that," he said. "Dead is dead."

No, she thought. Ben had left her, but he'd gone to God. The emptiness was there, but she would fill it. With Sundays full of hymnsongs that echoed off the barn rafters, and the uplifting cadence of the preaching, and the sharing of pots of bean soup with her neighbors and family afterward. With mornings full of tossing hay to the woolly monsters, and wetting down the cowlick in Benjo's hair. With afternoons full of the smell of bread baking in the oven and the sound of the Montana wind gusting in the cottonwoods. And nights when she'd sit in her rocking chair and the music would come, bringing God to her on a tidal joy of sound. All the days and nights full of work and prayer and music. Full of the love of those left to her, and the slow and steady sureness of time passing.

"Death *is* a hurtful thing," she said aloud, to the outsider and to herself, "but only to those left behind. The Bible says: 'The Lord giveth and the Lord taketh,' and in our sorrow it's so easy to dwell only on the taking part, to forget all about the giving. But He does give us so much. He gives us the sheep who love the winter, and a day like this one that is so pretty and full of the promise of spring that you ache with the joy of it. He gave me the years I had with Ben, and He gave me our son."

She spoke the words and she knew them to be true, and the thought behind them was true, and yet they didn't fill the emptiness.

"I'll kill them for you, if you want."

"What?" The word came out as a tiny squeak. She turned sharply to look at him.

He sat there in her chair, so sprawled out and lazy he might have been asleep. But his voice was as cold as winter earth. "I'll kill this Mr. Hunter of yours and his so-called stock inspector who hung your husband."

He'd said it so easily: *I'll kill them for you, if you want.* And God help her, but she could feel that burning emptiness, the need to make them pay for what they'd done to Ben.

"Killing is never justified," she said, her voice shaking. "Vengeance belongs only to the Lord." More true words that did nothing to fill the emptiness. Not like his words: *I'll kill them for you, if you want.* In one shattering moment he'd let loose this terrible need inside her, the need to make them all pay. It was like his gun—black and ugly—this need of hers.

He pulled that gun out of its oiled holster, slowly, lovingly. "The Lord taketh, Mrs. Yoder . . . but so does this." He pointed the revolver's barrel into the sky, as if he intended to shoot at the jays who were always raiding her vegetable garden. But he was offering that gun to her. His gun and the deadly skill of the hand that held it.

She lurched to her feet, almost falling over the steps, so that she had to grab at the railing. "Don't you say these terrible things!"

The outsider's hat brim rose slightly as he peered at her from underneath it. She could see his eyes now, and they were flat and bleak.

"You keep away from me!" She shouted it, as if he'd gotten up from that chair and was stalking her. But he only followed her with his empty blue gaze.

"It was just an offer, because I figure I owe you for taking me in and tending to me like you've done. If you change your mind—"

"I won't." Just then the wind kicked up hard, slapping her skirts and rattling the tin eaves. The wind was cold again, with no hint of spring at all. She wrapped her arms around herself, shuddering. "I won't," she said again.

She turned and walked away from him, out into the yard. She made herself walk slowly with her head up. She walked into the barn, all the way into the middle of it, and just stood with her arms hanging at her sides. She had no notion of why she had come there. Dust motes danced in the shaft of sunlight that shot through the open doorway. She breathed in the smell of animals and hay.

"I won't," she said, the words like a vow.

6

THE IRON HISSED AS it glided over the dampened cambric cap, leaving behind a knife-sharp pleat and the smell of hot starch.

Rachel returned the iron to the hob on the cookstove, releasing the handle a little too soon so that it settled with a loud clatter. She carefully lifted the freshly pressed cap off the ironing board and carried it to the kitchen table, where three others exactly like it sat in a row, like roosting white hens.

She glanced through the open door. The morning breeze had turned into a chinook, a wind hot and dry as summer grass. The sun shone weak in a pale sky, but the old wax-yellow snow glistened as it melted beneath the breath of the wind.

The wind brought the mulchy smell of wet earth into the kitchen to mix with the smells of starch and steam and hot metal. From where she stood Rachel could just see one of the outsider's glossy black boots. He'd been sitting out on the porch all day.

He kept his back to the wall, so no one could come up on him unawares. She knew that beneath his hat those restless eyes watched the road, as though waiting for someone fool enough to ride down it so he could shoot the poor fellow dead.

I'll kill them for you, if you want.

All her life she'd been surrounded by simple things: simple pleasures, simple people, even simple temptations. Then he had come staggering across her wild hay meadow and now her thoughts were going down twisted, dangerous paths.

The Bible said, "The light shineth in darkness; and the darkness comprehended it not." The outsider dwelled in darkness; he was the night. What she hadn't understood until now was that the night had its own compelling and seductive beauty.

I'll kill them for you, if you want.

She glanced out the open door again as she went back to the cookstove. She clamped a handle around the hot iron, then let it fall back on the hob with a loud clank.

When you wanted to chase away the darkness of night, she thought, you lit a lantern. Jesus had instructed Paul "to open their eyes, and to turn them from darkness to light, and from the power of Satan unto God."

She would show the outsider the light.

She smoothed down her apron, tucked the stray hairs beneath her prayer cap, and went out onto the porch. She stood in front of him. The hot wind slapped her skirts against the backs of her legs.

"What we spoke of earlier today, Mr. Cain . . ."

He pushed his hat back and looked up at her. "I remember having the conversation, Mrs. Yoder. Though I suspect you're now hell-bent on making me live to regret it."

"But it's about living and being hell-bent that I wish to speak more. Living, and then dying in God's own time, and being held to account for our sins. What Mr. Hunter did he must answer for, but he will do his answering only to God. As will you, as will we all when we are called."

"Yeah, well, I don't figure it's Him who's going to be doing the calling and settling up the accounts when my time comes around."

"But there's where you are all *wrong* in your thinking." She eased onto her haunches before him, so that she could face him eye to eye and he could recognize and come to know the truth as she spoke it.

"There is peace and joy to be found in God. And there is forgiveness and eternal life. It's never too late to make your soul whole by uniting with Him."

He leaned forward, bringing his face close to hers. Too close, so that she wanted to pull back from him, although she didn't. He wasn't smiling, but then she didn't trust his smiles. She did detect a softness, though, in the way he was looking at her. The wind blew between them in a gush of warmth.

"And there's where you're all wrong in your thinking, Mrs. Yoder," he said, and there was such a sweetness in his voice that she became lost in the sound of it and almost missed the sense of his words. "Because I like being damned. I positively wallow in my damnation like a fat pig in warm mud."

RACHEL RUSTLED THROUGH the straw in the hen roost, searching for eggs. She found one and added it to the two she already cradled in her apron. It was slim pickings today. The farm was home to half a dozen red bantams, but one or two were always wandering off to hatch a clutch of chicks.

She hurried back across the yard, one hand cradling the eggs in her apron, the other swinging out for balance. The wind filled her skirts like sails, pushing her along. She had to take big skipping steps as she picked her way through the rivulets of water that ran from the melting snow. The outsider sat on her porch, still and silent, watching her.

I like being damned. She couldn't imagine how anyone could say such a thing, even in jest. For the first time she understood how truly separate he was from her. She wasn't going to quit on him, though. She'd never quit on anything in her life.

She stopped alongside his chair. He'd gone back to passing the time by squeezing her pincushion. "That thing isn't going to be of much use to me," she said, "after you're done squeezing the stuffing out of it."

His clenching hand paused for just a fraction of a moment. "The world's full of pincushions. I'll get you another."

"Hunh." She put her free hand on her hip and turned to look back out over the yard. The warm wind kissed her face and fluttered the strings of her prayer cap. "I reckon it sure is a shame you can't just walk into Tulle's Mercantile and buy yourself another immortal soul as easily. Or pick a nice new unsullied one from out of a mail-order wishbook. But then it's only by living a Christian life that a soul can be cleansed and saved. And part of living a Christian life is understanding that we must love those that hate us, and not take revenge on our enemies."

The outsider had settled deep in his chair, and gone

back to hiding his eyes beneath the soft brim of his hat. He sighed. Loudly. "Are we back to trotting down that road again, Mrs. Yoder?"

"Indeed we are, Mr. Cain."

"Very well, then. In the first instance, the enemy we're speaking of here ain't my enemy, he's yours; I got no feelings one way or t'other about him. And in the second instance, I told you I'd be the one doing the taking."

"You would take the life of a man you don't even know?"

"I do it all the time."

His words shocked her so, her hand slipped its hold on her apron and one of the eggs slid out. She lurched to catch it and the other two went rolling after. One by one the eggs smacked and cracked open on the weathered pine boards, yolks and whites all running together.

She stared down at the broken eggs, then looked up at him. "You're not to do it to Mr. Hunter. You're not."

He lifted his shoulders in a careless shrug. "I offered and you said no-thank-you. So long as the man don't take a notion to come after me, I'm easy."

Her gaze fell back to the mess of burst yolks and shattered shells. She felt bewildered, disoriented. "What am I going to do . . . ?"

"I'll take mine scrambled," he drawled. "Like I said, I'm easy."

She turned her back on him and went into the kitchen for a bucket and rag to clean up the eggs. She stood in the middle of the room a moment, then strode back outside empty-handed. "I'll have you know that we Plain People have all offered up many prayers for the soul of Fergus Hunter," she said to the man who sat on her porch.

"Uh huh. And no doubt he's suitably grateful for 'em, too."

"As of this moment, Mr. Cain, I am praying very, very hard for you."

~

RACHEL SLAMMED THE rolling pin down onto the ball of dough. She pushed hard and the dough flattened. She pulled and pushed the heavy wooden pin, pulled and pushed, rolling out the dough with such vigor that flour floated in a white cloud around her.

She stopped pushing and stood in stillness a moment, bent over the table, her hands gripping the rolling pin.

She straightened, dusted her hands off on her apron, and marched out onto the porch. "The Bible teaches us, Mr. Cain, that 'whosoever shall smite thee on thy right cheek, turn to him the other also.'"

The face he turned up to her wore a polite expression, but his eyes were hooded. "In all my life the only times I ever turned the other cheek I wound up getting it slapped. I heard them Scriptures you keep throwing up at me read plenty when I was a boy. Seems like I remember Jesus Christ himself doing a lot of talking about loving your enemies. But on a day when *his* enemies were feeling particularly mean, he wound up getting whipped and crowned with thorns and hung up to die a bad death on a cross. That, lady, is what comes of turning the goddamned other cheek."

She flinched at his profane blasphemy. "Jesus died so that we might be saved."

"Yeah? So what did your man die for?"

She spun around, but his hand shot out, grabbing her arm. "Don't run off again. I'll quit doing it. I promise."

"I'm not running off, I've biscuits baking—quit doing what?"

"What I been doing to you. Like using a spur on a bronco, trying to make it buck so's you can break it."

"You've been . . . and here I thought I was . . ." Laughter burst out of her, surprising her before she could stop it, and surprising him, so that he dropped her arm. They'd been hurling words back and forth at each other, she thought, like children throwing balls in a game of Anti-I-Over. But they were too wide apart in their beliefs to ever really hit each other. They were so separate, he of the world and she of the Plain way, that no amount of words would ever put them on the same side.

And there was no need for it. She saw now that it wasn't the outsider she'd been trying to lead out of the darkness, it was herself. Because that burning emptiness inside her had allowed a terrible thought to take root, the Devil's weed of vengeance. But she had sought the light, and she had found the light, and the weed had shriveled and died before its awesome power.

She laughed again, feeling light-headed of a sudden. Feeling light-hearted. *Ye shall know the truth and the truth shall make you free.*

"You will never be able to break my faith, Mr. Cain," she said. "Certainly not with something as insignificant as a pair of spurs."

NOAH WEAVER HEARD HER LAUGHING.

He was slogging through the cluster of yellow pines and tamaracks that separated his farm from hers. He walked slowly, deliberately, his heavy brogans leaving deep furrows in the soggy pine straw and melting snow. His farmer's thoughts were on the weather. These chinooks always made him uneasy—hot as the Devil's breath, they were, and unnatural. A summer wind in winter.

The sound of her laughter startled him so that he jerked to a stop. The heel of one brogan slid on the wet mulch, and his legs went flying out from underneath him, landing him on his rump with a jar that knocked off his hat and rattled his teeth.

He got slowly to his feet, feeling suddenly old and aching in all the joints of his bones. He dusted off the seat of his broadfalls and anchored his hat back on his head. He looked around. No one had seen him, yet he felt foolish, and then ashamed of himself for his vanity.

He heard her laugh again as he came around the back of her barn. He slowed, more careful this time of where he was planting his big feet.

She was leaning back against the porch railing, her arms straight out behind her, her palms braced on the roughly peeled pine pole. Her skirts slatted in the wind, her cap strings danced. She was talking with the outsider. Laughing with him.

The outsider sat on one of her kitchen chairs with his back to the wall, but Noah barely spared a glance for the man. His gaze went straight to Rachel, and stayed there.

So many times over the years he had watched her like this, from afar. Coming to the Yoders' for a word with Ben about the shearing or the haying or the lambing, when it was really Rachel he'd come to see. Standing in the yard talking with Ben, one eye on the door, hoping, praying she'd come out, waiting to be invited in for coffee and maybe a slab of pie. Sitting at her table, drinking the coffee, eating the pie, talking with Ben. And watching her.

Watching the way her lower lip would puff out when she

blew a sigh up her face if she was tired. The way her skirts would sway around her hips as she moved from the cook-stove to the slop stone. The way her back would bow, supple as a willow tree, when she bent to pour more coffee into his cup, and he would look up and smile his thanks to her and she would smile back, and he could fool himself into thinking just for that one moment that she was his.

That was all he'd ever had of her, those times which had always felt stolen to him and somehow empty, lacking. Just those quick, passing moments in her kitchen, and when he saw her every other Sunday during the preaching.

Oh, it truly was God he went to worship on those Sundays, but a small corner of his heart always beat harder and faster at the knowledge that he would see her. No matter what barn the preaching was held in that day, no matter where on the rows of benches she sat, his gaze would find her in an instant. In a sea of brown-shawled backs, and black and white Sunday prayer caps, he would know her. He knew her voice in the hymnsongs and prayers. And afterward, when the women passed out the bowls of bean soup and platters of steaming bread, he'd know which hands were hers, without even looking up, he'd know. Although he always would look up, anyway, just to catch her smile, and he'd be close to pure joy in that moment. Close to God, and close to Rachel.

He approached her slowly now, not to sneak up on her, but only to prolong the moment when it would seem that she was his and his alone. The outsider must have seen him, made some telltale movement, for she suddenly jerked upright and whirled.

"Noah!" she exclaimed. Her face was bright, as if with happiness. But as her gaze settled fully on him, her eyebrows drew together in a slight frown. "What's the matter?"

Although she hadn't laughed again since he'd come around the back of the barn, he kept hearing the echo of it. He *felt* the echo of it in the pit of his belly. It made him uneasy, like the hot chinook wind.

The weather-rotted steps groaned beneath his weight as he came up to her. He allowed himself to drink in the sight of her. She stood now with her slender back straight, her shoulders flat and square. He always felt so hulking and clumsy around her, too big for his skin.

"Wie gehts?" he said to her. She'd been baking, for her sleeves were rolled up and there was a dusting of flour on her arms. Her skin was so pale he could see the blue veins on the inside of her wrists.

It was rude of him, Noah knew, to be speaking *Deitsch* in front of the outsider. The man was a guest in her home. Her gray eyes showed her disappointment in him, the way they darkened. Rachel's eyes had always been like a weather vane for her feelings.

"How nice of you to come calling, Noah," she said, enunciating the *Englische* words carefully, as if he'd suddenly turned into a big *dopplich* of a kid that needed teaching. "Mr. Cain, this is my good neighbor, and my particular friend, Noah Weaver."

Noah waited, though he wasn't sure what for. Maybe for her to say: This is the man I'll be marrying soon. Except she wasn't going to be saying that now. He'd asked her and asked her to marry him, but she hadn't said yes, and it was only a small comfort to know that she hadn't said no yet either.

He turned slowly, allowing his gaze to settle at last on the outsider. The man sat there looking all dandified and puffed up in his worldly clothes. His face was as bare and smooth as a baby's bottom. Noah felt the tight knot ease some in his chest. Rachel would find nothing pleasing in this flashy, beardless boy.

The outsider looked up at Noah through half-closed eyes that were a pale, cold blue. His face was as flat and empty as the prairie in winter, yet Noah felt the hackles rise on the back of his neck. Then the outsider lifted his hand and laid it on his thigh, and Noah realized that he'd had that hand resting on the handle of the Devil's tool he wore strapped around his waist. Had probably had it there from the moment Noah walked out from behind the barn.

"Good afternoon to you, sir," the outsider said. "And how d' you do?" He had a slight drawl, from Texas maybe, Noah thought. Or some other place way down south.

He'd spoken politely enough, but Noah still had no trouble allowing his contempt for such a man—a man who always needed to be touching a gun to feel safe—to show on his own face. "Myself, I'm doing fine, Mr. Outsider. As for yourself, I'd say you were fortunate in where you chose to get yourself shot."

The outsider's wide mouth curled into an easy smile. "Ah, but fortune is a two-faced wench, don't you know?" He cast a look over at Rachel and his smile changed, although Noah couldn't decide in exactly what way. "All because Mrs. Yoder went and saved my life, now I gotta be polite and let her take a crack at my black soul."

And in that moment Noah sensed something flash between the two of them, between the outsider and his Rachel. It made him think of the way Saint Elmo's fire arced and shot off blue sparks between the tips of cattle horns during a heat-lightning storm. Yet the impression was so startling to him, so impossible, that he told himself he must have imagined it.

"Whereas if it'd been your farm I'd've stumbled across

when I was dying, why, I suspect you'd have just let me go straight on to hell in my own merry way."

Noah knew the outsider was speaking to him. He could hear the edge in the man's drawling voice, and he could feel the impact of that insolent blue stare. But he couldn't take his eyes off of Rachel. He noticed suddenly that she had a smudge of flour at the corner of her mouth. He'd always had trouble looking at Rachel's mouth. With its bottom lip thicker than the top one, she looked like she was pouting even when she wasn't. When he looked at Rachel's mouth, Noah forgot it was the purity of her soul that he loved.

He tried to clear the gritty feeling out of his throat. "None of us knows if he is saved till he gets over yonder, so we don't worry ourselves about the salvation of others, Mr. Outsider. We leave that to God. And we don't accept converts into our church."

Rachel made a funny little jerking movement. "Oh, honestly, Noah—as if he should even want to. Mr. Cain is only joking."

Was that what they were laughing over when he came up, he wondered—over God and salvation and the immortal soul? He didn't like this conversation. He felt left out of it, horrified by it. His gaze roamed over the yard, the barn, the hay fields, as he struggled for something to say.

"Your ewes will be dropping soon."

Rachel looked over to the paddock where her sheep munched on scattered hay. "No, not for a while yet I should think," she said.

Noah felt a flash of irritation with her, even though he knew she was right about the ewes not being ready. A woman shouldn't contradict her man in front of another.

Rachel had turned back to the outsider, and her face had taken on an excited look. She tucked in her chin to hide a smile in that way she had when she was teasing. "But if they do start dropping while you're still here, Mr. Cain, we'll see if we can't make a lamb licker out of you."

"Lady, I sure do hope that ain't what it sounds like."

"Oh, it's much worse than what it sounds like. Much worse." And to Noah's utter shock, she laughed again.

He wondered where she'd come from, this Rachel he didn't know. How often had he himself testified at the preaching, about how a boisterous laugh and a quick retort betrayed a cocky spirit, the kind that God despised? He wondered now if Rachel had ever really listened to his words. She'd always needed a strong husband to guide her. Ben, he thought sourly, should have made a better job of it.

He cast a glowering look at the outsider. "Now that he's up and about, I reckon he'll be moving on directly."

"Mr. Cain is hardly cured enough to straddle a horse yet."

"He can walk. That's how he came; that's how he can go."

Stormy eyes flashed at him. "Noah!"

Noah grunted.

That same easy smile pulled at the outsider's mouth. "I fear, ma'am, that your good neighbor and particular friend don't have much use for a disreputable rogue like me."

Rachel almost laughed again. Noah saw the laughter rise up in her face and flood her eyes, making them sparkle, and she only stopped it from coming by sucking on her lower lip.

He looked from Rachel back to the outsider, looked down into that devil's face and those cold, cold eyes, and hatred roiled like a storm in his belly. He was astonished by the piercing purity of the hate that he felt. Astonished, and ashamed.

He closed his eyes and groped for a thought, a prayer, that would lead him back to God and away from the sin of his hate. *He that saith he is in the light, and hateth his brother, is in darkness even until now.*

Noah backed up, shaking his head. "I've a buckboard wheel at home that needs hooping," he said, thinking he probably wasn't making much sense and not caring. He groped for the porch rail, his big feet stumbling on the muddy steps so that he almost went sliding onto his rump again.

"Noah?" she called after him, but he pretended not to hear.

Once, a long time ago, Ben had said to him: "If she'd chosen you over me, it would have hurt. Hurt bad. But I could've come to accept it, through knowing she was happy. Look at her, Noah, really *look* at her, and not with eyes that only want to see what might have been. Rachel is happy."

Noah had looked at her that day. When could he not have looked at her? On that day she'd been out with the sheep, introducing the new lambs to Benjo. The boy was just learning to walk, and she was laughing at the way he kept grabbing onto the woolly backs of the lambs as he fought to keep his balance, and both lamb and boy would go tumbling down together into the soft spring grass.

"She would have been happy with me," Noah had said.

And Ben had sighed, his gaze settling gently, lovingly, on his wife. "Maybe so, but maybe not. She's like the water in that creek, is our Rachel, always flowing fast and clear. You can see through her plain enough, to the bedrock that is her spirit. But you can't hold all of her in your hands like you're always wanting to do. Like I try to do sometimes, even when I know better."

Now, when he got within the shadow of the barn, Noah looked back. She stood next to the outsider. He must have been saying something to her, for she stood as if listening, with her head slightly cocked, one hand on her hip and the other trying to capture her wind-tossed cap strings. Suddenly she leaned over and gave the brim of the outsider's hat a sharp tug, and she laughed.

Noah tried to breathe but his chest felt swollen shut, as though stuffed with cotton batting. He tried to remember if he'd seen her happy in the time since Ben had gone, if he'd ever once heard her laugh. Now this *Englischer* had come with his gun, with his easy smiles and his cold eyes.

Now this outsider comes and he makes my Rachel laugh.

MOSES WEAVER STOOD NAKED on a shelf of rock. He looked down, six feet down, into the still water. Wind rattled through the branches of the willow brakes and wild plum trees and stirred the dead marsh grass that limned Blackie's Pond. The wind was warm on his bare skin, but he knew the water would be freezing and he shivered at the thought.

He took a deep breath and dove.

The cold seemed to suck the air right out of his lungs, and the water closed over him, gripped him like a fist and pulled him down. He thrust his legs hard and shot back to the surface.

Judas, it was cold. He forced himself to swim two turns around the pond and then pulled himself out.

Shivering, he lay down on a bed of marsh grass, stretching flat out on his belly. He sighed as the warm wind and sun dried his goose-pimply skin. The water might be cold this time of year, he thought, but at least it was clear. Come summer, the pond would be cloudy and filled with skitter bugs and snaky reeds. If a body could stand the shock of it, winter was a good time to come swimming out here. Especially when the chinook blew.

Mose stretched, digging his fingers into the tangled roots

of the marsh grass, breathing in the loamy smell of damp earth. It was a luscious feeling just to lie there and do nothing, although he knew he'd pay for it later, once his father got a look at how that busted paddock gate he was supposed to have been fixing this afternoon was still busted. But when that gate got mended there'd still be another chore waiting, and another after that. Old Deacon Noah was always saying the Lord loathed idleness, and so he did his own level best to keep the Lord happy by loading his son down with work. Mose figured the draft horses at their place knew more moments of loathsome idleness than he ever did.

Mose sighed and stretched again. He closed his eyes and felt himself drift along on the hot wind, just drift along. . . .

The willow brakes crackled behind him. A pebble slid into the water with a soft plop. Mose looked up, and his heart did a flip-flop in his chest.

A girl stood among the rocks and willows and wild plum trees. She was dressed all in frothy white, and wore a big plaited straw hat with a white satin ribbon tied in a bow beneath her chin. Over one shoulder she carried a white lace parasol that seemed to be twirling like a carriage wheel in the wind.

Mose leaped to his feet, then remembered he was naked. He bent over, scrambling frantically for his clothes. He found his shirt and held it in a crumpled ball in front of his privates.

The girl was laughing at him. He couldn't actually hear her because his heart was pounding so hard, but he could see her parted lips and the white flash of her teeth. He felt a searing heat of mortification rise all the way from his bare toes to the tips of his ears.

"You want I should turn my back?" she said.

"Huh?"

"I'll turn my back so's you can put your trousers on. Then maybe you'll quit flushin' all the colors of berries in summer."

She did as promised, swinging around with a rustle of silky skirts. He stared at her, mesmerized. Her dress wasn't all white after all—it had tiny stripes going through it, the color of the cinnamon stick candy sold out of jars at Tulle's Mercantile. The silky material was ruffled and gathered in a pouf that rested on her bottom and cascaded over her hips like a lacy waterfall. And she had the tiniest waist he'd ever seen. He could have spanned it with his hands and still been able to link his fingers.

"I've never known anyone to get dressed so quiet. Did you fall asleep, or somethin'?"

Mose came to himself with a start. He didn't bother with his long-handles but went right for his trousers. He tried to put both feet through the same pant leg and had to hop about to get himself untangled. While he was pulling his shirt on, the yoke caught on his ear and he nearly poked out his eye getting it loose. His suspenders had gotten twisted, so he left them to dangle at his hips. He snatched up his coat and stabbed his arms into it.

The parasol dipped, and a straw hat brim peeked around the lacy scallops. "You decent now?"

Mose swallowed hard, making a funny clicking noise. "Uh, *ja*. Yes, miss. Sorry, miss."

She turned with another rustle of silk and walked right up to him, then past him. She gathered the ruffled hem of her skirt, revealing the lacy trim of a scarlet petticoat, and sat on her heels at the edge of the pond. She collapsed her parasol to lay it among the rocks. She peeled lacy gloves off her hands and dipped her cupped palm into the water and raised it, dripping, to her mouth.

She drank noisily, as if she enjoyed the taste of the water and didn't mind showing it. When she was done she wiped her lips with her fingers.

She looked up at him, flashing a bright smile. "I wouldn't mind restin' here a spell with you," she said, "but I don't want to get stains on my dress. Do you think I could trouble you, sir, for the use of your coat?"

He almost ripped his coat in his haste to get it off. He spread his precious new four-button cutaway, with its fancy satin-piped lapels, out on the wet grass for her to sit on. He felt awkward in his movements and yet rather gallant at the same time.

She settled onto his coat with a sigh, a waft of honeysuckle toilet water, and another flash of scarlet lace. She tossed a thick ringlet of hair back over her shoulder. It was pale yellow, her hair, the color of wheat just starting to ripen.

"This is a nice spot, this pond," she said. "I come here in the summer sometimes for picnics. But mostly I just come to be alone when I'm feelin' blue. Sometimes I go for walks out over the prairie, too. The other girls, they don't hardly stick their noses out the door, but I enjoy my prairie walks." She tilted her head back to look up at him and she smiled again. She had a crooked eye-tooth that caught at her upper lip when she smiled. "Do you ever go for prairie walks?"

"Yes, miss." He supposed herding a bunch of woolly monsters from one pasture to another might constitute a prairie walk.

Her bosom rose and fell with another sigh. "I like this country out here. It's so wide open, not at all like where I grew up in the Florida swamps, where it's hot and close and suffocatin'." She slanted another look up at him, and the sun seemed to catch at something in her eyes, making them sparkle. "It sure is warm as summer out here today, though, ain't it?"

"Yes, miss."

Mose felt foolish standing there bobbing his head like a windup toy and doing nothing. Yet he thought maybe good manners dictated that he should wait until she invited him to sit down alongside her. He rocked from one foot to the other, torn between standing and sitting. As he squatted down next to her, his knee joints popped like firecrackers.

"Yup, it's warm as warm can be today," he said, and then flushed.

She smiled at him again, a nice smile, not a mocking one. "So, what do they call you, boy?"

"Uh, Mose. Mose Weaver."

She wrinkled her nose. "Mose. What kinda name is that?"

"Well, it's Moses."

She held her hand out to him, her fingers pointing toward the ground in a delicate little arc. "I'm Marilee. That's my real name, too. I'm not like them other girls puttin' on airs with their made-up names."

He wiped his sweating hand on his pant leg and took her fingers. "Pleased to be making your acquaintance, Miss Marilee."

He thought she was the prettiest thing he'd ever seen. She had high wide cheekbones and a dainty, pointed chin that gave her face a sweet heart shape. Her lips were very red, as if she'd been eating berries. He wondered if she painted them—fast girls, he'd heard, always painted their lips. Her skin was like freshly skimmed cream. He could see a lot of her skin.

"D-do you work at the, uh, Gilded Cage?" he asked. Criminy, he was stammering worse than poor Benjo.

"Lord, I should hope to never sink so low!" she exclaimed. She lifted her chin and gave a proud little toss of her head. "I'm an upstairs boarder at the Red House."

She leaned into him and touched the front of his shirt. He jumped a little, and then he realized he'd missed a button in his haste to get dressed, and she was only doing him up again properly. For just a moment her fingers brushed the bare skin of his chest. He felt heat pulse deep in his belly, and a stirring in places he shouldn't even be thinking about.

"I don't know as how I've ever seen you there," she said.

Mose knew about the Red House. It sat on the very edge of Miawa City, between the creek and the cemetery. The house wasn't really red, of course. It might have been white once, but it had long ago weathered to a sooty gray. It was only called the Red House because of the red locomotive lantern that hung outside the front door most nights.

Mose had engaged in a lot of speculation with the other Plain boys about what went on behind that door. Last summer old Ira Chupp, whose wife had passed over five years ago, had gotten down on his knees during the worship service and confessed to the congregation that he'd been consorting sinfully with Jezebels. Although it had never been mentioned by name, everyone knew that the sinful consorting had been done at the Red House.

"I can't say for sure that I've ever been to *your* house," Mose said, trying to make it sound as if he visited so many houses of sinful consorting, and on such a regular basis, that he couldn't be expected to keep them all straight. "But now that I know you, now that we've been introduced, I mean, maybe I can come . . ."

A little laugh bubbled up her throat. "Land, *comin'* is what a bawdy house is all about, ain't it? So long as you got the proper tool and the price of admission." She leaned back and gave him a careful look-over, pouching her lower lip out in concentration. Her wet and very red lower lip. "You're a Plain boy, aren't you? Your hair's been barbered and you got on real clothes, but you're one of them Plain boys sure enough."

Mose could feel another flush burning on his cheeks, and a tightness in his chest. He felt shame for being Plain, and an awful guilt over feeling that shame.

His gaze fell to the hands he had clasped between his spread knees. "I've not joined the Church yet," he mumbled to his hands. "Maybe I'll choose not to."

The girl lifted her shoulders in a little shrug that caused the big sausage curls of her hair to slide over her shoulder. "At least you got a choice. Most of us don't ever get many choices."

She had a small beaded bag that dangled from a gold chain around her wrist. She snapped open the clasp now and took out a pocket-match safe and a cheroot. She struck a match on a nearby rock and put the flame to one end of the cheroot, protecting it with her cupped hand against the wind.

Mose watched while she sucked on the other end of the cheroot until her cheeks went hollow and the tobacco glowed red. She tilted back her head and blew a thin stream of smoke into the air, then held the cheroot out to him. "You want a drag?"

"Uh, well, I . . ." He wanted her to believe he was the sort of flashy gentleman who could smoke a cheroot with aplomb. But his back twitched in anticipation of the licks it would be feeling later on this evening. Once old Deacon Noah got a look at that still-busted gate and then sniffed out the stink of the Devil's weed on him, he'd give him a hiding for certain.

She smiled as she slipped the cheroot between his fingers. The end of it, he saw, was wet from being in her mouth. He thought about that as he put it between his own lips, about it being wet like that and why.

He sucked in hard like she had done, and swallowed fire.

The smoke seared his lungs and scorched his throat going down, and came back up again with a racking cough that tore at his guts.

She smacked him on the back. "Land, boy. You've turned green as a frog." Laughing, she pointed at the pond. "If you're gonna puke, aim it over thataway."

This must be what it was like to try breathing in hell, Mose thought. His eyes streamed tears. The world around him blurred dizzily, and his stomach rolled and flopped like a stranded fish.

He blinked hard, squinting at her through a haze of smoke. She'd taken the cheroot back from him and was sucking on it again. Her image wavered and cleared. Mose's gaze fastened onto her bosom. In she sucked, and her breasts rose and swelled, pushing against the ivory lace that trimmed her bodice. Out she blew, and her breasts settled slowly, gently, like a cloud floating to earth. A big, soft, fluffy cloud.

Lord God, please forgive me, Mose prayed. He ought to be plucking out his eyes, rather than look at what he was looking at. He ought to be cutting off his head rather than think what he was thinking. He was totally depraved, he was sinful, he was damned.

He was wishing she would put the Devil's weed to her lips and suck on it again. Harder.

She tossed the cheroot into the pond. Pulling on her gloves, she stood and shook out her skirts. "Lordy, it's gettin' late," she said. "I'd better be makin' tracks for home." She bent over and retrieved her parasol, unfurling it with a snap of lace and fringe.

Mose stumbled to his feet as she turned to him with another of those smiles that caught at her upper lip. "Thank you, Mr. Moses Weaver, for the use of your coat." She gave him a quick pat on the cheek. "You're a sweet one."

Her skirts rustled and whispered as she picked her way back through the rocks and willow brakes, back where she had come from. The pouf of silky material that rested on her backside bounced and twitched with every step.

"Hey, wait!" Mose cried out. He snatched up his coat and followed after her.

He caught up with her at the road, which was really nothing more than wagon ruts cut through the prairie grass. She'd driven a smart little black shay out to the pond. It had green wheels and fringed cushions, and was hitched up to a saucy-looking bay.

She had paused to look down the unfolding ribbon of wheel tracks toward the west, where the flat pancake clouds always built up during a chinook. "The wind's dyin'," she said. "It'll be turning cool again before I make it back. Would you help me to put the bonnet up?"

"Sure thing!" he exclaimed, then winced at the loudness of his own voice.

As he unfolded and fastened down the bonnet, he tried out what he wanted to say to her in his head, but everything he came up with sounded stupid. His mouth had suddenly gone dry, and his stomach felt as if he'd just swallowed a sackful of grasshoppers.

"Might I come pay a call on you, Miss Marilee?" he finally blurted.

He'd turned as he spoke, not realizing she was right on top of him, and they bumped into each other. He grasped her shoulders to steady her. She was looking up at him, her face serious. Time seemed to slow into a breathless stillness, and Mose would have sworn he could hear his own heart beat. That he could feel the heat and silkiness of her skin beneath her cinnamon-striped dress.

"You got nice eyes," she said. "Did anyone ever tell you

that? They're such a dark, deep brown. Like coffee beans. But coffee can be bitter and your eyes aren't bitter at all. They're nice. Nice and sweet-looking."

"You got pretty eyes, too." He tried to think of a way to describe them. Blue as the sky, blue as a bluebell, blue as . . .

But she was already slipping out of his hands, moving away from him and climbing into the shay. Too late, he realized he should have stepped up and helped her.

She gathered up the reins and looked down at him. She didn't smile this time; he thought she seemed almost sad. "You can come pay a call on me if you want, Mr. Moses Weaver," she said. "But if you do, you take a bath first, you hear? There ain't no token rich enough to make it worth puttin' up with the stink of sheep."

He watched the back of the shay sway and dip along the ruts until it was swallowed up by the rolling grassland.

He brought the skirt of his flashy four-button cutaway coat up to his nose and sniffed. He smelled of sheep all right, and of tobacco smoke.

7

BENJO SWIPED A SMEAR of apple butter off his mouth with his shirt cuff and stretched his hand across the table in search of another hoecake. But his mother got to the tin first, snatching it back out of his reach.

"You clean your plate of those pickled beets first, Joseph

Benjamin Yoder," she said, rapping his knuckles with the handle of her fork. "Then you ask, politely, for someone to pass you more hoecakes. And use your napkin, for mercy's sake, not your sleeve."

Benjo rubbed his stinging knuckles, and his bottom lip jutted out. "Yes'm," he mumbled to his plate, which had a little bit of sowbelly beans left on it, and a whole lot of pickled beets.

The kitchen fell back into silence, but for the occasional clink of a tin fork on a tin plate, and the tick of the tin-cased clock.

Another two days had passed since the outsider first tested his constitution by getting out of bed and taking the sun on Rachel's porch. But this was the first time the three of them had sat down at the table to take a meal together.

Meals were usually times of prayer and quiet contemplation in the Plain life, which seemed to suit the outsider just fine. He hadn't uttered one word since he'd taken a chair on the side of the table that backed up to the wall. While Rachel and Benjo had said their silent prayers, she noticed that he'd kept his head respectfully lowered. Nor could she fault the man's table manners. He ate with almost too much care, Rachel thought, as if he'd learned those manners late in life.

Thus far Benjo, too, had kept quiet, although with a considerably lesser show of manners. But he'd been watching the outsider with such wide eyes that Rachel could practically see behind them to the questions working their way from his head to his tongue.

While meals were indeed supposed to be a time of silence and prayerful contemplation, she and Ben had always indulged Benjo's questions during supper, hoping that any amount of talking at all would help him to get over his stammering. But she wished now they'd been more diligent in their discipline. Noah had warned her, time after time, that she was spoiling the boy.

Just then Benjo drew in a deep noisy breath, and Rachel held hers. "Huh—how muh—muh—muh . . ." he began and then got stuck, his throat spasming and clenching shut over the rest of it.

Rachel leaned over and gently touched his arm, trying to calm him. "The words might come out easier, our Benjo, if you didn't try to push them past the food that's already in your mouth."

The boy chewed and swallowed hastily. He wasn't going to quit on those words, Rachel could see, and she held her breath again, for a question from Benjo could know no bounds. Still, she nearly gasped aloud when it finally stuttered out.

"H-how many people have you shuh—shuh—shot s-stone dead, mister?"

The outsider slowly turned his head and looked at the boy as if he wondered where he'd sprung from. He laid his fork down gently on the plate and patted his lips with the napkin he had tucked into the neck of his shirt.

"Enough to make trouble for myself in this life," he said.

"Is th-that what they luh—locked you up in jail for?" Benjo asked, and Rachel dropped the hoecake she was eating into her lap.

He had stolen only that one look at the outsider all the time the man had been lying in her bed, so she couldn't imagine how her son could know Mr. Cain bore the marks of prison. Maybe the rumor of it had just gotten carried along through the valley on the Montana wind.

The outsider was staring at Benjo from beneath heavy-lidded eyes. He pulled at his lower lip. "Let's see, that time I got thrown into the hoosegow. I'm tryin' to remember, here.

I think maybe it was 'cause I didn't eat all my pickled beets like my ma told me to."

Benjo shot a wary look at his mother, then stabbed his fork into a beet. He cast a covert look at the outsider, and saw that the man was watching him in turn. He shoved the beet into his mouth, chewed, swallowed.

"I th-think it was 'cause you kuh—killed a man. Wh-what did he do to m-make you kuh—kill him?"

"I reckon he might've asked me one question too many."

Benjo's jaw sagged open, and his face flooded red. His gaze dropped to his plate. He stabbed at another beet.

Rachel tucked in her chin to hide a smile. In the fading winter sunlight she couldn't be sure, but she thought the outsider's eyes were crinkling at the corners. The man sure did like to tease, and he had a rather wicked way about it. Like Ben, she thought.

Neither shock nor fear could rein in that boy of hers, though. He squirmed in his chair and drew another breath, and Rachel knew the next question was working its way to the surface.

"You done your evening chores yet, Joseph Benjamin?" she said.

"No'm. B-but—"

"But get to it."

He heaved a loud sigh, then scraped back his chair, grabbed his hat and coat, and banged through the door, shoulders rounded and chin hanging low.

No sooner was he gone than Rachel wanted him back. Maybe, with all his pesky questions, Benjo could have pried some answers out of the outsider. His broken life fascinated her. She had been watching him closely, collecting thoughts and observations like quilt pieces, but she hadn't been able to make a pattern with them as yet.

These last two days he'd spent a good part of the time out of bed. He'd even taken a few short walks to the paddock to watch the sheep. But it had turned cold again, too cold for him to sit outside. So he'd done his sitting at her kitchen table, and they talked sometimes while she went about her work.

This much she thought she knew about him: His life had left a taint on him, wounds and scars that went beyond the ones on his flesh. Yet there was laughter in him, and unexpected wells of gentleness. He had no home, no family, and this more than anything struck her heart with pity for him. Family, friends, a home—those were what gave life meaning and joy.

Ach, the way he was sitting there now, with his back to the wall and his eyes flitting every so often to the door, waiting, watchful, careful. His hand lay flat on the table, next to his plate, but from time to time his fingers drew restless circles in the oilcloth. She wondered how he could live with such intensity inside himself. It would, she thought, be like trying to stare into the sun.

Rachel's chair made a loud grating noise in the quiet room as she pushed away from the table. She picked up her plate and Benjo's. On the way to the slop stone, she paused opposite the outsider's place. There were, she saw, a goodly number of pickled beets still left on his own plate.

Another thing she'd discovered about him was that he enjoyed being teased himself; he was like Ben in that as well. "I reckon, Mr. Cain," she said, "that you'd better finish off those beets of yours. Otherwise I just might have to send for the sheriff."

He looked down at his plate, then let his gaze slowly rise to meet with hers, his mouth curling into a roguish smile. "But, Mrs. Yoder, ma'am, what I really had my heart set on was some more of your deeelicious hoecakes."

She set down the plates and snatched up the tin of hoecakes, dancing just out of his reach. "Oh, no you don't. You can't sweet-talk me into breaking the rules just for—"

He exploded out of his seat, startling her so that she skidded backward, her feet tripping over each other. She grabbed wildly for a chair, dropping the tin with a loud clatter. The only reason she didn't scream was that he'd finally managed to scare the breath right out of her.

She pressed her fist to her pounding chest and stared at him wide-eyed. He had his gun in his hand, though for the life of her she couldn't say how it had gotten there. "What—" she began, and then from the yard she heard a horse's whinny.

"See who it is." He said it calmly, but his eyes were feral.

She swallowed, trying to clear her throat of her still wildly thumping heart. "You can't always be thinking that just any-old-body who comes to pay us a call—"

"See who it is, dammit."

Rachel quaked as she went to the window, fearing less whoever had ridden into her yard than she did the outsider already in her house.

She stared through the glass. A burly man in a mud-splattered duster and a sweat-stained brown Stetson was swinging out of the saddle and making to tie an apron-faced roan to the paddock gate.

"You know him."

She hadn't heard the outsider come up behind her; she jumped at the sound of his voice so close to her ear. And his words were not a question but an accusation.

"It's Sheriff Getts," she admitted. She jerked around to face him, suddenly afraid of what he would think. "I didn't send for him, truly I did not!"

The outsider gave no sign that he cared, or even heard

her. He braced the wrist of the hand that held his gun against the wall and leaned into the window for a better look. A grimace tightened his mouth, and he drew in a quick hitching breath. She thought he must have pulled the stitches on his wound, jumping up so quick like that. The wildness in his eyes had faded, though, replaced by the same flat stare he wore so much of the time.

She realized what a fool she'd been to let herself start liking him, even to think he was something more than what he'd appeared to be, a desperado on the run from the law. It was all because of his charming smiles and teasing manner. And because he'd reminded her in some strange way of Ben.

He shifted his weight, and his thumb cocked the hammer of his gun. The noise seemed obscenely loud in the quiet of her kitchen.

"Don't kill him," she said. "Promise me you won't kill him here, before me and my son."

This time the smile he gave her was pure mean. "Well now, lady," he said, drawling the words, "if I have to shoot the son of a bitch, you can be sure I'll go to the trouble to lure him out beyond your pasture fence first."

He turned back to the window. The sheriff didn't seem in any hurry to come in. He was leaning against the paddock gate, his elbows braced on the top rail, looking at the sheep.

"You said once, Mr. Cain, that you figure you owe me. And then you promised you wouldn't harm us. If you meant that at all, then you'll not allow your filthy violence to taint us. We haven't a back door, but maybe if I go out into the yard and distract him you can make a run for the barn. You can have our old draft horse. She isn't fast, but she'll give you a head start and—"

He snapped his head around to impale her with his cold, cold eyes. "I don't run," he said. And then he touched her face. He traced the curve of her jaw and brushed his fingertips once, lightly, over her mouth. "I won't kill him here, and not at all if I can help it."

She backed away from him. First one careful step and then another. "I'll go see what he . . . what the sheriff wants, then," she said. And she ran for the door.

She had a hard time slowing herself down as she crossed the yard. The outsider had said he didn't run. She wanted to run and keep on running, over the prairie and beyond the jagged mountains, to the very ends of the earth. And even then, she knew, she wouldn't be safe from what she had already allowed this man to do to her.

She drew a deep breath and squeezed her eyes shut for a moment. She kept feeling the brush of his fingers on her lips. She wanted to rub her mouth with her hand, to make the feeling go away.

The sinking sun seemed to have been snagged out of the sky by the hooked mountain peaks. It had turned the clouds around it a salmon pink and cast a pale yellow light over the fields that were just greening with the first shoots of spring. She searched the shadows by the outbuildings for her son, but she thought he'd probably taken off at the first sight of Sheriff Getts. Benjo held the man in part responsible for the hanging of his father and, in truth, Rachel felt the same. A man sworn to uphold the law, she thought, should have had more to offer than polite explanations for what had been done to Ben.

The sheriff touched the curled brim of his hat, all politeness even now, as she came up alongside him. "Evenin', ma'am," he said, then went back to looking at the sheep.

He was a man long past the prime of his life, with tired blue eyes and seamed, weather-glazed skin. His gray mustache hung down over the corners of his mouth, and his belly hung over the waistband of his black britches. He was pulling a pair of fringed buckskin gauntlets again and again through gnarled, big-knuckled hands.

"Them woollies of yours are gonna be droppin' pretty soon," he said in his deep, rough voice.

Rachel's eyes narrowed in perplexity as she studied the heavy-bellied ewes feeding on the scattered hay in the paddock. She saw no swollen udders, and their teats seemed to be hanging placidly. Not a single one showed the signs of imminent birth, and she wondered what had prompted the sheriff, and Noah before him, to say so. Maybe it was simply a need that men had to hurry time along.

"Did he tell you who he is?"

Rachel tried to calm her face, to make it look innocent, before she turned and met the lawman's eyes. "He said his name is Cain. Isn't it?"

He nodded slowly, sucking on one end of his tobacco-stained mustache. "Johnny Cain. It prob'ly ain't the name he was born with, but it's the one he's grown into. Johnny Cain." He said the name again, almost with relish. "He's a shootist by occupation, a man-killer. His purpose—some might even say his joy—is in killin'."

His joy is in killing. This was the piece of the outsider she'd known about all along and hadn't wanted to see, couldn't bear to see. It wouldn't fit into the pattern she wanted to make of him.

"Have you come to take him back to prison?"

"Did he tell you he's done a stretch in prison?" He rolled his big shoulders in a shrug. "Nope, that's a new one on me. He ain't wanted anywheres at the moment. I checked. I do need to have a li'l chat with him, though."

He pushed himself off the gate and started across the yard toward the house, his boots squelching in the mud.

Rachel stood rooted a moment, so that she had to hurry to catch up with him.

A slice of fading sunlight fell across her well-scrubbed pine floor as the sheriff opened the door. The back of the kitchen remained cloaked in shadows, and the outsider sat within those shadows, his back to the wall. His Colt lay on the table in front of him, his left hand resting lightly on the grip.

"You promised to put away your gun," Rachel said.

"Now, I doubt Johnny Cain ever made such a promise. He's only bein' cautious, ain't you, boy? He knows a tin badge ain't no guarantee I don't have it in my mind to build up my own rep by takin' on his."

The sheriff had kept the bulk of his body shielded by the door. He stepped fully inside now, though he held his hands spread out at his sides. "Now, what I'm fixin' to do," he said, "is hang up my gunbelt on that there wall hook, along with my hat, and then I'm gonna pull a chair up to Mrs. Yoder's table here and have myself a cup of coffee. That coffee do sure smell good, ma'am."

The kitchen didn't smell of coffee; if anything it smelled of pickled beets. The blue-speckled coffee pot sat cold on the fender of the stove. The hoecakes she'd dropped lay broken and scattered over the floor.

As Rachel knelt to clean up the mess, she glanced up at the outsider. His eyes rested solely on Sheriff Getts, and his face wore a slightly puzzled look, as if an innocent such as himself couldn't imagine what a lawman could possibly have to say to him.

The sheriff scraped a chair up to the table and collapsed into it with a heavy sigh. "There's three dead bodies I need to account for up on Tobacco Reef. I figure you can help me do that."

"I'm always willing to oblige the law," said Johnny Cain with a smile that held no warmth.

The sheriff grinned in kind. "That's fine, real fine." With slow, deliberate movements, he fetched a briarwood pipe and a buckskin bag of loose tobacco out of the pocket of his muddy duster. He said nothing more until he had the pipe smoking.

He settled his thick shoulders into the chair, puffed, and blew a cloud of smoke into the rafters. "My pappy was a mountain man," he said. He acknowledged the cup of cold, oily coffee that Rachel set before him with a nod of his head and a mumbled "ma'am."

"Even lived with the Chippewa for a spell, my pappy did. He taught me how to read sign to the point where I reckon I'm pret' near as good as most Injuns, if you'll excuse my own horn tootin'."

He took the pipe out of his mouth and rubbed the fringe of his mustache. He studied the man across the table from him, staring intently as though assessing the broken arm and the careful way he sat to accommodate the bullet hole in his side. Then the sheriff pushed the pipe back in his mouth and spoke around the bit.

"Now, this is what I figure happened up on that butte. It has its genesis, so to speak, with these three brothers name of Calder who ranched with their pappy up east of here. Them boys was down in Rainbow Springs a week or so back, where they spotted you in that high-stakes monte game what was happenin' then, and they got took with the sudden, stupid notion that braggin' rights to the name of Calder would sure be enhanced considerable if that name could be the death of Johnny Cain."

Rachel shot a startled look at the outsider, but he only watched the lawman with his flat eyes.

She had taken herself as far away from the two men as she could and still be in the same room. She perched on the woodbox next to the cookstove, cradling a bowl of beans in her lap to be picked over before soaking. But though her fingers sifted through the beans, her whole awareness was held by what was being spoken of at the table. This would be a tale of violence and death, she knew, and she didn't want to hear it. But at the same time she couldn't make herself cover her ears.

The sheriff inflated his cheeks and blew the air out in a gusty sigh. "Now, I ain't gonna speculate on how they knew just where you was headed and when you'd be passin' on through, though I suspect your kind can't step out to take a leak without hearin' hammers cockin' behind every bush. Suffice it to say them three boys waited for you up in the rocks of Tobacco Reef, figurin' to bushwhack you as you rode on by. Maybe you saw the sun flashin' off of a rifle barrel, or maybe you just *knew* they was there, like your kind always knows."

He paused for dramatic effect, and Rachel drew her feet up, pressing them hard against the slats of the woodbox as if to give herself support. Johnny Cain sat silent and motionless except for his hand, which stroked the smooth wooden grip of his gun once and then went still.

"However it was," the lawman went on, "you'd already turned and was firin' by the time they got off their shots. Which accounts for Rafe Calder windin' up dead in the rocks."

To Rachel's shock the lawman actually laughed then. "Yup, deader'n a can of corned beef, Rafe was—and still is, less'n he somehow managed to resurrect hisself. Shot plumb bull's-eye in the mouth." He chuckled again, shaking his head. "But then Rafe always did have a big mouth."

The air in the room had turned thick, until it had become an effort to breathe it in. Rachel couldn't take her eyes off the outsider's face, but it was as smooth as a weathered tombstone and just as difficult to read.

The sheriff suddenly leaned forward and stabbed the stem of his pipe toward the outsider's hooded eyes. Johnny Cain didn't so much as flicker an eyelash.

"Now, you might not know this," the sheriff said, "but them Calder boys had a rep in this neck of the woods for being crack shots. Hell, I once seen Rafe drive a nail into a fence post with the six slugs in his Colt. So if they had long enough to take aim at you, they was bound to hit you. Which they did, huh?" He looked the outsider over again slowly. "Which they sure enough did. One got you and another got your horse. Your horse went down, prob'ly rolled on you, which is prob'ly how your arm got busted."

He leaned back, and his fingers began to toy with his tarnished watch fob. But Rachel noticed that during all the lawman's fiddling, the outsider never once looked at the man's hands or anywhere other than into his washed-out eyes.

The lawman's spiky gray eyebrows drew together, as if tugged by complicated thoughts. "This is where it starts to get tricky, but this is how I'm picturin' it. You lose your six-shooter when your horse rolls and your arm gets broke, you can't reach your rifle what's still in the saddle scabbard, and them two livin' Calder boys is coming out of the rocks, their guns trained on you. So you make like an Injun and play dead."

The sheriff smiled slowly and nodded his head at the outsider as if acknowledging him a score in a game they were playing. "Yup, them Calder boys might not've known shit from wild honey, but they never was flat-out empty-headed. They come up on you slow, keepin' you covered the whole while. Maybe one of 'em kicks you a bit to see if you groan. Might be he even takes a lick at your busted arm, in which case you're one tough son of a bitch. Because you don't let out a peep, you don't so much as flinch. You just lay there playin' possum, waitin' for them to get closer. And you know they'll be gettin' closer if they're gonna take your scalp, or maybe your nose or an ear—"

Rachel lurched off the woodbox, dumping the bowl from her lap onto the floor. In the sudden silence she could hear the beans scattering over the bare pine boards.

"Yes, ma'am," Sheriff Getts said, not taking his eyes off the outsider, "them boys was gonna need a trophy, don't you know? To prove they kilt Johnny Cain." Shrugging, he rubbed the bit of his pipe over his lips as if in thought. "Otherwise there woulda been no point to any of it."

Rachel looked at Cain, wondering how he'd endured it, how heart and mind could bear such fear. She thought of the utter terror she had seen in his eyes that day in the hay meadow, when she'd first touched him.

"So you wait," the sheriff was saying, his voice a gruff whisper now. "You wait, because your kind are good at waitin'. You wait until Jed Calder puts up his gun and takes out his toad sticker and bends over you, and then you shoot him with that boob gun you carry in a holster under your armpit. And all the whilst you're killin' Jed, you're grabbin' the knife out of his hand and you're cuttin' the guts out of his baby brother Stu, and I reckon by then you musta been either real sore or real scared, because that boy looked like he'd been stabbed with a shovel."

Rachel trapped a moan behind her pressed lips. She shut her eyes and saw blood, smelled it. All that blood soaked and splattered on his clothes—it hadn't all been his.

"Mind you," the lawman was saying, "I ain't sure exactly how you managed to do that final bit, to take them both unawares like that. I only know you did manage it, because I seen the evidence with my own eyes." He wagged his head again and frowned. "Them boys shoulda known better than to go pokin' at a sleepin' rattler."

For the first time Johnny Cain stirred, but only enough to lift his head. He flashed one of his charming, easy smiles. "You sure do tell a fine story, Sheriff."

"Uh huh. And I suppose you're gonna tell me you shot yourself whilst cleaning your gun, and then broke your arm fallin' outta the chair."

"There ain't no law against being clumsy that I know of."

Sheriff Getts slapped his hand down on the table so hard the dishes rattled. Rachel jumped; the outsider smiled.

"There ought to be a law, though," the lawman growled, "against treatin' a man like a fool when he ain't one. There's some as say that to pit a man against one of your kind even in a fair draw is still murder, but I'm not so judgmental, myself. I've known them Calder boys to be dumb as fence posts and mean as polecats their whole lives, and so their deaths sure ain't no loss to civilization such as we know it. They came after you, and you only gave 'em what they asked for."

He leaned forward and tapped his finger on the silver star he wore. "But when I put myself on the pin side of this badge, I swore to uphold the law and protect the citizens of this territory. So I also figure I'd be derelict in my duty if I didn't suggest that you mosey on along, soon as you're able. And before this nice little valley is overrun with more bad hombres and fool boys who want to be known as the quick son of a bitch who shot Johnny Cain."

The sheriff stared hard at Johnny Cain, the pipe jutting upward as he clenched his teeth on the bit.

Johnny Cain said nothing.

"You are truly a tough bastard," the lawman said. "But then I figured you would be." He pushed the chair back from the table. Lumbering to his feet, he pulled the watch from his vest, then glanced at the window, glazed gold now by the setting sun.

"Thank you for the coffee, ma'am," he said to Rachel as he turned to leave.

And still Johnny Cain said nothing. Not even good-bye.

Rachel went with the sheriff out into the yard. The salmon pink light had seeped out of the clouds, leaving them a smoky gray. It would be full dark soon and a cold wind had sprung up. She was worried that Benjo wasn't back yet. She hoped he was only lurking in the barn, waiting for Sheriff Getts to leave.

The sheriff knocked the bowl of his pipe against the fence, the wind catching the sparks and embers and sending them winking like fireflies into the falling dusk. Leather squeaked as he put his weight in the stirrup and swung up into the saddle. He leaned over and patted the neck of his horse. Though Rachel knew his eyes were on her, she couldn't look at him.

"That Johnny Cain . . ." he began.

He had a strange way of saying the man's name, she thought. Johnny Cain—as if it was all of a piece, all run together.

But then she couldn't imagine anyone calling him just plain Johnny, the outsider who sat at her table with his hand always within easy reach of death. And Mr. Cain, the charming rascal with the lazy smiles and teasing ways—he was a made-up man. Made up by him to put her at her ease while he recovered from his injuries in her house. There was no Mr. Cain.

There was only Johnny Cain. The man who had offered to kill for her.

"Don't start to feelin' tender for him," the sheriff was saying. "A man like him is trouble, and trouble don't like bein' lonesome. Time and luck'll run out on him someday, they always do, and he'll wind up dyin' how he lives."

She crossed her arms beneath her breasts and flung her head back to stare up at him. "But what is a man to do if there are people always out there waiting to shoot him in the back, to cut off his ears?"

He gave a little nudge to the battered brim of his hat. "Which is my point exactly, ma'am. You and your boy have already had your share of woes. When his destiny finds Johnny Cain, you don't want to be standing anywheres near him."

8

JOHNNY CAIN STILL SAT at her table, his hand on his gun. Its long smooth barrel gleamed black and heavy against the brown oilcloth. By comparison his hand looked pale and ephemeral, almost beautiful. Deadly beautiful, Rachel thought. Yes, that was what his hand was to her—a thing that was horrible in its beauty, because it was an instrument of death.

Johnny Cain was looking down—at his hand, at the gun. But she could read nothing in the look of him. She didn't know if he felt the horror of what he saw, or if he felt nothing at all.

Rachel took the coal oil lantern down from its ceiling hook to light it against the coming dark. The scrape of the match sounded unnaturally loud in the still kitchen. She nearly dropped the chimney when she went to put it back on its base, and glass rang against copper, loud as a church bell.

Slowly he lifted his head. His eyes gleamed in the murky light, but there was no warmth there.

He had such a remarkable face, a truly breath-catching face. A face, she thought, that made you long to open its secrets. But maybe there were no secrets. Maybe there was simply Johnny Cain, man-killer.

He smiled, a smile with a hint of ruthlessness in it. "I've been telling you I'm the Devil," he said, "and you've been trying to argue me out of the notion. Now you're looking at me like you expect me to sprout horns and a pair of cloven hooves with my next breath."

"I know you are not the Devil, Mr. Cain."

He gave a hard, short laugh. He stood up, slowly this time, and pushed his revolver back into its oiled leather holster. "But you're still going to ask me to leave. Soon as you can think of a gentle way to do it."

He brushed past her, making for the door, as if he had it in his mind to leave that very moment. She went after him, although she didn't really know if she meant to stop him or see him on his way.

She nearly stumbled up the back of his boots when he halted, his hand on the jamb. "But what if there are others out there," she said, "waiting up in the buttes, waiting for you down the road, in the next town, behind the next rock?"

He kept his back to her. "There ain't no what-if about it.

They're out there waiting, all right. And I'll kill them for it, just like I did the Calder boys."

"You could put your gun away. Refuse to fight."

He studied his hand, pressed flat on the rough wood. He stretched his long fingers out wide, so wide the veins and bones of his hand pushed hard against the pale skin. "Turn the other cheek."

"Yes."

He spun around abruptly, facing her. "God, Rachel, what do you think'll happen then? You think some bastard hell-bent on taking on my rep is gonna come up and tap me on the shoulder and say, 'Excuse me, Johnny Cain, but I happen to notice you're not wearing your gun today, and I was sort of wondering if maybe you wouldn't mind strapping it on before I go ahead and shoot you in the back.'"

"But it's all so unfair! You shouldn't have to . . . have to *live* like that." *To die like that.*

He exhaled a laugh, flat and aching. He leaned back against the door as if he suddenly had no more strength to stand. "There's only the quick and the dead. You ever heard that said? Well, I reckon now you know what it means."

He stared at her, his head lifted, his gaze open and unwavering. And she saw the horror that lived deep within the wasteland of his eyes.

His hand came up, and she thought he was going to touch her mouth like he'd done before. But instead he let the hand drop.

"You make it easy for a man to take advantage of you. To hurt you."

"Would you hurt me, Johnny Cain?"

He said nothing, but he did touch her this time. He ran his fingers lightly, lightly down her throat, and her skin burned as if stung by nettles. He knows he's going to hurt me, she thought; he's sorry for it, but he's going to do it anyway.

He pushed himself off the door. He grabbed the latch, jerking it open with such force the hinges squealed. "I think I'll go on down to the paddock and take a look at the sheep."

She followed him out onto the porch, but no further. The chinook had scoured most of the snow off the ground, and the dead grass showed through. She felt scoured herself, washed clean to the bone.

She watched him walk slowly across her yard and she thought that he moved like what he was, a man sorely hurt.

She hadn't asked him to leave. He hadn't said he would stay.

She knew that anyone with a purpose could find him here on a Plain farm, same as anywhere else. And he knew that, too. She understood what the risks were for herself and for her son, and so did he. She thought that she was probably the only one, though, who was trusting in the Lord to take care of them all.

She saw Benjo come shuffling out from behind the lambing sheds, with MacDuff at his heels. The outsider saw them as well, and stopped. He said something that caused Benjo to shrug and plow the toe of his brogan through the mud. The dog trotted up to the man, and he stooped to ruffle its ears. After a moment the boy joined them. The three of them went to the paddock fence. The outsider put his boot on the lower rail and hung his left thumb off his back pocket. Benjo put his brogan on the rail, but he had no back pockets and so he simply rested his hand on his rump, which made him look a little silly and had Rachel smiling through a sudden prickle of tears.

She could tell by the way his head was jerking that her son was spouting his questions again. From time to time the outsider would look the boy's way, and she wondered if he was answering.

The moon was coming up full over the sloped roof of the barn, competing with the last glimmer of light from the dying sun, as the day gave way to night. Time passed. But no longer slow or sweet or sure for Rachel Yoder. She felt as if she were rushing headlong over a cliff, believing she could fly when she had no wings.

He'd called her Rachel. He probably hadn't even heard her name coming out of his mouth. But she had heard.

WHEN THEY CAME BACK INSIDE, the outsider went right to bed. She was sweeping up the cornmeal crumbs and the beans she'd spilled earlier, and he passed by without even looking at her. He said, "Good night, Mrs. Yoder."

The next morning she was rattling a fresh stick of wood into the cookstove, punching at the coals with it, when the door to the yard opened and she heard his step behind her.

She straightened and turned, her face flushed from the heat of the fire, to see that he carried a zinc bucket brimming with foamy milk.

"Why, you've done the milking," she said. She was surprised he even knew how to do such a thing as milk a cow. "And you managed it one-handed."

"Yeah, well, it sure wasn't easy. That brown bossy kept trying to kick the holy . . . dickens outta me."

She took the bucket from his hand and set it on the slop stone. He smelled of hay, and of the crisp morning air.

"That brown bossy's Annabell," Rachel said. "She has real sensitive teats. You need to use gentle hands on her. Ben used to say you got to squeeze her sweetly and slowly, like a man courting a skittish woman. . . ." She turned quickly back to the stove, flushing. She used the poker to wrestle the lid back into place, making a loud clatter.

"I'll have to remember that," he said, "if I'm going to be doing the milking while I'm here."

She swung around to look at him. She felt herself smile. She thought it was probably a very wide and foolish smile, and yet she couldn't seem to help it. "I'll make you into a lamb licker yet," she said.

"Now as to that, I'm kind of taking on a wait-and-see attitude. Wait until I figure out for sure what the heck that is, and then see if I can stomach it."

She laughed as she put a pan on the fire and began to stir up the batter for flapjacks.

He went to look out the window. "I was thinking maybe if you had a soogan," he said, "or some such thing handy, I could roll it out come nighttime and bed down in the barn."

"There's a sheepwagon parked out back of the lambing sheds. A herder's wagon. You could sleep there. My husband used to drive it up into the hills when it was his turn at the summer pasturing. It's all fixed up with a bunk, even a cookstove. A sheepwagon's a sight more comfortable than a barn."

He made a grunting noise that she took to mean he would be pleased to have the herder's wagon to sleep in.

She busied herself some more with the flapjack batter, whipping the wooden spoon through it. Beating out all the air, she thought; they'll likely be heavy as stones now. "Benjo sure will be grateful to hear you've done the milking for him. He'd laze away the whole morning in bed if I let him. Especially on a school day."

This time the outsider didn't so much as grunt a response.

"There's coffee fresh brewed," she said.

He turned from the window, but he didn't go for the pot. "What we talked about yesterday," he said, "about that trouble waitin' on down the road for me. I'll have a care that you and the boy don't get involved."

"Life is to be lived as it comes, Mr. Cain." She spooned a dollop of flapjack batter onto the hot fry pan. "Bad things happen, like floods and pestilence, and good things like babies being born and the wildflowers coming back to bloom every spring. They are not in our power to control. We can only put ourselves in God's hands."

"Lady, when are you ever goin' to figure it out that your God don't give a damn about me? He never has."

"Oh, for pity's sake!" She slammed the spoon back into the bowl so hard the batter splattered. She spun around to him. "You sound just like Benjo come Saturday mornings, when I make him take his bath and he whimpers on and on in just that poor-me, little-boy way. On and on about how if I really loved him I wouldn't be so awful mean to him, feeling sorry for himself, making excuses—"

His head rocked back a little, as if he'd just been slapped. "Mr. Cain . . ."

"I noticed there was some tack out in your barn needs soaping," he said. He snatched off his hat, then slammed it back down again. "Reckon I'll get at it."

His boots rapped across the bare pine floorboards. He jerked open the door.

"Mr. Cain? Do you like shoofly pie?"

He kept his hand on the latch, though he did turn to look at her. The cold morning air blew in, stirring up the rich smell of fresh warm milk. "I don't know as how I've ever had any," he said.

"It's what I make for Benjo come Saturday nights, if he's been a real good boy about taking his bath."

A quiet spun out between them. And then she saw the brackets around his mouth deepen just a bit. "You make that poor boy take a bath *every* Saturday? Lord-a-mercy, no wonder he questions your affections."

BENJO YODER WASN'T THINKING about baths as he walked later that morning through the jack pines and tamaracks that draped the lower slopes of Tobacco Reef. He was thinking that maybe he was almost as good at reading trail sign as any Indian scout ever was.

He squatted on his haunches to study the black droppings that lay scattered like lumps of coal over the pine straw. A bear had crossed over this deer trail not too long back, he thought. He pushed at one of the turds with his finger, rolling it over. It was still plenty fresh. Yes sirree he thought, a bear had sure enough passed this way, maybe as recently as this morning.

He looked up, squinting against the sunlight that splashed through the pine boughs. The trees were thick here but they thinned out further on up the slope of this butte, and there were plenty of caves in the rocks up there for a bear to snooze away the winter. It was just this time of year that bears first stuck their noses out their winter beds to get a whiff of spring—

The brush crackled behind him.

Benjo whirled, his fingers scrabbling for his sling. Ears straining, he stared hard at the tangled thicket of kinnikinnick bushes.

A breeze came up, stirring the leaves on the bushes and trees, rustling, whispering, crackling . . .

He let out a shaky breath. It was only the wind.

He sure hadn't wanted to meet up with any bear. He

had no illusions that he could take down a grizzly, or even a black bear, with his sling—no matter what David was supposed to have done to Goliath. Just like he knew he really wasn't any Indian scout.

Benjo ambled on down the trail, looking for more signs of the bear. A squirrel scampered ahead of him, disappearing into the trees, tail and whiskers twitching. He spotted a downed log cushioned with yellow lichen, and he sat on it. He opened up his tin dinner pail and smiled to see that Mem had made his favorite, a Cornishman's letter-from-home. He took a big bite of the beef and potato pie, licking the gravy off his fingers. It was a little early in the day to be eating dinner, he supposed, but his belly sure didn't care.

Just about now, Benjo thought, old Rabbitface Gibson would be breaking out the drill books and arithmetic charts. She would be scratching row upon row of numbers across the blackboard. In a moment some poor *Schussel* would have to properly fill in the empty spaces after all those equal signs, or get his hand whacked with a ruler.

Actually Benjo didn't mind working out arithmetic problems up on the blackboard, so long as he didn't have to open his mouth and talk about them. It was reading and answering questions aloud that made Benjo Yoder's school day a misery. The other kids would laugh, while old Rabbitface stood over him, waiting, waiting, waiting, and when the words just wouldn't come out, Benjo would feel the sting of her ruler.

But mean as old Rabbitface Gibson was, she had nothing on the McIver twins. It was supposed to be a sin to hate, Benjo knew, even to hate outsiders. But Benjo had trouble not hating the McIver twins.

It was probably also a sin to allow his mind to dwell on such thoughts, but Benjo couldn't help wondering why

God had chosen to afflict the Miawa Valley with such ornery specimens as those McIvers. They looked exactly alike, with the same fire-engine hair and freckle-mottled skin, and the same narrow-slotted pig eyes. The same big, knotty fists, too. The twins were two years older than he was, and twice his size. And with the way they kept pounding on him, Benjo figured he wasn't likely to grow any bigger.

Benjo didn't know what he'd ever done to earn the twins' enmity. It seemed that the mere fact of his existence on this earth was enough to get them riled. Every Friday for the past three months, regular as an eight-day clock, the McIver twins had stolen his Plain hat and run off with it to the boys' outhouse. There, they would threaten to drop his hat down the hole unless he begged them, saying, "Pretty please, don't." Once he hadn't been able to get the words past his tangled-up tongue. And once, pride had driven him to fight back. All that had gotten him, though, was beaten up, and his hat had wound up down the privy hole. He'd had to make up lies at home to explain away why his hats had gone missing.

The last time, he'd gotten caught out in the lie, and his mem had cried over his sin. He had hated that most of all. He would almost rather she'd given him a whipping. Which was why this Friday he'd decided to avoid the situation entirely by not even showing up at the schoolhouse.

Benjo figured those McIvers would never dare to beat up on him if his father were still around to put a stop to it. And Benjamin Yoder wouldn't have bothered with saying "pretty please" either. Once, two summers ago, when Mem was coming out of the mercantile loaded down with supplies, one of the Hunter cowhands had tripped her up with his spur, ripping her skirt. Da had gone after that cowhand with his fists and beaten the man's face bloody.

Later, Deacon Weaver had made Da get down on his knees during the worship service and confess about how he'd lost his temper and succumbed to the sin of violence. But Benjo remembered his father and Mem talking together that Sunday night, in quiet voices he probably wasn't supposed to be hearing, and his father had said that, confession or not, he would do it again because there were some indignities a man just shouldn't have to suffer.

Benjo figured the McIver twins were two such indignities.

He looked down the deer trail, his eyes suddenly blurring. Sometimes if he just held his breath and concentrated really hard, he could almost see his father. Almost see him bending over the ground to point out the bear droppings, almost hear him saying, "Look there, Benjo. This old she-bear's been feeding on huckleberries."

Benjo tried to swallow down the wad of tears that was building in his throat. It just hurt so much to think about his father being gone forever. It seemed like some days everything reminded him of Da, even his own name. His given name was really Joseph, but because there were three other Joes among the Plain People, folk had at first taken to calling him Ben's Joe, and before long it had gotten shortened to Benjo.

Even with Benjamin Yoder having been called home to God, Mem said he was still Ben's Joe. He would always be Ben's Joe.

Not like the outsider, who wasn't anybody's son. That's what he'd said just last night, out by the paddock gate, when Benjo had asked about his father. The outsider had said, "I ain't no man's son." Benjo knew, though, that you needed some kind of father just to get born. And when Benjo had told the outsider that, he'd laughed. Then he'd said his father had probably just been some poor, dumb son of a bitch passing through east Texas, who for once had managed to leave behind a little something more than his dust.

Last night Benjo had almost asked the outsider to walk along to the schoolhouse with him this morning. He figured all the man would have to do would be to show up wearing that six-shooter of his, and all of Benjo's worries would be over. But he hadn't asked the outsider for the favor, and now here he was hiding out in the woods instead of facing his indignities like a man. Like his father would have done.

But all he had to do was think about what went on out by that outhouse, of what was done to him, and the fear would rise up in his throat to choke him. And following on the heels of his fear would be a bitter shame that burned. Burned just like the tears that were now scalding his eyes.

He pounded his thigh, hard, with his fist. *Don't you cry, Benjo Yoder. Don't you dare cry.*

His mother had told him once that the fears and the sadness had a way of piling up inside a person until there was nothing for it but to cry them all back out again. But his mother was a female, and it was all right for her to cry. Men, like his father—they didn't cry.

The kinnikinnick bushes rustled again. Benjo looked up, blinking hard still against the tears.

But this time there wasn't any wind.

He tensed as the crackling, rustling noises came again, followed by a low whining whimper. It didn't sound at all like a bear, but more like a hurt dog.

Benjo took out his sling and dug in the dirt for a stone. Leaving the trail, he made his way cautiously through the thicket of trees and brush, and entered into a small clearing of bunchgrass choked with thistle and ironweed. The whimpers were growing steadily louder, breaking into an occasional mournful howl. Where the clearing blended back into the woods, he saw the caved-in edges of what looked to be a large pit. The whimpering was coming from down inside.

He approached slowly, his brogans crunching through the winterkilled grass. The whimpers deepened into a low growling. He peered over the edge.

A snoutful of snarling teeth lunged at his face. He yelped, and fell backward onto his rump.

He sat there a moment while the breath sawed in his throat and his heart jumped. He'd only gotten a glimpse of the animal in the pit, but he thought maybe it was a coyote.

He edged up to the lip again. He could feel his heart pounding, and there was a salty, bitter taste in his mouth that he knew was fear, because he had tasted it before. He made himself look down into the pit. This time the coyote didn't leap up at him, although it made snarling noises deep in its throat.

Dirt and leaves and pine needles slithered over the edge of the pit, raining down on the coyote and on a rotting log that lay next to it. The pit appeared to be at least eight feet deep. Too deep, Benjo saw with relief, and too steep-sided for the coyote to climb out, even if it hadn't been hurt. But one of its legs was twisted in a funny way. Its tawny gray pelt was wet and dark with blood from a deep gash in its side.

The coyote was a female and she looked to be growing pups in her belly. She stared up at Benjo, yellow eyes glowing wild, black lips peeled back over sharp canine teeth, bushy tail stiff and the hair of her white throat roached up in fear and anger.

Benjo thought the pit was probably some old deadfall trap, left over from when the Blackfeet used to hunt in these woods. The coyote's leg must have gotten broken and her side cut by the log that had been set to come crashing down on whatever prey stumbled into it.

Which was only good riddance, Benjo thought. Coyotes were sheep killers. In the summer they taught their young how to go after the lambs, and this one was going to have herself a full litter of pups to teach. Would've had herself a litter if she hadn't . . .

The coyote and the boy exchanged a long look, underscored by the coyote's low, rumbling growling and the boy's harsh breathing. Then the coyote's large pointed ears flattened back against her head, and her mouth snapped shut on a yelp of pain. She twisted her head around, trying to lick at the gash in her side.

Benjo sat back on his heels. It made him sad and slightly queasy to think of the coyote's suffering. She would die a bad death down in that deadfall trap. Unless a mountain lion got to her first. Or maybe the bear.

He pushed himself to his feet and ran back to the lichen-covered log where he'd left his dinner pail. He tossed what was left of his letter-from-home down to the coyote, who gobbled it up with a whimpering snarl. He killed a couple of squirrels with his sling and brought them back to her as well. He'd have to figure a way to sneak a bucket of water out here later, he thought, and a rope to lower it with.

He realized he was probably only prolonging her agony, though. Even if she didn't starve or some other wild animal didn't get her, she'd never manage a way out of the trap, not even if her busted leg somehow got healed.

It was funny, but he thought that if his father were here, he'd probably go get that old Sharps rifle he kept hidden out in the barn and shoot the coyote with it, if for nothing else than to rid the valley of another sheep killer. But not Mem. Instead, Mem would be wanting to feed her and give her water, just like he was doing. She'd be all worried about the coyote's babies, just like he was worried.

He scrubbed at his face with his coat sleeve, shaking his head. Judas. A moment ago he was all but bawling his eyes out, and now here he was fretting over some dumb coyote. He was scared of the McIver twins, and he was scared of old Rabbitface's ruler. He was even scared of a bear that probably didn't exist except in his own head.

He was worse than some disgusting girl.

He'd go back to the barn and get the rifle and he'd shoot that coyote—that's what he would do. It would be the merciful thing, he told himself. The manly thing.

He took off for home at a fast run, holding on to his hat. He broke out of the pine woods and descended into a coulee, his feet nearly skidding out from beneath him as he scrambled down the steep slope. Patches of snow still clung to the ground in the shady parts, and the mud sucked at his brogans.

He didn't see the two men on horseback until he'd nearly run right into them. He slewed to a stop, his knees loose, his belly quaking, and his heart thumping wildly in his chest.

The horse that was in the lead, a sorrel gelding, shied in fright. The sorrel's rider checked him with a soft curse. Benjo saw that the rider was a young man, not much older than Mose but with a hawklike face, thin-boned and high-nosed. Just then the other rider nudged his horse forward a couple of steps. He pushed his hat back to reveal a long face with droopy eyes and a beard like a billy goat's. His mouth was puckered around a thick wad of chewing tobacco.

Benjo's throat locked around a scream.

He was Mr. Hunter's stock inspector. The man who had hanged his father.

Benjo watched now, his eyes wide and dry, his breath whining through his throat, as the man unhooked a coiled braided rawhide rope from off his saddle.

"Well, now, what do we have here?" the man said. He spewed a thick glob of tobacco juice onto Benjo's brogans. "I'll be damned if we didn't just catch ourselves a cattle rustler."

9

QUINTEN HUNTER GRABBED THE man's arm, his fingers digging into fringed buckskin that was slick with old sweat and grease.

"Put it up, Wharton." He narrowed his eyes and made his voice smooth and slick as coal oil, a trick of intimidation he'd learned from his father. "Put up the rope."

For a moment longer the arm beneath Quinten's fingers stayed rigid, and a wildness flared deep in the man's pale eyes. Then Woodrow Wharton blinked and smiled, and hooked the rope back on his saddle.

Quinten's sorrel gelding danced sideways, its hind hooves sliding in the mud. The horse pricked its ears and tossed its head toward the stand of jack pines and tamaracks that climbed up the ravine. Quinten wondered if the boy was alone.

The boy certainly was terrified. Quinten could hear his breath scraping in his throat. The kid was skinny as a broom straw and he stood so rigid, he looked as if he would break in a stiff wind. He wore that old-fangled garb that marked him as one of the Plain folk who sheep-farmed the north end of the valley.

"You there, boy. What're you doing straying so far from home?"

The boy opened his mouth. He opened his mouth wide as if he would scream, but nothing came out of it but strange sucking noises.

Woodrow Wharton sent a thick stream of tobacco juice splatting into the grass and smiled. It was a wolf's smile, Quinten thought. Nothing behind it but teeth.

"Let's go ahead and string him up, Quin. Have ourselves a necktie sociable."

Quinten's gelding edged sideways again, jingling his bit chains. Quinten looked up into the empty pines. He heard only the sough of the wind, and the boy's harsh breathing. The boy's throat and jaw muscles were working hard, like bellows.

"Do you know this is Circle H land you're on, boy?"

The boy fisted his hands behind his back as if he needed to brace himself. "Muh!" he shouted with such force that Quinten saw his spit spray through the air. "Muh—muh—muh—"

"He thinks he's a woolly monster," Wharton said. His eyes were getting that crazed look again. "Are you a woolly monster, boy? Baaaa! Baaa!"

"Muh—m-my friend . . . huh—huh—he'll sh-shoot you all s-stone d-d-dead!"

The boy whirled and broke into an all-out run, scrambling back up the slope of the coulee toward the stand of jack pines. He ran awkwardly, with his coat flapping and his thin arms splayed out from his sides.

Quinten thrust his gelding into the path of Wharton's

horse and leaned over, grabbing the shank of the bit to keep him from bolting after the boy.

Wharton stared at him, still wearing that wild smile. "Scare him, Quin. I was only going to scare him."

Quinten looked up into the trees where the boy had disappeared. He shook his head. "You scared him. Half out of what little wits he seems to have."

Wharton wiped the wet tobacco flakes off the ends of his goatee. "I always knew Injun blood made a man's hide go red. I didn't know it also turned his guts yellow."

He dug his spurs cruelly into his horse, jerking its head around hard, and sending it back down the coulee in a spray of mud and chewed-up grass.

Quinten stared after him, frowning. It wasn't the insult; his hide might be red, but it had also grown thick over the years. Rather, it was Woodrow Wharton himself, and the wild unpredictability Quinten had seen in those spit-colored eyes. He'd known animals with eyes like that, eyes that couldn't be tamed, but he'd never seen them on a man before.

He wondered what had motivated the Baron to take on a man like Woodrow Wharton at the Circle H. No real hand would ever dude himself up in Wild West clothes, like chaps with silver conchas and fifty-dollar boots so skintight the man's feet were starting to curl like a ram's horns. No real ranch hand packed a pair of pearl-handled Colts rigged up for a quick draw.

Quinten felt his jaw tighten. Sometime during the months he'd been gone, his father had hired on a cowboy who seemed to know damn-all about cows. A hand more handy with a gun than a branding iron.

"Damn maggot-brained fool," Quinten swore aloud, then shook his head at himself. He hadn't been home a day and already he was letting his father rub him raw, like a poorly made saddle.

Quinten rode his horse up the coulee through the jack pines. If there had been someone else with the boy, hiding up in these trees, they were both long gone now. He went on climbing the slope of the butte. His horse shouldered through the timber, and he had to duck under low swags of pine branches or lose his hat. From time to time he caught the cold whiff of an old snowbank.

He broke through the tree line. The way was rugged here with shale and rocks thrusting out of the red earth. This was wild, tangled country. He looked up, squinting against the glare of the sun. The sky was so wide and empty and blue it hurt to look at it.

He stopped when he got to the shoulder of the high bluff. Up here, the wind was blowing strong, and he had to anchor down his hat with the bonnet strings. Yet the wind brought with it its own silence, he thought, until you began to wonder whether it was the wind you were hearing or the beating of your heart.

He straightened his legs to stand up in the stirrups, stretching out his body, stretching out his mind.

God, it felt so *good* to be home.

Sometimes it seemed that he could feel his very blood and breath in the big sky, wide as forever, in the ragged mountains and open prairie. Feel it so deep that it hurt, a sweet, sad seizing of the soul.

For almost two years he'd tried to please his father by attending college back in Chicago. He'd been shut up indoors all day, hunched over books in the winter, slaving in the heat and stink of the stockyards during the summer. He thought of Chicago, with its soot-grimed buildings that blocked out the sky and sun, its belching smokestacks and the blood stink of the slaughterhouses always thick in the air. To Quinten's mind that place had a jump on hell when it came to creating the miseries in a man.

But at least he'd discovered one thing of importance during what he'd come to think of as his time of exile. He was only nineteen years old, but already he knew what he wanted for the rest of his life.

He wanted that life to be here, on the Circle H. He wanted to wake up every morning and look out to see the mountains propping up the big sky. He wanted to ride the miles of prairie and not see another living thing, except maybe for a jackrabbit or a sage chicken, and his own shadow moving ahead of him on the thick buffalo grass. He wanted to raise cattle and horses and a family on this land, where you could ride and breathe and feel alive.

Below him a hawk had been riding the wind. The hawk banked suddenly now and flew straight off, like a shot arrow, into the deep and empty sky. From up here Quinten could almost convince himself he was seeing the Miawa as it had once been, back when it was new, before it had been claimed and tamed. Back when there were no towns, but only sagebrush and the wind. Back when this high mountain valley had been dark with buffalo and his mother's people had hunted the woods and fished the streams, and lived in tipis that left behind no mark on the land but a white circle of bare earth in the tall grass.

Now his mother's people lived on a reservation and bought their food from a general store with government scrip. And the only signs of buffalo were the bones left scattered among the rocks and sage and tumbleweed.

His father, who had been born near the coal mines of Glasgow, had once told him of a Scottish epitaph that went: "Here lies all of him that would die." Quinten didn't think often about dying—he was too young to worry much over the inevitability of death. But he did understand that epitaph. He wanted the heart and the guts and the spirit that were Quinten Hunter to live on in this land forever.

QUINTEN HUNTER PULLED HIS galloping horse up hard beneath the ranch gate.

So maybe it wasn't the prettiest place on earth, he thought. The signboard above his head was pocked with bullet holes. The cottonwoods that lined the road shivered naked in the wind. The grass was gray, the corrals were muddy, and the windmill was missing a sail. But the sight of the big white house, with its gables and dormer windows and stately spooled-rail galleries, still made him smile.

It was good to be home.

He rubbed his lathered horse dry with a gunnysack, and gave him an extra ration of oats. On the way to the big house, he walked by some of the cowhands, who were playing a game of pitch on the bunkhouse porch. He called out a good evening to those he knew, and nodded to those he didn't.

He paused on the gallery, sitting down on a bent willow rocker long enough to unbuckle his spurs so he wouldn't leave marks on the parquet floor. He used the iron foot scraper next to the door to clean the mud and stable muck off the soles of his boots.

Once inside, he paused again in front of a hall stand made of stag antlers to hook his hat on one of the points. He slicked down his shoulder-length black hair and rubbed the worst of the spring mud off his face with his bandanna.

From the winter parlor he could hear the sounds of two people talking. Or rather he could hear his father shouting in a voice roughened by thousands of cigars, and the cool, murmuring response of his father's wife.

"I built up this spread when there was damn-all out here but Indians and coyotes. You're daft if you think I'll brook the death of it."

His father's wife said something then, too low for Quinten to hear.

His father roared back in his gruff Scottish brogue. "We made a bargain, you and I, and for fourteen miserable years I've kept to my end of it. So you just go on keeping to yours, you bloody-minded bitch, or by God I'll—"

His father must have cut himself off then, for Quinten heard nothing more. Yet he held his breath, waiting. He knew the bargain his father spoke of had something to do with him, to do with that time when he had been brought to the ranch after his mother had died when he was a boy of five. For a lady born and bred as Ailsa Hunter was, to agree to take in the breed son of her husband's squaw, there had to have been one hell of a bargain struck. A Devil's bargain.

Quinten started when his father appeared suddenly in the parlor doorway. He stood spread-legged with his thumbs in his breast pockets, anger sharpening the prominent bones of his face.

The Baron had a face that was all blades: a bowie knife of a nose; a jaw shaped like an ax, as if he used it to chop his way through life; a mouth that curved sharp and down like a sickle. He was a bit bandy-legged after years of straddling a horse. The skin of his face and hands had been leathered by the Montana wind and the sweat of hard work, the grindstone life of ranching. His hair grew thick off his broad, flat forehead, white and flowing.

As usual, the Baron had emerged from his wife's presence in a riled mood. He looked his son over now with eyes that were hard and black, staring down at him as if sighting a rifle. "Where the hell've you been?"

"Out riding."

"I was led to believe that you were going to start in on taming those wild broncs for the spring roundup. Now you tell me you spent the time 'out riding,'" he said, with a mocking lilt on the last words. "You're a lazy scalawag, boy, and if you weren't my kin, I'd fire your bloody arse."

"When did that detail ever stop you before?" Quinten said with a wry half-smile.

The Baron had thrown him off the Circle H a half dozen times over the years, only to go after him and bring him back. And Quinten had let himself be brought back, because of the ranch that he loved with his every breath and heartbeat. And because of the woman, his father's wife, listening in the other room.

Quinten had to jerk his head back as his father's stiff finger stabbed at his face. "If you think, just because I'm letting you get away with quitting on college, that I'll tolerate you going back to the blanket, living up there on the res with your mother's people, to squat outside a bloody tipi, wearing a breechclout and tippling firewater like some no-good breed—"

"Not *like* some breed, Baron. I am a breed."

"What you are is my son. And, by damn, you'll stay here on the ranch and you'll work for your bloody keep, and you'll start by taking the buck out of those broncs tomorrow. Maybe getting your tail pounded proper will nail some sense into your thick head."

"Yessir," Quinten said. But he was talking to his father's disappearing back.

No sound came from the parlor, but Quinten knew she had heard. And that she would now be expecting him. He almost kept on going down the hall and into the kitchen to wash up, which was what he had been headed to do. It would serve her right, for once, for him to do the thing she did not expect of him . . . except that he knew it would serve her nothing. He could come to her, or walk away, and she would care not at all.

He went to her because he couldn't help himself.

He stopped just inside the door, and he let the old feelings come and settle deep, the yearning and raw longing that gripped his heart whenever he looked at her.

The room smelled of the lemon oil that had been polished into the gleaming satinwood wainscoting. The walls were papered in a pale green silk stripe to complement the thick forest green velvet curtains and cream satin upholstered sofa and chairs. Dried flowers were arranged in a spray of white in a gilded vase on the mantel. The parlor was elegant and beautiful and cold, and a perfect setting for the woman within it.

Her hair was the blue black of a crow's plumage, her skin a pale translucent white. She had violet eyes. Not dark blue, but the pure deep purple of hothouse violets.

Elegant and beautiful and cold.

She had been born Ailsa MacTier, the tenth daughter of a Scottish lowland squire. The family might have been titmouse poor, but they were gentry. The centuries-old kind of gentry where the bloodline was as cherished, and as fragile, as old crystal. It was a mystery to Quinten what had ever drawn her to this wild, crude place to marry a coal miner's son. He thought it was probably a mystery to her by now as well.

She was cleaning the milk glass globes of the parlor's brass chandelier. The arms of her gray silk dress were protected by a pair of white linen dust sleeves, which showed not a mark of soot or dirt. Even doing this mundane task, she moved with the fluid straight-backed grace of a princess at a ball.

It was not unusual to see her working, for she was a rancher's wife, after all. Yet in all the years of his life in this house, Quinten couldn't remember ever seeing her face damp with sweat, or a single strand of hair come loose from her tight chignon. He had never heard her shout. If she had a temper it was tamped down inside her so deep it never blasted loose. He had never heard her laugh. He had seen her smile only rarely, and never once for him.

And yet sometimes he thought that the only thing he'd ever truly hungered for in this life was something as simple as the touch of her hand in his hair.

He knew she was aware of him, aware that he had come into the room just to be with her. But she gave no sign of it. He thought he could stand there until he turned into a pillar of salt, and she would merely walk around him on her way out the door.

He went up to her, his boots making no sound on the thick Turkey carpet. He was conscious suddenly that he must smell of mud and horse sweat.

"Let me help you with that, Mrs. Hunter," he said. He'd always addressed her formally, since his first day here at the ranch, and she had never once asked him to call her anything different.

"Thank you, Quinten." She had a voice that was as silky and cold as dry snow.

As he took the polished globe from her hands, their sleeves brushed with a soft sigh and he caught a whiff of lavender water. He climbed the stepladder and began to screw the globe back into the chandelier. She stood beneath him and looked up at him in that way of hers that made it seem as if she wasn't seeing him at all.

An old Chesterfield clock chimed softly. The fringed drape on the fireplace mantel stirred. He turned his head and looked at their reflection in the gilded mirror.

He was struck by how they had the same crow black hair and slender build. Two years of living in a city had leached out his skin some, and he was dressed no differently than any other man on the ranch.

A stranger, walking into the room in this moment, he thought, could easily have mistaken them for mother and son.

HIS FATHER SAID: "It appears to me you spent precious little of your time back there book-learning and most of it girling about, behaving like a randy tom in a cathouse. And if you're opening your mouth to lie, then you can just shut it."

Quinten hadn't been opening his mouth to any purpose at all—unless it was to stuff in one last forkful of Saratoga chips. The crisp disks of fried potato were one of his favorite things, although he'd never told anyone that. If he had, he knew he'd sure never see them served at Ailsa Hunter's table again.

He glanced down the length of the table with its pristine lace cloth. His father's wife brought a crystal glass filled with whiskey up to her pale lips. Her violet gaze was lost in the red flock wallpaper above his father's head, but they both knew she was listening.

He looked back to his father and gave him a man-to-man grin. "Why should a fellow lie when he can brag, Pa? Soon as those big city ladies, with all their la-di-da airs, discover I'm part savage, they get all hot and bothered to discover the *particularly* savage part of me that stands tall beneath my breechclout."

His father laughed, puffing out his chest as if his son's

"girling about" somehow reflected on his own sexual prowess. Not that the old man needed a beacon to draw attention to himself in that regard. Hell, he didn't even need to strike a match. The Baron paid gentlemanly calls on the girls of the Red House every Saturday night, come blizzard or high water.

To Quinten's surprise he suddenly felt her watching him. Not just listening, but watching. When he turned his head and looked down the table and into her dark purple eyes, he thought he caught a glint of something—amusement, contempt? To his disgust he knew he was grateful for either one.

As it was, he thought, this was a conversation more suited to the bunkhouse than a proper dining room, and especially one with a lady present. But then the lady present was the whole reason for the conversation in the first place.

The Baron sat at the head of the table, wearing pearl gray California trousers, a black frock coat, and a gray silk four-in-hand tie fastened with a ruby stickpin. His flat belly was spanned by a watch chain hung with a half dozen gold seals.

At the other end of the table sat Ailsa Hunter, in a black taffeta gown and a shawl of jet-studded lace that glittered in the light cast by a matching pair of crystal candelabra. She wore pearl drops in her ears and a pearl choker collar around her neck.

They could have been a Chicago society couple, man and wife enjoying a quiet evening together in one of those fine mansions that graced the city's lakeshore, Quinten thought. Except for the man's red-skinned bastard and Wild West Wharton, hired gun, who were also in attendance.

The hired gun had placed a wad of damp chewing tobacco on one side of his gold-rimmed eggshell china plate while he ate. Now he put the plug back into his mouth and sucked hard on it.

Quinten looked again at his father's wife. As always, she sat straight as a hat pin. He knew she put Woodrow Wharton into the same category as what was scraped off the bottom of a horse's hoof, yet he knew as well that she would never question her husband's reasons for inviting the man to their table, any more than she would have questioned the topics he chose to converse about. To say anything would have been to admit a defeat.

Red-skinned bastards, Wild West Whartons, and conversations about whores—they were just some of the salvos the Baron fired in the daily war he waged with his wife.

His father's tobacco-fed voice cut into Quinten's thoughts. "Well, now that you are home, Quin, you can help me to rid the valley of those bedamned, holy-howling, Bible-banging mutton punchers. Christ, who would've ever thought they'd stick like they have for ten long years, like bloody cockleburs on a blanket."

The Baron had taken a fat cigar out of a silver case and was lighting it now with the candelabra. "I ask you," he went on when the cigar was drawing, "what kind of people is it goes to kirk in a barn?"

"The Son of God was born in a stable."

Quinten spilled a good part of the whiskey he'd been aiming for his mouth down the front of his vest. He looked at his father's wife, but she was back to contemplating the wallpaper again. She could do that—be silent for hours and then say something that would stop a person cold.

In many ways she was much better at war-waging than his father could ever hope to be.

She used to bring him to church with her sometimes, Quinten suddenly remembered, whenever the saddlebag preacher was passing through on his circuit. He went along to please her. Even after he came to understand that there was no pleasing her, or displeasing her for that matter, still he went with her.

That church in Miawa City was little more than a board-and-batten shanty with a tin roof that rattled in the constant wind. During its busy times, it probably smelled no better than those barns the Plain folk did their praying in. He wondered if she still went there on Sundays, if her faith was so strong. It surprised him to think of her believing in anything beyond herself.

The Baron was glaring down the length of the table at his wife. He puffed so hard on his cigar, a nub of ash fell from its tip, leaving a gray smear on his black frock coat.

"I don't give a sweet damn if those holy-howlers were born in the much straw right alongside the baby Jesus. They think they can come into this valley after the fact and reap the reward of those who came before. It took grit and brawn to make the Miawa what it is today. Grit and brawn. Not like those men you knew back in the old country, eh, Ailsa? Those pansy-faced lords, with their white hands and gilded titles—they couldn't have managed to make of this spread what I've made of it." He waved the hand that held the cigar, drawing smoky patterns in the air. "To wrestle all *this* out of nothing."

"Those men you speak of, Fergus, they have never felt a need to wrestle anything." Even with that silky lady's voice of hers, she'd managed to imbue the word "wrestle" with the same meaning it bore when used to describe a pair of drunks brawling in the mud in front of a saloon. And Quinten saw that she had cut his father deep.

The Baron stared at his wife, a hard glitter in his black eyes. Then his wide, handsome mouth broke into a sudden and dazzling smile.

"I've never flinched before anything, not even before

your tongue, my lovely Ailsa. And I'll not begin with a bunch of holy-howling mutton punchers."

Slowly, Ailsa brought the whiskey glass back up to her lips. Her face was as cold, as silent, as falling snow. And the cold silence drifted from her to settle over the room, until it seemed to Quinten that even the candles in their crystal holders shivered and dimmed.

"How come it is, Pa," he said loudly, his voice breaking like a raw boy's, "that you're back to wanting to rid us of those Plain folk after all this time? I'd've thought we all had pretty much gotten used to having them around."

The Baron said nothing, only shifted his glare from his wife to his son.

"Well, it seems to me," Quinten went on, "that any poor fool who tries to raise sheep suffers enough persecutions without you adding to them. Coyotes and bears, death camas and stomach bloat. I once saw a ewe roll over to scratch a tick itch—she wound up getting stuck on her back and suffocated to death before the herder could get to her. Sheep go out looking for ways to die."

"Aye, and I hope they find every bloody damn one of them."

Quinten opened his mouth, and then shut it. His father behaved as if there was something privileged, even sanctified, about raising cattle. As if a cow was somehow a higher class of animal than a sheep. But the truth was you could graze five to six sheep on the same ground it took for one cow, and they got along on a fraction of the water.

If left to graze in one place too long, though, sheep could chew the grass down to the nub. And what went in one end came out the other, creating an odor that was intolerable to cattle, and not easily stood by humans either. But Quinten suspected that what probably galled the Baron most about his "bedamned, holy-howling mutton punchers" was that wool now sold at a premium, whereas the glutted beef market had crashed last year to the point where you could hardly give even the hides away.

The glutted beef market also maybe explained why, after a good seven-year lull in his persecution of the Plain folk, the Baron had suddenly taken up the crusade again. The Circle H would need to put even larger cattle herds on just that many more acres of grassland for there to be a hope of seeing a profit in the coming years.

Yet Quinten thought he'd probably find himself knocked out of his chair and into next week if he suggested to the old man that they put a sheep band of their own out to graze on their range.

He settled for saying, "The open range wasn't going to last forever, Pa, much as we might wish for it. Didn't you always tell me that what you can't duck, you'd better figure out a way to welcome?"

The Baron pointed at his son with the wet end of his cigar, his eyes tightened into slits. But then he grunted and stabbed the cigar back in his mouth. "Ah, bloody hell," he said. "We'd only be doing those mutton punchers a favor to chouse them on out of here. This country is no place for pilgrims and amateurs."

For the first time all night Wild West Wharton unhooked his small clasp of a mouth for something besides spitting and chewing. "Something tells me that come spring it's not going to be a good time to be a woolly."

Quinten stared into the man's pale eyes, but he was frowning more over the memory of that skinny Plain boy. "Woodrow and I nearly rode down one of their young'uns while we were out searching the coulees for bogged strays this morning. *He* at least appears to have a friend who is willing to shoot us all stone dead if we don't mend our wicked ways."

Wharton scratched his head, plucked out a louse, and crushed it between his fingernails. Ailsa was watching him with a look of polite interest on her face. "He was probably talking about that stranger who got himself shot up while passing through here a while back," Wharton said. "One of them Plain women is supposed to've taken the sumbitch in. The widow of that Plain sumbitch we hung last spring."

Quinten's head snapped around to his father. "You hanged a Plain man? My God, for what—for being a cow thief? What Plain man even knows how to build a loop, let alone swing a wide one? Or was it for having the audacity to actually make a go of his few measly acres—"

"He was rustling our beeves, dammit! Leastways we caught him with a bunch of slick-eared calves, so what else were we to think?" The Baron's hand trembled slightly, and the smoke that rose from his cigar shimmered in the candle-light. "It isn't anything for you to get all wild-eyed about. It was an honest mistake. I told his woman, I've told everyone, it was an honest mistake."

"An honest mistake . . . Good Christ, Pa. You know as well as I do that a Plain man wouldn't pocket a bruised apple from Tulle's Mercantile, not even when there's a sign that says to help yourself."

Wharton let loose a ringing splatter of tobacco juice into the empty cast-iron hearth behind him. "You remember what that sumbitch was jawing about right before we hung him, boss?" His lips pulled back from his long teeth in a smile. "He said we were all gonna be done in by a rider on a pale horse—"

"'I looked, and behold a pale horse: and his name that sat on him was Death, and Hell followed with him.'"

That quiet snowdrift voice seemed to freeze them all in mid-breath.

Quinten looked at his father's wife. Her violet gaze was on the window that framed a fiery sunset. Streaks of copper and orange flamed across a blood red sky. The eerie light was suddenly reflected in the silver and china and crystal on the table, in the mirror of the mahogany sideboard, until it seemed the whole of heaven and earth had caught fire.

The faintest of smiles touched her pale lips. "His name was Death."

BENJO YODER CAREFULLY LAID the rifle across a pair of deer antler brackets mounted high on the barn wall. He wiped his sweating hands on the seat of his broadfalls and blew out a gusty breath. Maybe now that he was safe home again, and the gun was back where it belonged, maybe now he could quit being so scared.

He'd had to stand on a hay bale to reach the deer antlers, and he was about to climb down when the man's voice came out of the dark shadows behind him.

"I was wondering myself if that old Sharps could still fire."

Benjo whipped around and his feet shot out from under him. He landed on his rump on the hay bale and went scooting feetfirst to the floor. His heart was pounding so hard it was like a drumbeat in his ears. He looked up into Johnny Cain's face. But the sun, setting out beyond the barn's open doors in a blaze of red glory, dazzled his eyes so that all he saw was a black silhouette.

"I guess you been out doing some hunting this evening," the outsider said.

Benjo shook his head "no," then he nodded "yes," then

he realized he didn't have any dead game to show for a hunting trip, so he shook his head "no" again.

"If you're going to tell a lie, Benjo, it's always best to stick with it come hell or high water. Elaborate, but don't explain. Apologize, but don't make excuses. . . . Your ma was about to rouse the whole valley to go looking for you, she was that worried."

The outsider's hand gripped his shoulder, not hard enough to hurt, but Benjo still found himself being propelled toward the door.

"Huh—Hunter's m-men. Th-they were g-gonna huh—huh—huh . . . hang me!" he said, the last words shooting out of him with such force he choked on them. "F-for being a cuh—cattle ruh—ruh—ruh . . ." *Rustler.*

Then he realized that an almost-hanging wasn't going to account for a whole missing day, so he elaborated. "I ran off and huh—hid." And he *had* done that for a while, before he'd fetched the Sharps and a water bucket and gone back to Tobacco Reef and the coyote. "I'm suh—suh—sorry." Apologize, but don't make excuses.

What the outsider made of this story, Benjo couldn't tell. They were out of the barn now and heading toward the house, and although Benjo tried to drag his feet, they weren't slowing down any.

"I'm thuh—thuh—think . . . ing," Benjo said, stuttering so hard his head jerked, "m-maybe you m-might want to shuh—shoot them Hunters stone dead."

They stopped, and the outsider stared down at him from underneath the brim of his hat. The man made a sound that was partway between sighing and laughing. "I might want to. But I as good as promised your mother I wouldn't."

Benjo sighed, too, because the door to the house had just then banged open, and his mem had come flying out of it, and he knew he'd made her scared enough that as soon as she figured out he was all right, she was going to turn madder than a nest full of hornets.

She grabbed him, hugging him so hard she nearly knocked off his hat. She ran her hands all over him, feeling for broken bones, he supposed, and maybe gunshot wounds. Then she grabbed him again and shook him so hard his hat did fall off.

"Joseph Benjamin Yoder, you had me worried half out of my wits! Where have you been?"

Benjo opened his mouth, but the words piled up so thick and fast in his throat they made a dam there, and then nothing was coming out now, not even air. He gasped and choked and his eyes filled with tears, and he hated himself that he couldn't even *talk* like everyone else.

"He's only been lying low," the outsider said. "Your Mr. Hunter, the man whose soul you so enjoy praying for, his men threw a bad scare into him by threatening to hang him."

Benjo didn't like the way his mother's face got. She brought the back of her hand up to her cheek as if she was feeling to see if she had a fever, and above her hand her eyes were wide and dark with old pain and a fresh fear.

She reached for him, gently this time, and she smoothed his hair back off his forehead and touched his cheek the way she'd touched her own. "What were you doing clear over on Hunter land?"

"Truh—tracking bear."

"Oh, heavens." She surprised him by laughing, although it was a shaky laugh. "Go on into the house now, Benjo," she said softly. "Wash up for supper."

Benjo picked his hat up out of the mud and climbed the porch, but he stopped within the shadows just inside the kitchen door. His mem and Johnny Cain had their backs to him, both looking toward the buttes that divided the valley between cattle and sheep. The sun was mostly gone now, but it had left a ruby glow in the sky, and everything had a pink tinge: the barn and the sheep, his mem's prayer cap, the outsider's white shirt that had once belonged to his da.

It was hard to hear them from the house, but he thought his mother said, "What am I going to do?"

Johnny Cain must not have had an answer for her, because he said nothing.

She turned half around, and although the outsider still said nothing, she spoke to him as if he had. "No, never that way. Your way is wrong."

"My way is certain. He won't be able to hurt you from the grave."

"But what becomes of my soul then? What becomes of *me*?"

They were facing each other now, as far apart as the distance between two fence posts. Benjo thought, from the way the air seemed to crackle around them, that they were angry.

The outsider's voice had an edge to it. "They won't quit, Rachel. I know these men."

"Because you are one of them."

"Because I am one of them. They are capable of destroying anything, killing anything. Believe me, I *know*."

She shook her head once, hard. "I don't believe you've ever killed a child. I'll not believe it."

"Learn to believe it. There's only one way of stopping men like that."

"No!" Her hand came up as if she would touch him, but they were too far apart. "No, no . . . God's ways are often hard to understand, but He can be merciful. You are the one who must learn how to believe."

"Death stops us."

10

RACHEL HELD THE LANTERN high as she slogged through the icy mud in the yard.

It was after midnight, but she still was dressed properly, in her apron and shawl. She wasn't wearing either a prayer cap or a night cap, though, and her hair fell thick and heavy over her shoulders and down her back. The wind tugged and stirred the curled ends of her hair.

The moon, round and creamy, had risen above the cottonwoods, the first full moon of spring. It shed a soft light over the hay meadows, and over the sheepherder's wagon where the outsider now spent his nights. The wagon's big wheels cast spiky shadows onto the barn, and the battered tin stovepipe, poking out of the humped wooden roof, shone like polished silver.

She climbed the steps of the wagon's small stoop and knocked.

A moment later the top half of the Dutch door swung open, and she found herself staring at his naked chest. She took a startled step backward. "They are coming, Mr. Cain," she said.

She could almost feel his gaze moving over her hair, like the touch of the wind, before it shifted to the corral next to the lambing sheds, where the ewes milled and bleated in the cold spring night.

"Let me just finish getting dressed, then," he said.

She waited for him at the bottom of the stoop, facing away from the door.

When he joined her she saw that getting dressed to him included strapping on his cartridge belt. "What do you intend to do with that gun of yours tonight, Mr. Cain?" she said. "Aim it at some poor ewe's head and demand that she push harder?"

"No'm. I'm figuring to point it at you, lady, the first time you tell me to go lick something."

Their feet crunched through the half-frozen mud, the oil sloshed in the lantern she carried. Beyond, in the dark infinity of the prairie, a coyote began singing to the moon. Rachel felt herself smile, and she lowered her head, as the wind tugged and pulled and stirred her hair.

Benjo, with MacDuff at his side, appeared at the door to the sheds in a wash of lantern light. He had one gloved hand wrapped tight around a pole nearly half again his length and with a hook at the end of it. "You can go fetch some water from the creek," she said to him, "if you please. And by then I should have need of that hook."

The boy leaned the sheep hook against the sheds and snatched up a couple of empty creamery cans. He ran off, the cans banging against his legs, his dog loping at his heels, and was soon swallowed up by the black shadows of the cottonwoods and willows.

Earlier, in preparation for this moment, Rachel had hung several lanterns on the poles of the corral. She went around lighting them now, and yellow puddles spilled onto the muddy straw and the shifting gray woolly backs.

"Mr. Cain, if you would start separating out the ones who are about to drop . . ."

He stood in the middle of the bleating, milling sheep

and turned in a slow circle. "I'd do that, Mrs. Yoder, truly I would. But one sheep pretty much looks like another to me even in the best of times."

She ducked her head to hide another smile. "The ones with stiff teats, and those whose udder bags and female parts are pink and swollen—they're the ones whose time is near. That flighty one is going to be first off the mark." She pointed to a young ewe that had moved away from the flock and was digging almost frantically in the straw with her forefeet to make a nest. "It's her first spring as a mother, and she could have trouble."

Rachel could always spot the ones that were going to lamb in the next hour or so. She could tell right off which ones would need help and which wouldn't. Ben had said it was because she was a female herself that she was so good at reading the ewes.

Rachel thought it was the music. Come lambing time, she imagined she could hear a sweet trilling, like birdsong, emanating from the ewes who were about to give birth. Or rather, she didn't so much hear the songs as *feel* them as a stirring in her own blood. And if a ewe was headed for trouble, the birdsong became the jarring and discordant caw of the crow.

The outsider was now walking among the ewes, bending over from time to time to peer at them. "It appears," he said, "like there's gonna be a lot of 'em coming all at once."

"Indeed, Mr. Cain. It's going to be a busy night. Now, if you could just come over here, please, and give this new little mother your man's strong and sturdy leg to push against. She finds what's happening inside her belly very strange, I think, and so she's scared by it."

A thin white sac was showing now in the opening under the ewe's tail. She flung her head back, her neck stretching, her whole body straining, her eyes bulging. The opening widened, and more of the white membrane appeared. Rachel could see the emerging lamb's front hooves and between them a tiny black nose. This mother might be a frightened amateur, but at least her baby knew the proper way to make an entrance into the world.

The ewe collapsed suddenly into the nest she'd tried to dig for herself. She was laboring hard, her upper lip peeling back with each push. She was silent, though, except for a grunting deep in her throat and the instinctive slurping of her tongue.

The outsider had given the ewe his leg to brace against, and now he squatted down in the straw next to her rolling head. He threaded his fingers through the puff of wool between her ears, stroking her, over and over. "Why don't she holler?"

Rachel's gaze was held fast by those long fingers, the way they moved tenderly, almost lovingly over the ewe's head. But then, he touched his gun like that, she thought. And, once, her mouth.

"Sheep can bear a lot of pain," she finally said. "But I think more than anything they keep quiet because they don't want the coyotes and wolves to know when they're giving birth."

From the look on the outsider's face, he appeared to be suffering right alongside the ewe. It was funny, but watching a lamb come had sometimes twisted up Ben's insides like that, too. Maybe, Rachel thought, a woman understood better that birthing was just naturally going to be hard. That with life came suffering.

Benjo trotted up, bringing with him the hook and a piece of gunny sacking, just as the ewe lurched back onto her feet. She gave a mighty strain, her rear end jerking sharply. The lamb seemed to dive out of the womb, feet and nose first, landing in the muddy straw, a glistening, steaming nubby yellow sack of bones.

Rachel tore the membrane, peeling it away from the lamb's nose and mouth, laughing as she heard the squeaky *maa* that came with the little one's first breath. Her own boy was right there to hand her the sacking, so that she could quickly dry off the lamb's ears and keep them from freezing.

The ewe just stood there, *baa*ing frantically and shaking her hind end, as if she wasn't quite sure what all had been happening to her. Rachel began to fear she'd turn out to be one of those mothers who refused to accept her baby. But then, as if some wheel finally clicked over in her brain, she turned, stretching her nose out toward her lamb. She sniffed, and then began to lick the sticky yellow slime off its rump, making loud noises that almost drowned out the night wind, the rustling straw, and all the bleats and *baa*s of the other expectant mothers.

"And here all this time I've been worried you were going to make *me* do that," the outsider said.

"The night is young yet, Mr. Cain."

He laughed, then his gaze fell back down to the ewe, who was now trying to nudge her lamb to its feet by pushing up on its little rump. A gentleness she had never seen before came over his harsh face. He looked very young, she thought, and . . . surprisingly, the word that came to her mind was *happy*. He looked happy.

"M-Mem?"

She turned, swallowing down the lump that clogged her throat. She took the sheep hook that Benjo handed her. She slid it under the lamb's belly, in front of its hind legs, lifting the nubby yellow bundle of bones until it was dangling from the end of the pole, nose to the ground.

She offered the baby in this fashion to its mother, letting her see and smell it. But the ewe suddenly whirled and ran into the middle of the corral, scattering the whole rest of the drop band into a bleating, tail-humping panic.

"Oh, she sure enough is a flighty mother!" Rachel exclaimed in exasperation. "See if you and MacDuff can shoo her back over this way, Benjo."

Her boy, with both the dog's and the outsider's help, chased the ewe back over to the lamb. The ewe stretched out her neck, sniffing hard to be sure the baby was hers. Slowly Rachel backed up, the lamb dangling at the end of the pole. She made soft bleating noises low in her throat, a *beh-beh-beh*, to encourage the flighty mother. And the ewe followed them warily, sniffing the whole way, into the sheds.

The sheds, built long and low, had a mixture of straw and sawdust spread over the floor, and were divided inside into a honeycomb of pens, called jugs, that were just large enough to hold a ewe and her lamb. Once snug in its new home, the newborn pushed itself up onto its wobbly, knobby-kneed legs. Using gentle nudges, Rachel guided it to its mother's teat for its first meal. She couldn't linger to watch, though, for she could hear Benjo hollering that another lamb was coming.

They hit a flurry of birthings after that, so that she and the outsider had to work separately. She watched him, though, whenever she got the chance. Johnny Cain, man-killer, seemed to settle easily into the sheep midwifery business. His low and lazy drawl soothed the ewes like a lullaby, and the touch of his hands was gentle and sure.

Her eyes often sought out her boy as well, and her chest tightened with a bittersweet ache when she thought how proud of him his father would be. He seemed to be everywhere at once, handing them sheep hooks and pieces of sacking, scooping up the birth mess from the newly delivered ewes. And in between jugging the babies and their dams, they all took turns at forking hay into the pens and giving the new mothers buckets of water sweetened with molasses.

Only once did Rachel have to pick up a small wet yellow bundle and carry it outside the corral fence to the place that, one particularly bad spring, Ben had taken to calling the "bone pile." For it was inevitable that, even in the good years, some of the lambs died, and they always lost a few of the ewes as well.

Still, as Rachel carried the dead lamb over to the bone pile, she turned her head away so that the men, her son and Johnny Cain, wouldn't see her woman's tears.

RACHEL CLASPED THE SHEEP HOOK between her thighs so that she could use both hands to gather up her hair and work it into a braid.

Her hair had been falling into her face all night, when it wasn't being twisted into knots by the wind. She scolded herself for not pinning it up and covering it properly with a prayer cap. It had been prideful of her—and wicked, because she had done it for him.

"Rachel."

Her name, coming at her out of the night and in such a tone of urgency, startled her so that the sheep hook went clattering to the ground.

He had come up close behind her, and as she whirled, her flying braid wrapped around his throat. He reached up, his long fingers tangling in the thick loose plait. His fingers tightened their grip, pulling her closer. His head dipped, and his lips parted slightly as if he would kiss her.

It was as if she had roped him, roped him with her hair.

He let her go and took a step back. "We got trouble," he said.

Rachel's eyes flew to the road, expecting the trouble to belong to him. But then she saw that he'd already gone back into the lambing sheds, and she had to run to catch up with him.

The outsider led her to the jug where they'd put the first lamb born that night, the first lamb of spring. The little black-faced baby stood alone, ignored by his mother, his knobby legs shaking, his back humped up, eyes sunken, ears drooping.

"Oh, he's starving, the poor little *bobbli.*" Rachel squeezed into the jug with the lamb and his dam, stooping to keep from hitting her head on the sloping roof. "This flighty ewe of yours is bumming her lamb."

"Flighty ewe of *mine?* I don't recall marrying her."

"You hadn't ought to spurn her to her face like that, sir. Given how she adores you." And indeed, at the sound of his voice, the ewe had turned her head to look up at the outsider with an expression on her sweet clown's face that was positively besotted. "Help me to tip her over onto her rump, if you don't mind," Rachel said.

"I don't. But I ain't speaking for her feelings on the matter."

The drawling words were full of teasing laughter, and although she smiled back at him, there was a tightness in her chest now akin to fear. She thought of how his fingers had felt in her hair. No wonder the Bible said an uncovered woman ought to be shorn. It was a wickedness, what he had been about to do. What she had almost let him do.

They wrestled together with the stubborn ewe, their hips and shoulders bumping in the enclosed space, trying to upend her so that her baby could nurse. Once, Rachel's loosening braid curled around his arm, and she nearly upended her own self jerking away from him, but if he noticed he gave no sign.

When they got the ewe sitting up on her rump, Rachel worked her teats to get the milk to flow. Soon the shed filled with the slurping sounds of hungry suckling, the slap of a little black nose against the bag. They didn't let go of the ewe, though, until her baby's belly bulged with milk.

The outsider stepped aside to allow Rachel to precede him. But she couldn't go past him without brushing up against him, and her unruly braid caught in the buttons of his coat. She spent a frantic moment trying to tug herself free, while he said, "If you'd just quit wriggling like a cut worm, I can . . ." And once again she had to endure the feel of his fingers in her hair.

When they were safely, and separately, outside the cramped jug, he straightened to his full height, bracing his good hand into the small of his back. He rolled his shoulders, easing out a deep groan. "I could stretch for a mile, if it weren't for the walk back," he said. "This is a downright indecent hour to be working. There's only one thing a body ought to be doing this time of night."

"And just what is . . ." A blush rose in her cheeks, as her head caught up with her tongue.

"I was going to say *sleeping*, Mrs. Yoder."

He turned away from her, but not before she'd noticed how the lines had crinkled at the corners of his eyes.

He took off his coat and slung it over a peg where the sheep hooks hung when not in use. Although the night was cold, the crowded sheds were warm and they'd been working hard. He grabbed up a pitchfork now with his good hand and dumped hay into the feeding trough that ran along the back of the flighty ewe's jug.

He hadn't bothered to put on his vest when he'd dressed.

Beneath the thin, wash-worn flannel of Ben's shirt, she could see the muscles of his back and shoulders flexing as he worked. His black suspenders seemed to cling to those muscles, to move with them.

Plain men never wore suspenders.

She touched the middle of his back, above where the suspenders crossed. It was supposed to be a light, brief touch, meant only to get his attention. Yet like his suspenders, her hand seemed to cling there, and she felt the heat and hardness of his flesh.

He turned, slowly, so that her hand trailed for a moment across the width of his back before it fell to her side. "I've been meaning to thank you," she said. "I don't know how ever Benjo and I would be managing on our own tonight, without you."

"I suspect your good neighbor and particular friend would've come hightailing it on over here, tripping over his own big feet in his rush to lend you a hand."

"Noah doesn't have big feet. Well, yes, he does. But you shouldn't mock him. He's a good man."

The outsider said nothing. He stabbed the pitchfork back into the hay bale just as Benjo came into the sheds with a splashing bucket. The outsider took the bucket from the boy and set it inside the jug. The ewe immediately stuck her nose into the molasses-sweetened water.

"Besides," Rachel said, "Noah's probably having plenty of his own lambs to worry over just about now."

She suddenly realized that MacDuff was whining at her. Benjo gripped her arm, and she turned. The boy was looking up at her with wide eyes. His throat worked, his tongue pushing so hard against his teeth that he was spitting.

She laid a gentling hand on his shoulder. "Hush, now, and take a breath. I'm listening."

"Muh—Mem! Y-you know that old gappy-mouthed ewe? Huh—huh—her baby's c-coming out all wrong!"

THE EWE LAY ON the ground, quiet except for her contracting belly. Rachel could see only one tiny black hoof thrusting from her rear. Her water had broken some time ago. The music that Rachel felt, emanating in radiant waves with each hard shudder of her body, was like the wild and plaintive howl of a coyote. Yet as Rachel knelt in the straw, the ewe looked up at her with those serene eyes that had always made her seem such a gentle, wise old thing.

"You poor old dear. Your baby's trying to come out all backwards, isn't he?" She thrust her fingers through the ewe's thick gray fleece, massaging her clenching belly. "I'm going to need to pull her," she said to the outsider, who had squatted down alongside her. "Benjo, fetch me a bucket of water and some of that lye soap. And a piece of baling twine."

As they waited in silence for the boy to come back, kneeling side by side, watching the ewe labor, Rachel was so very aware of him. Of the way those black suspenders cut his shirt into white diamonds lit by the moon, and the way his sharp cheekbone cast a deep shadow onto his beard-roughened cheek. Of the way his hand, like her own, rubbed and pulled through the wool of the sheep's shuddering belly.

And her awareness of him made her aware of herself. Of the heaviness of her braid lying on her back. Of the way her breasts pushed up against the cotton of her shift, and her thighs rubbed together when she shifted her weight to bend closer to the ewe.

Benjo came running up so fast he stumbled and sprawled

onto his knees in front of her, nearly dumping the bucket of water in her lap. "M-Mem! Is she g-g-going to d-die?"

"I don't know," Rachel said, rolling up her sleeves. "I'll try to save her and her baby both. But the Lord always knows what's for the best." She plunged her arms in the water, scrubbing hard with the soap. "So we must leave it all in His hands and strive for the patience and the courage to surrender to His will."

The outsider made a small movement, and she thought he was going to say something, but then he didn't. She thought he'd probably been about to say that the good Lord surely had more pressing business to attend to than the fate of an old gappy-mouthed ewe and her lamb.

"God is all-knowing, and all-loving," she said, answering him as if he had spoken aloud. "A sparrow doesn't fall from the sky without Him knowing of it." *Even you, Johnny Cain.*

She pushed her hand up inside the ewe's hot womb. The lamb's head was turned backward, and its other hind leg seemed to be bent up around it. The ewe stretched her neck forward and rolled her head as a fierce contraction shook her body. The squeezing muscles bore down hard, crushing Rachel's hand between the lamb's skull and the ewe's pubic bone. The bruising pain was so intense tears started in her eyes.

When the contraction ended, Rachel pulled out her hand, slimy now with the ewe's blood and the birth mucus. She tried to wipe the wetness off her cheek with her shoulder, but more tears followed, for she knew now that the ewe and her lamb would both surely die.

"The lamb's head is twisted around all funny, and my hand's too big. I can't get it up in there far enough."

"Let the boy try," the outsider said.

Benjo reared back. "Nuh—nuh—nuh—!"

Rachel cupped her son's face so that she could look into

his eyes. They'd gone big and round as cartwheels. "You don't have to do it. I'll not make you. But this poor old gappy-mouthed ewe, you are her only hope."

Benjo pulled his head out of her hands to look at the outsider. The man's face showed nothing—to Rachel, at least. But her son must have found what he was searching for, because he turned back to her and nodded solemnly.

"All right, then." Rachel's breath eased out in a sigh. She had smeared the ewe's blood on the boy's cheek and she used a gunnysack now to wipe it clean.

"The trick is going to be to get your fingers around the lamb's nose and jaw and ease its head around until it's pointed right." She tucked a strand of his long shaggy hair behind his ear. "You can use a piece of the baling twine then, to help you, but you're going to have to stay with it, to stay with the head and pull the baby out. And Benjo . . ."

She gripped his hand, his small boy's hand that she was asking to do a man's job. She could feel a fine trembling going on inside him. "Benjo, the ewe's belly is going to be trying to squeeze out her baby, and when that happens she's going to squeeze your hand, too."

"Wuh—will it h-hurt?"

"Yes."

"Luh—luh—lots?"

"Probably. Yes."

"He can do it." The outsider clasped her boy's shoulder, giving it a rough shake, the kind of touch men gave one another. The kind of touch a man gave his son. And he smiled—the first all-out, genuine smile she'd seen from him. It was as bright and dazzling as hot sunshine.

Her boy tried for a brave smile himself, but his mouth only trembled a little.

Benjo had to lie flat on his belly to push his hand and

arm up inside the ewe. With every one of the ewe's contractions, he screamed aloud. Tears ran down his cheeks, leaving white streaks through the straw dust and grime, but he never once let go, and Rachel had to cover her mouth with her hand to keep him from hearing her sobs.

Each time the ewe labored, the lamb came down only an inch or two. Then, finally, she gave a mighty heave and the lamb slid, bloody and sticky, out into the straw.

Rachel knelt unmoving, with her hand pressed hard against her mouth. But the outsider was right there to cradle the lamb. His fingers tore away the membrane from the tiny black nose. "Breathe, damn you, breathe, you little bastard." He was chanting the profane words like a prayer. "Breathe, breathe, breathe."

The lamb wasn't breathing.

Rachel grabbed the yellow bag of bones from him by the rear hocks. She stood up and swung it hard in a full and violent circle through the air. Once. Twice.

The lamb let out a loud, indignant *baa!*

Laughing, Rachel collapsed back into the straw, cuddling the bawling lamb in her lap.

Through it all, Benjo had been choking over hysterical words, while the outsider had stared at her, wearing a wide-eyed look of pure wonderment. Now as she sat hugging and rocking the bleating lamb, she laughed just to see him like that. Then he let his own laughter go.

"I thought you were going to . . ." he sputtered. "Lordy, I don't know what I thought—the way you were swinging that poor lamb like a lasso." His laughter wound down and then came back again. He shook his head. "If you aren't the damnedest woman I've ever seen."

"No, no," Rachel said. "That's how it's done, truly. It's supposed to help them start breathing."

"Helps to scare the breath right *out* of them, I would've thought."

Her boy had been laughing as well. But now he gripped her arm. "M-Mem? Wuh—wuh—wuh . . ."

She touched his tear-streaked face. "He'll live, our Benjo. He'll live." She laid the lamb gently back into the straw, then pushed a burlap sack into the outsider's hands. "Here, rub him down with this, Mr. Cain. Or you can go on ahead and use your tongue, if you like. Then you can lay full claim to the title of 'lamb licker.'"

That dazzling smile blazed across his face again. "Lady, you sure don't cut a man any slack, do you? I've a mind to . . ."

She was so caught up in his smile that it took her a moment to realize his voice had trailed off. The whole world suddenly seemed to have fallen silent, and in the next instant she saw what he had just noticed: that the ewe was lying too quietly. It was hardly to be expected that she would bounce right up after such a hard delivery, but still . . .

Rachel pressed her hand to the ewe's brisket. It rose once and then subsided, softly, gently. She looked down into those quiet, all-knowing eyes in time to see the life fade out of them.

The outsider came up onto his haunches, shifting his weight so that the ewe was shielded from Benjo's sight. His gaze met hers and then, together, they looked at the boy. Benjo had taken up the burlap sack himself and he was absorbed with wiping the lamb clean. His face glowed bright as a lighthouse beam, with joy and pride over what he had done.

"Hey there, partner," the outsider said, as he gripped the boy by the back of the neck and gave him another of those rough manly shakes. "Come along and help me to carry this youngster of yours into the shed and out of the cold."

Rachel watched them go. Once, Benjo started to look

back, but the outsider said something, snagging his attention. She knew he would find out soon enough about the ewe's death, but she couldn't bear for him to be told of it just yet.

When Benjo was out of sight inside the shed, she turned back to the ewe. That old gappy-mouthed ewe—she should have been culled from the band last fall, but she'd always been such a good mother. Such a sweet, gentle mother.

Tears came again, stinging Rachel's eyes. She threaded her fingers through the tight curly wool between the ewe's ears. She leaned over and kissed her bony nose.

"Good-bye, old dear."

RACHEL STOOD IN THE middle of the corral. The drop band was quiet now, the only sound coming from the low-burning lanterns that hissed and guttered. Beyond the fence, the night was just beginning to soften into dawn.

She sighed and stretched, feeling loose-jointed with weariness. She had just checked on all the expectant ewes; there would be a respite of several hours before the next flurry of birthings. Her arms ached from carrying so many lambs into the sheds, for tiny as they were, they could still feel heavy when dangling off the end of a long hook.

Her chest ached, too, with the mixture of joy and pain that always came with spring and the lambing time.

She drew in a deep breath of air sweet with the smell of warm ewe's milk. From inside the sheds she could hear the soft *buuuuh* of ewes crying to their babies, and the tiny lambs answering *maaaaa.* The ewes would be settling down to sleep. The new lambs would stretch out across their mothers' front legs, and the ewes would rest their chins on their babies' heads. It was a sight that never failed to pull at Rachel's heart.

A creaking noise broke her reverie, and Rachel turned.

Benjo emerged from between the shed's crossbuck doors. He carried a green willow stick, upon which he was adding another notch with a whittling knife. He hadn't cried when she'd told him of the old gappy-mouthed ewe's death. He'd cinched his mouth together and tugged his hat low over his eyes, but he hadn't cried.

"What's the tally, then?" she said to him now, smiling.

Grinning back at her, the boy made a show of counting the notches he'd made in the stick, slowly and carefully. "Tuh—twelve!" he announced.

"Eleven."

The outsider stepped out of the sheds. He had his own hat pulled low to shade his eyes against a sun that wouldn't be up for an hour yet. His mouth was set tight. He carried one of the newborn lambs cradled in his good arm, as gently and tenderly as if it were made of spun glass, but the lamb was dead.

"I went to check—the little fella was so hungry before, and I wanted to make sure that flighty mother of his had gotten the hang of feeding him. She'd gone to sleep. I reckon she didn't know any better, but she laid right down on her baby and smothered it with her wool."

The outsider turned away from them and headed for the bone pile. He laid the tiny carcass down next to the other ones, arranging its head and tiny legs so that it seemed only to be sleeping. In the first days of its life, a lamb's wool felt more like the matted nap of a worn-out old rug. But Johnny Cain stroked that flighty ewe's dead baby as if he were touching the softest thing on earth.

RACHEL CUDDLED THE BUM LAMB to her chest as she tipped the pap bottle's black nipple into the gaping, pouching mouth. "Drink up, little one, drink up," she crooned, tickling him under his little yellow tail to stimulate the suckling instinct. Through the kitchen window she could see the sun casting its first long light onto the land, reddening the bluffs and etching the cottonwood branches into a pale sky.

She sat on the floor in front of the cookstove, two cracker boxes filled with straw flanking her. She had two bums to care for after this first night of the lambing season. The lamb she fed was a twin whose mother had only enough milk to nurse one. And snug in one of the cracker boxes slept the old gappy-mouthed ewe's orphaned baby.

The door to Benjo's room opened, and she looked up. The outsider stood there obscured in shadow. Then he stepped into the kitchen, shutting the door behind him with a soft click.

"That's one tired boy you have," he said. "He and that ol' dog of his both went out the moment their heads hit the pillow."

The morning sun, pouring now through the window, caught him full on the face. You looked into that face, Rachel thought, and you longed to possess all its secrets. If the Devil walked the earth, he would have such a face, for what better way to seduce than with sublime mystery.

He came toward her, padding across the floor in his stocking feet. They'd all had to leave their shoes on the porch, filthy as they were with the muck of the lambing sheds. He squatted on his haunches in front of the cookstove, his face turned away from her.

"Your boy did you proud tonight."

"I'd be busting my buttons, if I had any," she said. She tried to smile, but her mouth couldn't manage it. She was more afraid of Johnny Cain in this moment than she had ever been. If the Devil walked the earth . . .

She watched him as he shook down the ashes in the stove, adding more wood. Watched the way his long fingers curled around a piece of splintery kindling, the way the bones and veins of his hand stood out against the pale skin. His hands fascinated her—perhaps because every time she saw them, she couldn't help thinking of all the violent, terrible things those hands had done.

He turned gracefully on the balls of his feet to sit Indian fashion across from her, their knees almost touching. She looked away from him, toward the window that now framed a morning sky of dazzling blue. The new wood settled into the fire with a pop and a hiss.

The lamb had slowed in its suckling. Milk dribbled from the abandoned nipple into Rachel's lap. The lamb's tummy, round and warm and replete, pressed into her own belly.

There were so many things she could say to the outsider in this moment. She chose what seemed the easiest, the safest.

"He's different around you, Benjo is. I think he wants to show more of what he is, of what he can be, when he's with you." She settled the sleeping lamb into the empty cracker box. "Those aren't the sort of feelings I'm very good at inspiring, making him feel like a man."

His unsettling eyes stared at her across the small space that separated them. His voice, when he spoke, was clotted and rough. "You're good at it."

And then time slowed and slowed and . . . stopped, as his hand came up. His fingers caressed her neck as they followed the length of her thick, loosely woven braid, down over her shoulder, down where the feathery, wispy ends of it curled around her breast. Dreamily, she realized he was loosening it further. He was loosening and unraveling her hair.

His mouth was so hard, so hard. But his fingers combing

through her hair were gentle. She felt a strange seizing, deep in her heart—as if it, like the whole rest of the world, had ceased beating.

"Rachel," he said, though it was more of a sigh, an easing of the breaths they'd both been holding.

He had her hair undone now, he had all of her undone. Strands of it caught on his callused fingers, clinging. He brushed his knuckles along her jaw, so lightly it was as if he'd only thought about touching her. "Rachel," he said again, so soft it was as if he'd only thought her name.

But she heard in his whisper, she saw on his face, echoes of the same longings that cried inside her. She wanted to touch the hard edges of his mouth. She wanted to touch his mouth with her own.

One of the lambs let out a loud, indignant blat. They both started, jerking away from each other.

His hand, that a moment before had so briefly touched her face, fell gently to the cracker box and was now fondling the lamb, the old gappy-mouthed ewe's baby. She thought of that hand, of what it had done and what it could do. Of what a terrible, terrifying, tender man he was.

The lamb bumped the outsider's hand with its head, thinking the rough, scarred palm was its mother's udder bag. "That poor little bum, I guess he woke up hungry," Rachel said, shocked at how hard it was to get the words out her tight throat.

He picked the lamb up, one-handed, by the scruff of the neck. She'd never seen anyone do that before. "You'd better go on and get some sleep yourself," he said. He pried the pap bottle from her stiff fingers. "I'll take care of this one."

He didn't sound as if he was having any trouble at all getting his words out. Whatever she'd seen in his face, it might never have existed. He could do it so easily, empty his face of all thought, all feelings, until it looked made of stone.

"Go on to bed," he said again, for she hadn't moved.

She wanted to stay with him, talk with him more, have him touch her again. And she wanted to touch him.

Instead she pushed herself to her feet and walked away from him on legs as unsteady as any newborn lamb's. At the door to her bedroom, she turned and looked back.

He had the old gappy-mouthed ewe's baby cradled in his strong left arm, nestled against his chest, and the bum lamb was suckling hard on the pap bottle, its little tail flopping up and down. The man's eyes, his smile, his touch were all for the lamb.

"Johnny," she said. But softly, so that only she would hear.

11

OH, YOU POOR THING. Whoever's tied you up like this?"

Rachel knelt in the damp grass and began to pick at the knots in the wet rawhide rope. MacDuff welcomed her with a whimper and a heavy thump of his tail. He lay with his ears drooping and his nose buried between his paws. One end of the rope was tied around his neck, the other around one of the corral posts.

As Rachel's fingers worked to loosen the knots, her eyes searched the creek bank and hay meadows for Benjo. She saw sheep, of course, and a beaver sitting next to a chewed log, combing its fur with its toenails. She saw a pair of red-winged blackbirds trilling in the willows. But no boy.

She couldn't imagine where Benjo was off to so early on a preaching day, what he was doing that he didn't want MacDuff along with him. He took that dog with him everywhere, sometimes even to school, and never mind that a herding collie's main purpose in life was to be following after sheep and not Benjo Yoder.

Rachel stood, wrapping the rope around her bent arm in a cowboy's coil. MacDuff didn't seem to care that he was free. He buried his nose deeper between his paws and looked up at her with sad eyes. Rachel thought of what had happened to Benjo the last time he'd strayed too far from home, and she could actually taste the fear in her mouth.

Suddenly MacDuff lurched to his feet with a joyful bark and took off for the woods that separated their farm from the Weaver place. Benjo burst out of the yellow pines and tamaracks, running so hard he was throwing up pine straw in his wake. Rachel's legs went weak with relief.

The boy saw MacDuff and jerked to a stop. His head whipped around toward the corral. His shoulders sagged when he saw her. She could almost hear the sigh he let out as he turned reluctant feet in her direction. He came slowly, his gaze on the ground. MacDuff pranced along beside him, beating the boy's coat with his tail.

"What've you been doing?" she said as he shuffled up to her, her voice sharp-edged with the residue of fear. He was sweaty and out of breath, as if he'd been running not only hard but for a long way. His broadfalls were soaked to the knees and splattered with mud. He wouldn't meet her eyes.

"Joseph Benjamin Yoder, I've asked you a question, and now I'll thank you for the answer to it."

His face paled and then turned pink as a spring strawberry. "Nuh—nuh—nuh . . . thing!"

"And just what sort of 'nothing' was it that you didn't want MacDuff along with you?"

He pursed his lips, shrugging. He dug a trench in the mud with the heel of his brogan—a brogan she'd put fresh blacking on just last night. She was about to scold him for it when she saw the blood beneath the nails and in the creases of his hand.

"You haven't been killing rabbits with that sling of yours just for the sport of it, have you?"

His face changed hue again, paling. He shook his head, but his eyes looked guilty.

She gave him a little push in the direction of the yard pump. "Go wash up, then. Go on. We don't want to be late for the preaching, today of all days. . . ."

She let her voice trail off, for by now he and that dog of his were already halfway to the pump, both of them running with the carefree gait of sinners freshly shriven. She stared after them, frowning. Her boy was doing something he wasn't supposed to be doing and he was lying about it as well. She wanted to shake him until the truth rattled out of him. She also wanted to tie him up to a corral post with a rope, keep him home, keep him safe.

"Oh, Benjo." His name came out of her on a sighing breath.

Squaring her shoulders, she turned back to the corral and lifted her black bonnet from the fence post where she'd set it before freeing MacDuff. She pulled the bonnet on her head over her prayer cap, and tied the wide black ribbon beneath her chin, tilting her head back to stare up into the soft and hazy sky of a Montana spring.

She loved this time of year, when the earth seemed to

be warming up from within, erupting into a rainbow glory of color. The willow trees were swelling with brilliant red buds. Blossoms of phlox pillowed the ground, pink and sweet. And high on the slopes of the buttes, the sage at last was turning from the steel gray stalks of winter to a soft feathery green.

Rachel laughed as, out in the pasture, a lamb awoke with a start and jumped stiff-legged like a grasshopper into the air. When he lit, he butted heads with another young male, spooking the whole flock.

A horse's loud, nose-clearing snort cut across her laughter, and she turned, smiling wide. The outsider had led their old draft mare from the barn and stood now in the yard, his hand wrapped around the harness reins, looking at her.

Rachel felt a shiver of precognition, as if this moment would someday prove to be more important, sharper, truer than other moments. But perhaps it was only that the sun had just then lifted full above the hazy horizon to brighten the world, and a breeze had come up to blow soft and sweet against her face.

"Isn't this the most glorious day?" she said as she came up to him. "It's as if the whole world has gotten caught up in God's smile."

He turned away from her and began backing the horse between the shafts of her small buckboard, letting her words and her smile hang suspended in the air, until they both began to fade.

"What's put you in such a fine mood this morning?" he finally said.

He was having trouble fastening the traces to the swingletree, for although he'd discarded the sling some days ago, Doc Henry hadn't removed the surgeon's plaster from his arm as yet. She leaned over to help him with the harnessing, their shoulders brushing. He smelled good, of laurel soap and coffee.

"I'm that pleased you're coming to the preaching with us, Mr. Cain."

"Yeah, well, I'm thinking you ought to hold off on being pleased until we see how it goes."

It had been two months since he had come into their lives, and nearly a month since that first sweet night of the lambing season. In that time the last traces of winter had run off into the creeks and coulees, the days had grown longer, and the land was greening. During that time, every other Sunday, as was the Plain way, they had all gathered to worship the Lord. But not the outsider. Then last night, while they were feeding the newest bum lambs in front of the stove, she had said to him, "Come with us to the preaching tomorrow."

And he had said, not surprised, indeed almost smiling, "Why?"

"So that you can come to know us, to see how we are . . . and this Sunday the preaching is at my father's farm."

A silence came between them then, as it often did, and then he said, "They won't want me there."

She couldn't deny the truth of that. And what would it serve him, what would it serve her, for him to know the Plain and understand their ways when he could never be one of them?

But then he said, "I'll come."

And it was her turn to ask, "Why?"

"Because," he had said, "you asked."

NOW, THIS MORNING, his cheeks shone from a fresh shave and his hair was still damp from washing. He had polished his boots and brushed his coat and put on a clean shirt of Ben's. Those shirts didn't look the same on him as they had on Ben. He made them look flashy, even without a collar and neckcloth.

He was coming with them to the preaching, and the day was bursting with spring; Rachel smiled as she watched him reach up to take a kink out of one of the kidney link rings. But then his coat flared open to reveal the leather cartridge belt and holster hanging heavy around his hips.

She took a stumbling step back, away from him. "Mr. Cain, you cannot bring that gun along with you. We're going to a preaching, not a turkey shoot."

His hat brim lifted as he swung his head to stare at her. His eyes, his face, all of him, had turned hard.

"You're asking too much," he said.

"Still, I am asking."

He left her, striding back across the yard to the sheep-herder's wagon. He went inside without bothering to shut the door behind him, and she thought: *He will leave now. He will leave without another word spoken between us, and he will be gone forever.*

When he came back out, he had his Winchester with him. He carried that rifle like it was grafted to his hand, but he had taken off his six-shooter. His hips looked slim and strangely naked without the cartridge belt.

His gaze lifted from the rifle to her face, and for once she saw something in his eyes, a son of wary pride. "I'll leave it stowed in the buckboard when we get to your father's farm," he said.

She nodded, her throat too full for words, and climbed into the open carriage. Benjo came running, shaking the water from his hands, MacDuff at his heels. The boy looked up at her, a pleading question in his eyes, but Rachel shook her head. Sighing loudly, Benjo sent his dog back to watch over the sheep. The outsider gave him a boost up onto the plank seat alongside her, and then he joined them.

He spanked the reins against the mare's rump, and the harness jingled. The iron wheels creaked into motion, squelching through the mud in the yard.

They rattled over the corduroy bridge that spanned the creek, and started up the rise. Rachel looked back. The last bunch of ewes and new lambs had been put out to graze. The lambs, heady with life, butted heads and kicked up their heels. The ewes, thin from nursing their babies, munched hungrily on the sweet green grass.

Another lambing season nearly ended, she thought, another spring unfolding. She remembered all the Sundays she had done this, looked back this way to the farm as the buckboard rolled across the bridge and started up the rise on the way to the preaching. During their first year here in the Miawa country, Benjo had been but a baby and he'd slept in a cracker box on the seat between her and Ben. Now her baby was barely even a boy any longer, but edging up to being a man. And the outsider sat on the other side of him, in her husband's place.

She wanted to tell herself it was not the same, having him on the buckboard alongside of her in place of Ben. No, it wasn't the same at all, for he was only like Ben in small ways, like the way he could make her laugh with his teasing, and the way he moved so gracefully for all of his man's big size and hard strength. But then she remembered how just looking at him a few moments ago from across the yard had changed her world. Changed not only the sun and the wind, but how she felt about herself, deep inside. She'd been that way with Ben, when they were courting, and sometimes even after seventeen years of sharing a bed and a table and the day-to-day chores of life. Breathless, her chest aching, her belly heavy. Her skin tight all over, too tight for her body, so that it seemed she would burst apart if he so much as touched her hand. Or spoke her name.

And he had taken off his six-shooter. He had done that for her. She was sure he had done it for her.

Rachel turned her back on the farm, settling down on the hard board seat. For once the wind wasn't blowing wild, and the buckboard's wheels clicked and creaked along in the silence. Benjo kept slanting calculating looks at the outsider. He pursed his lips, and the muscles in his throat clenched as he worked on dredging up his words.

The first word burst out with a misty spray. "Guh—good thing you're finally c-coming to the p-preaching with us, Cain. 'C-cause now you'll be able to see all those men who want to muh—marry Mem in c-courting action."

Rachel's head snapped around. She poked a stiff finger into her son's ribs. He jumped and squirmed, but he kept his face turned carefully away from her.

The outsider slapped the reins and clicked his tongue at the plodding mare. "Your ma's got lots of suitors, does she?"

Benjo nodded vigorously. "Fuh—fuh—first there's Deacon Weaver. Everyone f-figures he's got the best chance at it."

"Yeah, I bet everyone does. Good neighbor and particular friend that he is."

"Thuh . . . there's also Joseph Zook. Buh—but everyone f-figures he's the long shot 'cause he's real old. He's got hair growing out his n-nose and ears, and he's got st-store-bought choppers." Benjo made a face. "And he farts during the p-preaching, then he looks around and g-glares at you, as if you were the one causing the big stuh—stink."

"Benjo!" Rachel shot a glance at the outsider over her impossible son's head. Those blue eyes were squinting in a smile beneath the soft brim of his hat. One corner of his mouth twitched.

"I think you'd better cross that fella off your list, Mrs. Yoder," he said. "A man who farts in church . . . well, no tellin' where else he might do it."

Benjo's head bobbed with exuberant relish. "Th-then there's Ira Chupp. His wuh—wife died a while back and now he con-consorts with those Jezebels who live in the Red House."

"Joseph Benjamin Yoder!"

"And he s-sneaks s-sips of rhubarb wine even when it's not Com-Communion Sunday."

The outsider sucked on his cheeks so hard, he looked as if he was about to burst into a whistle. "He sounds like a real bad hombre, this Ira Chupp. Better cross him off, too. Who else is there?"

"Euh—Ezra Fischer. He talks real sweet but he's got . . . smuh—small, squinty eyes, like p-pumpkin seeds. And he's suh—so stingy he'd skin a flea for the hide."

"Ezra Fischer is a good man," Rachel stated. "He's our *Vorsinger*, he leads the hymnsongs during worship. His voice can warble up and down like a wren in the spring. What's more, he's not stingy. He merely believes that if he's careful with his pennies, the dollars will take care of themselves, and it's uncharitable of you to say such a thing, Benjo, even if it were true."

Benjo made his eyes go all round and innocent. She'd have thought him a living angel if she didn't know better. "Muh . . . *Mutter* Anna Mary said the exact suh—selfsame thing, and n-nobody yelled at her for it."

Johnny Cain and her son exchanged a look. The outsider drew an imaginary line through an imaginary list in the air.

Rachel fastened her own gaze hard on the space between the mare's ears. She also jabbed her son in the ribs again, this time with her elbow. She couldn't imagine what was possessing the boy to carry on such a conversation. She would almost have suspected him of playing matchmaker, except that he knew full well a Plain woman and an outsider could never marry. It was forbidden.

"That's quite some inventory of suitors your ma's got herself there, Benjo." The outsider spanked the mare's rump with the reins again. "Gee-up, you lazy ol' glue pot. If you went much slower we'd be travelin' backwards. . . . I bet all of 'em, Deacon Noah Weaver included, wouldn't mind gettin' their hands on them creek-fed hay meadows of hers."

"It's not the Plain way to take pride in one's own worldly possessions, nor to covet those of others," Rachel said. "And there are rules against trying to use such a thing as land to increase one's stature within the church."

"Rules, huh? You can make up all the rules in the world, but they don't change a man's nature. And it's in a man's nature to covet creek-fed hay meadows."

Rachel said nothing. She lifted her head and looked toward the distant mountains, blurred by the haze of spring. She couldn't help herself—it hurt a little that he so readily assumed it was her land the men wanted and not herself. If he'd been in their place, in all likelihood it was her creek-fed meadows he would be thinking most about. If it crossed his mind to court her at all.

But then, after that one night she had never again allowed her hair to be uncovered in his presence. And not once had he come close to touching her in any deliberate way, not once had he called her Rachel.

At the end of the first week of lambing, she had said to him, "I'll hear no more talk about you earning your keep. I'll pay you the proper wages of a hired man."

His mouth had taken on that teasing look of his. "Just how much would that be?"

"A dollar a day and found."

"Yeah? Well, I reckon that's more'n I ever made. By any honest means, anyways."

"Oh, you!" she'd exclaimed, flustered by his joking. He had been joking, surely. . . . For she didn't want to be reminded of the ways he wasn't at all like Ben. Reminded of the sins he must have committed, of the wicked life he must have lived before he'd come stumbling across her wild hay meadow.

So she had said, "I'll hire you on through the end of summer and mating season." Just so he'd know that she understood there would be an end to it someday. Just so he wouldn't think she was some lonely Plain widow who'd fallen into a wild crush for a flashy, handsome outsider.

Then he had said, "Just through the end of summer, Mrs. Yoder." And she had known that, of course, there really would be an end to it someday. As there should be.

Because anything else was forbidden.

THE BUGGIES AND BUCKBOARDS and spring wagons were lined up in Bishop Isaiah Miller's pasture like pigs at a feeding trough. No Plain family ever missed a preaching if they could help it, not even during the lambing season.

As the outsider squeezed their buckboard into a shady spot along the north side of the lambing sheds, a gangly boy came running up to them. He was supposed to help with unhitching the horses, but when he caught sight of Johnny

Cain at the reins, he skidded to a dead stop. His eyes grew wide and his shoulders hunched, as if he expected the man to explode into crackling gunfire at any moment, like a Fourth of July celebration.

"The way that mouth of yours is gaping open, Levi Miller," Rachel called down to her youngest brother, "it'll be a pure wonder if you don't catch yourself a fly."

The boy snapped his mouth shut and turned a half dozen shades of red. But of course Levi, fifteen and the baby of the Miller family, flushed over everything.

Laughing, Rachel climbed out of the buckboard. The Plain People weren't ones for public displays of affection, or private ones for that matter, but Rachel gave her brother a hug anyway and set off another string of blushes. His gray eyes, still round as silver dollars, stayed riveted on the outsider.

In spite of the way he was behaving, this was hardly the first time Levi Miller had set those big eyes on the notorious desperado. Indeed, even though it was lambing season and the busiest time of year, nearly every Plain man and boy in the valley, and a good many of the women, too, had found a spare moment during the last month to come around to the farm and take a gander at Johnny Cain. Rachel thought she'd probably told the story of how he'd come staggering and bleeding across her wild hay meadow dozens of times, yet even repeat visitors never seemed to tire of hearing it.

Then they would say to her in *Deitsch,* so that he couldn't understand: "So, what's he like, then, this outsider? What sort of man is he?" And Rachel would wonder herself.

The outsider, given what a skittish man he was beneath those charming manners and easy smiles of his, had shown remarkable forbearance while being gaped at and jabbered over in *Deitsch* by all her friends and family. Still, he'd always slipped that six-shooter of his from its holster, every time he heard hooves or wagon wheels turning into the yard.

He wasn't wearing that gun of his this morning, though, and all because of her, to please her. He was even pretending not to notice how her brother was gawping at him.

Rachel nudged the boy's bony shoulder. "Are you putting down roots? Go show Mr. Cain where to pasture the horse."

She gave the bow of her bonnet a straightening tug, then smoothed her hands over the skirt of her apron. She didn't need to look around to see that the knots of people, who'd all been standing outside the front doors of the barn, gossiping before the preaching, were suddenly staring stock-still, wide-eyed, and open-mouthed at the Yoder buckboard.

Benjo ran off to join the other youngsters, who had crowded around a pond in back of the lambing sheds where tadpoles hatched this time every year. "Don't you go using that sling of yours on the poor frogs," Rachel called after him, and he, of course, pretended not to hear.

Rachel waited while Levi and the outsider led the mare through a gate in the nearby snake fence, built of peeled and whitewashed pine poles. It wrapped around hay fields as lushly green as any of her creek-fed ones.

In one large meadow, which was shaped like a horseshoe, a flock of ewes and lambs grazed on the sweet spring grass, quietly growing their premium wool. In another, smaller meadow the drop band huddled, those few ewes still awaiting the arrival of their babies.

The meadows surrounded her father's house, which was two stories high and made not of rough cottonwood logs but of milled lumber. Snuggled up next to the big house on either side, like step blocks, were two smaller houses. In one, her elder brother Sol was batching it. The other, called the *Daudy Haus,* was where her great-grandmother, *Mutter*

Anna Mary, lived. It was tradition for the old folks to live in houses separate but not apart from the younger generations. A white-spooled railed porch wrapped around all three houses, linking them like a daisy chain.

Bishop Isaiah Miller had the biggest and finest sheep farm in all the valley, mostly because of her older brother Sol. A solemn, gentle man and a lifelong bachelor, Sol had filed his claim alongside their father's, and they had combined the two homesteads. The bishop spent a good part of his days praying, studying the Scriptures, and shepherding his human flock, while his eldest son tended to the sheep.

Rachel wondered if the outsider would believe that Isaiah Miller's stature within the church really did come from his prayers and spiritual guidance, and not from the size and wealth of his farm.

The outsider came back through the gate alone, without Levi. He flashed one of those sweet-rascal smiles at her. She wondered what sort of look she was wearing on her face that he felt he had to smile at her that way.

They walked together toward the front of the barn where the preaching would take place. They passed along the rows of buggies and wagons, all of them Plain, without backrests or dashboards, whip sockets or booster steps, the seats all simple plank boards. The outsider's restless gaze lingered a moment on a large gray wagon, which had the look of a hearse.

"That's our bank wagon," she said. "We use it to carry the benches for the preaching service. Since we worship in a different barn every time, the family who hosted the service last time brings the benches along for the next preaching in the bank wagon. Our church is a body of believers, not a single place."

He said nothing. He wasn't looking at the bank wagon anymore, and she couldn't tell what he was thinking. She could never tell what he was thinking. Not during all his teasing talk and lazy smiles that drew her to him, or the hard and brutal silences that made her fear him—she never knew what he was really feeling.

But then she wondered about herself, what her own thoughts and hopes were on this day. She had wanted the outsider to see this because it was so much a part of her, the backbone of her life. And yet she had known that even seeing it, he would never really understand. It could never matter to him anyway.

As they drew closer to the silent crowd in front of the barn, Rachel felt a nervous quiver in her belly, and she unconsciously smoothed her apron again. There would be consequences to face over what she had chosen to do. It was one thing to take in an outsider who'd been found gunshot and bleeding to death in your hay meadow. It was quite another to make him your hired man. And another thing entirely to bring him along with you to the preaching.

Rachel looked for her father. Of all those here today, he would have the most influence over whether the outsider would be allowed to stay among them for a time. But he was already in the barn, meeting with the community's other two ordained ministers, Noah Weaver and Amos Zook, as he did before every worship service.

Her brothers certainly appeared to have made up their collective Miller minds. They stood in a row, looking like a chain of cutout dolls in their freshly brushed Sunday sack coats and broadfalls and wide-brimmed felt hats, all of them glowering at the outsider as if they wished him in perdition.

Or rather, Abram and Samuel glowered. Levi gawped and blushed. Sol, whose big and gentle heart was incapable of glowering, looked only at her, with concern shadowing his face. Sol wouldn't send the outsider away, at least not without a lot of prayer and thought. Not so the others. Samuel was the sort to leap headfirst into a raging river without a care for whether it was deep enough. And where Samuel leaped, Abram followed.

It was Samuel who broke away from the group to stride toward her and the outsider, with the others trailing after him like wind-stirred leaves. He stopped in front of her, hands on his hips, long black beard jutting.

"What the die-hinker do you think you're doing, bringing *him* here?"

Rachel thrust her own chin into the air. Samuel always had something to be angry about, and Rachel had learned long ago that the only way to handle him was to stand up to him. "Mr. Cain has come to witness the preaching. It's not a forbidden thing."

A loud snort punctuated the air. This came from their brother Abram. Some people thought Abram was skewed in the head, mostly because he never had a thought there that hadn't started out in Samuel's head first.

"It is not forbidden," Rachel said again. "And you just now sounded like a sick hog, our Abram."

"He'll not understand a word he's hearing," Samuel said. "He'll be bored."

"He'll be bored stiff as a corpse," Abram echoed.

Since they were already speaking *Deitsch,* presumably he couldn't understand a word he was hearing now. But Rachel thought the man could probably make a pretty good guess at the sentiment behind the words.

"So what's it to us all if he is bored," she said, in *Englisch.* "I've told him he can leave whenever he wishes and we won't be offended. You would deny him an opportunity to pray and worship God in fellowship with us?"

"He's an outsider," Samuel said, in *Deitsch*.

Abram's lips curled. *"Englischer."*

"He's a man in the sight of God," Rachel said, in *Englisch*.

"The Devil's own son, more like," Samuel said. In *Englisch*.

Four pairs of gray Miller eyes looked the outsider up and down, four wide Miller mouths flattened into frowns. Even Sol's. The Devil's own son stared back at them with lazy, hooded eyes, and that empty face he could slip on like a mask.

"She's right," Sol said. Sol's words were so soft, they sounded as if they came out of his shirt yoke rather than his mouth. But when Sol spoke, others always listened. "About the preaching, at least," Sol went on. "It's not forbidden if he wants to come and witness."

"Aaugh . . ." Samuel waved his hand as if brushing away a pesky fly. "He'll grow tired of it all soon enough anyway. Long about the time his back starts to feel like it's going to crack in two and his butt goes numb."

Levi snickered. Samuel and Abram exchanged knowing grins.

Just then, as if they'd been given some invisible signal, the Plain women began to file into the barn. The children came running up from the pond, the girls going with the women, the boys joining the groups of men. Benjo seemed to have something in his hat and he was laughing and showing it to Levi, who had gone trotting over for a look. Rachel wouldn't have put it past that boy of hers to bring a frog into the preaching.

But even a frog would be more welcome than Johnny Cain. She turned to him, feeling this strange need to stay with him, to keep him safe—which was ridiculous, for her brothers would do him no terrible harm, nor even a small harm. There was probably no safer place on this earth for Johnny Cain than here, in this place, at this moment.

"I must go," she said to him. She wanted to touch him, simply touch him in some small way, but she didn't dare. She wouldn't have touched him even if they'd been alone. "We women always sit separate from the men."

He gave her a probing look, one she couldn't read. Then his mouth broke into one of those reckless smiles that had a touch of wildness in it. "Don't you worry none about me, Mrs. Yoder. If I waited till I was invited, I'd never go anywhere.... But then I *was* invited, remember? By you."

"It's not that the others don't want you, it's just..."

But they didn't want him, and it was hardly to be wondered at. Looking at him standing across from her brothers, she realized how separate he was from them all.

Oh, her brothers might look different from each other. Samuel, with his hair and beard black as a starling's wings, and his big square jaw always thrust forward, plowing through life. Abram, Samuel's shadow, but a lighter man with his butternut hair and beard. Sol, with no hair at all on his head and a beard as tangled as a crow's nest. And Levi, still growing up into his features and his self. Yes, different they were to look at, but underneath they were much the same man, in their faith and values and tradition.

Her brothers, with their open, honest faces and their Plain dress, standing shoulder to shoulder, God-fearing men, good men. Whereas he...

He was Johnny Cain, man-killer. And an outsider in every way there was.

"I must go," she said again. And she left him, almost running.

She crossed over to the side of the yard where the women stood in their own tight little knots. Her steps faltered when she saw her mother. Sadie Miller's mouth and eyes were etched with shame. Her shoulders bowed with the weight of it. In a world where a woman was judged by the daughters she raised, Rachel was her mother's singular failure.

Standing close to her mother, on either side of her as if she needed shoring and bolstering, were her daughters-in-law. The two younger women each held a baby resting on a hip. Together, they raised their free hands to pat Sadie on the arm. Together, they lowered their heads as if in silent prayer.

Abram, who followed his brother Samuel everywhere, had followed him into marriage as well, taking the same woman to wife, or as close as he could get without being sinful. Velma and Alta were twins and so alike that no one but their husbands even made an attempt to tell them apart. It was more than a matter of them sharing the same moon-pale hair, dimpled chin, and bow-shaped mouth. They had the same squeaky voice, the same whimsical smiles, the same way of blinking their identical big hazel eyes whenever they were simultaneously confused. They lived, they thought, they even breathed in synchronization.

Next to the three Miller women, and yet somehow apart from them, was Noah's spinster sister, Fannie. She stood with her shoulders pulled back and her bosom lifted high, as if she'd just sucked in a deep breath and now didn't want to let go of it. She turned her head to stare at Rachel, with her nose wrinkled and her mouth puckered.

Still, Rachel wanted to go to them so badly her chest ached with it. She thought she could face the twins' blinking eyes and Fannie Weaver's puckered mouth, but she couldn't face her mem's shame.

So instead she went alone to the snake fence and took off her bonnet, looping it over the top rail with the others. The black bonnets all hung upside down off the fence rail in a row, looking like coal scuttles.

She stood there by herself a moment, feeling lonesome, even shaky. By the time she turned around again, all the older women, the wives and widows, had already passed through the big sliding double doors into the shadowy coolness of the barn. Rachel was left to join the *Meed,* the girls and young unmarried women.

The *Buwe*—the young bachelors—flanked the barn doors to watch as the girls walked through. The girls' eyes stayed straight ahead, but their lips curled into pleased smiles and blushes pinkened their cheeks. They wore white shawls and white aprons and crisp black prayer caps to mark their virginal state. But those smiles and blushes, Rachel thought, would still have given them away.

She remembered what it was like to be young and watched, to be wanted. But Rachel had never been like the other Plain girls. Always, at the last moment, as she passed by the *Buwe,* she would brazenly turn her head to catch first Noah's shocked eyes and then Ben's laughing ones.

And because she was remembering, she was careful not to turn her head on this Sunday. For Ben wouldn't be leaning there, one shoulder braced against the barn door, his dark eyes peering at her from beneath his hat brim, watching as she walked by. But others were there. On this Sunday, an outsider was there to watch. And perhaps to want.

THE SILENCE LAY HEAVY and warm over the barn.

It was a time of waiting, of moments that passed slowly, yet were rich with the promise of what was to come. She breathed in the barn smells of horse and cow and hay, the Sunday smells of starch and soap and shoe blacking. Her gaze moved lovingly over the checkerboard of white and black prayer caps in front of her.

This was her life.

It was not as if she felt God more, in this moment, in this place, for God was everywhere and with her always. But in this time of waiting, of silence, with her family and friends close around her, Rachel Yoder felt safe. She felt loved. She sat on the hard, backless bench and lost herself in the silence. For her, just being here was an act of worship.

Rachel's gaze roamed over the men's benches. The outsider sat pressed between two of her brothers, Sol and Samuel. Her son also sat with the men, sat properly with his hands resting on his knees and his head respectfully lowered. But just then he shifted around on his bottom, caught the outsider's eye, and pointed to the back of the man in front of him, Joseph Zook's back. Benjo wafted his hand through the air and pinched his nose. Rachel had to bite her lip hard to keep from laughing.

She closed her eyes. *Oh, Lord God,* she prayed. *Thank You for blessing me with the gift of my son. Thank You for blessing me with life and love and laughter.*

Her prayers drifted, became formless thoughts. The silence spun out and out and out, until the men reached up, as if in one motion, and took off their felt hats, putting them under the benches. They made a soft *husssh* of sound, like a suppressed sigh.

And Ezra Fischer shuffled slowly to his feet.

Ezra Fischer did have small, squinty eyes; they were like two dimples tucked into the smooth roundness of his cheeks and forehead. His coat was worn bald at the elbows and frayed at the cuffs, and even his patches had patches. Everyone knew Ezra wouldn't gift himself with a new coat until this one had fallen off him. But he was a good man otherwise, Rachel thought, although she couldn't imagine being married to him.

He opened his mouth, and for a moment it seemed he would be smothered by the thick, enveloping silence. But then his voice took flight. A trilling tenor so pure and sharp, it pierced the soul.

His head thrown back, his eyes on his Lord, Ezra Fischer drew out the first note of the hymn as if it were so precious he couldn't bear to let it go. Then the rest of the men joined with him.

The men's voices, deep and dark and rich, rolled in slow waves up to the rafters. The women's voices, high and sweet, melded into the low, tolling tones of the men to become one pure song rising up, up, beyond the rafters now, beyond the sky, to reach the ears of God.

It was an old hymn they sang, mournful and yet beautiful, about exiles wandering through the land. Each word stretched out long and slow, into a chanting cadence, until the hymn itself became its own world of waiting.

They sang not with many voices but with one, and the glorious sound of it was an embodiment of their unity. For three hundred years the Plain People had sung this hymn in just this way, and so it would always be. "For thine is the kingdom, and the power, and the glory, forever." Forever. The whole of our lives are lived as we sing our hymns, Rachel thought. Slow and unchanging, always together. One flesh, one mind, one spirit.

And for her, for them all, she supposed, there was such sweet comfort in that. You could never become lost, if you always walked the straight and narrow path.

Rachel's head fell back as the hymn thrummed through her blood and seized her heart, creating a tempest of joy and wonder within her. The slow chanting washed over her, purifying her and making her feel one with God. On and on and on they sang, as if they'd been caught up in eternity.

And then they stopped, abruptly, cutting off the last word, the last note, as if the hand of God Himself had covered their mouths. Silence descended once more, silence and the sweet sense of waiting.

Rachel sat on the hard, backless bench, with her face lifted toward God and her mouth parted, her eyes closed, and not until she felt a sharp pain in her chest did she realize she'd stopped breathing. She drew in a draught of air, and slowly she opened her eyes to a world that tilted and blurred dizzily. She was so filled with joy and the glory of the Lord, she could have burst with it.

Once, Ben had told her that when she sang the worship hymns she looked to be in ecstasy. Dazed still, and breathless, she looked over to the men's side of the barn, almost expecting to see him there, her Ben. Her gaze locked with the outsider's instead.

He was staring at her hard, his face fierce and intent. She jerked her head away. And time, which had seemed suspended, as if floating in the rays of sunlight that poured through the cracks in the rafters, rippled suddenly . . . and broke.

NOAH WEAVER STOOD BEFORE the congregation.

His gaze moved slowly, carefully, over each man, woman, and child, seeing if all were according to the *Attnung,* if all followed the straight and narrow way. He counted the pleats in prayer caps; he looked for buttons, for suspenders, for other forbidden things. When he saw that all were dressed Plain and as they should be, he nodded his approval. As deacon it was his duty to do this, and he was known as a man who took his duties seriously.

Before resuming his seat, he once more surveyed the silent and bent heads. If he was surprised to find the outsider among them, he gave no sign of it. But then his eyes met Rachel's, and a look of stark pain crossed his face. Rachel's hands curled into a tight ball in her lap. He could find no fault with her dress, she knew, but what if he could see beneath her carefully crossed and pinned Plain shawl to the confused yearnings, to the doubts stirring in her heart?

Noah sat slowly and heavily in his place on the front bench, moving as if he carried a log on his big shoulders to round them and weigh them down. Rachel stared at the back of his head, her throat tight. His hat had left a mark, like a ring, in his hair. It made him look oddly vulnerable, she thought, that indentation in his hair. It made him look less a deacon and more a man, with all of a man's weaknesses and frailties. She wanted to go up to him and smooth his hair, to make that mark go away.

For more long and silent moments, they all sat and waited. And then Bishop Isaiah Miller rose to his feet, which meant that he was the one who'd first gotten the call to preach on this day. There would be two sermons preached, testimony given, prayers and Scripture read, more hymns sung—and the whole of it would last for over three hours.

He stood strong and tall in the middle of the floor, Rachel's father. His beard was black and fleecy, but his hair had a white streak going down the very center of it, like the stripe on a skunk's back. He had awakened with that stripe the morning after he'd had the vision-dream that had led them to leave their homes in Ohio and settle in this wild and empty land. It had been taken by all as a sign of divine benediction, that white streak appearing suddenly in Bishop Miller's hair.

He raised his head now and began to speak.

He talked of days long ago, of a time in the old country when the Plain People suffered terrible torments for their faith: burnings and stonings, crucifixions and whippings, the severing of tongues and hands and feet. He preached the way they sang their hymns, in a slow singsong rhythm. Yet in the dusk of the barn his gray eyes flashed with the passion of his words.

Sometimes Rachel listened to these old, familiar stories. Sometimes she just let the words flow through her while she drifted on her thoughts. She could smell the bean soup simmering in the big iron kettle out in the yard. She listened to the chickens clucking and scratching in the barn straw, to the *baa*s and bleats of her father's sheep out in the pasture. The air grew heavy and thick, as before a storm. Her father's voice flattened into a deep hum. . . .

She came back to the world. Much time must have passed. Her father was preaching now of how the righteous, persecuted and driven from their homes, had brought the one true faith with them across the perilous ocean waters. Yet even here there were hardships to suffer, even here in this land of freedom and plenty there was pain, there was loss.

My Ben, she thought. Oh, my Ben, my Ben, choking to death at the end of a rope. If we are truly God's chosen people, then why does He make us suffer so?

She pushed the thought away. She listened to her father, the bishop. He spoke of the will of God, of how salvation always came through submission, through acceptance. The familiar words rose and fell against her ears, like gusts of wind, and she imagined God offering those words to her with His cupped hands—words of truth and light and comfort—while that voice, the voice of her father, rose and fell, rose and fell, gentle, soothing. She remembered all the mornings of her childhood, kneeling in the kitchen and listening to that dear voice read the morning prayers.

The memory was as deeply etched on her heart as were the words of God in the big black family Bible.

Those mornings kneeling in the kitchen . . . Rachel searched the rows of prayer caps, needing suddenly to see her mother's face. Sadie Miller's eyes were closed, her mouth slack; she was sleeping. Wisps of gray hair curled out from the edge of her cap. Her face looked worn, etched by time, and empty.

Those mornings, kneeling in the kitchen . . . bright sunshine streaming through the bare windowpanes, hands clasped, heads bent, Rachel and her brothers casting their shadows on the worn oak floor. And their *Vater*, with his faith that was so deep and so severe and yet so gentle, throwing his large and loving shadow over them all. Only Mem's shadow was ever missing in her memories. Had the sunlight never reached where Sadie Miller knelt in silence?

But then, Rachel thought, none of them had ever looked on Mem as a being of substance, something separate from them all. They'd never thought to wonder if Sadie Miller had feelings, dreams, desires of her own.

Whenever Rachel looked back on all the moments of her life, both small and wondrous, even the shadow of her mother was always missing. That morning of her marriage to Ben, when she'd knelt in the kitchen of her childhood for the last time, that morning her father had ended the prayer by putting his arm around her and holding her close as if he couldn't bear to let her go. Her brothers had grinned at her and made teasing jokes about poor Ben not knowing what he was letting himself in for, and Rachel had wanted to hold that moment of laughter and love tight to her breast as she was holding her father. To make it last forever. And yet where was Mem in that memory? Had her mother not been there, or had Rachel never turned around to see her?

A dipper of water was being passed down the rows of benches. Velma handed it to her mother-in-law, not realizing that she was asleep. Water slopped into Sadie's lap. Her head jerked, her eyes snapped open. She looked surprised at first, to have been caught napping during the preaching. And then a deep flush spread up her neck and over her cheeks. Rachel felt a painful tightening in her chest and breathed to ease it. She wished Mem would look her way so that she could smile at her, but Sadie Miller's gaze remained fixed on the spreading wet stain in her lap.

Bishop Miller was approaching the climax of his sermon. His head was bobbing, and the singsong cadence of his words came faster and sharper now.

Several worshipers shifted their bottoms on the hard benches in anticipation of the end. Benjo swung his feet through the straw, making a loud rustling noise and getting a rap on his knee from his uncle Samuel's knuckle.

Isaiah Miller was explaining how, through all their sufferings, the Plain People followed the example set by Jesus Christ, who had yielded so completely to His Father's will that He suffered and died on the cross. Rachel listened to her own father's words and tried to stow them away in her heart for later, when the doubts would stir.

"They spat upon Him and they scourged Him with reeds. And then they led Him away and crucified Him. They passed by Him, hanging up there on His cross, and they wagged their heads at Him and mocked Him, saying, 'If you are truly the son of God then why don't you save yourself, why don't you come down from that cross and save yourself?' They said to Him, 'If you trusted so much in God, then let Him deliver you now, you who say you are the Son of God. . . .' "

Rachel's eyes had drifted closed. She saw a mountain

and three crosses silhouetted against a black, tormented sky. She saw a man, bleeding, tortured, dying. Saw him throw back his head and scream in his despair.

And she knew suddenly what had been behind the terror in Johnny Cain's eyes.

My God, my God, why hast thou forsaken me?

12

RACHEL WALKED OUT OF the dark coolness of the barn and blinked against the sudden wash of sunlight, almost stumbling. After all the stillness and silence and waiting of the worship service, she felt the world rushing past her now in a whirl of sound and motion.

She fetched her bonnet and leaned against the snake fence, bracing her forearms on the whitewashed rail. Clouds were building up over the mountains. But here in the valley it was spring, periwinkle skies and a warm whisper of breeze.

She spotted a cocoon hanging from a pokeweed leaf. The tiny silk case trembled once and then went still. She broke off the leaf at its stem, cradling the cocoon in her cupped hand.

She heard footsteps behind her, moving through the grass. As she turned she saw the outsider coming toward her, his stride so fluid and elegant. He should have been stiff, she thought, after three hours of sitting on a hard, backless bench, listening to preaching and prayers that to him must surely have seemed like only so much babble. During the long worship service Johnny Cain had sat as quiet and unmoving as the rest of them. But through it all, Rachel had felt his awareness of her, like a warmth that just barely touched her on the air.

"You appear none the worse for wear, Mr. Cain," she said as he moved to the fence and stood next to her, "after such a long and perilously close brush with salvation."

"It was a near thing, though. Y'all got me so worked up, I was almost shoutin' hallelujahs."

She looked away. She had astonished herself, making a joke out of such a serious thing as a soul's salvation. She wanted the words back, but of course it was too late. That was the dangerous thing about words—once said they couldn't be unsaid.

She would have to remember that he had a way of making her say things, do things, that were not herself.

He noticed the cocoon in her hand and leaned over to see it, leaned so close his breath bathed her cheek. He touched the wriggling cocoon with the tip of his finger. "We don't have enough bum lambs at home to feed that you got to be taking in bum butterflies now, too?"

At home. She knew he hadn't really meant to say such a thing, but it did make her smile. "By evening this little one will be flying free on the wind."

They stood together in silence a moment, then he said, "I've never heard hymns sung like that before. They sounded like the bells that're played sometimes during a funeral. Slow and sad and lonely."

She wondered if that meant he'd liked their singing. She wanted to ask him if he'd been given even a glimpse of God in the silence, in the waiting, in the hymns that had sounded to him like funeral bells. "There's someone here I want you to know," she said instead. "And I want her to come to know you."

"Your mother?"

She shook her head. Her mother—if she brought Johnny Cain to her mother and said, "I want you to look at this man, Mem, and see not an outsider but a man I have come to . . ." She shook her head again. She couldn't finish that thought, not even to herself.

She said nothing more to him, but pushed away from the fence and started across the yard, leaving him to come with her, or not.

The Plain People had gathered together again in groups of friends and family in the yard. The men talked about what kind of lambing season they were having, and how the open winter meant a poor hay crop this summer. The women talked about their next quilting frolic and a new recipe for sour cream cake. But a hush fell over everyone as they turned to watch Rachel and the outsider walk side by side toward Bishop Miller's big house.

They skirted a huge iron kettle hanging from a tripod over a fire. Steam thick with the smell of bean soup billowed around them. "Are you hungry?" she asked him.

He glanced back at the bubbling kettle. "Well, I was." He tilted his head to study her. "But with the way you're looking so solemn-mouthed all of a sudden, you got me feeling like a horse thief on his way to meet the judge."

"I'm taking you to meet *Mutter* Anna Mary. She's what we call a *Braucher,* which means she can heal the sick with her touch alone. It's a wondrous gift of God and comes from a faith that runs deeper than the core of the earth. She is very old and very wise, and you mustn't mock her."

He made a show of patting his pockets. "Well, shucks, lady, I think I got me some manners in here somewheres." He smiled at her, but when she didn't smile back, he said, "I'll be good."

"She's actually my father's grandmother, but all of us from the youngest babe to old Joseph Zook call her *Mutter*, mother, for she's connected to so many of us here, either by marriage or blood. She is our roots."

SHE SAT IN A willow rocker on the gallery of her *Daudy Haus.* She'd never been a big woman, even in her youth, but the years had worn her down until she was little more than parched skin and frail bones. As Rachel climbed the porch steps, the old woman lifted her head. Her skull was bald beneath her prayer cap, her marbled skin pulled taut over the bones. Her eyes were like two smooth milky white pebbles. She had been stone blind for over fifty years.

"Rachel, my wild child," she said, although Rachel had yet to make a sound but for the tap of her heels on the floorboards and the rustle of her skirts. "What have you done?"

Rachel knelt and put the leaf with its fragile cocoon into the old woman's hand. "I've brought you a butterfly. It will be a spring azure, I think, when it hatches." The silk shell shivered and trembled, and the old woman's sunken mouth curved into a smile. "And I've brought Johnny Cain."

Rachel stood up. The outsider settled down on his haunches in her place before *Mutter* Anna Mary. The old woman still held the butterfly cocoon cupped in her parchment brown palm, but she reached out with her other hand, and he took it. She stared at him with her milky blind eyes, and he stared back.

"You have slain your brother."

She'd said the words flat out, brutally. He didn't answer her accusation. But neither did he pull his hand from hers.

The old woman's chest rose and fell with her breath. "And will you give to your God only silence when He says to you: 'What hast thou done? the voice of thy brother's blood crieth unto me from the ground'? Are you so full of pride, Johnny Cain?"

"Yes."

The word had come out of him almost like a gasp, but he said, "I make no excuses for what I've done, and I'm not looking to change what I am."

The old woman turned her face toward the tenuous warmth of the spring sun. "The farther you run, the longer the road back becomes. I would have thought you tough enough for anything, Johnny Cain. Even repentance."

"Well, ma'am, the way I see it: repenting ain't so hard. It's giving up the sinning that can get to be a challenge."

"Do you think that because your words are the truth that they are any the less hurtful to God?"

She pulled her hand from his and let it fall in her lap. She was silent for a time, and the outsider remained where he was, staring up into blind eyes that no longer looked at him and yet saw everything.

"That hand of yours, it has done more than its share of living," *Mutter* Anna Mary said.

"And hurting," he acknowledged. "But then your hands have done more than their share of healing, or so I've been told. Might be it's just nature's way of evening things out. You heal, and I kill."

Rachel jerked, bumping into the back of her great-grandmother's chair, making it rock with a soft creak. "The men have started setting up the trestle tables and benches for the fellowship meal," she said. "Perhaps you ought to go help them, Mr. Cain."

The outsider pushed the flat of his good hand against his thigh, stretching slowly to his feet. "It was a pleasure to make your acquaintance, ma'am," he said. His eyes met Rachel's for one enigmatic moment, and then he turned away. His boot heels rapped a slow beat as he walked the length of the gallery and down the steps.

"You sent him away," *Mutter* Anna Mary said.

Rachel knelt beside the willow rocking chair. She laid her cheek on her great-grandmother's knee. After a moment she felt the old woman's fingers stroking the crisp black cotton of her bonnet.

"What did you see?" Rachel said. Neither thought it an odd question to ask of a woman who was stone blind.

"He is broken," *Mutter* Anna Mary said.

His joy is in killing. He was more than broken; he had been shattered, and Rachel knew there was no mending him. It wasn't even right that she should try to mend him.

The old fingers, gentle, sure, moved beneath the brim of her bonnet to stroke her cheek.

"You brought him to me because you hoped I would see a goodness buried deep inside him, a soul worth nurturing. And then you became frightened that I would see too much and you sent him away. He has a soul, Rachel. Even that most wicked of Cains, who slew his brother Abel, had a soul. But for what he did God made him a fugitive and a vagabond and banished him from the face of the earth."

Rachel raised her head. She hadn't known she was crying until she felt the air cool the wetness on her cheeks. "But, *Mutter,* why can't God forgive him? If you could have seen his eyes on the day he came to me."

Mutter Anna Mary neither moved nor made a sound.

She still held the cocoon cupped in the palm of her hand. Rachel could see the butterfly's blue wings now, through the opaque skin of the chrysalis.

The cocoon trembled again, and the thin brown hand curled around it for a moment, as if she would protect it. "'And Cain said unto the Lord, My punishment is greater than I can bear.' And perhaps it was, but it was no greater than he deserved. Whom do you want to save this outsider for, my wild child—God or yourself?"

Rachel could feel the truth searing her face, her cheeks burned and flushed as if she'd been bending too close to a hot stove. But it was easier, in a way, for someone else to name her sin. Easier, then, to admit to it at last—if only to herself.

"I want to come to know him. I want to understand how he can be as he is," she said.

"But what you know and understand, you might come to love."

Rachel was quiet. Out in the yard the children were playing a hand-clapping game, their laughter bright as sleigh bells.

The old woman's chest shuddered with her deep sigh but she, too, said nothing more. For Rachel to love an outsider was a thing so wrong, so impossible, it was beyond words.

The cocoon wriggled suddenly, almost jumping. *Mutter* Anna Mary breathed a soft laugh. "Look, Rachel. It's hatching."

Rachel leaned closer. The chrysalis was splitting open at one end. "Soon it will fly."

"IF THE WEATHER KEEPS UP like this, it's going to be hot as this soup come shearing time," Samuel Miller said as Rachel set a clay bowl filled to the brim with bubbling bean soup in front of him. He wasn't speaking to her, though, but rather to the other men sitting with him at the trestle tables.

The fellowship meal was the only time the Plain didn't eat in silence. The women always ate separately from the men, though, and they always served the men first. Rarely did they join in the men's talk.

"Aw, our Sam's only worried about his sweat fouling the wool," Abram said. He tore off a crusty chunk of bread, dunked it in his soup, and stuffed it in his mouth. He grinned and winked at his brother, while the others all laughed at his joke.

Bishop Isaiah Miller stroked his beard as if he was about to pontificate, but his eyes were smiling. "These hot days of spring do serve as God's warning that summer is coming. So I'm thinking we had better clip my Samuel's sheep first, wouldn't you all say so, my brothers in Christ? Before he has a chance to build up a good head of steam."

The men laughed again, and Rachel smiled. She tried to catch the outsider's eye, but he and her son, who were sitting side by side, seemed to be sharing a joke of their own as a platter of pickled cucumbers and beets passed beneath their noses. Benjo pinched his face up into a knot of exaggerated disgust.

Deacon Noah Weaver, on the other side of Benjo, saw what they were doing and frowned.

The men had made a place for the outsider at the table and then ignored him. They spoke in *Deitsch* and let their eyes slide over him as if he were a ghost they couldn't see. His separateness from them was understood and accepted by all, including himself.

But then perhaps he is used to being the outsider, Rachel thought. Even among his own kind.

She heard a step behind her and she started, aware that

she'd been caught staring at the man. She whirled, nearly knocking a bowl of soup out of Fannie Weaver's hands.

"Oh . . . Fannie. Is that my *Vater*'s soup?" Fannie's face was bunched tight, like the knuckles of a closed fist. Rachel tried on a smile. "Give it here and I'll take it on down to him."

Her hands closed around the bowl, but the other woman held fast, so that they wound up tugging it back and forth between them. Boiling hot bean soup slopped over the rim, scalding Rachel's fingers.

Fannie's, too, probably, for she suddenly let go, and turned on her heel and stalked off. Rachel sucked on her burning fingers.

She used her apron to wipe the soup off the side of the bowl before she carried it down to the end of the table, where her father sat waiting. As bishop he should have been served first, but in a display of proper Plain humility he had insisted on going last.

The men had fallen into a serious discussion about the coming summer's work, about the hay that would need cutting next month, and the wool crop that would need reaping as well. Come July the sheep would have to be driven from their home pastures up onto the mountain, where they could grow fat on the lush buffalo grass.

Rachel waited for a lull in the talk before she set the soup in front of her father. "If you men are going to speak of such things as haying and shearing schedules and the plans for the summer pasturing," she said, "then you best do it in *Englisch*. For I've hired him on to work my farm through the breeding time."

The silence that fell over the table had the impact of a thunderclap from out of a clear sky. The men's heads all swiveled to look first at her, then at Bishop Miller.

But Rachel's father said nothing for the moment. He

brought a spoonful of the steaming soup up to his mouth and blew on it. In the tense quiet the huff of his breath sounded as loud as a gust of wind.

Her brothers exchanged long worried looks. Noah Weaver's head jerked around to the outsider, then back to her. Harsh color blotched the skin above his beard.

Rachel's belly felt queasy, but she held her head high and stiff. It wasn't against tradition for an outsider to be hired on to work a Plain farm. Many a man sitting at these tables had paid Basque herders to watch over their sheep in the summer. And back in Ohio, even her father had often taken on outsider help during the harvest.

But she knew her father would say those hired hands had been boys, too young yet to grow beards, and thus not so lost to the world.

"I thought it would answer," she said, "to hire on Mr. Cain. He can be taking Ben's turns with the haying and with the summer herding."

Noah forced a laugh that seemed to come ripping out of his throat. "And will he be taking Ben's turn at the shearing, too?"

"A man needs two good arms to properly clip a sheep, and one of his is broken."

"He isn't even wearing a sling anymore, and he'll have that plaster off long before shearing time." Noah swung his head back around, pointing at the outsider with his beard. "Such a worldly man as that one, with all his guns and his flashy dress and his *knowledge* of things, why, I expect he probably figures that to shear a hundred-pound woolly monster has got to be as easy as spitting out a straw. For such a flashy, worldly man as he is."

Since they were speaking in *Englisch* now, the outsider had no trouble understanding the Plain man's words. Or the insult behind them.

But the smile he gave Noah might have been dipped in honey. Only Rachel, who was coming to know him, saw the danger at the edge of that smile. "Well," he said, drawling the word out to its fullest potential, "the sad truth is that up till now sheep shearing hasn't much figured in my line of work." His eyes hardened. "I've had me plenty of practice, though, at recognizing a challenge when I'm given one."

Samuel barked a sharp laugh and cocked a thumb at the outsider. "You're trying to wring shame from the unshamable with that one, Brother Noah."

Abram hooted. "*Ja,* you'll have as much luck getting shame from that one, Brother Noah, as that one will have separating a ewe from its wool. The rest of us will be clipping our tenth woolly before he's done with his first."

"You can't have a shearing contest with a man who's never done it before," Rachel protested. "It wouldn't be fair."

"Who said anything about a contest?" Noah said. Benjo was anxiously trying to hand him a pitcher of cider that had been making its way around the table, but he ignored the boy. He cast a contemptuous look at the outsider, and stretched his mouth into a hard smile. "I'm saying he'll not last out the first hour of shearing, let alone the day."

"And if I don't?"

Noah showed more of his teeth. "I'm already saying you won't. Outsider."

"And I reckon y'all *humble* Plain folk will sure have shown me up properly then, huh? Your God gives out a prize, does he, to the man among you who shears the most sheep?"

Noah's eyes winced shut, his head bowed, and Rachel knew he felt shame to have been caught out in a vanity. Especially by an *Englischer.*

But her hotheaded brother Samuel leaned across the table to point the handle of his spoon in the outsider's face.

"Might be we'll allow you to take a crack at summer herding the woolly monsters, then. Might be all those guns of yours will come in handy when the coyotes come to pay you and the woollies a call."

Johnny Cain's gaze swept down the table and stopped at Rachel's father. Isaiah was carefully wiping the bottom of his soup bowl with a piece of bread.

"I reckon," the outsider said, "that your bishop would say 'the good shepherd giveth his life for the sheep.'"

Slowly, Isaiah raised his head. He nodded, his long thick beard brushing the yoke of his shirt. "*Ja.* It was the Lord Jesus Christ who said as much."

There was a moment of stunned silence, then Samuel flourished his arm in a dramatic arc. "How fortunate we are then to have this brave outsider among us, my brothers in Christ," he scoffed, "to take on the coyotes."

Abram snickered. "The big, bad coyotes."

Noah had folded his hands on the table, pressing them together so hard they trembled, his head bent as if in prayer. But then he lifted his face and Rachel saw that it was flushed, although whether with shame or a new anger she couldn't tell.

Benjo, who sat between the two men, had turned a pasty white. He still held the cider jug which he clutched tightly to his chest.

"You ever watch a coyote kill a lamb, outsider?" Noah said. "He goes for the throat, so he does, and the last thing that poor lamb sees is his life's blood spilling down the front of him as he dies."

Noah laughed.

And Benjo upturned the jug of cider into his lap.

Noah's laugh turned into a bellow. He reared to his feet, his belly and thighs knocking into the table so hard it rocked. He pulled back his hand. Benjo squawked and flung his arms over his head.

"Noah!" Rachel cried.

The outsider's arm shot up and caught Noah's wrist before the flat of his big palm could slam into the side of Benjo's head. The two men stared at each other, breathing heavily. Noah tried to wrench free, but the outsider held him fast. Benjo cringed between them, his shoulders jerking as he choked over his words.

"Nuh—nuh—nuh!"

"Noah, don't!" Rachel had started around the table toward her son, but her father grabbed her arm, stopping her. "He didn't mean to do it," she said. She was sure he hadn't meant to do it. It was that talk of coyotes and blood spilling down a lamb's front—it must have frightened the boy, for the pitcher had just seemed to slip from his hands. "He didn't mean to do it."

Benjo scrambled off the bench and took off running. The outsider let go of Noah's wrist. Noah's hand clenched into a fist. His nostrils flared as he sucked in a sharp breath.

Rachel's father had tightened his grip on her arm to keep her from going after her son. He cast a stern look down the length of the table. "Brother Noah."

Noah's chest shook as his breath rushed in and out his throat. "The Proverbs admonish us not to spare the rod."

"My daughter coddles that boy too much, 'tis true. But you ought not to have given way so to the sins of anger and pride."

Noah's head rocked back. He closed his eyes, and his lips moved in desperate prayer.

His whole body shuddered hard, as if he were trying to throw off the sins that had gripped him. Then he swung around and pointed a shaking finger at the outsider. "You see! You see what corrupting influence this man has on us all. He is of the evil world, and he has brought the evil world among us!"

He turned and tried to climb over the bench that had him trapped against the table. His big feet got all tangled up with the table and the bench and each other, and he went sprawling onto his hands and knees in the dirt.

He picked himself up, brushed off his broadfalls, and walked off, his hands folded together and his head bowed.

Joseph Zook and Ira Chupp snickered in their beards. The others pretended a sudden fascination with what was left in their soup bowls. Noah's son, Mose, stared after his father and then lowered his head in bewildered shame and contempt.

Bishop Isaiah reached for the bread and tore off a piece. "The fellowship meal is no place for such as this," he said.

The tables fell quiet except for the clink of tin against clay. Rachel stood next to her father, rubbing her arm where he had held her. Johnny Cain looked up, and their gazes met, but she could see nothing in his eyes. Throughout all that had just happened, he had shown not a shred of anger, nor even said a word, yet he had stopped Noah from striking her son. He had cared at least that much.

Still, she thought that when the fellowship was done her father would tell her that the outsider must go.

THE WOMEN SPREAD QUILTS to sit beneath the shade of the cottonwoods that grew along the east side of the big house. Rachel found a place next to her mother and the twins. She wanted so badly to talk with her mem, simply talk. But then, sitting there with her arms wrapped around her drawn-up legs and staring at the blue dahlia pattern of the quilt, she could think of nothing to say.

Alta's baby started fussing. Rachel watched the other woman as she unpinned her shawl and bodice and put the baby to her breast.

"Yours suckles so much better than mine," her sister Velma said.

Smiling, Alta kissed the downy crown of her son's head. "But look at yours. He'll be crawling long before mine."

Velma's baby had caught sight of a cattail waving in the breeze, just off the quilt, and he was going after it. He hadn't yet learned how to coordinate his knees with his elbows, though, and he pushed his bottom high in the air and fell forward onto his nose.

"He thinks he's an inchworm," Rachel said.

"Whereas my Thomas thinks he's nothing but an old slug," Alta said, laughing, for her Thomas had chosen just that moment to let out a loud, satisfied belch.

Rachel leaned over and picked up Velma's wriggling baby. She stood him on her thighs. He rocked back on his heels and blew bubbles at the sky.

She turned her head in time to catch her mother staring at her. But when the two women's gazes met, Sadie looked away.

Rachel rubbed noses with the baby, and he squealed in delight. She hugged him to her, breathing in his baby smell. Oh, how she wished he were hers. The Plain had a saying: A new baby every spring. Velma and Alta both had six children in only ten years of marriage, and all of them still living. No one even thought to tease them anymore, when the twins started increasing at the same time and gave birth to their babies on exactly the same day. Rachel remembered her own marriage bed, remembered lying in Ben's arms and whispering dreams in the dark of all the babies they would make together. But the nights had passed into months and the months into years, eight of them, before Benjo had been born. They had called him their miracle baby.

And Rachel had stopped mourning the lack of other babies. Benjo had been all that they had needed, to make their world complete. Their wonderful, precious, God-delivered miracle. But her Ben was lost to her now, and her world was complete no longer.

She almost didn't feel the touch of a hand on her shoulder, so light it was, so tentative. Afraid even to breathe, Rachel turned her head and looked into her mother's face. She couldn't remember the last time her mother had touched her in any way, even accidentally.

"When you were a little girl," her mother said, "you used to say you were going to have thirteen babies. A baker's dozen."

Tears blurred Rachel's eyes and filled her throat. She had to swallow twice, before she could speak. "Did I?"

Her mother nodded, so serious, so solemn. Her mother, Rachel thought, wore her solemnity as naturally as she did her shawl and prayer cap. "Thirteen children and a hundred and sixty-nine grandchildren."

A startled laugh burst from Rachel's tight chest, and a smile flickered over her mother's lips. A smile so quick and faint, Rachel wondered afterward if she'd really seen it.

"Oh, yes. For each of your babies was going to have thirteen babies of its own, you see," her mother went on. "You were only three at the time you made this declaration, but you had your brother Sol work out the mathematics of it." A crease appeared between her eyebrows as she searched Rachel's face. "But we always thought, your father and I, that Deacon Noah would be the one you would choose to marry."

"You never said so at the time."

"It was your life to live, Rachel."

My life to live as long as I kept to the straight and narrow path, she thought. And of course she had. She always would.

The baby flung his head back and whimpered. Rachel set him belly-down on the quilt, and he immediately started inchworming his way back toward the waving cattail. She picked up a doll, dancing it in front of his eyes to distract him. Plain dolls never had any faces painted on them.

Rachel glanced again at her mother. They'd never talked this way before and she was afraid of saying the wrong thing, of ruining the moment. Sadie's whole attention was now on her grandson. There was a look about her that reminded Rachel of the old gappy-mouthed ewe that had died this spring.

"Mem, have I changed so much from that little girl you remember?"

Sadie made a jerking motion with her hand and turned her head away, and Rachel nearly gave up then. A Plain woman was judged by the daughters she raised, and she was surely her mother's failure.

"In here," Rachel said, pressing her hand to the hollow between her breasts where her shawl ends crossed, "I don't feel as if I've changed at all."

The silence stretched between them. Rachel started to push to her feet.

But then Sadie reached up and gripped her sleeve.

Rachel looked down at the hand that held her and she was startled. This wasn't Mem's hand. This was an old woman's hand, webbed with wrinkles and liver-spotted. She looked up into her mother's face, so beloved and familiar, and it was a face she knew not at all. There were deep lines around Sadie's mouth and eyes, and the hair that showed from beneath her prayer cap was the gray of a winter's day. Yet into Rachel's head came a memory of her father saying: *She had the merriest laugh in the whole of Sugarcreek Valley, did your mother. The merriest laugh.*

"It's not too late," her mother said.

Rachel sucked in a breath and nearly choked. "What?"

"It's not too late for you to have more babies." Sadie's hand fell to her lap. She looked down, watching her own fingers make a pleat in her apron. "He's always wanted you, has Noah Weaver. That man has always wanted you worse than a mudhen on a tin roof wants rain."

Her mother's words shocked Rachel, their frankness cloaked in country wryness. No Plain woman ever spoke aloud of a man's desires, no one even acknowledged the existence of such a thing in the Plain life, let alone made a joke of it.

Sadie raised her head. A smile flickered in her eyes, and then was gone.

Yet for Rachel it was enough. She felt herself smile in return and then heard herself laugh. Her smile widened to include the twins, who laughed with her even though they'd been talking between themselves and missed what Sadie had said. Rachel's gaze took in all the women, spread out over their hand-pieced quilts, and then went beyond, to the men at the trestle tables lingering over their empty soup bowls, to the children who had gathered around the pond again to play with the tadpoles.

A thousand times her eyes and heart must have taken in such a scene. It was all the same, and so was she. She hadn't changed at all, not at all.

This is what it means to be Plain, she thought, this certainty of changelessness, of always belonging. This is what she'd really brought the outsider here to see. Mem, Da, her brothers and Noah, even Fannie: these people defined not the means to her life, but life itself, and she wouldn't know who she was without them. They were a part of her, as much a part of her as her guts and heart, as her soul. They would always be a part of her in ways she could never be to others. To any outsider, even him.

She thought that if she lost all this, if she lost any more, she would never be able to bear it.

THOSE WHO DIED PLAIN were buried in a cemetery on a hill behind the Miller big house. It was a pretty spot, this hill, shaded by cottonwoods and box elders and carpeted with lush buffalo grass that bowed and danced in the wind. A snake fence had been built around the graves to protect them from the winter snowdrifts. But one grave lay outside the fence, separate from the others. No stone or wooden cross marked this resting place, though everyone knew it was there.

Rachel's steps faltered as she passed by that grave on her way to the gate, but she didn't look at it. Couldn't bear to look at it.

Ben's grave was with the others, safe inside the fence. She had picked wildflowers and put them in an empty tomato can. Spring colors and smells—yellow holly grape, white Indian pipe, and pale lilac monkshood. She knelt in the grass and wedged the can of flowers into the sunken earth beneath a rough-hewn granite marker. Into this stone she herself had scratched with a hoof pick his name and the years of his life.

Usually Benjo came with her when she did this, when

she brought Ben things like flowers and holly sprigs and a wreath of fall leaves. She wanted Benjo with her now, but he'd run off to hide somewhere again. Nursing wounded feelings after that incident with Noah and the cider. Maybe Ben would have known where to look for him. Or maybe Ben, like her own father, would have said to leave the boy alone.

She arranged the flowers in the can so that they made a pleasing picture to the eye. "Here you are, Ben. A little something just for pretty." That's what he'd always said to her. *A little something just for pretty.* No sooner would the year's first Indian pipe and monkshood be poking their heads through the spring grass than he'd be out picking her a bunch. *A little something just for pretty.* It was one of the rituals of spring, like feeding the bums in front of the stove and watching the newborns take their first steps—Ben picking her flowers. Now she did it for him.

"We had us a nice crop of fat lambs this year, including six sets of twins. And the bone pile's been small."

He'd been killed during the haying time. On this day last year, he'd still been alive. He might have picked her flowers on such a day. A month later she'd been scratching his name into this stone. This afternoon the sun shone warm and bright in the sky, but on the day they buried him it had been raining. Life and death, they were so close, she thought. All that separated them was a solitary breath, a single heartbeat, and the will of God.

Then it had been raining. The earth had been wet and heavy, and it had made loud plopping noises as it slid from the shovels onto his coffin. He had been dressed not in his brown sack coat and broadfalls but in a suit of the purest white. *Der Herr gibt und der Herr nimmt.* The Lord giveth and the Lord taketh. She had said, weeping, to her father, "Where was God when my Ben died?" And her father had said, "Where was God when His own son died?"

The rawhide hinges of the gate squeaked as it opened. Rachel scooted around on her knees, squinting against the sunlight that splashed through the trees, hoping to see Benjo. But instead it was Noah.

She said nothing, only got stiffly to her feet. She didn't want him here.

But her annoyance faded when Noah Weaver raised his head, and the broad brim of his hat lifted to reveal his face. His eyes looked like two bruises in the paleness of his face, and she knew she had done that to him.

He stopped in front of her, not looking down at Ben's grave, but searching her face, as she searched his. The silence between them grew heavy.

She wanted to do something to make it better, to make him better. He wasn't a man often given to smiles, but she wanted to make him smile.

"I was just telling Ben what a sweet crop of lambs we have this year."

"And did you tell him how you've been letting an *Englischer* work his evil wiles on you?"

Rachel pushed past him, but he grabbed her arm, swinging her back around so hard she fell against him.

His lips tightened and twisted down at the corners, making him look mean. "That outsider, he sure does think he's somebody, he does. And now he's got you thinking you're somebody, too."

She tried to pull free of him, but his grip tightened, hurting her. "Let go of me, Noah."

"*Ja,* I'll let go of you, Rachel Yoder. I'll let go of you. But not before I've spoken plain." He let go of her, but only to span her bonnet with his big hand, twisting her head back around toward the gate and the solitary grave that lay beyond it. "That's what comes of pride, of thinking you're somebody. Is that how you want to wind up, first shunned in life and then shunned in death, shunned by all, even by God?"

She squeezed her eyes shut. She wouldn't look, she couldn't even bear to think of it.

He gave her head a little shake. "Do I need to tell you what to think, Rachel? How to be? 'Be not unequally yoked together with unbelievers; for what fellowship hath righteousness with unrighteousness? What communion hath light with darkness?' "

She wrenched loose of him with such force she stumbled. She flung out her hand to break her fall and scraped her knuckles on one of the rough gravestones. Lurching upright, she backed away from him.

"I've done nothing wrong. Do you think I could come up here and face Ben if—"

"Ben is dead!" He closed the space between them and grabbed her shoulders. "Dead!" He shook her so hard her teeth cracked together, shocking a cry out of her. "Aw, Rachel, Rachel." His hands gentled and moved up her neck to cradle her face. "Ben's dead and you've a life still to live, a straight and narrow life, a Plain life. Homesteading to be done and a boy to raise." He lowered his head, bringing his face close to hers, breathing hot, harsh gusts. "More children to bear for the glory of God and the church."

His lips came down on hers, desperate, smothering. She tried to pull away but he held her fast, his fingers pressing into her cheeks. She pushed against his chest and twisted her face aside, cutting her lips on his teeth.

He let her go. He was panting, sucking in great gasps

of air like a drowning man. He pressed his hands to his mouth. "*Lieber Gott, lieber Gott.* Rachel . . . I'm so sorry, so sorry. . . ."

Her legs were shaking so hard she had difficulty standing upright. She could feel herself swaying. She wiped her mouth with the back of her hand and tasted blood.

"That you could do such a thing, Noah Weaver, and right on top of Ben's grave." A harsh sound tore out of her. She had meant it to be a laugh, but it wasn't. "And you accuse me of thinking I'm somebody."

He dropped his hands and lifted his head. "You don't . . ." He drew in a deep breath, his chest shuddering. "Listen to me, our Rachel . . ." He came at her. "No, no, I won't hurt you," he said when she scuttled back a step. He spread his arms out from his sides, pleading. "I'll not touch you. Only you must listen. Send the outsider away. Make him go before it's too late. Light cannot be found in darkness. Or truth among lies."

She shook her head, not understanding him, not knowing him. Yet he looked so hurt, so frightened and broken, and she couldn't bear it.

She held out her hand to him, but she was too far away to touch him. "Oh, Noah. Surely you know nothing can seduce the truth from my heart."

He stared at her with eyes that were wet with anguish. "Once. Once I thought I knew you. But no longer."

This time she was the one to take a step toward him. She thought at first her legs weren't working right, the way the grass trembled and the ground shuddered beneath her feet. A heavy rumbling was pounding her ears, growing louder and louder, like thunder rolling across the sky.

She saw Noah's face change, contort with horror as his

eyes focused beyond her onto the farmyard below. She spun around.

A herd of cattle about a hundred strong stampeded down the lane that led to the farmhouse. Eyes wild, rolling and white. Mouths bawling and nostrils snorting, hocks clattering and horns clashing. Hooves drumming, churning up the grass and mud.

The sheep in the meadow waddled in panicked retreat, their frenzied bleating adding to the din. In the farmyard men shouted, women and children screamed, running, knocking over trestle tables and benches, scattering quilts, running, running for the shelter of the barn and the houses, and still the cattle came, thundering down the lane. The pretty white pasture fences, those poles so lovingly hewn and peeled and whitewashed by her brother Sol, acted as a funnel for the crazed beasts.

And standing alone in their path was Benjo.

13

THE HERD OF CATTLE bore down on Rachel's son with hooves that could trample bones to dust. She screamed his name, although she knew he couldn't hear her over the churning roar of those deadly hooves. She lunged for the cemetery gate, but her half boots got tangled in her skirts and she went sprawling.

Noah grabbed her arm, pulling her to her feet with his man's hard strength. "Rachel—" She turned on him, snarling and clawing like some rabid thing, and he let her go.

She plunged down the hill faster and faster, all the while knowing she'd never get to her son in time. She could see his head jerking. His tongue, tangled up with his words, had tied his feet as well.

"Benjo!"

The shout hadn't come from her, although her mouth was open and she was screaming, a silent scream that tore through her belly and seared her breath.

"Benjo!" the outsider shouted again, and he was there, running down the lane, running so fast his boots kicked up gouts of mud in his wake. And still he was too far away.

The earth shook. The thunder of the pounding hooves reverberated against Rachel's ears. The outsider launched himself the last few feet, knocking the boy to the ground, covering him with his own body as the panicked cattle swarmed and crashed over them. Rachel could see nothing but motley red hides and slashing hooves and tossing horns and black bawling mouths in white faces and, once only, the flash of something pale that might have been his shirt, or his hand.

Rachel screamed, over and over, but the scream was trapped inside her throat, flattened the way her son was being flattened between the pounding hooves and the unforgiving earth. She would have run right into the path of the stampede if Noah hadn't caught up with her. He wrapped his arm around her waist, holding her fast while she flailed and clawed at him and screamed her silent scream.

For just a moment the bellowing, trampling herd parted around the man and the boy, as rushing water breaks around a rock in a stream. They seemed nothing but a pile of clothing in the mud of the road, but then the man stirred. He pushed himself up on his elbows and in his one good hand he had a pocket pistol. He fired point-blank into the crush of wild cattle that was once again bearing down on them.

The rumble and roar of the thudding hooves drowned out the shots. But Rachel saw one of the steers slew sideways and stumble to his knees. The front-runners in the herd parted to go around the flailing steer. More kept coming—until suddenly one reared up on his haunches, bellowing and tossing his horns, and fell in a tangle of slashing hooves.

The rest turned then, bolting in rolling-eyed terror. They crashed into Sol's pretty whitewashed fence, smashing it to splinters. They exploded into the pasture, trampling the bunch of frenzied sheep in their path.

The long and silent scream that was tearing out Rachel's throat must have ripped through her ears as well, for she could hear no sound. She watched the shattered pieces of whitewashed wood fly tumbling end over end across the blue sky, watched the cattle's hooves churn over grass and bloody scraps of wool, watched the panicked ewes and lambs scatter and fall, their black mouths open wide. But she could hear no sound.

Hands were holding her, fingers digging into her arms. She twisted free and ran to her son through the silence of her scream.

She threw herself onto her knees beside him in the mud of the lane, ran her hands over him, over and over every inch of his body, over the solid and yet giving warmth of his living flesh.

"He's all right."

The words were like a slap against Rachel's ears, breaking through the shroud of silence. She could hear bellowing cattle now, bleating sheep, men shouting, someone praying. A woman's sobs.

She looked at Johnny Cain. A gash below his eye showed the white of bone. His clothes were in tatters, exposing bruised and bleeding flesh. A deep cut in his hand, the hand that still held the fancy pearl-handled pocket pistol, dripped blood into the hoof-churned mud.

Rachel took that hand. She lifted his hand and brought it to her mouth. She rubbed her lips over his hand, tasting his blood, and the mud of her father's lane, and the metal of his gun.

His hand trembled beneath her lips, and then he pulled it away from her.

His gaze narrowed on the bloodied pasture, on a single sweat-foamed horse coming toward them. Rachel realized that she had seen men on horseback with the cattle all along. Men who might have been trying to turn the cattle, if they had not been driving them to this destruction. Fergus Hunter's men, who hated the Plain People and wanted them gone.

The outsider got slowly to his feet. Rachel stood as well, bringing Benjo with her. She looked across the ruined pasture. Her throat burned raw. Her skin felt as if it had been peeled off in strips.

Sheep carcasses lay in bloody mounds on the ripped and flattened grass. The thick stand of jack pines at the edge of the horseshoe-shaped meadow had finally blunted the cattle's wild stampede. Men on horseback, Hunter men, had the herd bunched beneath the trees now, a churning, milling mass of bawling steers.

The sheep that weren't dead bleated wildly. The cattle too were nervous, humping their tail ends, shaking their heads, lowing. Yet they seemed less dangerous now, with their matted tails and swayed backs, their coarse motley hides and dark wet eyes. One cowboy was singing, a lilting song that was like a lullaby. Another of the men had left the herd and was trotting toward them.

"Take your boy," Cain said, "and run on back to the house." His voice was flat, quiet, and he stood with his hands loose at his sides, his head a little bent. But the air around him pulsed and thrummed.

Rachel grabbed Benjo's arm. He pulled away from her. She grabbed him again. His throat was fisting over his words, his lips peeling back from his teeth. She dragged him back down the road.

Her father and her brothers and Noah all stood unmoving at the front of the yard, with the rest of the community behind them. But they would come no further, they would shout no warnings or challenges or curses, for it was the Plain way to meet threats from the outside world with silence and with acceptance.

"Nuh—nuh—nuh!"

Benjo dug his brogans in the mud, jerking her to a stop. They were still far from the yard, far from safety—although, as the outsider had once told her, there was no such place.

The rider reined his horse up in front of Cain in a slurry of wet mud. A man with a short pointed beard, a cheek bulging with tobacco chaw, and a big, long-barreled buffalo gun in his hand. A man who had once taken his rope and hanged a woman's husband, a boy's father, from the limb of a cottonwood tree.

A lone lamb bleated loudly, crying for its mother. A cloud floated across the sun, and shadows spread like a stain down the lane and across the bloodied pasture.

The man on horseback spewed a fat glob of tobacco spittle out the corner of his mouth. "My name's Woodrow Wharton. You ever hear of me?"

"I can't say that I have," the outsider said in his easy drawl.

The man nestled the gun's butt into his shoulder and cocked his head, sighting down the barrel. He had strange eyes, Rachel thought, nearly colorless, yet shimmering with light, like sun-struck ice. "They say you're the genuine article, a dead shot."

And she waited for the outsider to raise his own gun and kill him with it, kill this man who had hanged her husband and sent stampeding cattle to trample her son.

Woodrow Wharton's lips lifted off his teeth like a snarling dog's. "But then a man," he said, "can't be a dead shot with nothing but an empty boob gun to hand. Can he, Johnny Cain?"

One of the other cowboys had left the cattle and was riding hard toward them now, shouting something. It distracted the stock inspector for a moment, then his eyes burned brighter. "It's a pure shame, it truly is, for me to have to put a hole in a man of your rep."

Johnny Cain stared up into the gaping black maw of the gun, and he smiled. "Are you going to do it, sir, or is it your intention to bore me to death talking about it?"

The light faded from Woodrow Wharton's eyes, and the hand that cradled the gun tightened its grip.

A harsh, strangled sound erupted from Benjo's throat. He started to run toward the outsider. Rachel made a wild grab for him and then she was running herself, running past Benjo now. She tried to scream, to beg, to pray, but it felt as if her chest were being crushed.

Something flew past her eyes, like the blurred beat of a hummingbird's wings.

The stock inspector's horse leaped as if bee-stung, shrieking and rearing, just as the buffalo gun fired. The roar of it smacked against Rachel's ears, and stopped her heart.

White smoke hazed the air. Her eyes filmed and burned. Then she saw him and he was still alive, his gaze riveted on Woodrow Wharton, who now knelt in the mud. Wharton no longer had his buffalo gun, but he was reaching for the revolver at his hip while trying to cling to the reins of his spooked horse.

A bullet whipcracked through the air. The frightened horse reared again, jerking loose the reins, and cantered off. Wharton fell back, his hands flailing at the air as he choked on the chaw he'd swallowed.

At first Rachel thought the outsider had somehow managed to fire his empty pistol after all. But Wharton's watering, angry eyes were on the other Hunter man, the one who'd come riding at them hard, shouting. Smoke wisped from the gun in the cowboy's hand.

Wharton choked and wheezed, his eyes streaming. "You're starting to annoy the hell out of me, breed."

The cowboy kept his revolver pointed at the stock inspector. The click of the hammer cocking sounded hugely loud. "That's enough," he said, his voice soft and dry.

Wharton shook his head hard, as if he weren't hearing right. "You keep forgetting which side you're on, boy, dithering like a virgin in her wedding bed when it comes to these Plain folk. You know your pa'd be the first to tell you we're not gonna chouse them outta here by treating them kindly."

"I said we've done enough."

He wheeled his horse's head around, turning his back on Wharton as if finished with him, careless of him. He walked his horse through the shredding smoke. He drew abreast of the outsider and the two men exchanged a long look, and then he turned his gaze on Rachel.

She saw that he was closer to a boy than a man. A boy with long sleek black hair and a sharp bony face and a silk handkerchief, the color of wet blood, sagging from his brown throat.

Rachel had drawn Benjo up against her, one hand pressed to his heaving chest, the other smoothing his hair over and over. The young man stared down at them, his eyes dark and intense beneath the curled brim of his hat. He seemed to be absorbed with the movement of her hand stroking Benjo's hair. His mouth tightened.

"Is he your son?" he said.

Rachel's hand slid off Benjo's head and gripped his shoulder so hard he flinched.

"I'm Quinten Hunter, the Baron's . . . son." The young man's gaze fell away from them. He patted the neck of his sweating horse. "I'm sorry we spoiled your frolic." He twisted sideways in the saddle, to look at the pasture where his cattle milled and bunched and tore at the tender spring grass. Where the bodies of trampled sheep were already drawing flies.

His Adam's apple bobbed above his silk kerchief. His jaw pulled rigid. "They're wild this time of year," he said, "after the winter and all. We were doing some cutting out for branding when a sage hen flew up from her nest cackling and set them off."

Rachel said nothing. She didn't believe him. There was a bitterness in her mouth, hot and powdery, like the taste of ashes after a prairie fire.

"That's it, Quin. Why don't you just coddle them some more before the slaughtering." Woodrow Wharton had gotten to his feet and he was now trying to knock the mud out of his hat by slapping it against his thigh. He slammed the hat down on his head and clawed the mud out of his beard. His gaze sheared off the outsider and fastened on Rachel. His eyes glittered with hatred, and though Rachel knew little of outsider ways, she understood that this man had been humiliated, and would be even more dangerous now because of it.

"You woolly punchers aren't wanted around here," he said. "Maybe you ought to think about moving on." He jerked around and limped off down the road to chase after his horse.

Fergus Hunter's son watched him go, then he turned back to Rachel. He sucked hard on his lower lip, as if he had words he wanted to say that would hurt coming out. But in the end he kept the words to himself. The other Hunter men had started to haze the cattle, quieted now, out of the Miller pasture and back down the lane. Quinten Hunter tipped his hat and rode off to join them.

He left behind a breath-held quiet, as if the very heart of the earth had suddenly stopped beating. Yet it seemed to Rachel that she could still hear the gunshots ringing in her ears, that the rank stench of gunpowder still pinched her nose.

The bleat of a lamb broke the silence. The Plain People walked slowly down the road, praying as they came. Sol stopped before the shattered fence. He seemed unable to look beyond it to the blood-smeared pasture. Levi knelt beside a dead ewe. Fannie screamed and threw her apron over her head. She screamed again and then began to sob, and Sadie wrapped her arms about her, pulling her head against her breast.

Rachel knelt and began to wipe the mud off her son's face with her apron. She made her eyes as wide as possible to hold back the tears, but it didn't work. She felt as if a fist were squeezing her heart.

She had nearly lost him. If she had lost him, she could not have borne it—not Benjo, her son, her heart, her life.

She gripped his face between her hands and pressed her lips hard to his forehead. She closed her eyes and saw churning hooves and tossing horns, and a man with a buffalo gun, a man who had hanged her husband and sent stampeding cattle after her son. She had waited for Johnny Cain to raise his pistol and kill that man. She had wanted Woodrow Wharton dead. With all her heart she had wanted him dead.

"M-Mem!" Benjo twisted away from her, swiping his cuff across his forehead, and then the outsider was there before them, and he was holding out his hand to Rachel's son.

"I'd be honored to shake your hand, Benjo Yoder."

Surprise held the boy still a moment, then he reached up, and the outsider's hand closed around his in a man's firm grip. "You got a quick eye with that sling of yours. A man can be mighty grateful to have himself a partner with a quick eye."

Benjo's chest swelled and his face came alight with the outsider's praise, and Rachel's eyes stung with fresh tears. She blinked and reached up to brush the hair out of her boy's face. "You did a . . . remarkable thing, and I am so very proud of you," she said. "But it is only for the three of us to know, to share. You mustn't speak of it to the others."

Benjo nodded, his mouth set serious now. He wasn't too young to understand that what he had done was not strictly in the Plain way.

"A brave deed don't need words anyway. It speaks for itself," Cain said, and the boy's whole face broke into such a beaming smile that Rachel had to look away.

She stood up, facing the outsider. She searched for words, spirit-lifting words like those he had given as a gift to her son. Words that she could give to him in turn, to thank him for what he had done.

He was the one who spoke. "Let me kill him for you, Rachel."

"Lieber Gott," she cried. That he could speak such hateful words, when but a moment ago he had used loving words as a gift for her son. "Do you still understand so little about us, about me, that you could say such a thing?"

Her own words echoed hollow with her lie. She had wanted Woodrow Wharton dead, if only for a moment. She shuddered as if a cold wind had blown through her soul.

"That man, he hanged my Ben," she said, willing the lie back into truth again. "Who are you to speak of hate and revenge in front of Ben's son? He would have killed our son, that man, our son who is all of life to me, and if in the face of his persecution and his cruelty I can still hold fast to the tenets of my faith, then who are you to do otherwise in my name?"

"Maybe I'm mistaken, but I seem to remember staring down the business end of a buffalo gun for a while there."

"If you fear for your own life, Mr. Cain, then all you need do is leave us."

His mouth tightened, and a muscle jumped in his cheek. "I don't know as how I've ever been called a coward in quite such a righteous way before." He touched the brim of his hat. "If y'all will excuse me, I believe I'll go see about washing off some of this mud."

But she stopped him from leaving by laying her hand on his arm. The wool of his coat sleeve was rough and warm from the sun; it had been ripped by the slashing cut of a steer's hoof. "We are separate from each other, you and I, outsider and Plain. But you saved my son's life, and there are no words, no words to tell you what is in my heart."

He reached up to straighten her bonnet, and he let his fingers slide softly down her neck. His touch made her tremble and that frightened her, but his words frightened her even more.

"We're not so separate, you and I."

"We are, always we are," she said, and she backed away, out of his reach.

"Rachel. Rachel, my child."

The sound of her father's voice, full of comfort and love, was nearly her undoing. She pressed her lips together and closed her eyes. And when she opened them again it was to look into her father's dear face. The bones of his cheeks were white above the black fleece of his beard. His eyes, like hers surely, glittered too brightly. For a moment she thought he would throw his arms around her and pull her close, but it was not the Plain way.

"I'm all right, Da." When she tried to smile, the skin around her mouth felt stiff. "We're both all right." She draped her arms over Benjo's shoulders, linking her hands together over his heart. She kept having to touch him, to reassure herself that he still lived.

"Rachel. The Lord has indeed been merciful."

This time it was Noah who spoke, and she tried to smile at him as well, and at her brother Samuel who stood with him. And then her gaze widened to include them all, all her brothers and Mem and her family and friends, all so very precious and dear to her. Her eyes met Fannie Weaver's, and this time she did manage a smile for the other woman.

Isaiah Miller turned to the outsider. He took off his hat, but he did not lower his head or his eyes. He would humble himself, but not so far as he would humble himself before the Lord.

"Outsiders sought to take my grandson from me," he said in his careful *Englisch,* "but you, an outsider, gave him back to me."

Cain's gaze flickered over to Rachel, and his eyes didn't smile with his mouth. "Yeah, well, I wouldn't be countin' on me for next time. Y'all ought to do what the man said: sell out and move on."

"Ja." Isaiah nodded slowly. "It's all in the Bible, how Isaac, when the warring Philistines stopped up the wells for his cattle, he moved to new lands and dug other wells. So now you, an outsider and an unbeliever, a man who kills men, you tell us we should leave. I say, what if God is only testing our resolution? 'They that trust in the Lord shall be as mount Zion, which cannot be removed.' "

"Hunter and his hired guns sure enough seem resolved to remove you folk. And if they can't remove you, it's not too big a stretch before they resolve to bury you."

Noah made a hacking sound of disgust deep in his throat and turned away. But Samuel stepped up to thrust his finger in the outsider's face. "You speak of death and you smile your devil's smile and think you're somebody. But you'd be stone dead now if God hadn't caused that horse to spook when it did."

Benjo jumped and paled, and his left hand slid up to cover the sling that was tucked into the waist of his broadfalls.

The outsider gently pushed Samuel's finger aside. He flashed the most devilish of his devil smiles. "Well, sure enough it must've been a miracle."

THAT EVENING THE HYMNS did sound sad and lonely, like funeral bells.

Rachel listened from the porch of her father's house. It was tradition for the young people to gather at the end of a worship Sunday to have a sing. It was a time of courtship, with the girls sitting on one side of the long trestle table and the boys on the other, with the day slowing down to greet the coming night—and with eyes going where they shouldn't and hearts occupied with thoughts other than the Lord.

In the air was the sickly sweet stench of burning sheep carcasses. It was the only way to get rid of them fast and clean, and spare the farm an invasion of vultures and wolves. The woolly monsters burned easily because of the lanolin in their fleeces. They went up, so the saying was among sheep farmers, like pitch torches.

The young people ended their singing with a crisp, sharp note that echoed in the dusk. Rachel glanced down to the other end of the porch, where *Mutter* Anna Mary was healing the outsider. She could see the old woman's lips move, chanting Biblical phrases as she stitched the cut below his eye with sheep gut.

"You're to come in now."

Rachel turned. It was her brother Sol, and it was too dark to see his face. He reached out, though, with his big, clumsy fingers and pushed a loose strand of her hair back under her cap.

Their father sat at the long oilclothed table in the kitchen, with the rest of her brothers and Noah on their feet behind him. Mem was at the slop stone with her back to the room and her head tucked low, peeling a basket of potatoes, making herself disappear, even down to her shadow.

Although Rachel had never lived in this house, had never spent a night in it, she still knew this place as her home. This table where her father sat, she would always have a place at it. They were bound, she and her brothers, Mem and Da, with ties toughened by life and love, too tough to break. Surely, surely, they were too tough to be broken by anything.

They all waited for Isaiah to be the first to speak. Yet he sat in silence, with the big family Bible open before him, combing his thick beard with his fingers while he gathered the words he would need from his heart and his head and the book he lived by.

"We have been thinking," her brother Samuel said, though it was not his place to do so, "that you don't need to hire some outsider to work your farm. Your brothers and your good neighbor Noah will give you the help you need."

She knew what they wanted, especially Noah, and so she would shut her ears to their opinions. But if you were Plain, you never outgrew the commandment to obey your parents. What her father said, she would do.

She knelt beside her father at his chair, settled back on her heels, folded her hands in her lap, and bowed her head. "Is this what you think, Da?"

Isaiah pressed his hands flat on the table as if he could draw strength from what it symbolized, the unity of their familial spirit. "I will tell you what I know. I know that he's not one of us. That he can never be one of us."

"He's not like other outsiders," Rachel said.

A scoffing snort burst from Samuel's nose, so loud the rafters echoed with it. Beside him, his shadow Abram snickered.

"He doesn't drink the Devil's brew," Rachel said, "or smoke the Devil's weed." Since he said he'd won that harmonica gambling, she was careful not to mention games of chance. "He's careful not to blaspheme, except for those times when he was out of his head with fever. He—"

Samuel's hand slashed the empty air. "He kills, is what he does!"

"He's trying to stop. He has come to us for sanctuary, and so that he might stop." Johnny Cain was staying for a reason. She believed, she had to believe, that in his heart he wanted an end to the death and killing.

"He brought a gun with him to the preaching," Noah said, and the words came out of him flat and hard.

"A gun that saved our Benjo's life."

"If it had been God's will for the boy to die—"

"Don't say that!"

Sol stepped between them, as if they'd been about to come to blows. "He didn't mean that as it sounded," he said. He turned to Noah. "It would be uncharitable to deny the good the outsider has done for us all on this day."

An angry flush streaked Noah's cheek like a slap mark.

Rachel felt her father's hand settle on her head. "But still," he said, "for all the good the outsider has done for us, for all the good he might want to do for himself, there is but one faith that counts with God. He is not one of us. He can never be one of us."

Rachel felt the heaviness of her father's hand on her head, and the starchy stiffness of her prayer cap, and these things reminded her of what she was. "You should forbid it if what I am doing is against the Plain way. I only sought to hire a man to help with the farm until I marry again."

"That's easily solved," Samuel said. "Marry tomorrow."

Rachel raised her head. She looked not at her brother, nor at Noah, but at her father so that he might know the truth of what she said. "Ben is still in my heart."

Samuel spat out a short laugh with something sharp in it. "Are you sure it's not the outsider who's come and put down stakes there?"

"You think deviant thoughts sometimes, Samuel Miller. He sleeps in the sheepherder's wagon."

He flung his arms out from his sides. "So you say. But four sons our father's raised, and none has been as much trouble, as much pain to his heart as his one daughter."

Rachel surged to her feet. "*Five* sons he raised, not four. What stone do you carry inside of you for a heart that you can deny our brother like that? To speak as if he never existed? He might be dead, but you can't deny he ever lived. He was our brother—" She felt as if she were choking on her own breath. "Our Rome."

It echoed in the suddenly quiet room, that name. The name that had not been spoken for over five years.

Their mem was gripping the edge of the slop stone with both hands as if she needed it to hold her up. "How can you deny him?" she said to her mother's back, though she had to swallow hard when she did it. "You carried his body and soul in your womb, you nourished him from your breast. He was your son. Rome was your son."

Sadie whirled and fled from the room, and the slam of the bedroom door reverberated like Rome's name.

Their father rose slowly to his feet. He stood before Rachel and she saw on his face a terrible fear that she was being lost to the world as her brother had been lost.

She reached for him. She gripped his sack coat with her two hands and clung to him, pressing her face into his chest. But he took her by the arms and set her away.

Samuel shoved their father aside to thrust a stiff finger in her face. "I say that if the *Englischer* stays through the summer, then, mind you, come mating season he'll be gone and you like the sheep will be ready to marry."

At any other time she would have laughed, for it was such a preposterous thing. To tell her, a grown woman and with a child of her own, whom she must marry and when. But she couldn't laugh, not looking into her brother Samuel's face, flushed as it was with anger and even revulsion.

Her gaze went to Noah. He stared back at her through eyes dark with anguish. He had never been able to hide the love he felt for her. She didn't want to believe that such a love could be a burden as well as a gift. That it could hurt.

"If he stays," she said, holding Noah's eyes with her own, "then I promise that come mating season I will marry again."

She waited for her father to speak, but he gave her only silence. She thought she should leave before she started to cry or said too much. She'd already said too much.

Yet she couldn't bear to leave things this way between her and Samuel. She made sure to pass by him on the way to the door, and she put her hand on his arm, squeezing it a little. It wasn't until she was back out on the porch that she understood the gift her father had given her with his silence.

The gift and the burden.

NOAH STARED AT THE door as it shut behind her, and his eyes burned as though there were sand under his eyelids.

"That's that, then," Samuel said. "She gave her promise. You heard it." He looked at Noah, waiting for him to speak. But Noah couldn't seem to get his tongue to work, even get enough air into his lungs to breathe.

Samuel snatched his hat off the wall hook and stomped from the house, with Abram at his heels.

"I should take a look at what's left of our sheep," Sol said after a moment that passed long and heavy. He too lifted his hat from its hook, although he paused with it in his hands, turning it around and around by the brim. Then he pushed out a sigh that sounded as if it hurt, settled the hat on his head, and left.

"Levi, go milk the cows," Isaiah said.

Noah thought the boy was so frightened at what was happening to his family that he shook with it. "But I just did already, Da," he said, his voice breaking.

"Go."

The door whispered shut behind Levi's slender back. Only two hats were left on the hooks now. Noah stared at those hats as if he found them fascinating. It seemed impossible to look anywhere else.

Isaiah fell back heavily into his chair, causing it to scrape on the bare wooden floor. He laid his hand on the Bible, his blunt fingers stroking the black leather lovingly.

Noah pushed out the words he knew needed saying, even though they didn't want to come. "Why are you doing this? Why are you letting an outsider such as that one come among us?"

"If we come across a lamb lost in the wilderness, do we leave him to stay lost, to perish? Or do we lead him back to the flock of the Lord? *Ja,* there is much wisdom in the Scriptures."

No, Noah thought. That is not the reason, not the only reason. You think that for Rachel's sake Johnny Cain will be as our sword, cutting down our enemies, while we keep our hands clean of their blood. But though you are our bishop, you are wrong in this, wrong in the path you are choosing for us.

Noah knew he should speak to Isaiah Miller of the wise words in the Bible, words about how you shouldn't do evil so that good will come of it. But this time his tongue stayed pressed to the roof of his mouth.

Isaiah stood up and laid the Bible in its place on the

crockery shelf above the table. "The outsider will do what he will do. And God will give him his punishment, not us."

Noah's gaze fell back down to his feet, and the words he should have spoken stayed locked in his heart. He turned away from his bishop and crossed the kitchen to get his hat. He felt that he was moving like an old, old man.

Out on the porch he filled his lungs with clean Montana air, but it didn't ease the pain that gripped his chest. Deacon Noah Weaver, puffed up in his wicked pride, keeping quiet about his misgivings, hoarding his thoughts. Knowing in his heart the right thing and choosing to do wrong.

And all because Rachel, *his* Rachel, had looked him in the eye and promised to marry after the breeding time.

14

THE CROAKING OF THE bullfrogs by the pond rumbled in the blue dusk. Rachel waded through the thick grass looking for wildflowers. An ache pulsed behind her eyes. She felt unstrung down to her soul.

She knew the outsider would find her, wanted him to find her. Yet when he came, she turned her back on him. She ripped through a patch of mountain bluebell, twisting and yanking at their stems so hard she pulled them up by the roots. Dirt rained on her skirt and shoes. She started to sneeze, but the sound that came out was closer to a sob.

"What did they do to you?" he said.

"Nothing." She straightened up, but still she wouldn't look at him. "Did you think they would beat me? Shout at me?" The bluebells in her fist trembled. "Oh, Samuel and I, we shouted aplenty. We exchanged terrible words. We've hurt the family, so badly I wonder if . . ." She caught at her lower lip, tears blurring hot again in her eyes.

He thrust his hands in his coat pockets and turned away from her, toward the mountains that were stark flat silhouettes against the ivory light of the fading day. "They want me to leave," he said.

"I promised Noah I would marry him after the breeding season."

To that, he said nothing. But then he didn't understand the cost of her promise, or perhaps he didn't care.

She cut through the grass with long strides, heading for the hill behind the big house. When he didn't come along with her she stopped, turning, and waited for him, and after a moment he caught up to her.

At the cemetery, she didn't go through the gate as she had earlier that day. She knelt beside the grave that lay outside it. "My brother Rome is buried here," she said. "Do you know why he's apart from the others?" Do you care? she wanted to ask him.

He studied the neglected grave. "He was an outsider," he finally said.

"No, not in the way that you're an outsider." She took in a deep breath, closing her eyes for a moment against the pain and loss. "Rome went to one of those revival meetings one day, just for a lark, and this saddlebag preacher there laid his hands on him, and the next thing Rome is coming home and saying he'd been born again in Jesus, that he'd been saved."

She brushed her hand across her face, breathed again.

"How this happened, we don't know. He wouldn't confess to being wrong, and so he was placed under the *Bann* by the church for having a *fremder Glaube,* a strange belief. He was shunned."

Her throat clenched. "Shunned by us all, even his own family. Food was made for him, but he had no place at the table. He worked side by side with us, but no one could speak to him, or smile at him, or acknowledge him in any way. He had a bed in the bachelor house with Sol, but his own brother would have nothing to do with him, for if you break the *Bann,* then you are shunned by all in turn."

"Why didn't he just leave, then?"

She looked up at him, her eyes wide. "This was his home. How could he leave his home? Only to us it was as if he had died. He moved among us, but he was dead. And then one day he did die."

She laid the ragged bluebells with their bruised petals and ripped roots on the weed-choked earth. She didn't realize he had knelt beside her until he took her in his arms. She didn't realize she was weeping until he said, "Go on, now. Get your cry out."

She clung to his coat the way she had her father's. But he did not set her away as her father had done. He held her, stroking her back. And after a while he rested his chin on the stiff pleats of her prayer cap and held her closer.

"I want you to stay," she said.

"... AND THEN THE OLD LADY, she yelled, 'So *now* you do tell me! *Mein Gott,* his cock, you say? And no wonder the fish they were biting so good. I thought it was an angleworm and I used it for bait.'"

Mose pretended to laugh. He leaned against the rough

boards of the lambing shed, crossed one foot over the other, dangled a piece of timothy hay from his lower lip, and pretended he was one of them, one of the *Buwe*. But he wasn't.

It was like this at the end of every worship Sunday. The *Buwe* would gather out by the wagons to chew hay and be rowdy, or at least what they thought of as rowdy, which was to swap stories having to do with shitting and farting and screwing, and the more dirty words the better.

None of them had ever really done anything more sinful than to nail his big brother's brogans to the floor or smear apple butter around the privy hole. They were all nothing but talk. The truth, Mose thought, was that they couldn't tell their own dicks from an angleworm even with the help of a lantern at high noon.

Someone cut a loud fart, and the *Buwe* let loose with another burst of laughter. Mose's lips curled in a sneer around the hay stem.

Their laughter had caught the attention of the *Meed*. The girls still sat at the trestle tables where they'd all been having a sing earlier. Their white aprons and shawls glowed in the gray dusk, catching the last pale light of the dying day. They weren't supposed to be looking over at the *Buwe*, but most of them did. Not Gracie, though; she'd probably never broken a rule in her life.

Even from where he was by the wagons, Mose could pick out Gracie Zook from among the other girls. She had a shoulders-back way of sitting. A way of holding her head just so. Because of that some people accused her of being proud, but she wasn't proud. She was only being Gracie.

Mose plucked the hay out of his mouth and pushed himself off the shed wall. He headed for the trestle tables, his heavy brogans cutting a swath through the thick buffalo grass.

Gracie was careful not to look at him as he approached. It was tradition to try to keep your courtship a secret from the others, even though everyone knew who was bundling with whom.

One of the other girls touched a match to a lantern wick just then, and light spilled over the tables. Before, all his eyes had been able to make out of her was her white apron and shawl. Now he could see all of her, down to the little wisps of honey brown hair that curled out of her crisp black prayer cap, and the tiny mole, like a cinder, caught between her lip and her uptilted nose.

He'd known her all his life, but sometimes out of nowhere the sight of her could snatch away his breath and make his chest hurt.

He hung a thumb off the waistband of his broadfalls, threw his weight onto one hip, and tried on a cocky smile. "*Har*, Gracie."

She blushed red as a beetroot, but she answered cool enough. "*Har* to you, too, Moses Weaver."

"Come take a walk with me?" he said.

"Now? Here?"

"No, I was thinking more like in San Francisco next Fourth of July."

A tiny smile crimped her mouth. He held out his hand to her, and after a moment she took it.

He helped her to climb over the bench and he kept her hand as they left the pool of lantern light. They walked to the west end of the Miller farm, where a line of cottonwoods stood black against the twilight sky like the posts of a stockade.

Her hand was rough in his, chapped from hard work on her folk's sheep farm. Not at all like Miss Marilee's hands. He'd been thinking a lot about the two girls lately, comparing them. He'd been wondering how they would both look naked.

He thought Marilee's breasts—he'd already seen a good part of them—would be heavy and full, with rosebud pink nipples. Gracie's breasts would probably be small, just big enough to fill his hands, and her nipples would be round and brown, like acorns. The hair between Marilee's legs would be golden and crinkly, while Gracie's secret hair would be dark blond and sleek.

He shook his head hard, trying to dislodge the pictures he had put there. Judas, he was truly depraved, to deliberately let such thoughts steal into his head, especially on a Sunday.

He slid a glance at Gracie, half afraid and half hoping the evening breeze had managed to rip off all her clothes. But no, she was still all pinned up from heel to head in apron, shawl, and prayer cap. He sighed. She was being unusually quiet, and her lips were puckered as if she'd somehow been given a glimpse of his nasty thoughts.

"That mouth you got on you looks weaned from a pickle," he said.

She pulled her hand from his and turned to face him, folding her arms across her chest. "Why are you behaving so crazy and wild?"

"I haven't done anything," he protested, his voice breaking on the last word so that he sounded as guilty as he felt. He spread his hands out from his sides. "Look, I even dressed Plain today."

"You know I'm not talking about today."

It was getting dark, too dark now to see her face, and he was glad for it. He knew there was a hurting going on behind those deep brown eyes.

He felt all tangled up inside like a snarl of yarn, but he

kept hoping that if he just found a loose end, he could unravel the mess and everything would be all right again. She was so strong, his Gracie, the strongest person he knew. Maybe if he could just get her to understand what was wrong with him, then she could show him how to make it right.

"Haven't you ever wanted to go to a minstrel show, Gracie? Or how about a circus, one with elephants and tigers?"

"A cougar came out of the hills last week and slaughtered three of our lambs. They have this terrible scream, cougars do. I heard it and went running outside and there he was, ripping out the belly of a newborn lamb." She shook her head at him. "And you think I should want to see a tiger?"

"Forget about that, then," he snapped, impatient with her, impatient with himself. "Do you know that there's a city, New York City, that has three million people living in it, some of them from countries we've never even heard of? And they've all sorts of new inventions there, like telephones and electric lights."

She stared at him. He knew she was trying hard to understand him, and she wasn't even coming close.

He himself couldn't grasp what it was inside of him, where it came from, this terrible urge that drove him to try wicked things like the taste of whiskey and the feel of flashy clothes against his skin. He wanted to see if he could touch and taste and smell the moon.

And there she stood, his Gracie, with her shoulders back and her steady eyes gauging him, and he knew he could lose her if he wasn't careful. If he didn't stop wanting things he shouldn't want.

"These inventions you talk about, those things are evil," she said. "What good is knowing about evil things that we shouldn't have?"

"Maybe it helps to know the truth about evil in order to understand what is truly good."

She gave him a little flex of her lips that didn't quite make up a smile. "But we've always known what is truly good, Mose. It's this." She swept her arm in a broad arc and then folded it up against her chest, as if she'd just gathered to her heart all that their eyes could see. "Our families and the church. The life we will make together, the children we'll have."

And what could he say to that—that those things weren't good? He knew they were; he wanted them as much as she did. Or once he had.

She'd gone quiet beside him. Above their heads, the cottonwood leaves stirred. A loud whoop came from the pond in back of the lambing sheds. The younger boys were down there throwing rocks at the bullfrogs and trapping fireflies. Mose almost wished he could be down there with them. He could get Benjo Yoder to teach him how to bean a frog with that sling of his.

Benjo Yoder. When those cattle had come roaring down the road, they'd all run like skeeters out of a smokehouse, except for poor Benjo. And the outsider.

"That was something, what Johnny Cain did," he said aloud, expecting Gracie to jump right into the middle of his thoughts. "That's how I want to be, like him. To know enough things, to have done enough things that I can feel strong and brave inside. Brave enough to walk out into the world and face down the Devil himself."

She tilted her head, thinking, then she said, "The outsider doesn't face down the Devil, he sits down to sup with him. He isn't strong and brave, he's lost. You should be pitying him for his lostness."

"But what if we're the ones who are lost? If it wasn't for

the outsider, Benjo Yoder could have died today, and all we'd have done about it was to *pray.* We're like those poor dumb lambs who got trampled, and we don't even know it. We're always patting ourselves on the back and telling ourselves that we're smarter than the world. But what if they're the smart ones? What if we're wrong in what we believe?"

He seized her by the arms, desperate to make her see, to understand. "Aw, Gracie, Gracie. Do you honestly believe you would be a sinner if you woke up one day and decided to wear four pleats in your cap instead of three? Is an extra pleat going to damn you to hell?"

She pulled away from him, rubbing her arms where he'd grabbed her. "You make it sound too simple. And stupid. But you know it's not."

He tried to laugh, but it felt like he had a tough scrap of jerky lodged in his throat. At the moment everything he'd ever been taught to believe sounded too simple and stupid, their church, their whole way of life that allowed for no doubts, no bending. No mercy.

That was the hardest to accept of all, that for those who strayed, for those who doubted, there could be no mercy. It was get down on your knees and swallow the whole *Kitenkabutal* or be damned to you, Moses Weaver.

And there she stood, his Gracie, looking at him with her forthright eyes, waiting for him to be something he wasn't.

He thrust his face close to hers, making her flinch. "I know what it is you really want; you want what every girl always does. You want me to settle down and join the church so we can get married. You got those quilts piling up in your hope chest and you're starting to wonder if you'll ever have a bed to put them on."

He wrenched away from her with such force he almost stumbled. "Well, you can just go on wanting and quilting,

Gracie Zook," he shouted at her over his shoulder, "because I'm not ready to be tied to a woman's cap strings yet."

He got almost all the way back to the big house before he looked back. He could barely make her out, still standing there among the sentinel trees.

THE SLOP BUCKET SAT THERE beside the door, waiting to be taken outside and emptied into the pig trough. A simple enough chore, but every time her glance strayed that way, Fannie Weaver screamed inside.

Outside the night waited, and the sky, the black and empty Montana sky. The night brought the sky closer. Even within the stout log walls of the house she could feel the sky looming over her, big and black and brutal, pressing down on her. Crushing her.

The slop bucket sat there, a silent and smelly reproach. If she left it until morning it would stink even worse, and Noah would scold. She could see her brother through the half-open door of his room. He sat on the edge of his bed, etched by the lantern light. His Bible was clasped lovingly in his hands, his lips moving silently as he memorized the day's verses.

"Noah?"

He looked up, looked through her, and then his gaze fell back to the open book in his lap.

Fannie wiped her sweating hands on her apron. If Mose had been here she would've told him to do it. But he was out somewhere, lost to the night, running wild.

She wiped her hands again. It was a small kitchen with little in it, for it was Plain, as it should be, with a bare pine floor, a square oak table with four ladder-back chairs, a black potbellied stove, and a trundle bed tucked into one corner where Mose slept. Yet by the time she crossed that bare pine floor to the door, her ragged breathing was louder than the hated Montana wind. Her heartbeat thundered in her ears.

Her hand fumbled with the latch. Slowly she cracked the door open, just as a bat flew out from beneath the eaves with a frantic flapping of black wings.

She shrieked and slammed the door so hard the whole house shook.

"Vas geht?" Noah called out. But she was already past him. The house shook again with the slamming of her own bedroom door.

She fell back against the wall, sucking in great gasps of air, breathing, breathing, breathing frantically, as if she dared not stop even for an instant.

"Fannie?"

Her breath caught.

He knocked. "Fannie? *Wie gehts?*"

Her whole body was so rigid it shook. A high-pitched whine hummed in her constricted throat. She heard his booted feet thump back across the floor and the click of his own door latching closed.

She sagged, sliding down the wall until she was sitting on the floor with her legs drawn up tight against her chest. "Leave me alone," she said, too loud, too loud with only her to hear it. She smothered her mouth with her knee, but now she was shouting it, screaming it, inside herself, *Leave me alone, leave me alone, don't leave me, don't leave me, don't leave me alone....*

She threw her head back and squeezed her eyes shut against the burn of tears, but they came anyway. They poured like hot, silent rain over her face, into her nose and mouth and ears to drown her, poured back down her throat to flood her heart. Poured and poured, until she was empty and full, both at once, of tears.

And she was left staring wide-eyed up at the open rafters, feeling foolish. No, not foolish—betrayed. Surely, she thought, so many tears should have earned her more than just burning eyes and a sore throat. She fumbled for the handkerchief she always carried in her sleeve and blew her nose. She creaked slowly to her feet, leaning against the wall. She was only thirty-five, but she felt so old, and so alone.

Although a coal oil lamp already burned bright in the room, she lit the fresh candle that sat in a stick by her bedside. Later, when she was calmer, she might extinguish the lamp. But she would leave the candle to burn until dawn.

Noah was always telling her she'd burn the house down around their ears one night. So now she was careful to set the stick in a saucer of water. He told her she was being wasteful, so she bought the cheapest candles, made of buffalo tallow. Noah said they stank. "It's my nose to suffer," she'd answered back, standing up to him for the first time in her life. But it was worth it to her putting up with the smell to have the light.

She said her evening prayers in private silence, as was the Plain way, while she undressed. She put on her nightrail and night cap and climbed into bed. The sheets were cool and rough against the bare skin of her legs and smelled of the lye soap she'd washed them in. The bed was large, big enough for two. She spread her legs wide from corner to corner, feeling its emptiness.

There were no windows in the room, so she couldn't see the night and the sky. But she knew they were there.

She prayed some more until she heard Mose come in. At least, she thought, he wasn't bundling with that Gracie Zook tonight. Fannie hated Gracie, even though she knew she wasn't supposed to hate, that it was a sin. It was just that Gracie managed to remind her of Rachel, the way she was always acting lofty, always thinking she was somebody. And now Gracie was trying to take her Mose away from her. Just like Rachel had taken Ben.

"Ben."

She turned her head into the pillow to stifle the sound of his name in her empty bedroom. She wrapped her arms around the pillow and pulled it to her belly, pressed the pillow to the hollow ache that ate at her belly, and she curled her body around it.

15

IT GOT HOT EARLY that spring of '86, the spring the outsider was hired on to work Rachel Yoder's sheep farm.

A haze built up in the mountains and hung there like tobacco smoke in a saloon. But overhead the sky blazed so blue it hurt to look at it, and stayed empty but for a few feathers of cloud. The mud dried to a cracked crust that was scuffed into dust by hooves and boots and wagon wheels.

Folk said a drought was in the making and everyone, even those with only a nodding acquaintance with the Lord, prayed for rain. But no rain came. Not even enough dew collected overnight on the tall grass to wet the ewes' udders. And on the morning the outsider paid his first visit to town, the sun came up smoking and the wind died early, so that by midday the whole valley lay sweltering, beneath a blanket of gummy, heavy air.

"Isn't this a fine summer's day we're having in spring?" Rachel said to the outsider as he was loading the wagon with crocks of her clotted cheese. "The grasshoppers started singing even before the sun came up."

Cain swiped at the drop of sweat that clung to the end of his nose and growled something about how now they wouldn't shut up. She laughed back at him, not caring that the heat made him grumpy. It was hot, true, but there was a canopy of deep and endless blue sky overhead, and the smell of sun-ripe grass and sage spiced the air. A patch of fireweed in front of the barn had exploded overnight into bright pink blossoms, so pretty that Rachel smiled every time it caught her eye.

The wagon made a song as it creaked and clattered and rumbled its way to town over the washboard ruts in the road. The harness chains jingled and jangled, and the old mare's plodding hooves beat a sleepy tattoo on the baked dirt. Rachel had often dreaded going into town before, the outsiders all stared so and could be so mean. But today a feeling of excitement gripped her, as if they were off on some grand adventure.

She knew a part of her happiness came from him, because he was here with her, sitting in her spring wagon with Benjo between them. He almost looked as if he belonged with her now. His flashy clothes, all but the black duster, had been ruined in the cattle stampede, so Ben's broadfalls, sack coat, and felt hat had been added to the Plain shirt. Except it was too hot for the sack coat today, and he couldn't seem to put on the big floppy broad-brimmed hat without tilting it at a rakish angle. He still wore his own fancy stitched boots and black suspenders. And, always, his gun.

Like the road they traveled on, the Miawa Valley itself had the undulating shape of ripples on a washboard, with

Miawa City tucked into the lowest dip of the rolling buttes and hills. The first thing a body saw when topping the rise before town was a meandering creek lined with diamond willows and aspens, whose silver leaves always quivered even in the stillest air. Surely the creek was the only pretty thing about the town, which otherwise was a sparse collection of ramshackle buildings roofed with rusty tin and made of logs weathered to the color of old buffalo bones.

Only one road led in and out, but a fingerboard had been planted at the top of the hill pointing the way for those who'd perhaps harbored a faint hope of avoiding the place. Cain pulled the wagon up, looked from the fingerboard to what awaited them down the road, and said, "If you asked me, to call itself a city is to give itself airs. Fact is, if you was to ask me further, I'd say it's got to stretch itself a bit even to be a burp in the road."

Rachel squinted against the sunstruck piles of tin cans and bottles that had been dumped along the creek. "It does have a church," she said, "although the circuit preacher only comes through twice a year. And it's got a schoolhouse, with a flagpole. Except a man got drunk one afternoon and shot at it, at the flag I mean, so now it's got a couple extra stars on its field of blue."

Benjo bounced up and down on the seat, sputtering. "Tuh—tuh—tell him how the Miawa g-got its name, Mem."

She glanced at Cain. He was watching her in that intense, heavy-lidded way of his that made her feel as if he measured the depth and length of her every breath.

"Once, a long time ago," she said, trying to copy his drawling way of telling a tale, "before the white man came to this valley, there was a Blackfoot warrior name of Mia-Wa, who was afflicted with the worst case of hard luck of any Indian ever born. One night he went to light a campfire and wound up setting the whole prairie ablaze. One day he rode off to kill a buffalo and instead caused a stampede that trampled all his tribe's tipis flat as flapjacks. Another time he took his bow and arrow and went hunting for supper. He saw a plump willow grouse and he took aim, but he missed the bird and shot his chief in the foot instead—"

"Th-that's not the way Da used to tuh . . . tell it," Benjo interrupted. "He suh—said ol' Mia-Wa's arrow got his ch-chief smack in the ass."

Rachel gave her son a look. "Anyway, the other Indians eventually got so tired of the walking disaster that was poor Mia-Wa, they banished him from the valley forever. So don't ask me why they then decided to go and name the whole place after him."

"Might be," the outsider said, "that they were so glad to see the back of him, they decided to commemorate the event."

Rachel laughed. Their gazes met and lingered, and parted. He gathered up the reins and started them on their way again.

Alongside the creek some tame Blackfeet lived in tipis made of antelope hides. As they drove by, Rachel saw smoke puffing from one of the tipis, and her smile faded. She thought of that Indian, poor Mia-Wa, who'd failed at everything he'd tried to do. To be banished from your home and family, to be ripped up by the roots from the very earth of your life, was a fate too horrible to be borne.

They passed the cemetery next, where a pair of boots dangled from a freshly hewn cross. Then came a two-story gray clapboard house that was encircled by a double gallery, and had a red locomotive lantern hanging from a hook next to the front door. Three women in silk wrappers and hair papers sat perched on the upper balcony rail like a flock of bright-colored finches.

"Th-that's the house where all the Jezebels live," Benjo declared, loud enough for the Jezebels to hear, and to laugh.

Rachel hauled her son's pointing finger back into the wagon. "If you're going to flap at something, make it those flies that are feasting on my cheese."

Benjo twisted around to pick up the bundle of willow branches that lay in the wagon bed. He waved the makeshift fan over the crocks of clotted cheese that Rachel hoped to trade to defray the cost of their monthly supplies.

As for Rachel, she kept her eyes carefully on the road ahead and off that house of sin. Keeping her mind from wandering inside was more difficult. In that house were beds. She could imagine those beds, with goose-down comforters deep and white and soft as fresh snowbanks. There'd be lace edging on the pillow slips and sheets so silky they'd whisper under a woman's bare skin. There'd be a piano playing in the parlor below. A mahogany piano. A piano below, and above a man and woman lying on a bed in a hot and shadowy room, clasped together, moving together, and the music from below pulsing over them and through them. . . .

"You going to roost up there all day?"

Rachel looked from the outsider's raised hand to his upturned face. He stood in the road, in the middle of Miawa City, waiting to help her climb out the wagon, and he didn't look at all like he'd been thinking of bare legs entwined on feather beds in houses of sin. He only looked hot.

Her fingers were curled around the edge of the seat beside her thighs, and she couldn't seem to loosen them. Her face burned like a stoked fire. She hadn't known it was in her to conjure up such wicked imaginings.

He took a step closer and clasped her around the waist, swinging her out of the wagon and all the way onto the warped boardwalk. She gasped aloud and clung to his shoulders like a child.

"You don't want to be getting your feet wet," he said.

It had been a polite thing to do, nothing more. Yet she had been so aware of the hard strength of his hand and arm pressing into her back, of the way her skirts had whispered as they brushed against his leg. Of how, just for an instant, their faces had been close enough for his lips to have touched hers.

"Wet?" she said. And then she realized that Mr. Beaker had just stepped out of his barber shop to empty a bathtub. Gray sudsy water flowed through the shallow trough that passed for a gutter in the road.

She didn't notice how the barber had stopped to stare, how the few people who were about on such a hot morning had all stopped to stare, not so much at her and Benjo this time as at the infamous shootist Johnny Cain. She looked around her, feeling disoriented, as if she'd never seen Tulle's Mercantile, Wang's Chop House, the Slick As a Whistle Barber and Bath, the town's four honky-tonks and dance halls. A covered jerky clipped past them, throwing up a cloud of dust and dung flies. She let the dust settle over her without even blinking.

"We better get those crocks out of the hot sun," Cain said to her son. "How about you handing them down to me?"

Tulle's Mercantile sported a ratty green-and-white-striped awning over its bay window. Cain set a couple of the cheese crocks beneath the awning's dubious shade, and as he straightened up she saw him grimace and press a hand to his side. The day after the cattle stampede she'd come upon him shirtless, scrubbing himself at the yard pump trough. His whole torso was a purpled mass of weals and welts and bruises.

"Since Doc Henry's going to be cutting that surgeon's plaster off your arm this morning," she said, "you ought to go ahead and have him take a look at those ribs."

"Aw, they ain't busted, Rachel. I should know."

She looked away so he couldn't see her face. He'd called her Rachel. He did it sometimes now, when he forgot about keeping his distance.

She wondered why he would know how busted ribs felt. The life he'd had before he'd come staggering across her wild hay meadow, the paths he'd followed before his had intersected with hers—it was all a source of constant, gnawing curiosity to her.

Yet when she stole another glance at him, she had to laugh at the face he was pulling. "What is it about you men and physicking? Wave a bottle of cod liver oil under your nose and you run like a prairie chicken. Then come winter let that same nose catch a rheum and to hear you moan, one'd think you were dying. And what are you snickering over, Benjo Yoder? You're the worst of the lot."

Cain and her son rolled their eyes at each other, as if to say, "Women!"

"After I'm done being tortured by the doc," Cain said to the boy, "I'm going to go buy me a horse. Want to help me pick it out?"

Benjo looked like he'd just been given the moon.

"A horse?" Rachel said.

He grunted as Benjo slapped another crock of clotted cheese into his hands. "Lady, if I ever do got to make a quick getaway, it sure ain't gonna be on that slug mare of yours."

"Oh." Of course he would need a horse. After all, he wasn't going to stay forever. When he left he would certainly need a horse.

"Horses are expensive."

His face took on a look of pure astonishment. "You don't think I can afford one on my dollar a day? Well, shucks. Guess I'll have to hold up the stage, then. Or use some of this."

Rachel didn't see where it came from. It was suddenly flying at Benjo and he snagged it out of the air. A man's leather boodle book.

The boy popped the boodle book's button lock and spread open the flaps, his eyes going wide. It was stuffed fat with treasury notes and greenbacks. "*Barmlich!* Wuh . . . wuh . . . where did all this money come from?"

"It was in my coat pocket all along. Back in the days when I had any pockets worth mentioning." She could hear the mischief in Cain's voice. But all she could think of was that he was buying a horse.

"All those hours you kept me flat on my back and as good as naked," he said, his eyes on her now, "and I guess you never thought to look and see if I had a purse you could lift."

"I would never!" she cried.

His eyes laughed at her.

She pulled her gaze away from him and resisted the urge to fan her face with her hand. "We were only wondering, Benjo and I, how you managed to come by so much?"

"Monte winnings."

A democrat wagon rolled by, its axle squealing loudly. Benjo clambered out of their wagon, the boodle book still clutched in his hand. At least, she thought, the man hadn't admitted to robbing a bank.

"I assured my father that you didn't partake of the Devil's pastimes," she said stiffly.

"Well, now, that depends on what the Devil does to pass his time." The laughter in his eyes was both teasing and knowing. "Shouting fire and making hell howl?"

"Games of chance," she said. "For one thing. There are others."

"Uh huh." He took off his hat to cuff the sweat off his forehead. He raked his hair back out of his eyes with his fingers. It was getting long, as long as any Plain man's.

He dropped the hat back on his head and gave its brim that rakish slant. "I'll try not to do any misbehaving today, but I ain't promising." His arm settled over Benjo's thin shoulders. "Come along, partner."

Rachel watched them walk off down the boardwalk, feeling strangely left out. He was taking her son along with him to buy a horse that he would then use to leave them. Benjo got invited along, and all she'd gotten was a little nudge to his hat.

"Do you really think you'll be needing a quick getaway, Mr. Cain?" she called after him.

He cocked his head around and flashed his rascal's smile, the one she didn't trust. The one that belonged to Johnny Cain.

"Don't you know, Mrs. Yoder? The guilty man runs even when no one's chasing him."

"SPREAD YOUR LEGS."

Marilee shifted her hips on the black leather cushion, letting her knees fall apart. She hummed a breath out her tight lips and focused her eyes on the ceiling. As ceilings went, she supposed she'd looked at worse. At least this one was pocked with knotholes instead of bullet holes.

"Wider," Lucas Henry said from between her legs. "And for God's sake, try to relax. One would think you'd be used to this, the practice you've had."

A pain stabbed at Marilee's belly, a pain that had more

to do with the doctor's words than with his probing fingers, which were actually rather gentle. She'd certainly been given plenty of rougher pokes of one sort or another in her young life. And he was right—she'd had plenty of practice at spreading her legs. The words had hurt her, though, because Luc had been the man to say them. She'd been knocked around by a lot of hard words as well. Men never thought a whore had feelings. She was only a hole to put it into.

"There ain't no call for you to be so mean," she said, and to her surprise the hurt she was feeling roughened her voice and stung her eyes. She was usually better at hiding her wounds.

The room fell quiet. It was so hot she could practically hear the heat, as if the very air were panting and sweating. He straightened up, going to a white porcelain basin to wash his hands. "Marilee, my sweet Marilee," he said, weariness—or maybe just booze—slurring his voice. "That remark was uncalled for, and I do apologize."

She lay there looking up at the ceiling, her bent knees still spread wide, even though the doctor appeared to be done with her. Sometimes he could go from behaving like a swine to being such a gentleman and then back again so fast he'd make her head spin. Yet she just went on loving him like crazy no matter what he did, no matter what cruel things he said. And she knew that made her a fool, because all she was to him was a fifteen-minute French Trick every other Saturday night.

His face appeared upside down before her eyes. His spectacles winked at her, and a swatch of fair hair slid across his forehead. His mustache quirked up at one corner, surprising her into a smile. "You are, by the by," he said, "in an interesting condition."

Her smile perished into a wail. "Aw, shit-fire!"

She sat up. Her stomach lurched, flopped, and threatened to erupt. She folded her hands over her middle, swaying dizzily. She held her breath.

He had taken a couple of steps back to lean against a glass-fronted cabinet filled with thick tomes, medicine bottles, and gruesome looking instruments. He had one arm folded across his chest, the other hanging loose with his spectacles dangling from his long fingers.

"Do you need the pot?" he said.

She pressed her lips harder together, shaking her head. Her belly churned, flopped, and settled; churned, flopped, and settled. When it seemed to have settled for good, she dared a breath, and then another.

She wiped her mouth with the back of her hand. "This is all your fault, Lucas Henry, damn your miserable hide."

He lifted one finely arched pale eyebrow. "*My* fault? What fascinating quirk of womanly logic has led you to—"

"That female preventive you been givin' us girls up at the Red House didn't prevent nothin'. First Gwendolene and now me. Lord, Mother Jugs is gonna throw a pure hissy fit when I tell her."

"Every occupation has its hazards and its failures." He unfolded his arms and pushed himself off the cabinet. "While you put your lovely gown back on, I'll put together an herbal infusion for your morning sickness."

She twirled her finger in the air. "Whoopee. If it works as well as your preventive did, it'll likely have me pukin' clean into next year."

He laughed, and the sound of it, deep and a bit ragged, made her chest ache sweetly. He wagged his finger at her. "Marilee, Marilee. Shame on you for your blasphemy. Don't you know we doctors are God?"

As she slid off the tall, claw-footed examining couch, she

could feel herself smiling at him. She did so love the way he said her name: *Marilee, Marilee.*

She jerked on her petticoat and knotted the tapes. She sucked in her belly until it felt pressed against her backbone, so she could fasten the sateen buttons on the front of her corset without having to loosen the back laces. She tied on her crinoline bustle, giving her bottom a little wriggle so that it settled properly. It was so blasted hot, and her corset stays dug painfully into her ribs, cutting off her breath.

She was already feeling fat and she wasn't even showing yet. In a few months she'd be wide as the back end of a cow and twice as ugly. She thought of Gwendolene: that chippy hadn't just swallowed a watermelon seed, it was the whole darned patch.

Fear cramped in Marilee's belly, making her queasy again. She didn't want to lose her looks; they were all she had. Marilee had figured out early where all her blessings, and all her miseries, would come from in this life. She had a face sweet and pretty enough to break a man's heart and a body that made him want to howl at the moon. And she had beguiling ways. Someone had said that to her once, and she'd liked the sound of it. She'd liked it even more when she'd found out what it meant. And she practiced them, too, her beguiling ways. Even the other girls up at the Red House, who were all jealous bitches with each other, thought she was sweet as a sugar tit. But then her daddy, who himself was as mean as they came, always used to say that when his little Marilee called the tune, even the 'gators had to dance.

And everybody danced, except for Doctor Lucas Henry. She'd tried everything she could think of to beguile him. She'd even tried being herself, and a risk that was, what with him being an educated Virginia gentleman and her being pure ignorant trash from the Florida swamp.

But then, it didn't take a lot of fancy words and genteel manners to make a good whore. When Lucas Henry, gentleman physician of Virginia, came to the Red House, he always picked her. She was the best at giving the French Trick, and everybody in the Miawa country knew it. He came to satisfy his carnal urgings, nothing more. She was the fool who'd fallen in love.

Oddly, it had only been lately, when she'd started just being herself around him, that they seemed to have progressed as far as being friends, or at least friends of a sort. They'd actually shared laughter, and had conversations outside the purview of their sexual transactions. And, once, he'd come upon her on one of her prairie walks and he'd given her a ride back to town in his buggy.

Marilee thought of that buggy ride with a smile as she carefully pulled her pink foulard dress over her head. She'd worn this dress for him. He must have noticed, for he'd called it lovely, and she smiled again to think of that. She loved the feel of the silk as it settled over her bare shoulders and arms. It put her in mind of standing naked in a soft summer swamp rain, which was how she and her sisters had bathed when they were young, since the only tub of any sort they'd owned had been used by their pa to brew his corn squeezin's.

She'd come far since those days, thank the Lord, but not nearly as far as she intended. Luc had called her gown lovely and it was, for she believed in investing her earnings in herself. But then, he appreciated fine things, and he seemed to have plenty of East Coast money to spend on his appreciation. If he married her . . . Marilee went still, her smile turning into a soft hum as she became lost in the dream of being Mrs. Lucas Henry. If he married her, they wouldn't live in this godforsaken bit of nowhere. She'd beguile him into taking her to a big city, San Francisco maybe, or Chicago. They would live in a grand house, and she would have a dozen wardrobes full of lovely gowns. And a built-in enameled bathtub with hot-water taps so that she'd never have to bathe in the rain again.

Luc's prodding at her insides with his fingers had left her feeling like she had to pee. She peeked behind the lacquered peacock screen that filled one corner of the room and was pleased to see he had one of those newfangled patent toilets, with a china bowl and an oak water tank. She lifted her skirts and squatted with a soft sigh, thinking that a patent toilet was one luxury she would surely enjoy as Luc's wife. She finished and stood up, but then bit her lip in indecision over whether to pull the chain or not, since she'd never actually used a patent toilet before.

She gave the chain a jerk. Water gushed into the bowl so loudly that it sounded like a hundred geysers going off at once.

Marilee pressed her hands to her fiery cheeks, as the noise echoed and echoed. She listened, breath held, for some sound of him in the next room, but all she heard was a close, heavy silence. She crept out from behind the screen, feeling hot and shaky, but she also had to laugh at her own foolishness. To think the noise of a patent toilet could make her blush after the kind of intimacies that had passed between her and Luc—both acting in their professional capacities, of course.

Her fingers still trembled, though, as she put on her English straw bonnet, anchoring it to her pouf of curls with a faux pearl pin. She fastened her chatelaine pocket to the hook at her waist. She tiptoed to the door, slowly eased it open, and poked her head out into the parlor. It was empty.

She straightened her back and glided into the room with

her head held high, pretending for the moment that she lived here and was entertaining company for tea. It was a small house, consisting of only four rooms: this parlor, the room he did his doctoring in, his bedroom, and a kitchen. But the parlor was filled with so many fine and pretty things, it seemed to Marilee like a house from a picture in one of those mail-order wishbooks.

She trailed her hand along the back of a brown leather wing chair. She picked up a crystal pen holder, marveling at its weight. She caught her reflection in a glass-fronted cabinet packed tightly with row after row of books. The books frightened her because she sensed they were filled with things she ought to know and never would, and that this lack of knowledge would someday be her undoing.

A brown tweed frock coat hung from the arm of a bentwood coat tree. She lifted one of the sleeves and rubbed it against her cheek. It smelled fresh, with just a hint of sandalwood. It was one of the things she liked most about him, his clean smell. In her experience most men were filthier than rutting pigs.

A beautiful hide trunk with brass hardware stood against one wall, and above it hung an army officer's sword. He'd once done his doctoring in the cavalry. That was one of the few things she knew about him.

Next to the sword a valentine had been hung on the wall in a gilded frame. As Marilee stared at the collage of gold lace and red velvet flowers, of pearl clusters and pink satin ribbons, she felt a sinking sensation in her belly. The valentine had been given to him by a woman, surely, a woman he must care for still to keep this token of her affection always within his sight. Perhaps she waited for him in Virginia, perhaps he'd kept her valentine and hung it on his wall to remind himself that he was going home to her someday.

Marilee heard a footstep behind her and swung around. He stood at the threshold of the kitchen, holding a small wicker tray of dried flowers. A shaft of sunlight from a window behind him cast him in shadow, so she couldn't be sure, but she thought she saw him smile. A blush warmed her chest and rose to her cheeks.

"I was fetching the chamomile for your infusion," he said.

She could smell the sharp tang of the dried flowers even from across the room, and she couldn't help smiling back at him. "You're like someone's old granny, you know that? What with the way you're always growin' them herbs and roots and such to make potions with, 'stead of dosing people proper with patent medicines like other docs do."

He lifted one shoulder in an elegant shrug as he stepped into the room. "Dulling one's pain with alcohol is certainly an option. But ounce for ounce, a bottle of Rose Bud whiskey is cheaper and far more effective."

Her smile faded slightly for she hadn't understood him; she never understood half of what he said. And as with the books in the glass-fronted cabinet, this frightened her.

He was, though, underneath his fine manners and educated ways, a man, and she understood men's natures all too well. She heaved an exaggerated sigh that puffed her painted lips and lifted her bosom. The bodice of her dress was filled with an ivory lace jabot sheer enough to reveal the hint of the pink flesh beneath. She slanted a look up at him from beneath her kohled eyelashes, pleased to see that he was taking a good long look at her. Smiling to herself, she turned and lifted the cascade of thick curls off her neck and bowed her head. "I need your help, please, with hookin' up."

She heard his footsteps, a pause as he set down his tray of dried flowers, more footsteps, and then his shadow fell over the soft pink bell of her skirts. His fingers brushed against her bare nape, and she shuddered.

"Still feeling a bit queasy?" His hands moved lower, pressing into the small of her back as he fastened the hooks.

"Oh, no." She had to tighten every muscle to keep from trembling again. "It's just been such a shock an' all, findin' out that I'm goin' to have a baby."

He finished with the last hook and turned away from her, but not before giving her bustled bottom a friendly pat. Marilee hid another smile.

She watched while he made up the potion for her morning sickness. He worked at a big rolltop oak desk which had bottles and jars and tins in all the cubbyholes and drawers where most men kept their bills and accounts.

"I reckon neither my belly or my head's quite settled into the thought of it, of havin' a baby, I mean," she said.

"A damned inconvenience for you, I'm sure. So I suppose you'll be wanting to rid yourself of it."

She was still so caught up in looking at him—at the way the muscles of his shoulders bunched beneath the thin white linen of his shirt as he crushed the chamomile with a mortar and pestle—that it took a moment for his words to sink in. When they did, hurt punched into her chest like a blow.

"God, Luc. What is there about me that makes you want to do that?"

He raised his head and turned to look at her, genuine puzzlement on his face. The hurt skewed deeper and then flared into anger.

"I know I'm nothin' but a worthless chippy, a whore, a tart, sportin' gal and fancy gal—oh, there's plenty of names for girls like me and I've been called them all, so you don't need to be throwin' it up in my face all the time like you do." Her hand made a fist that pressed unknowingly into her chest, as if to ease the pain there. "But my bein' what I am don't mean I ain't got feelin's and sensibilities same as anyone else."

She stood with her head thrown back, her bosom heaving above her clenched fist, her blue eyes wide and sparkling with tears. She looked magnificent, and for once in her life she didn't know it.

She was aware, though, of him staring at her, and of the strange smile that started to pull at his mouth beneath the concealing droop of his thick mustache. "'If you prick us, do we not bleed. If you tickle us, do we not laugh? . . . And if you wrong us, shall we not revenge. If we are alike you in the rest, we will resemble you in that.'"

She flung her hands into the air. "Oh, God, now you're throwin' Bible words at me! I swear, I'd rather be cussed at a blue streak than to—what? What're you laughin' at?"

It had started with a rumble but he was laughing all out now, wild laughter that stung her feelings even more.

He leaned back against the desk, wheezing as he tried to bring the laughter under control. "Life, sweet Marilee. I'm laughing at life, because it is just so sublimely ridiculous that there's nothing else to do but laugh—or drink." He stared at her a moment, then sighed. "I was only trying to convey that I'd rather deal with this condition of yours myself than have to clean up the mess left after Mother Jugs gets done butchering your insides with a knitting needle."

Her throat hurt as if something were caught there, but she managed to get her chin up. "Gwendolene's keeping her baby. Might be I'll keep mine."

He had turned back to the desk, to his herbs and medicines. "Well, don't dawdle over the decision. I'll induce an abortion for you, if I must. But I won't commit outright murder."

Marilee felt the clot of tears expand in her throat until she could barely get the words out. "Luc. Did you ever think this baby could be yours?"

He laughed again. "It would be one for the medical journals, rightly enough, and a babe well worth preserving. Imagine the stir you would cause. The first girl to get knocked up after taking it in her mouth."

She'd been a whore since she was twelve, but no one had ever sat her down and explained to her the way a woman's insides worked. She supposed she hadn't really thought it possible to get pregnant in that way, but she'd never been sure. Well, now she was sure, thanks to Luc and the way he had of making her feel more stupid than she knew herself to be.

And he made her feel unwanted, unworthy. Unloved. The utter hopelessness of her yearnings hit her in a rush of anguish. Her shoulders slumped and her head bowed as she turned away.

She stiffened when his hands settled on her shoulders, but she didn't resist as he pivoted her around to face him. "Oh, Christ," he said. "You're crying."

Her chest ached from sobs swallowed down, and her eyes ached from tears held back. "What d'you expect, Luc? Them things you say to me."

He pulled her against him, gathering her in his arms. She pressed her face into the sun-warmed linen of his shirt, which was slightly damp with sweat. His chest was so strong, so solid, a girl could lean on it forever. He held her with a sweet tenderness she'd never known from a man before. But such a tenderness was not meant for her, she thought, not for Marilee, but was simply some innate part of him that he usually managed to squelch and hide.

His hands rubbed her back. "Even when I'm stone sober, I suppose I'm not the nicest person. And there you are, always coming at me like a puppy, head up, nose wet, and tail wagging. The temptation is just too much to see if I can make you whimper."

"I don't guess I'm much of a challenge to you, am I?"

"No, not much of one."

She pushed against his chest with both hands, separating them. He was so tall, she had to raise her chin to see his eyes. And he was so fine to look at that she wanted to smile at the sheer wonder of him, even in the midst of her weeping. "What if I do decide to go ahead and have the baby?"

She knew it was a stupid question the moment she uttered it. What did she expect him to say? *Why then, my sweet Marilee, I reckon I'll have to marry you, won't I? I would be plumb privileged to be a daddy to this babe of yours, what could belong to any of the dozens of men who've had you this past spring.*

Gently, very gently, he brushed his fingers over her cheek, but his words were his old self, careless and a little mean. "The world's full of bastards, my dear, both accidents of birth and self-made men. I shouldn't think one more or less will matter much."

He finished making her potion after that, wrapping it up in an old scrap of newspaper, telling her how to brew it into a tea to drink every morning before she got out of bed. She put the small parcel in her chatelaine pocket and took a dollar out of it to pay him for his doctoring. He accepted the dollar, just like she took the three-dollar token from his hand every other Saturday night. Gentleman to the end, he saw her to the door, his hand resting just above her rear flounce.

She cocked her head to look around her shoulder at him, a panic in her that she'd made an utter fool of herself, and that he'd want nothing more to do with her, not even another French Trick. "I'll see you tomorrow, then?"

"Of course, my sweet Marilee. After all, too much virtue can lead to too little vice."

She laughed and tossed her head, and she swiveled her hips as she walked away from him, bouncing her bustle, twitching her skirttails, all the while trying to puzzle out what he'd just said. They were probably more Bible words, she thought, only they'd sounded backward or something.

She waited until she heard his door close behind her before slowing her steps. The air was so hot and heavy, it seemed to press into her, weighing her down. She could feel her face sagging, feel a band of misery tightening around her throat, feel the tears and the hurt welling up again in her chest.

She stumbled along the boardwalk and into the small alley that cut between Tulle's Mercantile and a saloon that was still only half built. The tang of new-cut wood pinched her nose.

She collapsed onto an upturned nail keg and she breathed through her mouth to keep from crying, but a fierce pain was pressing against her chest so hard it seemed her ribs would crack. She was dimly aware of activity out in the street: a Plain wagon pulling up in front of the mercantile, water splashing, a boy's laugh.

From deep within her the sobs came, exploding in a downpour of tears, tears that weren't only for this moment but for all the hurting of her life, all the hurting suffered and gone and the hurting that was to come. She doubled up, curling into herself, pressing her head to her knees, hugging them. She rocked and sobbed out words she didn't know she was saying: "Mama, don't let them do that to me, please don't let them do that, Mama. . . ."

And then someone touched her shuddering back, and cut off her crying as if a hand had been clapped over her mouth.

She flung her head up and found herself looking into the face of one of those Plain women she saw in town occasionally, depressing looking women who went around in their black coal-scuttle bonnets, black shawls, and homespun dresses dyed an ugly dung brown. Except this woman wasn't plain at all. She had fine pewter gray eyes and a mouth on her, Marilee thought, that most chippies would die for. Lush and ripe, what a man would call tempting.

"Are you ill?" the woman asked.

Marilee straightened up slowly. She clutched at her sore belly, trying to draw a breath through her clenching throat.

"I'll fetch Doctor Henry."

She reached out and snagged the Plain woman's sleeve. "No, don't. I've just come from the doc's. I ain't sick."

A soft pity filled the Plain woman's eyes, stinging Marilee's pride. "Hell, no, I ain't sick at all," she went on, her voice turning hard and ugly. "It's just that some damn son of a no-good bitch has gone and knocked me up, and I've turned into a regular waterin' pot because of it. I reckon you know how 'tis, the way you Plain folk're always droppin' babies."

She was glad to see the shock on the woman's face, and yet sorry she had done it. Plain or not, the woman had only been trying to help.

"Look here . . ." Marilee reached out her hand, but she pulled it back when the woman flinched. She was probably terrified of having her holy Plain self defiled by a chippy's touch. "I'm all right, truly I am. But you better hie yourself away from the likes of me before someone sees you. People do like to talk."

The woman's head jerked around, and her face paled even more. She swung her gaze back to Marilee but she was already backing up, her hands twisting in the folds of her heavy apron.

"We'll pray for you and your baby," she said.

"Amen to that, sister, and pass me the barleycorn," Marilee shot back. But the woman had already disappeared around the corner.

Marilee wiped the tears off her face with the backs of her hands. Her eyes were swollen and aching. She snapped open her pocket and rummaged through coins, Luc's potion, lip paste, and cheroots, until she found a small bottle of iris water. She sprinkled some onto a handkerchief and laid the damp cloth over her eyes. *We'll pray for you and your baby.* Hunh. Imagine being prayed over by those mutton-punching, hymn-singing, Bible-banging Plain folk. She didn't need prayers from the likes of them; she didn't need anybody's prayers.

She realized she had her mouth cinched tight, and she made her lips relax. Frowning like that only gave a girl wrinkles, and she must have a care for her good looks, because from them all her blessings would come.

She had a face to break a man's heart, after all, and a body to send him howling after the moon, and she had beguiling ways. She mustn't forget her beguiling ways.

DOCTOR LUCAS HENRY SAT in his brown leather wing chair, his bleary gaze focused on the surface of his big roll-top oak desk. A single celluloid hairpin lay on the green felt blotter.

He'd found the hairpin on his examining couch a few moments ago. It must have fallen from Marilee's hair. Poor, sweet Marilee, the whore. A memento of her momentous visit. His mouth curled. He'd been such an ass, and he'd been cruel. He didn't like himself much when he was cruel, and he often was.

He'd brought the hairpin back with him into the parlor, along with a fresh bottle of Rose Bud. He didn't know why he'd brought it—the hairpin, that is. He knew damn well why he'd brought the whiskey. He had also fetched a relatively clean glass from the kitchen, but then he hadn't bothered with it, choosing instead to drink straight from the bottle. The glass had seemed like an unnecessary detour on the whiskey's journey to the fire in his guts.

The hairpin was crimped in the middle, and he wondered why they made them that way. But he didn't wonder too hard, for the heat was making his head pound. It was also making the whiskey curdle in his belly, but that didn't stop him from tilting the lip of the bottle to his mouth and pouring more of it down his throat.

He picked up the hairpin, rubbing his thumb over the pronged ends, but they weren't sharp. *If you prick us, do we not bleed. . . .* He flipped the pin over and over between his fingers until he dropped it. This time when he picked it up, he tossed it into the empty fire grate, just as there was a knock on the door.

He took another swig from the bottle, almost choking, and his breath came in ragged gasps. He felt the black depression settle over him. Some days, most days, it felt as if he lived in the bottom of a well that was deep and wet and slick with moss, and with no hope of crawling out of it.

The knock came again, louder.

"'Physician, heal thyself,'" he quoted aloud, and that made him laugh, for in many ways he was no less a fool and surely no better off than poor sweet Marilee, who didn't know Shakespeare from Jesus and rightly didn't care.

He stood up, swaying as his booze-sodden legs sought a

safe purchase on the Turkey carpet. He took his spectacles from his pocket and hooked them with exaggerated care over his ears. He made his way to the door and flung it open, blinking against the too bright, too hot sunlight.

"Please, do come in," he said, slurring the words. "I seem to be doing a roadhouse business today, and all of it of the best sort, too. Whores and desperados."

Johnny Cain was nothing if not brave, for he walked through the door.

"I suppose you're here to get that plaster sawed off," Lucas said.

Cain took off the Plain hat he was wearing and hooked it on the bentwood coat tree, then he smiled. But there was something about his eyes that made Lucas want to take another drink.

"So long as you don't saw off my arm along with it," Cain said.

Lucas tried to draw himself up tall, but teetered instead. "You'd be amazed at the daring and complicated feats I can perform while half soused."

It was a simple matter, anyway, to remove the surgeon's plaster and splints. Lucas cut through the hardened gypsum with a surgeon's saw. When he was done Cain stretched out the healed arm, flexing his fingers.

"Your killing hand, is it?" Lucas said.

"Killing and other deeds, both wondrous and wicked."

Lucas laughed, although his gaze was held by that hand, the long fingers and fine-boned wrist. He wondered if God, when He created a man's hand, had thought beyond all the good the instrument could perform to the evil it would do.

He nodded at the desperado's killing hand. "That one might not serve you so well for deeds of any sort in the future. It was a bad break. Your arm may seem much as before, but the bone's been weakened. Like a rope that's been frayed once and then mended. I wouldn't, for instance, trust it with my life."

"I never figured on dying in bed anyway." Johnny Cain looked up at him smiling, but Lucas saw that his eyes were empty.

"How about a drink?" Lucas said. He opened the glass-fronted door of a cabinet, shoved aside a box of lancet blades, and extracted a fresh bottle of Rose Bud. He brought out a silver caddy of tobacco and cigarette papers as well. "Or a smoke?"

"No, thank you. I'll take some water, though."

"The kitchen's in there, back through the parlor."

He followed behind Cain, bringing the whiskey with him. He longed for a cigarette himself, but his hands had the booze tremors too badly to build one. "So you only indulge in the larger vices, do you? Murder and mayhem and such. But then I suppose a young man in your profession must always keep a clear head. No whiskey to dull your brain, or smoke to cloud your eyes."

He leaned against the doorjamb, watching as Cain worked the pump and cupped his hand under the running water. "Are you sufficiently impressed with our great metropolis? You have certainly impressed *us*. You've been the sole topic of conversation for weeks now. Everybody's been busy speculating over whom you're going to shoot dead next."

Cain bent over the sink to drink, the well-scrubbed hickory of his Plain shirt pulling taut across his back.

"There's a *Harper's Monthly* been making the rounds," Lucas went on, "with a story in it that has you killing your first man when you were but a tender fourteen. Or was it twelve? In any event, twenty-seven more are said to have followed that first poor unfortunate into the grave in the intervening years, dispatched there by your lightning-quick draw. Have I got the tale right?"

Cain splashed water over his face and straightened up, combing back his wet hair with his fingers. "I haven't stopped to do a tally recently. Are they counting those three I was supposed to've killed up on Tobacco Reef?"

"Hell, I don't know." Laughing, Lucas waved the hand that held the whiskey bottle. "You probably noticed, by the proliferation of stray dogs scavenging in what passes for a street around here, that our fair and charming town doesn't have an excess of law enforcement. Hence, you may slaughter the citizenry with reckless abandon and relative impunity. Although, as I'm both physician and undertaker for these parts, you might want to spare a thought for the trouble you'd be putting me to."

The kitchen was small, barely large enough for an old sawbuck table and a potbellied stove. Cain stood at his ease in front of the big stone sink, his quick and dangerous hands hanging loosely at his sides.

"Tell you what," he said. "I'll be a friend to you, sir. I'll shoot them stone dead so's you don't have to do any doctoring, and I'll do it where it don't show so's you'll have little work in making them pretty for the burying."

Lucas laughed again. And then the laughter faded as he stared into Johnny Cain's eyes and realized that, if the man had ever had a soul, the Devil had long ago claimed it. To Lucas, looking into those eyes was like that first shuddering razor-edged rush that came from a whiskey bottle, but now the horror and excitement of seeing his own dark potential was reflected in someone else.

Only two other people in his life had ever been able to

do that to him, to force him to see through the amber fog of booze in his brain to the unbearable truth about himself and the human condition. One was his brother, who had been killed in the war. The other was a woman, and he had married her.

"Why do you do it?" he said to Cain.

"Do what?"

Lucas shrugged. He took another pull of whiskey, for he had lost his thought. But then he found another. "Live the way you do. Hasn't it occurred to you that it's a flamboyant, self-indulgent, and rather prolonged form of suicide?"

"So's drowning yourself in a bottle."

Lucas smiled painfully. He thought of all the whiskey bottles laid out like dead soldiers, stretching in a long line through all the years of his life, and in that moment he both relished and regretted every one of them.

He rubbed the bottle back and forth over his mouth. "Ah, but I have found a way to go to hell without dying. This is my solace, my lover, and my joy. What is yours?"

He said nothing, but Lucas knew the answer. Killing was this young man's whiskey, to be embraced, celebrated, drunk deep. It was his obsession and his addiction. Johnny Cain was intoxicated with death.

Lucas tried to swallow through the tightness in his throat. "And what of our dear Plain Rachel?" he said. "Have you spared a thought for what you're doing to her? She who is not plain at all, with her fine red hair and those big solemn gray eyes that can see through to the dark side of a man's soul. She who is so damned innocent, so pathetically innocent. You could destroy her utterly."

Cain's voice and face expressed only mild inquiry. "Why do you care? Unless you want her for yourself?"

Lucas shook his head. "I do like her, though. And when

I'm not wallowing too deep in my drunkenness, I admire her, bound as she is by her faith that is gentle and yet so severe. In this world, but not of it. If I thought there was even the remotest shred of hope for the salvation she believes in—"

He cut himself off. He wasn't going to bare all of his soul to this man, at least not yet.

"Thanks for the water," Cain said.

As he started to pass through the door he stopped and turned. His stare was an insult, filled as it was with that cold indifference. "You're right, Doc, I do have it in my mind to seduce Rachel Yoder. But not for all the obvious reasons."

DOCTOR LUCAS HENRY FOUND himself back in the brown leather wing chair, not sure how he'd gotten there. The whiskey bottle in his hand was still mostly full. A fine sheen of sweat coated his skin, sticky and cold, in spite of the stifling heat in the room.

He stared with longing down the bottle's slender neck into brown liquid oblivion. He wanted to crawl into the bottom of that oblivion and stay forever. He'd been there before and he knew it for a gentle, numbing place where no one could touch him, no one could hurt him, where he couldn't feel and he didn't care anymore about the horrors that he still managed to drag down into the bottom of the bottle with him.

His brother had told him once that he dwelled too much on the dark side, that he wallowed in thoughts of sinning and evil and death, especially death. He had become a doctor to fight death, and a cavalry officer to wage it, and he drank to escape both his fear of death and his fascination with it. Or so his brother had once said.

But after many years and many bottles of Rose Bud, years of killing himself a swig at a time, Lucas had arrived at the hardly original conclusion that it wasn't death he feared so much as living.

He looked at the wall, where hung his officer's sword and the valentine his flamboyant and beautiful wife had given him the first and only year they were together. But he seemed to see them through a watery film, like rain on a windowpane. These mementos of his disgrace and his damnation.

He toasted them with his bottle of Rose Bud. His mouth twisted, starting out as a smile and becoming something much more painful.

"Here's to conduct unbecoming an officer and a gentleman."

The words echoed in the hot, empty room. And Doctor Lucas Henry thought of how some of the hardest blows life dealt fell not on the body, nor even on the heart, but on the soul.

16

THE WANTED POSTERS HUNG limply in the hot, still air, papering the side wall of the town's sprawling livery stable. They shared the space with "for sale" notices, old stage schedules, and an advertisement for a McGrady's Big Top Circus and Extravaganza which, as much as anyone could remember, had only made it as far west as Fort Benton.

Waiting in the gray twilight shade cast by the livery, Benjo Yoder had already read the whole wall at least once. Some of the wanted posters had sketches of the outlaws. None of them looked like anyone he knew. But there was this one poster that drew his attention. It didn't have a picture, only a description. It was rain-spotted and curling at the corners, but it wasn't as old as most of the others, which were so shredded they looked like mice had been at them. The poster described how a man had stolen one hundred and fifty-seven dollars in greenbacks and treasury notes last winter from a bank in a place called Shoshone, in the Wyoming Territory. The bank teller had been shot dead through the heart "by a tall and slender man, well dressed, in the third decade of his life and with a Southern way of speaking. He has dark brown hair, a handsome visage, and the cold blue eyes of a man-killer."

Benjo stared at the poster and wondered how big a wad one hundred and fifty-seven dollars would make. If it would be enough to make a black leather boodle book bulge at the seams.

"Were you thinking to run me in to the law?"

Benjo jerked around. Guilt more than fright had his heart thudding in his chest.

Johnny Cain's gaze lifted from Benjo's upturned face to the poster-papered livery wall. The floppy felt brim of the Plain hat cast a shadow over his cold, blue, man-killer eyes. "Might be you could collect a reward, huh? And then later, you could issue invitations to my necktie party and sell off pieces of the rope they hang me with, as souvenirs."

Hot words of denial knotted up in Benjo's throat and

tangled his tongue. He could feel his chin jerk as he tried to force them out.

"Uh—uh—uh . . . I w-would never do that. Whuh—what you said. Not for nuh—nuh—nuh—" *Nothing.*

He thought suddenly of his father, and his belly made a sickening lurch. He wondered what had happened to the rope the cattlemen had used to hang Ben Yoder.

The outsider had hooked a thumb in his gunbelt and half turned, so that he was looking at the creek now. In the tangle of wild plum thickets that choked the bank, two jays were having an argument. "What do you want most in this world, Benjo, above all other things? Want bad enough to make your teeth ache."

What Benjo Yoder wanted he couldn't even formulate as a thought, let alone put into words. Certainly not words he could ever say to this hard-eyed man, who gave him the same shaky-excited feelings he got listening to the wind gust through the big cottonwoods at night, or watching a herd of wild mustangs gallop across the prairie.

He searched his mind desperately for a wish that Cain would believe. Something flashy, worldly, something an outsider boy would want badly. Then he remembered the marvel he and Mem had seen last time they were in town, displayed behind the sheet-glass bay window of Tulle's Mercantile.

"I wuh—want a s-safety bicycle," he said, and it was only half a lie. For that shiny black machine, with its nickel-spoked wheels and genuine lizard-skin saddle, had sure been something grand.

The answer seemed to satisfy the outsider, for he nodded. His gaze left the creek and came back to the wall of posters, paused there, and then settled on Benjo's face.

"Would you turn me in to the law for a bicycle?" Cain said.

Benjo could see the words in his head, white on black, like chalk on a slate board. He could see the words and he could feel them form in his throat and curl around his tongue. He could see them and feel them, but he couldn't get them out. Frustrated to the point of tears, he could only shake his head hard.

And then he remembered that he'd lied about the bicycle anyway, and the things he wanted most.

Cain reached up and ripped the wanted poster off the wall. He crumpled it up in his fist, but he didn't throw it away. He gave it to Benjo.

"Let's go see about that horse," he said.

The livery was the only building in town to wear any paint, and the paint it sported was the bright red of a spit-polished apple. Even on hot days, passing through those sliding double doors was like dipping your toe into a pool of spring water. Dark cool moist air enveloped them, redolent of hay and manure. Today the livery's back doors were open, and from the yard there came the tang of burning charcoal and the *pang-ping-pang* of hammer on steel.

They found Trueblue Stone, the hostler, at the smithy out back, fastening a new handle onto a battered black-bottomed boiling pot. Trueblue wore only a pair of tattered trousers and a big leather apron that fell all the way to the domed toes of his hobnailed boots. The bare skin of his arms and back was shiny and black. He had the biggest muscles Benjo had ever seen on a man, thick and knotty as cottonwood logs, and he spoke to his horses with words no one else understood. He'd once told Benjo the words came from a place called Africa.

While the men fell into a conversation about horses,

Benjo rummaged through the pile of horseshoes that stood nearly as tall and wide as a haystack in the middle of the yard. Trueblue liked to tell a story that he'd once fashioned a horseshoe out of a piece of falling star and then accidentally went and tossed it onto the pile. Benjo didn't believe the tale, but he always looked for the lucky horseshoe anyway, whenever he came to the livery.

Except for this time. This time he dug a hole deep into the pile, stuffed the wadded-up wanted poster in there, and covered it with dozens and dozens of bent and rusted horseshoes.

When Trueblue was finished with the pot, they went to the corral to look at the horses. There were five of them for sale, four geldings and a young mare.

"Which one do you fancy?" Cain asked.

It took Benjo a moment to realize the question had been directed at him, and his chest stretched with surprise and pleasure. But with Trueblue standing there—a man who could speak to horses with words from Africa—Benjo knew he had no hope of getting any of his own ordinary words out from around his twisted-up tongue, so he pointed to the mare, a chestnut with a blaze on her face and white stockings.

"She is the prime one of the lot, all right: nice fat sleek coat, bright eyes, a long arch to her neck, thick cannons, and a clear-footed gait. You've a good eye, partner," Cain said, making the boy's chest swell even more. "Trueblue allows as how she can be a bit of a bangtail when the mood takes her, though. I'm looking for a real sugar-eater of a horse. One that's been gentled, not broke."

Benjo watched, fascinated, as he checked all the horses over carefully, peering in their mouths and up their nostrils, running his hands over their legs. He even squatted down in the dirt of the corral and studied their droppings. He narrowed the horses down to two candidates, the mare and a big gray gelding, riding them both bareback with only a hackamore bit. To Benjo's proud delight, he settled on the mare, even though Trueblue had said she could be a bit of a bangtail when the mood took her.

He dickered with Trueblue for a long time over the price—what the hostler wanted for the mare was an ocean apart from what the outsider appeared willing to spend—and then they dickered some more over a saddle and bridle. And not for a minute during it all was Benjo bored. He loved watching Johnny Cain, and he loved listening to him talk. He even pretended to be him sometimes, tilting his hat low over one eye and moving in that easy, loose-jointed way Cain had. But even when Benjo was alone, with no one but himself to hear, he couldn't talk in that cool, slow way of Cain's.

Afterward, out again on the hot and dusty street, Cain wiped the sweat off the back of his neck and said, "You know, Benjo, I sure have got me a touch of dry throat, what with all the argufying I had to do with Trueblue Stone over the cost of that mare you talked me into. How about if I was to buy us a couple of sarsaparillas?"

Grinning, Benjo nodded. Then, remembering his manners, he said, "Puh—puh—puh . . ." *Please.*

They walked side by side down the boardwalk, and although Benjo felt the stares, he didn't care. In truth, he relished the looks and the whispers they were attracting. It was a sinful thing, he knew, a worldly thing, this thinking you were somebody. But walking alongside of Johnny Cain, he *felt* like somebody.

And when they stopped in front of the Gilded Cage saloon, he thought he would explode from nervous excitement, although the moment lost some of its shine when Cain said, "Maybe you better wait out here, else your ma'll have both our hides."

Benjo waited until the saloon's summer doors had stopped swinging behind the outsider's back before he stood on tiptoe to peer inside. But he couldn't see much beyond an old moose head hanging on the far wall and a coal oil lamp with a red paper shade.

He dropped down on his knees and peered beneath the batwing doors. He saw a tobacco-stained puncheon floor sprinkled with sawdust. He craned his head, looking up. A whiskified man sat slumped over a table, snoring. A long string of flypaper coiled down from the ceiling above the man's head, but it didn't seem to be doing much good, for half a dozen flies buzzed around his oiled hair. Two more men stood at a brown felt-covered table, knocking ivory balls around with long skinny sticks.

He didn't see any dancing ladies with naked bosoms.

He saw the big gold-framed mirror that Mose Weaver had talked about, though, and the barkeep with the purple lips and the jowly cheeks. "Soon as I serve Gramps here," the barkeep said to the outsider, who must have just put in his request for the sarsaparillas.

The barkeep jerked on a big silver handle and a dark stream purled out of the tap and into a glass. He set the foaming glass in front of the only other man standing at the counter, an old-time prospector, to judge by his sourdough coat and slouch hat.

The prospector slapped a coin on the slick wood, making it ring. He said, "Here's how," and drained most of the Devil's brew in one swallow.

Benjo heard the ring of jingle-bobs and the scrape of spurs on the boardwalk behind him. He backed up on his hands and knees, out of the way of the saloon's door. His gaze went up winged, silver-studded black leather chaps to a fringed and greasy white buckskin shirt and a cowhide vest, settling finally on a face with a billy-goat beard and a bulging cheek, and pale wet eyes.

A strange light appeared in those eyes when they fell on Benjo.

"You sure do keep turning up where you don't belong, don't you, boy?" Woodrow Wharton said.

Benjo's head jerked as the words began to pile up in his throat. His left hand went to the sling at his waist.

But Wharton was already turning away. "I don't mean to wound your feelings any, but your daddy should've thought about using a French letter."

His lips peeled back from his pointed teeth, and he sent a stream of tobacco juice whizzing so close to Benjo's face he felt the spray. Laughing, Woodrow Wharton slammed the flat of his hand on the swinging door and disappeared into the murky shadows of the Gilded Cage saloon.

MIAWA CITY WAS A dangerous place. Most especially, thought Rachel Yoder, it was a dangerous place for a Plain woman who sometimes forgot to keep to the straight and narrow way.

First there had been that girl crying in the privy alley, sobbing as if her heart had shattered. Rachel knew she shouldn't have gone to her. The church's teachings were clear on that: outsiders, with all their corrupting ways, were better left to their own hurts and worries. And such a girl as that one, who lived in the house with the red locomotive lantern, ought to be doubly shunned for the wickedness she had fallen into.

The girl had been coarse, with her harlot's paint running in streaks down her face and her Jezebel dress that showed all of her bosom. And she had been lewd, brazenly admitting to being with child after lying in sin with a man. Yet Rachel had felt a disturbing empathy for her, as if her tears could have been the tears of any woman, of all women. And she'd felt an even more disturbing curiosity to know of the forbidden things that this girl could tell her of: feather beds and silk sheets and mahogany pianos. And all the ways in which a woman's body could please a man.

More than from that girl, with her harlot's paint and her sinning ways, Rachel had fled from herself. The church's teachings were clear; it was only when she forgot them that Rachel ran into trouble.

And it was when she'd fled from the alley that she'd heard the music. It came bellowing suddenly through the slatted wooden doors of one of the saloons, along with shrieks and whoops and a burst of pungent profanity. It was bold music, with walloping bawls of sound. Never had she heard its like before. Deep and rich and echoing, it made the hot air rumble like summer thunder.

"Oh, what is it?" she cried aloud, startled into pure wonderment.

"Why, 'tain't nothing but a concertina. The fellow sure can make them bellows wail, though."

She turned to meet the round and shining face of Mr. Beaker, the barber. His long waxed mustaches lifted with his big smile.

"Kind of gets a body's feet to agitating, don't it? No matter the heat."

Rachel's gaze fell to the sun-bleached boardwalk. She turned and walked quickly away, leaving Mr. Beaker to mumble to himself about "them uppity Plain folk who think themselves too good to pass the time of day." But the music followed after her, made her want to cross the street and look through the doors of the saloon so she could see what sort of worldly instrument this was that made such swelling, wailing, warbling sounds. The music—oh, it was a terrible danger indeed.

Like the danger there, in the mercantile's bay window. It was always an adventure, coming into town, to see what was displayed in Mr. Tulle's window. Last time it was a safety bicycle, and how Benjo's eyes had shone to see it. And once, while Ben was still alive, there'd been a four-in-hand road harness made of polished black leather and fitted with etched silver buckles and copper rings. Afterward, on the drive home, Ben had joked that with a harness like that—with so much sparkle—a man needed to wear sun goggles to look at it or he'd be blinded. But Rachel had always wondered if deep in some secret corner of his heart, he hadn't coveted that fancy harness.

This time there was a dress in the window, a dress so beautiful it took Rachel's breath away. It was of soft velvet, the blue of forget-me-nots, with an overskirt that was caught up in the back to make a foaming waterfall of ecru lace. A hand-lettered sign identified the dress as a "watering place costume" imported from Paris at a cost of five hundred dollars. Rachel's mouth fell open in shock. She tried to imagine that much money accumulated all at once and in one place, but she couldn't.

She wondered if Blackie's Pond qualified as a watering place, and if even the most extravagant outsider would be foolish enough to wear such a costly and delicate gown among all those thickets and rocks and brambles.

Yet the image of the beautiful dress stayed with Rachel as she entered the mercantile. Mr. Tulle had sprinkled the floor with water to lay the dust, so the place smelled strongly of wet wood. And of oilskins, which were piled on a deacon's bench just inside the door. She thought it optimistic of Mr. Tulle to have so many oilskins for sale in the middle of such a hot dry spring.

Whenever her father preached of the Plain being strangers in a strange land, it put Rachel in mind of Tulle's Mercantile. Today, with shafts of bright sunlight streaming through the bay window to haze the air with dancing dust motes, it especially seemed a mythical place, full as it was of so many tempting things.

Most of the foods for sale there she easily provided for herself, like pickles, and chokecherry preserves. She was certainly capable of potting her own chickens and deviling her own ham. And she wondered what woman would pay such a ruinous price for a tin of butter when she could so easily churn some. Still, she supposed, there was something about store-bought things that made them seem special.

Of course there were some foods she had no earthly way of providing for herself, even if she should want to, like the cans of sugarplums and white grapes.

Faced with the many marvels on display in Tulle's Mercantile, it was easy to become forgetful of the great goodness of God and all that he provided them from nature, easy to hunger for vain, store-bought things. Like those wispy lisle stockings and those tortoiseshell combs, like that chased gold watch and those dainty button shoes, rainbow-colored ribbons and frilly lace collars. . . .

Like that bolt of yellow sateened muslin, so shimmery it looked shot with sunbeams. She reached out a tentative hand to stroke the soft, shimmery cloth. What did one make out of such a bright material? She wished she could think of a purpose for it that wasn't worldly. A Plain woman wasn't supposed to covet such a thing, but she did.

"How there, Miz Mutton Puncher. What can I do for you today?"

Rachel jerked her hand back and whirled, hot color flooding her cheeks. Mr. Tulle had a nose like a crow's beak and a whittled brown face, and his black button eyes were scowling at her as if he suspected her of trying to steal, or of soiling things with her sheep-grubby hands.

Like most outsiders, he'd always made her uncomfortable and she stumbled through her list of purchases: flour, salt pork, soda crackers, hominy, brown sugar, a five-gallon tin of coal oil, a bag of Arbuckle coffee beans. A couple of yards of that yellow muslin.

Mr. Tulle's head snapped up at that, and his thin lips pulled even thinner. "Falling off the wagon, are you?"

She didn't understand his words, or the sneer she'd sensed lying beneath them, so she chose to answer him with silence. As a result he called her a snooty Plain bitch under his breath, and he refused to take her clotted cheese in trade. But then it was probably close to spoiling anyway, what with the miserable heat.

He packed her purchases into empty hardtack cases, but he didn't offer to help her carry them out to the wagon box. She had to make several trips, and was just coming out of the mercantile for the third time with the tin of coal oil when she saw Benjo running down the boardwalk toward her. Mouth and eyes open wide, legs pumping hard, one arm flailing and the other holding down his hat, he ran as if he were being chased by a swarm of yellowjackets.

Suddenly she realized that Benjo wasn't the only one running. Mr. Tulle came bursting out of the mercantile, bumping into her and running past without an apology.

Mr. Beaker dashed by, long stiff mustaches quivering. Big Mr. Trueblue Stone was lumbering down the street from the livery, his leather apron slapping his calves. People were spilling out of the shops and Wang's Chop House, shouting and excited.

Benjo slammed into her, spitting and sputtering, his throat unable to disgorge his words. She dropped the coal oil and let him drag her after him, fear burning a hot path up her chest.

It was the outsider, she knew it was the outsider. Everyone was running and converging on the saloon. He'd killed someone, was going to kill someone. Someone had killed him.

Benjo wormed his way through the knot of men at the slatted wooden doors, pulling her with him.

She'd never been in a honky-tonk in her life, never even looked inside one. She stopped on the threshold, blinking against the sting of tobacco smoke and the sudden darkness after the bright sunlight. Rank smells assailed her: beer-soaked floorboards, stale sweat, slopping spit boxes.

". . . how hard-boiled eggs tend to be yellow inside," she heard a man say. She heard chairs scrape against rough wood, and a stifled yelp of alarm. Shadows moved, flattening against the wall, and suddenly the very air itself seemed empty.

A huge mirror on the far wall caught and refracted the light that poured through the doors in back of Rachel. In front of the mirror was a long, high, narrow wooden bar polished to a glossy sheen. The bar had a vaguely religious look to Rachel, like the altars she knew existed in cathedrals, although she'd never seen one. Two men stood before the bar. One, Johnny Cain, faced the mirror, his hand wrapped around a bottle of sarsaparilla. The other man was Woodrow Wharton, and he had a gun in his hand.

He spat a viscous stream of tobacco juice onto the sawdusted floor. "I believe that I spoke to you, sir," he said. Even in the muted light his face looked pale and slick with sweat.

Slowly Johnny Cain turned his head, tilting it slightly so his eyes could clear his hat brim. "Pardon me," he said, and he smiled.

His shoulder dipped as he backhanded the bottle against the bar. The bottle burst into a spray of sarsaparilla and shattering glass. The jagged shard left in Cain's hand flashed, slashing across Woodrow Wharton's mouth.

The man screamed. One hand, the hand without the gun, flew up to his mouth to catch a bright gouting spill of blood.

"No!" Rachel cried and took a step toward them.

Johnny Cain's head whipped around to her, his eyes flaring brightly.

Wharton's hand fell from his bleeding mouth, and the hand with the gun came up, pointing, but Cain was already snatching his own gun from its holster as he whirled back, so fast that all Rachel saw was a flash and a puff of smoke.

An explosion ripped through the air, sharp as a whipcrack.

Wharton was slammed backward with the force of a mule kick. His cowhide vest twitched and tore. Blood misted in a red cloud. His back slammed against the bar and he hung there for a heartbeat, staring slack-jawed as if in surprise. Johnny Cain fired four more shots and his white buckskin shirt blossomed with scarlet flowers.

Blood and tobacco spittle gushed from his mouth. His pale eyes rolled back in his head. Slowly his legs folded and he slid to the floor. He knelt there for another heartbeat, then slumped onto the beer-soaked sawdust.

Powder smoke drifted past Rachel's eyes. A smell like

brimstone pinched her nose. As she stared, a pool of blood began to spread from beneath Woodrow Wharton's still body. It was thick and gummy, and very red.

Hard fingers dug into her arm and she was spun around abruptly. Johnny Cain slapped the batwing doors open, dragging her behind him, and people were suddenly scurrying out of their way, scattering like prairie chickens.

She looked around wildly and saw Benjo trotting along the boardwalk after them, whole and safe, and she breathed her first breath in an eternity.

The outsider pulled her into the street just as a dray piled high with cut lumber rolled past. He nearly walked them right into it, as if he hadn't seen it.

When they got to their own wagon, he turned her to face him. It hurt to look into his eyes.

But all he said was, "You and the boy better stay here by the wagon."

As he walked off, she could feel her heart beating, and each breath needed a deliberate effort to make it in and out of her throat.

After a time she and Benjo climbed into the wagon. Her mouth was dry, her belly sour. A muscle in her thigh kept twitching.

"I told everyone he doesn't drink the Devil's brew."

She hadn't even realized she'd had the thought, let alone voiced it aloud, until Benjo jumped.

His head jerked once, and then the words burst out of him, whole and complete as they so rarely did. "We got thirsty buying the horse. He only went in there to get us some sarsaparillas."

Rachel shocked and horrified herself by laughing.

"That man," Benjo stated, "he's the one who hung Da. I'm g-glad he's duh . . . duh . . . duh . . ."

"Dead," Rachel said.

She stared at the dark spots of sweat on the mare's sides, and shivered. She wondered what the outsider was doing now. Maybe he was seeing about burying the man. No one had checked to be sure the man was actually dead; they'd all just left him lying there. The street was as empty now as a ghost town. But then there was no marshal in Miawa City for anyone to summon, and Sheriff Getts might be anywhere in the territory. Johnny Cain had no law to answer to. Except God's law.

He came out of the livery, leading a tacked-up chestnut mare. The closer he came to them, the harder Rachel's heart thumped. He lifted his head and met her eyes. His face was as smooth and flat and cold as pond ice.

He knotted the horse's reins around the wagon's tailboard. The wagon dipped and rocked as he climbed aboard. He had, Rachel suddenly saw, Woodrow Wharton's blood splattered on his shirt.

As they pulled out of town, the wind blew up. Dirt stung Rachel's eyes and turned into a gritty paste on her tongue. The brim of her bonnet slatted in the wind. Dark clouds choked the mountains, whiplashed by sharp, white cuts of lightning, and with each flash, Rachel flinched, over and over, as if they were gunshots.

~

BY THE TIME THE WAGON clattered over the log bridge and pulled into the yard, the storm had moved in low and heavy overhead. Sheets of lightning backlit the clouds, followed by great claps of thunder that seemed to rip the heavens apart.

The skirling wind tore at Rachel's skirts. She wanted to throw back her head and shriek along with the wind.

But the way of life was strange. Terrible things happened, earth-shattering things, and life just went on as it always had. A man gets shot in the chest and lies bleeding on a saloon floor, and the cows still need milking, bellies need filling up with supper. A storm was coming and she had sheep to see to.

She and Benjo and MacDuff herded the ewes and lambs to the lee of a gently sloping hill, away from the danger of flooding coulees and lightning-struck cottonwoods. She didn't see what the outsider did or where he went. They hadn't spoken once on the drive home. She wondered if she would ever be able to speak another word to him. She despised him for what he had done, and she despaired of him, despaired of his soul. But a dark, ugly corner of her own soul was in awe. And gratified. Oh yes, gratified. Woodrow Wharton was dead and she was glad.

She tried to pray for the soul of the man who had murdered her Ben, but she could not. She prayed for Johnny Cain's soul instead, which was surely damned for all eternity.

They stayed with the sheep, to keep them bunched, but although the storm was bright and noisy for a time, it gave up no rain. Only after the storm had passed did she go to see if the outsider had put his new horse in the barn, or if he had used it to ride away.

The clouds and wind had brought little relief to the heat outside, but the barn was cool. Lavender shadows filled the rafters. Her old gray draft horse was in one of the stalls, crunching on oats. In another, his flashy chestnut mare was drawing up great mouthfuls of water from the trough.

He hadn't moved or made a sound, but she knew somehow where to go to find him. At the far end of the barn, where the sheep hooks hung along the rafters and the roof sloped down low.

He sat in the packed dirt of the barn floor with his shoulders pressed hard to the wall, his arms hanging loosely over his bent knees. He lifted his head as she walked up to him. For a moment she thought she saw through the cold glittering windows of his eyes into his shrouded, tangled soul, but then his eyelids came down like shutters.

She stood looking down at his dark hair and the knob of bone at the nape of his neck, at the smooth hard flesh of his back beneath the worn hickory shirt, the shirt stained with another man's blood.

She laid her hand on him as she would have with Benjo, to comfort him, and he uncoiled, surging to his feet, backing away from her.

"Don't touch me," he said.

She took a step toward him and he flinched, backing away again. "I said, don't touch me!"

But she kept coming, until she was close enough to wrap her arms around his waist and press her face against his chest. She could feel him trying to hold himself very still, as if he feared to draw even so much as a single breath.

"Please, don't touch me, Rachel. I'm filthy," he said, and she knew he wasn't talking about dust and sweat.

But though he didn't touch her himself in any way, he let her hold him until he stopped shuddering.

THE COYOTE WAS NEVER going to get tamed.

Benjo approached the pit slowly, as he did every time, crooning to her in the sweet singsong he used with the lambs. And every time, she lunged up at him, snarling and baring her teeth as if she would bite his head off if she could. He'd brought her food and water, and still the coyote hated and feared him.

This evening he didn't bring her any rabbits and squirrels. The thought of killing something made his stomach lurch.

Once, a boy in school had shown him a thing called a stereoscope. It had a slotted piece of wood at one end, where you put two photographs that looked exactly alike. Then you looked through the two eyepieces at the other end of the stereoscope and the two photographs somehow became one image that took on depth and life. Only nothing in the image moved, so that it was more like a slice of life, frozen forever in time.

What had happened today in Miawa City he kept seeing like images in a stereoscope. Johnny Cain turning away from the bar, smiling. A jagged piece of sarsaparilla bottle slashing across a man's mouth. Fire spitting out the end of a gun. Blood exploding from Woodrow Wharton's chest in a red mist.

And himself laughing.

It was the memory of his own laughter that bothered him the most. He tried to tell himself that maybe it hadn't happened that way, but he knew it had. He'd felt the laughter erupt out his throat and he'd heard it, as plain as he'd heard the gunshots. Blood had exploded from a man's chest in a red mist, and Benjo Yoder had laughed.

The bunchgrass around the deadfall trap was thick and green now, and scattered with pink shooting stars and mountain bluebell. It muffled his footsteps, but he knew the coyote would smell him. When he looked down at her over the lip of the pit, she arched her back, the black hair along her spine standing up. She showed off all her teeth and growled.

He'd picked her a hatful of huckleberries and he emptied his hat into the pit. She gulped the berries down, then lifted her head and watched him with a blinkless stare.

He felt bad, for he knew the huckleberries weren't enough.

She had three pups now to feed, as well as herself. She'd gotten so skinny lately her ribs showed through her grizzled buff-gray hide. He wondered if she was slowly dying, trapped down there.

It had taken him a while to figure out how he was going to get her out. Then one day, while mucking out the barn, his gaze had fallen on the ramp leading up to the hayloft and it had come to him. He'd lashed a bunch of small logs and branches together with rawhide rope and made her a ramp. His plan was to slide the ramp down into the pit, and then run off before she could come after him.

Only he hadn't done it yet. Every time he thought about doing it, he got a cold queasiness in his belly. He couldn't forget that coyotes were sheep killers.

Benjo loved every ewe and lamb on the farm. People mostly thought sheep were all alike, but that wasn't so. They had their own ways and peculiarities. One would always run away whenever you got near, while another would come right up and eat hay out of your hand. One would be so lazy, you'd have to always be prodding her up or she'd get stomach bloat. Another would be so flighty, she would forget to feed her lamb. Even their *baa*s were different from one another, and if you listened close enough you could learn to tell them apart.

It was hard sometimes, though, loving the lambs, because so many of them were always dying. They slid into the creek and drowned; they rolled onto their backs, bloated up and suffocated; they fell over cliffs and into bog holes; they poisoned themselves by eating death camas and lupine.

And sometimes the coyotes got them.

He thought again of what had happened today, how the man who'd hanged his father had come to die and how Johnny Cain had come to be the instrument of his death.

How he, Benjo Yoder, had in a way been a part of it all just by nodding his head to that offer of a sarsaparilla. And he had laughed about it afterward.

You did one thing that led to another, and that led to another thing, until suddenly you found yourself at a place where there was no going back, and no escaping.

He should have gotten his da's rifle out of the barn and shot the coyote cleanly the day he'd found her. Instead he'd fed her and brought her water, and then her pups had been born, and now those pups were getting big and getting hungry, and Benjo Yoder was at that place where he was going to have to either let them go free or kill them after all.

UP IN THE BUTTES a coyote bayed a mournful song to the moon. But down in the valley, at the big house, a piano waltz floated sweet and lilting out the parlor's open windows.

Quinten Hunter stood outside in the shadows of the gallery and watched his father's wife. Her back swayed gently as her hands stroked the black and ivory keys. In the candlelight her hair gleamed like polished obsidian.

Every once in a great while Ailsa Hunter would play her piano, and when she did she would let him watch and listen. But only from the gallery. It was her way of reminding him, he supposed, that he would forever be on the outside looking in, would forever be a breed and his father's bastard.

The music, the sight of her at the piano, always made him ache. Yet he always came to watch and listen. There were times in his boyhood when he had come out on the gallery during raging blizzards just to hear her music. Because she would play for him so rarely, and only if he was on the outside looking in.

At least this night it was warm, and the waltz she played

was one of his favorites. He was starting to tap his boot in time with the music when the front door to the house opened, and the floorboards creaked and sagged beneath heavy feet. A match hissed and flared in the night, lighting the sharp bones of his father's face.

"That you out here in the dark, Quin?" the Baron said. "I thought you were hellcatting it in town with the rest of the boys."

The waltz stopped abruptly on a jarring chord, and for a moment all Quinten heard was the pulse of his own blood in his ears. Then the darkness filled with nightsounds, the saw of crickets, the low of cattle, the rustle of wind. Quinten tightened his jaw against a rush of disappointment and turned away from the window, for there would be no more music tonight. It would be just like her to close the fallboard over her piano keys and never touch them again.

"Woody's being buried in the morning," he said to his father. The Baron was only a bigger, blacker shadow among many, marked by the glowing tip of his cigar. "I didn't go to the Red House with the others because I don't believe in going to funerals with a boozed-up head. It's disrespectful."

The Baron blew out a snort along with a puff of cigar smoke. "Who made up that rule of etiquette? Besides, Woodrow Wharton was a bloody-minded fool to let things get personal between himself and a shootist of Johnny Cain's rep, then try to best the man in a quick-draw contest."

"You're the one who hired the bloody-minded fool in the first place. You saying now he would've done better to bushwhack Cain and shoot him in the back?"

Quinten could feel his father's aggravation come floating down the gallery, thick and acrid as the cigar smoke. He looked back through the window at his father's wife. She still sat before her piano, her hands quiet in her lap. Her head was slightly bent, as if in thought. The nape of her neck shone white in the lamplight.

The Baron pushed a sigh up from deep inside his chest. "What I'm saying, what I'm thinking, is we ought to be able to chouse those mutton punchers on out of here without having to come up against Johnny Cain's gun. What's it to him if those Bible-bangers decide to sell out?"

"He's living with them, for one thing," Quinten said. "Maybe he figures that gives him a stake in the issue."

"So he should be getting a real education, then, on how perilous is the life of a sheep farmer. What with droughts and coyotes and the death camas. And these hot dry days like we've been having." The Baron drew deeply on his cigar, then waved it in an elaborate arc through the air, trailing tiny pinwheels of fire. "You can never tell, for instance, when a stray spark is going to come flying along on the wind and set those woolly farms to blazing like pitch torches."

Quinten leaned his head back and closed his eyes. "Pa, don't . . ."

"Don't what?"

He turned his head, trying to see the Baron's face in the night. He wanted desperately to understand, to know, this man who was his father. He supposed, at the heart of it, he wanted to know if Fergus Hunter really loved and accepted his half-breed son.

But that knowledge was as elusive as the strains of a waltz coming through an open window, and he was always on the outside looking in.

"Why are you that hell-bent on pushing things so far with those Plain folk?" he said, though he had no hope of getting an answer. He had never been allowed a say in the running of the ranch. Except for sleeping in the big house instead of the bunkhouse and addressing the boss as "Pa" on occasion, he was no different from any other of the Circle H's hands.

But then his father spoke, surprising him—and frightening him, for the words seemed to come ripping out of the man's big chest with a dark desperation.

"I'm in deep as a tar baby to the stockyard banks, Quin. Deep and stuck fast. The beef market is still sucking on a dry hind tit, which means I got to run more cows this year to make even half of what I made last year—"

"*More* cows. But we're already overstocked and overgrazed as it is."

"You're making my point for me, boy. Those cows, they got to eat. Throw in this bloody killing drought to play billyhell with the equation, and the simple fact is I need what those Plain folk got. I need their grass."

"But they don't want to sell out to us. To you, I mean," he amended, flushing. "You can't just make them give it up—"

His father laughed and turned, pointing at him with the red end of his cigar. "Aye, that I can, lad o' mine. Ride on up to the reservation and take a good look at what's left of your ma's people, at what's left of the pride of the great Blackfoot Nation, then tell me if the world's not divided into those that take and those that are made to give it up."

Quinten swallowed hard and looked away, toward unseen buttes that rose out of rolling grassland that went on for mile after mile, and would never be enough.

He sensed a movement on the other side of the window. When he looked around, he saw that Ailsa was standing next to the piano with the candelabra in her hand. Their gazes met, the woman and the boy's, and although the light shone full on her face, it gave him nothing. She turned, leaving the room and the piano that was shrouded now in darkness and silence.

17

RACHEL LOADED A WATER BUTT onto a small dump-cart and dragged it out to where the men were making hay.

Windrows of the freshly mowed timothy grass ribbed the meadow. The hot wind blew thick with the smell of it, sweet and rich. Two days ago the hay had been mowed and raked and left to dry, today they were stacking it. Benjo drove the wagon, while Mose Weaver and the outsider did the forking. Noah did the layering and rolling, because that required the most skill. It surprised her, but the outsider seemed to like making hay. He called it "sweet and sweaty work."

Rachel had always loved watching the hay rise into stacks; they reminded her of fresh baked bread loaves, light and fluffy. Every year Noah and Ben had helped with the haymaking on each other's farms. It was the Plain way for neighbor to help neighbor, and Rachel was pleased that Noah had chosen to carry on the tradition this year, even though he sure enough resented Johnny Cain's participation in the task. But then Noah thought that no outsider could ever work as hard as a Plain man, or could know as much about farming.

"That outsider, he doesn't know beans about hay," he'd grumped to her after the first day, making her smile. "And he swings a pitchfork like his elbow joints are screwed on backward."

The men finished off the window they were loading before they came for the water. The hay crackled as it was forked and stacked. Prickling dust swirled into the hot air, coating their faces and hair so white their heads looked dipped in cornstarch. Rachel knew from personal experience that on sweaty hot days, hay dust itched like the very dickens.

Benjo and the outsider were the first ones to the water butt. She gave them each a dipperful and they slurped it down. She watched the water spill out the corners of Johnny Cain's mouth, watched as a single wet rivulet ran down the pulsing vein in his neck, over his collarbone, to be soaked up by his shirt. His shirt, already drenched with sweat, clung to his chest.

When he lowered his head, he caught her staring, but she didn't look away. The first time she'd seen him, it had been in this very hay meadow. She was about to ask him if he remembered, when Noah and Mose joined them.

Rachel waited until the men had drunk their fill before she scooped out a dipperful of water for herself. She drank as the men did, with her head tilted back and the water running out the sides of her mouth and down her neck. When she was done, she flicked out her tongue and tasted water and salty sweat on her upper lip. The air was steamy and thick, but through it she could feel the heat of Johnny Cain's gaze on her now, on her mouth. It was so still she could hear water dripping into the hay stubble at her feet.

"Is it hot enough for you, Mr. Cain?"

"Heck, no," he said, drawling out the words teasing and lazy. "Back where I come from we call this middlin' weather.

We don't say it's hot enough till the water in the creek gets to boilin'."

"Wuh—we don't say it's hot enough," Benjo chimed in, "till the r-rocks start to melt."

Laughing, Rachel looked from the man to the boy and back to the man again. They looked like big-lipped clowns, their mouths and chins washed clean while the rest of their faces were still chalky white with hay dust.

"If you two aren't a pair of a kind," she said.

Cain's eyes crinkled at the corners as he cocked a thumb at the boy. "He's the young one. I'm the one who's wind-broke as an old trail horse."

Noah Weaver tossed the dipper back into the water butt with a splash. His jaw had taken on a tense bulge. "Hard work is good for a man's soul," he said.

Mose rolled his eyes up to the sun-bleached sky. "Da!" he exclaimed with such force that he blew off the sweat dripping from the end of his nose. "It's a haymaking we're at here, not a preaching."

"A preaching or a haymaking," Cain said with an easy smile, "to my way of thinking they're both plumb hard on the back."

Mose started to grin back at him, then tamped it down at the look on his father's face.

"Noah has always built the best haystacks in the valley, haven't you, Noah?" Rachel said. "High and tall and straight."

Noah stared at her. She saw a tightness around his eyes and a hollowness to his face, a sort of bewildered agony. "The righteous man doesn't swell up with pride in his work, he just works." He turned on his heel and started off, saying over his shoulder, "There's still plenty hay that needs stacking sometime before next winter." And the tone in his voice made the boys jump and trot after him.

The outsider lingered behind, though, his gaze following the Plain man's stiff back.

"I'm sorry," Rachel said. "He doesn't mean to always be scolding. He's just . . . being Deacon Noah."

Cain rolled his shoulders in a half shrug. "Aw, he can't rile me so long as I don't let him. I've been ridden with sharper spurs."

The hot wind plucked at her loose cap strings, making them dance. She tossed them out of the way, over her shoulders, then peeled a strand of loose hair off her sticky cheek. She sucked her chapped lower lip into her mouth to wet it; she was thirsty again. And she could feel his eyes on her again, hotter than the summer wind.

"We're having rivels and puddins for dinner," she said. "It's a haymaking tradition. And there's peppermint tea cooling in the creek."

"I ain't asking what rivels and puddins are, in case I don't want to know."

She spun around, laughing at him, with him, just laughing. "Hunh. Once you're done building me a haystack to the moon, Mr. Cain, I expect you'll be hungry enough to eat anything."

She took off for the house at a run, her skirts tossing gaily. But as she crossed the yard and climbed the porch steps, her feet slowed and her smile faded.

Through the open door she could see Fannie rubbing the soft dough of the rivels between her palms and dropping them into a pot of boiling broth. In a fry pan next to her, the fatty pork puddins were crisping and popping in hot lard. A snitz pie that Rachel had baked that morning was cooling on the windowsill, filling the air with the smell of apples and cinnamon spice.

Most times she would have enjoyed the company of another woman in her kitchen, but today Fannie was pushing her nose into the air and pulling her skirts aside every time Rachel came near her.

The broth hissed as Fannie dropped in another batch of rivels, but Rachel lingered on the porch. The furnace-hot sun leached the sky of its blue and gave the mountains a gray sheen, making them appear forged of steel. The hot wind laid a skein of hay dust over the men at their work. From here she could make out nothing but the lean and graceful shape of the outsider, and the flash of dark hair sliding across his shoulders from beneath the slouching brim of his hat. Yet he could have been pressed up hard against her, belly to belly, breast to breast, heart to heart, so close did she feel to him in that moment.

She felt a movement beside her and turned to look into Fannie Weaver's face. And Rachel knew that all she was thinking, all she was feeling, showed on her own.

Fannie folded her arms over her chest, gripping herself hard. The harsh lines at the corners of her mouth pulled deeper. She'd always been a thin woman, but now she looked gaunt and shriveled, like a thing left too long in the sun.

"I know you, Sister Rachel. I've always known you."

Rachel turned away from her, saying nothing.

"You're doing it to him again, to our Noah. You think I don't remember how you already shamed and hurt him once, letting him think things he shouldn't, want things he shouldn't? And you all the while with your eyes and your thoughts dwelling on another man."

"That other man was Ben. My husband. And I could never help what your brother thought and wanted."

"Ha, so you say. But I saw what you did with our Noah the night Gertie died, how you led him into sin."

"I held him, is all," Rachel said, and her soul shivered faintly as if a ghost had touched her. She'd often wondered how her husband had come to hear of that private moment with Noah. Well, now she knew. Fannie Weaver and her spying eyes.

I held him, is all.

Sometimes the heart remembered things better than the head, holding both the hurt and the joy, as if it all had happened only yesterday.

She had come home late that night to find Ben sitting at the table, his hands wrapped around a cold cup of coffee. He faced a day of plowing on the morrow and he should have been in bed and asleep hours before.

His dark eyes had looked up at her, glittering with hurt. But his mouth, his mouth that could kiss her so tenderly, was pulled taut and hard with anger, and his thick black beard bristled with it. So did his words, when he finally spoke.

"And where have you been all this long night, my Rachel?"

"You know I've been with Noah. He's so sore with grief, I—"

"Sore, is he? And did you soothe his soreness then, my Rachel? Soothe him with your sweet body, with your soft mouth." His big and callused farmer's hand slapped down hard on the table. "Did you lie with him?"

"How could you even think it?" she'd shouted back at him. Shouted to hide a surge of guilt that had no logic and no basis, but came anyway to burn her cheeks with a hot flush. "And of him? How could you think it of him?"

He shook his head slowly, heavily, as if the weight of his thoughts was almost more than he could bear. "I know what he's always wanted, *ja*. It's you I've never been sure of."

And she had said, "I held him, is all."

Ben had scraped back from the table then and gone into the bedroom, undressed, crawled between the sheets, and all without another word to her. In the dark silence she had joined him. But she couldn't bear the anger that had crawled into the bed with them, the anger and the mistrust.

She moved over to fill the emptiness in the middle of the bed, curving her body around his, laying her head on his chest. He held himself rigid, but she could hear his heart beating, and she thought what a sweet, comforting sound that was to a woman: the beat of her husband's heart.

"Ben, I love you. Only you."

She'd never said the words before, because it was not the Plain way. A man and wife, they would speak aloud of loving God, never of loving each other. But they did love each other, she and Ben.

She felt his flesh grow warm and melt beneath her, as if she were the flame and he the candle. His arm came around her back and he held her tight. "Promise me that it will always be so," he'd said.

And she had promised.

TO RACHEL THE CLANG of the lead-wether's bell was a joyous song marking the end to a good day.

She drove the herd of ewes and their lambs onto the rough stubble of the newly shorn hay meadow. MacDuff padded slowly back and forth along the rear edges of the flock. He knew his business; a smart herding collie never nagged or drove his sheep, but gently guided. Rachel liked it that nobody, and no dog, could rush sheep. They got where they were going in their own sweet time.

She and MacDuff saw the woollies settled and munching happily. But although she had dishes to wash and a kitchen to scrub down, she stayed in the pasture. She stood with her feet planted firmly in the hay stubble, her hands hanging loosely at her sides, and she let the hot wind blow wild through her.

Slowly, she tipped her head back and let herself be drawn up, up, up into the deep blue of the evening sky, the endless and empty sky.

"A body could get lost up there if she isn't careful."

He stood leaning against the trunk of a jack pine, one booted foot crossed over the other, his hat dangling from his fingers. She stared at him, at his reckless face with its flaring cheekbones, his fierce mouth, his eyes. . . . Those eyes weren't cold, not cold at all.

She looked from his eyes up to the heavens, then back to his eyes again, as if judging which were bluer. "How do you feel when you look at the sky?"

He hooked his hat on a pine branch and walked toward her through the grazing woollies until they were only a handspan apart. He'd just washed up, for the ends of his hair dripped water and he smelled of soap, with a lingering whiff of green hay. His shoulders lined out level and wide, blocking her view of the horizon. His eyes were definitely bluer than the sky.

"Lonesome," he said. "The kind of lonesome that can make you feel good and sad and wild, all at the same time. Almost crazy like, so that you want to howl with the coyotes or climb up on a horse and ride till you get to the edge of the world."

He leaned toward her, although he was being careful

not to touch her. But the words pulsed out of him, soft and deep. He touched her with his words.

"The kind of lonesome that's like a sweet hurting inside you, so that you aren't sure if you should laugh with it, or cry. Because you know it comes from a wanting, a reaching for something you ain't ever gonna have."

She stared up into his face, a face that had somehow become beloved to her, and a wild yearning swelled and cracked open inside her. It was more than love she felt for him. Love she could live with from afar, but not this. She needed him, needed him in her life, and it was a need so elemental, so consuming, it was like needing air to breathe, like—

"Cain! Cain! I w-washed up real good just like you s-said. Oh . . . hey, Mem."

She stepped back and turned to smile at her son as he came running up all breathless with a big grin on his face. A face that shone red with sunburn and a good scrubbing. She wondered what threat or bribe or miracle Johnny Cain had worked to get her son to bathe.

She reached down and pushed her fingers through her son's wet hair. Even the backs of his ears were clean. "You men baled a fine batch of hay this day."

"Benjo's the best hay stacker I've ever had the pleasure to work 'longside of," the outsider said, looking serious.

The boy preened like a jaybird, and Rachel's heart swelled again. "I hear Annabell lowing like she's fit to die," she said. "Don't you think you ought to go milk her and ease her misery?"

Benjo heaved an enormous sigh and said, "Aw, Mem."

He obeyed her, though, and she was alone again with Johnny Cain. But the closeness of before had been lost.

She let her voice go light and teasing, the way she knew

he liked her to be. "So, and just how many hay stackers have you worked with that you're suddenly such an expert?"

"That boy does you proud, Rachel."

"It's you he's aiming to impress," she said. But she flushed, pleased for Benjo's sake, and pleased also that he'd called her by her given name. He was doing it more often now.

Just then one of the lambs took a notion to buck, jumping stiff-legged and sideways, and landing with a loud bleat. He spooked the whole flock into a run, so that they flowed around Rachel and Cain and down the sloping meadow.

They laughed, and their laughter—his mellow and deep, hers light and airy—became a carol of bells. The woollies bleated and *baa*ed, bass and tenor notes. Grasshoppers rasped in the grass along the creek. A killdeer trilled sweetly and a chickadee burbled. The wind roared a song through the tops of the cottonwoods.

"Oh, do you hear it, Johnny! Do you hear the music?"

She whirled to face him in her excitement and caught the look on his face. He stared at her with such fierce intensity that she could almost feel it, like a warm gust of breath on her flesh.

"I hear them, you see, all the sounds the earth makes," she went on, as if he'd said to her, *What music*? "I hear the wind and the creek and all the noises the animals make, the sheep and birds and frogs, I hear them all in my head and it comes together into music. I don't know. I can't explain it, except that I know it's wicked."

A muscle ticked in his cheek. He lowered his head slightly, so that his long thick eyelashes shielded his eyes. "What's wicked about taking the songs of life and making a symphony out of them?"

She turned away from him, suddenly shy. She began to walk toward the house, and he fell into step beside her.

"I know of such a thing as a symphony orchestra," she said. "That is, I've heard it spoken of. Tell me what it sounds like."

"I've never heard one myself. I did go to an opera once in Leadville, Colorado. It seemed mostly just a lot of fat ladies caterwauling." His mouth crooked slightly, not quite forming a smile. "And once, somewhere down in Texas, I heard this phenomenon called a cowboy band. It was mostly a lot of brassy horns. It was led by a man with a baton in his one hand and a six-shooter in his other, I reckon so's he could kill the first man who blew a sour note."

They laughed together again. She felt light-headed, and light-footed. She wanted to lift up her skirts and twirl around and around and around, until she became dizzy and collapsed into a heap in the grass, the way she used to do when she was a little girl.

"Have you ever done any dancing?" she asked him.

"Now, I have indeed been to more than a few fandangos in my time."

Somehow they had stopped walking and were facing each other. The wind fluttered her cap strings. He took one in each hand and pulled them down until they were stretched taut, with his fingers barely brushing her breasts, and yet she felt his touch all the way to her toes.

He surprised her by starting to sing, a lilting song about a girl named Annie Laurie, filling in with la-di-das when he forgot the words, and at some time he had let go of her cap strings to take her hand, and he was now fitting his palm to hers, entwining their fingers, while his other hand had lifted her arm by the wrist and was draping it over his shoulder, and he was sliding his arm around her waist.

And they were dancing.

He twirled her around and around in dipping, sweeping

circles, and his knee came in and out between her thighs, and her skirt wrapped around his legs. She could feel every inch of her own skin, every prickling hair on her arms. She could hear her own breathing, and his.

She clung to him as he turned her faster. Her head fell back and she opened her eyes to the wide blue sky spinning crazily above her while the earth tilted and swayed beneath her floating feet. The dance and the wind snatched away the last of his song, and they were laughing, laughing.

And then suddenly they weren't laughing anymore. Their bodies slowed and drew closer and his mouth came down over hers, pressing her lips, opening them, filling her with his breath, with his heat, with his tongue. She dug her fingers into the hard muscles of his back to hold on, hold on. And they might have been dancing still, for the way the sky spun and the earth tilted.

It lasted forever and ended too soon. His mouth let go of hers, but slowly, slowly, coming back to touch her lips with his once more, and then again.

"I want you, Rachel," he said, his breath washing hot and urgent over her face. "I want to lie with you."

She put her fingers on his mouth. Her heart was fierce with panic, because she needed him so and loved him so, and she was so very weak. "No, we can never," she said, her voice breaking over the words. "You know we can never. Not only is it a terrible sin, but what you would take from me is so much less than what I would end up giving. And what you would give to me can be nothing."

His mouth moved beneath her fingers, but she pressed them harder to his lips.

"There's nothing you can give me," she said, pulling away, letting him go, taking one step backward and then another and another and another, so that they were no longer within touching distance of each other. "Not even if you somehow came to love me, because you are an outsider."

She turned and walked away from him. She kept her back stiff and her head up because she didn't want him to know how hard this was when she needed him and loved him so much.

"You ask too much, Rachel," he shouted after her. "You ask too much."

THAT NIGHT THE WIND blew hot and smelled sweet, of fresh cut hay and sun-baked earth.

The men on horseback pulled up on the north bank of the creek, where they were shielded by the thick willow brakes and cottonwoods. The small logwood farmhouse, the sloped-roofed barn, the squat lambing sheds all looked quiet. Nothing stirred but an empty milk bucket which the wind blew tumbling across the yard.

"You sure you got the grit for this, lad o' mine?"

"I'm less worried about my grit than about your good sense," Quinten Hunter said. "The whole valley's like a tinder box and you've taken a notion in your head to play with fire."

His father's laughter came to him from out of the dark, carried on a gust of tobacco-laden breath. "You don't intend to ease up on me, do you?"

"No, sir."

"But in the end you'll do what I tell you, where I tell you, and how I tell you. Won't you?"

"Yes, sir." Quinten's lips pulled back from his teeth in a hard smile, but the branding iron he carried was heavy in his sweating hand. The Circle H mark glowed fire-red in the dark, like a giant eye.

He made himself think of the grassland they had ridden

through to get here, of how it was grazed down to the roots in places, and cut up by hundreds of sharp and pointed hooves. He remembered the first time he'd ridden over this end of the Miawa. He'd been with his father then, too, only so small he'd been riding a pony instead of a horse. The grass had grown as high as his stirrups that summer.

When Quinten thought of the grassland, of how it had been before the Plain folk had brought their sheep into the valley, the burning brand didn't feel so wrong.

"Let's get it done, then," the Baron said, and sent his horse splashing across the creek and toward the stacks of fresh mown hay.

Quinten spurred his own horse to catch up with his father. Three other Hunter cowhands crossed the creek on their heels. These others had joined up with Quinten and his father shortly after they had left the small campfire they'd built to heat the iron, and Quinten had paid them little mind. The Baron had made it plain that tonight at least he was putting the Circle H brand and all that it stood for into the hand of his breed son.

They rode through a flock of sheep, scattering the bleating animals into broken streams of gray wool. Inside the farmhouse a dog barked. One of the cowhands fired two shots from his six-shooter, and a door slammed shut.

Quinten clamped his legs tighter to his horse, urging the big gelding to go faster. Fear and excitement pulsed through him, and a wild shout surged up his throat, hot and wet, like the thrumming of his blood. He threw back his head and let it loose into the starry, wind-swept sky. The Blackfoot war cry.

Whooping, Quinten put the burning brand to one of the haystacks. The timothy grass was fresh and green and slow to catch. But then spirals of white smoke curled up from the end of the iron, and the hay melted into tongues of orange and red flame.

From out of the night, a gun fired. The cowhand next to Quinten slumped over in his saddle with a soft cry.

"Christ. Ailsa!" the Baron shouted. He pointed his gun toward a sheepherder's wagon which was parked next to the barn, and fired off three quick shots. The two other Circle H men opened fire on the wagon as well.

His father's words had so shocked Quinten that he dropped the branding iron. He twisted around trying to peer through the veil of smoke and flickering light. The cowhand, what he had thought was a cowhand, was sitting up in the saddle again, one hand gripping the other arm.

"Ailsa!" the Baron shouted again.

"Regrettably you must delay the celebration, Fergus," said that snowdrift voice. "I am not yet dead."

"Aw, woman, why are you always saying such things? Quin, what in hell are you doing to set that fire, rubbing two sticks together?"

Quinten bent over his horse's neck, searching for the branding iron. The gun fired again from the sheepherder's wagon, and he heard a bullet kiss the air where a moment before his head had been. He couldn't see the brand, and then he did—a glowing red Circle H in a spilled shaft of hay.

He stretched out his hand for the iron just as the haystack went up in a sheet of flames, spitting sparks, lighting up the night bright as day. And silhouetting them against the horizon like wooden ducks at a shooting gallery.

"Let's get the hell out of here," his father bellowed, but Quinten had already dug the heels of his boots hard into his horse's sides.

They all rode low on their horses' necks back across the creek and through the cottonwoods, firing off random shots.

When they were sure they weren't being pursued, they pulled up their mounts and looked back at the sheep farm. They could see figures with buckets running to and fro between the burning haystack and the creek and a yard pump.

But Quinten could only look at his father's wife. In all the years he had been at the ranch he had never seen her on a horse, and yet she sat the saddle as if born to it. He had never known her to wear anything but silk and taffeta. Now the sleeve of the man's shirt she had on was black and wet with her blood. Her face was alight with a wild and desperate excitement.

He didn't understand what she was doing here, why his father had allowed her to come. Quinten's throat felt thick with what he realized to his shame were tears of jealousy.

"I left our branding iron back there, Pa," he said, his eyes still on Ailsa.

The Baron pulled his horse's head around, toward home. "Don't fret about it."

The two other cowhands followed him, but Ailsa Hunter lingered, and so did Quinten. She took off the man's hat she was wearing, and her hair fell thick and heavy over her shoulders. He had never seen her hair down before. It shimmered in the starlit night.

Quinten brought his horse closer and leaned toward her. He was compelled to touch her, although in the end his courage failed him. He pulled his hand back and gripped the pommel of his own saddle instead.

The word tore out of him, heavy with years of uncertainties and fears, and desperate longings. "Why?"

She looked at him. A glaze had come over her eyes, like a film of ice. And then, although he hadn't been able to touch her, she touched him. For the first time in all his memory, she touched him.

She laid the tips of her fingers against his mouth. "What

a poor fool of a boy you are," she said. "Shouldn't you be asking that question of yourself?"

"THE DEVIL SHOULD BE well pleased with his work on this night."

Rachel pulled her gaze away from the blackened, smoldering stack of hay that Noah had built so high and tall and straight for her. She looked at him, her good neighbor and friend. He had seen the fire from his farm and ridden over to help put it out. Now his long beard was singed, his face streaked with soot, his eyes red rimmed and watering from the smoke.

She lifted the Circle H branding iron that she held awkwardly in her hand. "It wasn't the Devil," she said.

He shook his head, his mouth set stubborn. "This happened because the outsider killed that stock inspector."

She turned away from him and threw the branding iron into some willow brakes. The outsider, along with her son and Noah's boy, Mose, were soaking blankets and gunnysacks in the creek and laying them over the smoldering mound of hay to prevent the wind from fanning an ember back into life or stray sparks from setting more fires.

"Perhaps you're right," she said. Her eyes stung. Her throat was so raw and gritty it hurt to swallow. "Perhaps if Mr. Cain hadn't provoked them, they would've set fire to your haystacks instead."

Noah's big rough hand grabbed her arm. "Send him away, Rachel. For the sake of your immortal soul, send him away."

"No."

He let go of her, although she hadn't tried to pull away. His gaze searched her face, then went slowly over the rest of her. She had run out of the house to fight the fire barefoot, wearing only her nightrail. She had on her night cap, but most of her hair had fallen out from underneath it. She knew she should feel shame to stand before him with her hair uncovered, but all she felt was tired.

Noah made a strangled sound deep in his throat. "You've said you'll be marrying me come the mating season. But who is the woman I'll be taking as my wife?"

The outsider had left the boys and was coming toward her. Noah's gaze flickered to him, then back to her.

"Rachel," he said, but then he turned and strode away.

The outsider's face was so blackened by the smoke, all she could make out of his features was the white glint of his eyes reflecting the rising sun. He too was barefoot and he wore his Plain man's broadfalls with no shirt. But his gun was strapped around his hips.

When the men on horseback had come riding out of the night, howling louder than the hot wind, she and Benjo had huddled against the wall, out of the way of the windows, and she had heard the outsider firing back at them from the sheepherder's wagon. It was not the Plain way to fight, to shoot guns at your enemies. But she couldn't help wondering if those Hunter men would have managed to put their burning brand to all of her haystacks instead of just the one, if Johnny Cain hadn't been here to shoot his gun.

They could survive the loss of one stack. If they ran short, Noah and her brothers and others in the church would share their own. It was hard to think of winter, though, when the wind still blew hot and the sun came up bright and searing onto another summer's morning. But the wind would blow cold again soon enough, and the sun would lose its heat, and this winter would have been a bad one for her and her sheep without all her hay.

If the outsider hadn't been here to shoot his gun.

He stopped in front of her. His naked chest was streaked with soot and sweat, and marked with red blisters from flying sparks and embers.

He searched her face just as Noah had done. "This time I'm killing them for you," he said.

She closed her eyes; she was so tired. And she felt that terrible burning emptiness in her belly, the need to make them pay for what they had done. She thought of how all she had to do was keep quiet and let JohnnyCain, mankiller, do what he wanted.

She exhaled a deep, painful breath. "You gave me your promise you wouldn't. It was understood between us when you said you would stay."

"And I've told you before: you ask too much."

She couldn't meet his eyes. She pressed her hands flat against her belly, but the burning emptiness didn't go away. "What you are thinking, what you're wanting, would destroy my soul. And you say I ask too much."

18

JOHNNY CAIN STOOD EASY, feet spread and hands hanging loose at his sides. The slouching brim of his Plain hat shaded his eyes from the glare of the midday sun. A soft smile played at his mouth.

As Benjo watched, the gun suddenly seemed to leap into

Cain's hand, spitting fire. The six bottles lined up along the top rail of the Yoders' south pasture fence exploded in quick bursts, and shards of glass fell, glittering, into the grass.

"You didn't miss a one!" Benjo exclaimed, so excited at this display of crack shooting that he forgot to stutter.

The outsider swung around, his eyes glowing and wild, like the coyote's. Skeins of gunsmoke drifted through the air.

He slipped his Colt back into its open-topped holster. "It's easy not to miss when the bottles don't shoot back at you," he said.

Benjo hesitated a moment, but then he approached Johnny Cain, slowly. He carried a string of black-speckled trout in one hand and a hickory pole in the other. A wicker creel, slung over one shoulder, bounced against his hip. His brogans made the sun-seared hay stubble crackle. The loud popping blasts of the gunfire had seemed for a moment to silence the earth, but now the insects that lived in the grass resumed their dry song.

It was so hot that the thick air shimmered in waves before Benjo's eyes, one of which was swollen nearly shut. Sweat dripped off the shaggy bangs of his hair, stinging the cut that split open his eyebrow. His lips felt thick and pulpy.

The outsider was snatching his six-shooter from its holster and releasing the hammer onto an empty chamber with a loud click, over and over, snatch and click, snatch and click, so fast Benjo couldn't see the individual components of the motion, only the end result of the gun barrel pointing level at the fence where the bottles used to be. And, every time, that fateful click of the hammer striking steel.

His mother had forbidden Benjo to be anywhere near the man while he practiced his gunplay. She'd tried to forbid Cain to do it in the first place and he'd answered her with a *no*, a *no* that offered no excuses or explanations or apologies. So now Benjo figured the outsider's stern face and grown-up lecture about bottles not shooting back was only his way of making up to Mem for that flat-out *no* he'd given to her.

"On the other hand," the outsider went on as if there'd been no pause in the conversation, "it looks like them trout must've put up one heck of a fight."

"Huh?" Benjo jerked the string of black-speckled trout up into the air as if he'd suddenly forgotten he had them. He flushed, and words piled up like a dam of stones in his throat. The outsider said nothing more, only looked at him. Ashamed, Benjo's gaze dropped to the domed toes of his brogans.

"Come here." Cain's hand fell on his head, propelling him toward the creek.

Benjo sat on a flat-topped rock. He slid the creel off his shoulder and wedged his hickory pole into the elbow of a chokecherry branch. The outsider squatted on his haunches on the gravelly bank. He took off the flashy blue bandanna he'd taken to wearing lately tied around the neck of his Plain shirt. He soaked the bandanna in the lazily running water, wrung it out, folded it into a pad, and handed it to Benjo.

"Hold this to your mouth. You're bleeding onto your shirt."

Benjo glanced down and saw that his shirt looked like he'd dribbled chokecherry jam all over it. He took the wet bandanna and pressed it gingerly to his tender lips.

Cain looped the string of trout around an outcropping of rock so that it would dangle into the creek and stay cool. Benjo waited for the man to ask how his face came to look like a side of butchered beef, but he said nothing more. Cain was leaving it up to him to tell what had happened, or not.

It was cooler here by the creek, shaded by a thick stand

of lofty cottonwoods and yellow pines, but Benjo thought the sun must have been baking the rock he sat on not so long ago, because it burned right through the seat of his broadfalls. He squirmed, wincing at the bruises a pair of pointed-toed boots had planted on his rump.

He cast a covert look at the outsider, who had sat down himself on a beaver-chewed log, hooking his elbows around his bent, widespread knees. He had picked a stalk of monkeyflowers and was twirling it between his fingers.

"Muh . . . muh . . . muh— . . ." Benjo took a deep breath. "My hat!" he spat out.

"I noticed it has gone missing" was all Cain said.

The muscles in Benjo's throat clenched and spasmed. Tears of frustration burned his eyes, but he kept them tamped down. It took him a long time to get it out, what with the way shame and fear acted like a snakebite to his tongue, swelling it up so thick it tangled over every word.

The McIver twins had come upon him fishing down by Blackie's Pond. They'd snatched his hat and gone running off with it. Only this time they didn't make him say pretty please to get it back. They'd filled it full of stones and sent it to the bottom of the pond, and then they'd beat him up proper and for no reason that he could tell, except maybe pure meanness.

"And now," Benjo finished up on a rush of spent breath, "whuh—when Mem f-finds out I lost another hat, she's g-gonna be muh—mad enough to chew nails."

"You could always tell her the truth of how you 'lost' it."

"Wuh . . . would you t-tell her if you were me?"

The outsider plucked the red petals off one of the flowers while he considered this. He raised his head, his eyes squinting against the glare of the sun on water. "Probably not."

Benjo sighed. It wasn't a man's way to go around making

excuses or explanations or apologies—his da had taught him that. He thought of his da, and of that time his da had beaten that Hunter cowboy bloody for tripping up Mem. And of how his da had later said there were some indignities a man just shouldn't have to suffer.

It took Benjo an especially long time to get these next words out because they were so important to him. "Wuh . . . would you tuh—tuh—tuh—t-teach! . . . T-teach m-me how to f-fight?"

The outsider's fist closed over the last monkeyflower, crushing it. He opened his hand, letting the bruised petals fall into the creek. "I didn't think fighting was allowed on the straight and narrow path."

Benjo swallowed hard. It was right what Cain said, about the Plain and narrow way, and not succumbing to the sins of violence and anger and hating your enemy. But he just kept thinking that if he stood up to the McIver twins once, if he struck back with even a single blow, then maybe they would leave him alone once and for all.

The outsider nodded slowly, as if he'd managed to hear Benjo's thoughts. "I reckon fighting back does help sometimes. Other times it only gets you a worse beating." His gaze shifted to the sling that hung out the waistband of Benjo's broadfalls. "I would think a fella who's as handy as you are with that sling wouldn't have to take a lot of gaff from the other boys."

"Mem m-made me pruh—promise n-never to use it in anger. I'm only suh—supposed to use it to hunt f-food wuh . . . wuh . . . wuh . . ." *We eat.* He flushed hot to think of the lie he was telling, of the lie he'd been living. All those rabbits and squirrels and rodents he'd killed for the coyote and her pups, they sure didn't count as food for the Yoder table. But the coyote was gone now. She was gone.

"But she didn't make you promise not to fight with your fists?"

It took a moment for Benjo to catch up to the outsider's thoughts. "She didn't thuh . . . think of it," he finally blurted.

He stood up and held out his hand the way the outsider had done with him once, and this time he barely stuttered at all. "You said we were p-partners, that we watched each other's backs. Partners t-teach each other things, too, like how to f-fight."

A tight look came over Cain's mouth and eyes, as if he were suffering a hurt somewhere. But he took Benjo's hand and gave it a good shake.

"She sure is not gonna be happy with me for doing this, though," he said.

Grinning, Benjo shrugged off that worry. "She w-won't see us. When you pruh—practice with your gun, she always stuh—stays in the house."

RACHEL COULDN'T IMAGINE what they were about. At first she thought they were dancing, and the silliness of it made her smile.

Until Benjo slammed his fist into the outsider's stomach.

She covered the last few feet at a run, stumbling over the rough hay stubble. The outsider must have seen her coming, but he didn't so much as flicker an eye in her direction.

"You're starting to pull back on your punch the instant it lands, boy," he said. "You got to follow through with it. Think of my belly here as a McIver face and smack his freckles right on through the back of his head."

Benjo cocked his arm for another blow. Rachel grabbed his wrist and whipped him around—and saw his face.

"What devil has done this to you?" she cried. For a moment she thought it was the outsider, but then she made better sense of what she'd just seen and heard.

Her hand hovered over her son's bruised eye, afraid to touch him. "Oh, my poor *bobbli.* Who did this?"

"Nuh—nobody. I f-fell."

"Benjo Yoder, don't you lie to me. Please don't you lie to me."

His gaze darted once to the outsider, then his chin set at a stubborn tilt. He backed up a step, and she realized he was about to bolt. She made a grab for him but he was too quick, running off along the creek in the opposite direction from home.

"Let him go for now," Cain said. "He's trying hard to grow up and learn how to fight his own battles, and you shame him when you make a fuss like that."

"I'm not making a fuss. My son is beaten bloody, and you say I'm . . ." She pressed her fist to her mouth. She closed her eyes and saw an image of her son, her *Plain* son, punching his fist into the outsider's stomach. She spun around to him, anger burning so hot and raw in her that she could only choke over the words she wanted to fling at his head.

He hooked his thumbs in his gunbelt and cocked one hip. His mouth pulled into a wry grimace. "So, you want me to go cut you a willow switch now," he said, "or wait till you're done scolding me?"

"Don't make a joke of it. Not this."

"You got to allow—"

"No, I will not allow it, Mr. Cain. I will not allow you to teach my son how to push his fist through another's face."

"One thing I was trying to do was save wear and tear on his own nose."

"While putting his soul in jeopardy."

"Look, right now your boy's having himself a little tussle

with life. He already knows and understands your way. So he's asked me to show him my way—"

"The ways of violence!"

"Ways he's *seen,* Rachel. And been on the hurting end of, to judge by the look of him. Ways he can't help seeing, no matter how much you and your people try to shelter him. Maybe you ought to let him make his own choices as to what sort of man he wants to grow into?"

She looked at his revolver, hanging heavy at his hip and snug along his thigh, looking as if it belonged there the way his hand belonged at the end of his wrist. "Like you've made your choices."

His eyes held hers for a moment. Then he slid the gleaming Colt from its holster, snapped open the gate, and began feeding cartridges into the chambers, one by one.

She averted her gaze from the sight of that hand loading a gun, and for the first time she noticed the shattered green bottle glass littering the ground beneath the fence. He'd been teaching her son how to fight with his fists. He could have been showing Benjo how to shoot, as well. To shoot and to kill.

He snapped the gate closed. "What did you come down here for anyway?" he said.

"Benjo. He was—"

He shook his head slowly. "Uh uh, Rachel. You didn't know about your son getting beat up on by those other boys until you got down here. You've been listening to me practice my shooting for weeks now, and you've been wanting to come and not wanting to come." His finger moved gently, lovingly over the trigger guard, but his eyes were locked with hers. "Because it excites you, doesn't it?"

Her breath left her in a gasp. "No!"

Casually he stretched out his arm, pointing the gun barrel slightly downward.

She didn't see the battered tin plate lying in the grass until he struck it with the first shot. It leaped into the air, ringing like a dinner triangle, only to be struck by the next bullet, and the next and the next and the next, ringing, ringing, ringing. He made that plate dance, and she couldn't imagine how he did it, how his eyes could follow that flash of tin so fast, to strike it again and again, five times in all, before it at last clattered to the ground.

He stood there with his arm outstretched, the gun wedded to his hand and his eyes on fire with an unholy delight. She stared at him repelled—and enthralled. Caught up in his wild and ringing power.

She breathed, ran her tongue over her dry lips. "You're right-handed," she finally said, surprised her words sounded so everyday, as if she were discussing the sheep or what she was going to fix for supper. "You managed so fine with your left hand while you were injured, I thought—"

"I've taught myself to manage fine with either hand."

"To kill with either hand."

"That most especially."

His smile was cold, but something terrible flared in the depths of his eyes, as though the shutters there had cracked open an instant to reveal the passion that lived inside him—a passion stark and black, and infused with the most frightening pain.

She leaned forward, her voice softening. "It's possible to change, Johnny. With prayer and effort and the help of God's holy grace. Oh, I'm not saying it won't be hard—"

He grabbed her arm, his fingers biting deep, hauling her roughly up against him. With his other hand, he brought his revolver up to her face and pressed the barrel against her cheek.

"Rachel, darlin'," he said. "Who are you fooling?" He pressed the barrel harder into the soft flesh of her cheek, forcing her mouth to pucker. He wet her lips with his tongue. "You want to change me, Rachel, to reform me and make me God-fearing . . . but only so's your conscience won't put up a howl when you finally take me into your bed."

He took her mouth, then, in a kiss that was both sweet and brutal, and she let him. When he was done he released her. He dropped the hand with the gun to his waist and fired the sixth bullet, making the tin plate dance one last time.

RACHEL LAID HER FOREHEAD against the cow's warm broad belly. Her throat felt so raw and hot her sigh hurt coming out. But it hurt even more to hold it in.

She hiked up her skirts, pulled the tin milking pail between her legs, and leaned forward, balancing easily on the one-legged milking stool. The cow's hairy udder bag, heavy with milk, swayed as she washed it. The milking actually was Benjo's chore, but he hadn't come home since he'd run off. When he did, she would bathe his cuts with witch hazel and rub a raw potato on his bruises, but she knew she would get precious few confidences in return. He'd confided his trouble to the outsider, though, and it hurt to think of that.

She pulled and squeezed on the cow's pink teats, and the milk hit the bucket with a sweet ringing. Cain had said her boy was trying hard to grow and learn how to fight his own battles and she had shamed him with her fussing. She wondered if Ben, confronted with the sight of their son's bruised and bloody face, would have done the same as the outsider and taught Benjo how to fight back. How to fight his own battles.

It wasn't the Plain way, though.

And it wasn't the Plain way to kiss as she and the outsider had kissed. Two people not married, kissing with their open mouths and tongues.

She'd always known he was tainted—what he'd seen, done, how he'd lived and sinned. But she could only think of that with her head, not with her heart. Not down deep where it really mattered. She couldn't think of him in terms of right and wrong anymore, or of good and evil. At some time during the long hot spring, her soul had come unstrung.

"Rachel."

She looked up, twisting half around on the milking stool. He stood within the door frame of the stall, his feet spread slightly, his hands hanging loose at his sides, the way he did just before he fired his six-shooter. Rafter shadows fell in bars across his face.

"I'm sorry what I did to you out there," he said.

"Don't you dare tell me you're leaving."

"I'm hurting you, goddammit."

"Don't blaspheme; it's wicked. And you're not hurting me. Leastways, no more than I deserve to be hurt."

His throat clenched around a harsh laugh. "All right, maybe I'm not being too kind to myself either. But no woman deserves me, especially not a woman like you."

The cow chose that moment to slap her in the side of the head with a manure-caked tail, and Rachel went back to her milking. Hunh. A woman like her, with stinky green cow poop likely smeared now on her prayer cap and cheek. It made her want to laugh, probably because she was so close to crying.

"You're sounding like Benjo again, feeling sorry for yourself for having to bear the fruit of your sinning when you've only yourself to blame. And whether I deserve you or not bears no relation to whether you are leaving or staying. You said you'd stay and work my farm until the mating season, so I'm holding you to your word."

"Jesus God Almighty, save me. Rachel, you know what I want from you. I don't know how to make it any plainer."

Oh, she knew what he wanted all right, and she wanted it as well. But she also knew how to wage that particular battle. "We are two very strong people, Mr. Cain, who can and shall resist temptation. Salvation has always required suffering and sacrifice. God doesn't expect us to let Him do it all."

He stared at her hard awhile longer, and then he laughed, a soft, easy laugh of genuine amusement. "That boy of yours," he said, "he sure did ask the wrong person to teach him how to fight."

LATER THAT EVENING Moses Weaver stood among the wooden markers and decaying boots of the Miawa City cemetery, trying to screw up the courage to go screw his first woman.

The cemetery was as close as he'd been able to bring himself yet to the Red House. Mose figured he might as well get used to the cemetery anyway, since this was likely where he would be ending up real soon. His father would kill him for what he was about to do, and then, since he would have died unsaved, he would be planted for eternity among outsiders, here in this Godforsaken place.

And it would all be worth it, he thought, if he could have but a few moments of heaven on earth between the soft white thighs of Miss Marilee.

But before he got himself inside of Miss Marilee, first he had to get himself through the front door. He'd ridden to town on an old knock-kneed plow mule. But he hadn't wanted to arrive looking any more the bumpkin Plain boy than he could help, so he'd stopped at the cemetery. He'd looped the mule's halter reins around the trunk of a quaking aspen, intending to walk on over to the house of sin. The ground had saved up most of the day's blistering heat and was now releasing it back into the night air. He was sweating rivers beneath his flashy mail-order clothes.

He was sweating oceans by the time he climbed the steps of the Red House's broad verandah. The famous locomotive lantern was lit, casting a red glow onto the warped floorboards. The lantern swayed in the wind and its red light flickered in the half-moon window above the door, making Mose think of the flames of hell.

He gave the door a timid rap and was surprised when it opened almost immediately. He found himself staring down into the slit-eyed face of a man as shriveled as a seed husk. Mose had never seen an Oriental before, but he'd heard they had one working at the Red House. He wondered if it was true what they said about Orientals having yellow skin. In the puddle of red light cast by the locomotive lantern he couldn't tell.

He realized he was staring and he flushed, jerking his gaze away. He slapped the hat off his head. "I'm here to see Miss Marilee."

The front top of the man's head was bald, but a long black braid swung over his shoulder as he bowed. He said something in a scratchy voice that Mose couldn't understand. He hoped it was the Chinese for "come right on in," because that was what he did.

He felt awkward and stumble-footed standing on the

worn carpet of the hallway. The Oriental waved at a curtain of blue glass beads and squawked more Chinese. A string of brass bells suddenly appeared in the little man's clawlike hands. He rang them with vigor, then shuffled off on silk slippers into the shadows.

Mose passed through the beads, clicking and clacking, and entered a room stuffed from floor to fanlight with things: plaster busts and glass vases, brass spittoons and lacquered boxes, and other things he couldn't have put a name to. Even the furniture was all doodadded up, with tidies on the chairs and sofas and Arab scarves draping every conceivable flat surface.

His gaze drifted from a hurdy-gurdy with yellow stars and a moon painted on it, to the china pug on the hearth, to a pair of dragon candlesticks, and stopped dead at the huge gilt-framed painting that filled one wall, of a man apparently being ravished by three naked nymphs. He stared at it, his mouth agape. He supposed this was what the Bible meant when it said: "He goeth after her straightway, as an ox to the slaughter."

Beneath the painting, a small sign in black letters read:

SATISFACTION GUARANTEED,
OR SECOND TOKEN GIVEN FREE.

He thought at first the room was empty—of human habitation, that is. But then something stirred over by the nickel-plated parlor stove. The something was a cowpuncher, to judge by the pointed-toed boots and dusty Stetson, a cowpuncher sitting stiffly on a ladder-back chair. The stove wasn't lit on such a hot night, but Mose thought it sure probably drew a crowd come winter.

He settled himself on a plush purple sofa and saw right away why the cowpuncher had chosen the chair. The sofa's feather cushions closed around him until he felt in danger of being smothered. He rested his hat on his knee and tried not to fidget.

He drew in a deep breath and nearly gagged over the foul stink emanating from a nearby china cuspidor. He moved down to the other end of the sofa; the cushions billowed up to his armpits.

The cowpuncher didn't look any more comfortable than Mose felt. The man kept tugging at his creased and yellowed celluloid collar, stretching out his neck. It looked as though he'd scraped himself shaving, because he sported a mark under his jaw like a strawberry stain. The cowboy gave his neck another stretch, took a twist of chewing tobacco out of his pocket, and gnawed off a piece. His gaze floated up to the ceiling, where a fan was slowly going around and around in the still hot air.

The beaded curtain was slapped open with a loud clatter. A woman came into the room, and Mose felt his jaw come unhinged.

She was the fattest woman he'd ever seen, doughy and white as a dumpling. A three-hundred-pound dumpling. She was also the most woman he'd ever seen, for she had on nothing but a corset and a pair of drawers. She headed right for him, and Mose's heart sank into his belly.

"Well, hey there, handsome," she cooed. She leaned over him until his nose nearly disappeared into the chasm between her two mountainous breasts. "Were you waitin' for me, sugar?"

"I'm here to visit with Miss Marilee," he said, and he could have sworn the words echoed back at him from the valley of her bosom. Judas Iscariot! He could see her nipples, big as chestnuts.

The woman took a floor-shuddering step back to plant a

dimpled fist on her ample hip. "Marilee, Marilee. Ever'one always asks for Marilee. What's she got that I ain't?"

"It's what she's got less of, you old cow."

The woman who followed that remark into the room was skinny—so skinny she would've had to walk twice to make a shadow. At least she had all her clothes on, although they weren't much to crow about. Just a simple black skirt and bodice, with long cuffed sleeves and a high neck. Not too different from what Plain women wore. She went over to the hurdy-gurdy and began to crank the handle, banging out a tune so loud it made Mose's ears jangle.

The mostly naked, fleshy woman went over to the cowboy. They exchanged a few words and then left the parlor together, the cowboy still trying to stretch his neck out of his tight collar. The spindling woman continued to work the hurdy-gurdy crank.

Mose took another gander around the room. On second look he was able to see the flaws beneath all the gimcracks and foofaraws. The cabbage rose wallpaper was spotted and stained by damp, the Turkey carpet moth-eaten and faded, the plaster crumbling. There was a tainted smell to the place that was more than just tobacco slop and wood rot. The stink of sin, he supposed.

He heard a knock at the door, footsteps, and a voice rough as a whetstone bellowing a greeting. The Oriental's brass bells rang, and the skinny woman stopped her hurdy-gurdy cranking. The bead curtain clicked and clacked open and Mose's heart, which had been lying heavy but quiet in his belly, suddenly thrust up into his throat and nearly choked him.

Fergus Hunter strolled into the room.

The cattleman's gaze flickered over Mose and dismissed him. He exchanged howdies with the skinny woman, who left the hurdy-gurdy to pour him a glass of whiskey from a decanter that sat on a tarnished silver tray on top of a paisley shawl-draped table.

The Baron finished off the whiskey with one flex of his elbow. He took a cigar out of his vest pocket, struck a match on the silver tray, lit up, and tossed the spent lucifer into the dirt that littered the stove grate. He sucked smoke deep into his chest, his cheeks hollowing.

Fergus Hunter's face had always been all sharp bones, but now it was as if the hot sun that parched the countryside had melted the last of the flesh off it. He was dressed fine, though, in a dark suit, white brocade vest, and gray silk tie with a pearl stickpin. The gaslight glinted off his thick gold watch chain, which was hung with many seals and a crystal fob.

The beads clicked and clacked again, and a young man entered the parlor. Mose recognized him as the Baron's son, who they said wasn't his legitimate son at all but only his get by a Blackfoot squaw.

"Why, good evening, young Mr. Hunter," the skinny woman said with a false smile. She had teeth like a squirrel's.

"I decided to let my boy loose on the town tonight," the cattleman boomed in his rough voice. "You randy young bucks get quarrelsome when you aren't allowed your weekly spree, isn't that right, Quin?"

Two red spots the size of dollars appeared beneath the boy's thin, sharp cheekbones. He seemed embarrassed by his father, and Mose could sympathize with that. His own father managed to dream up new ways to mortify him every day of the week.

Mose saw that the Baron had now returned his attention to him and was giving him a slow once-over, with hard eyes. Mose swallowed and burrowed further into the soft purple cushions. He shifted his gaze to a red-lipped plaster cupid that hovered on a stone pedestal by the window.

"Why, I didn't think you pious Plain boys ever succumbed to the calico fever," the Baron said, shaking his head in mock surprise. He laughed, a short, sharp laugh. But then a genuine smile stretched his wide mouth as the beads clacked open again. "Well, now, if it isn't the best little whore in all the Miawa."

Mose snatched his hat off his knee and pumped his arms, propelling himself out of the sofa and onto his feet. Marilee entered the parlor on a waft of honeysuckle toilet water and wearing a wispy silk wrapper the scarlet of hellfire. The wrapper hung open down the middle to show off frilly-legged drawers, black stockings with pink garters, and a corset decorated with black lace. Another girl followed after her, a girl with hair the brassiest yellow Mose had ever seen.

The Baron stuck his cigar in his mouth and smacked his palms together. "Come here, Marilee m'girl. Let's you and me take a walk upstairs." Grinning around the cigar between his teeth, he tried to slide his arm around Marilee's waist.

She eluded him, although she gave his cheek a pat as she drifted by. "You can just wait your turn, Fergus Hunter." She turned a smile that was as bright as new paint onto Mose. "I see I got me a special caller tonight."

The Baron's face colored, but he smiled amicably enough. "Sure, then, Marilee. You go and take care of the woolly puncher, first. I'll bide my time here till you're done." He tugged at his watch chain and slid a gold hunter out of his vest pocket. "I doubt that one'll last for longer than a ten-second spine tingle."

"Which leaves me with this one." The brassy-haired girl sidled up to the Hunter boy. She rubbed her near naked bosom up against his arm and blinked eyelashes at him that looked coated with wet soot. "I hear tell his ma wore moccasins." She pushed vermilion painted lips into an exaggerated moue. "Oooh, maybe we'll all be scalped in our beds."

The skinny woman snorted a laugh. "At least in your case, Jewel, he'll be able to tell your head from your pussy, since one's yellow and the other ain't."

Everyone laughed at that, except for the Hunter boy. A flush stained his hawk face again, and his mouth tightened at the corners.

Marilee slipped her arm through Mose's and pulled him out into the hallway, toward a spooled banister staircase. The bead curtain swayed and clicked shut behind them.

"Don't pay them all no mind," Marilee said. Mose had forgotten how her upper lip caught on that crooked tooth when she smiled. He liked her smile, although it stirred feelings in him that were definitely wicked.

The skinny woman came through the curtain, gave Marilee a sharp look, then disappeared down the hall to the back of the house.

"Doesn't anyone feed that woman?" Mose said, but softly, because he didn't want the poor thing to overhear and get her feelings hurt. She probably didn't get many gentleman callers, not like Marilee did.

Marilee's smile was gone, and a crease had appeared between her pale eyebrows. "Feed who? Oh, you mean Jugs." She gripped his sleeve tighter and edged him over toward the stairs. "Honey, she could dine on chocolate cream cakes and champagne every night if she wanted to. She's the mother."

He craned his head for another look at the skinny woman, and nearly tripped over a shell umbrella stand. That scarecrow was this exquisite girl's mother? He must have misunderstood. "Why do you call her Jugs?"

" 'Cause she ain't got tits enough to fill a pair of thimbles."

Mose tried to puzzle that one out and couldn't.

He followed Marilee up the stairs. There was a cherub on the newel post, with a candle stuck in the dimple of his bottom. A fringed oil lamp hung from the ceiling on a long brass chain. It creaked and swayed even though the air was hot and still. But then someone was banging hard on the wall above, grunting and groaning with the effort of it.

Marilee mounted the stairs slowly, her hips rocking from side to side. Mose felt his heart quake, his belly tremble. Beneath the straining fly buttons of his worldly checked trousers, he was as iron-hard and rigid as a plow.

She startled him by suddenly whipping around and snapping her fingers beneath his nose. "Thunderation, where's my head tonight? I nearly forgot to collect your token."

"Huh?"

She rolled her eyes toward the pressed tin ceiling. "I told you not to come payin' me no calls without your three dollars."

He fumbled for the coins in his vest pocket. "I brought it. I just didn't know when was the proper time to give it to you—"

She cast a furtive look around, lowering her voice to a whisper. "You can give it over now." Her fingers curled around the dollars, making a fist, but she flashed that bright, crooked-toothed smile at him. "I'm goin' to show you such a time, Mr. Moses Weaver. You watch and see if I don't have you singin' hallelujahs afore I'm done."

Just then the banging, groaning, and grunting stopped. There was an instant of utter silence, followed by a great trumpeting bellow, like a bull moose in rut. Mose nearly jumped out of his skin, but Marilee continued on up the stairs as if it hadn't happened.

She paused before a half-open door and turned to him,

rubbing her palm over the satin-piped lapel of his worldly coat. She leaned into him, took his hand, put it between her legs, and pressed herself up against his palm so hard he could feel her crinkly woman's hair through her silky thin drawers.

"You did take a bath, didn't you, Moses? 'Cause you know I can't abide the smell of sheep."

Lord Jesus God in heaven. She felt sinful. She felt wonderful. He tried to tell her that he'd scrubbed himself down proper right before he came, that he'd even washed under his union suit. But he was having too much trouble simply breathing. She stirred again beneath his hand. A deep groan burned up his chest like a belch.

Her fingers closed around his coat, pulling him into the room. Unlike the parlor downstairs, this was furnished simple. Just a small two-drawer dresser with a blue enameled pitcher and wash basin on top of it, and a bedside table with a smoking white glass oil lamp. The bedstead was iron, rusting through in places. The tick looked too lumpy to be filled with feathers. It was probably stuffed with prairie grass, like his own bed at home.

She took the hat from his hand and set it on the table next to the oil lamp. She turned over an egg timer. Beside the egg timer was a bowl of butter, which was melting in the thick heat. Mose figured the egg timer and the butter had to have some relevancy to what was about to happen, but he couldn't imagine what. His gaze roamed over the roses and ribbons that were climbing the wallpaper. He blinked, feeling dizzy. The room smelled of the twist of dried sweetgrass burning in a tin saucer. But there was another smell, moist and musky, underneath. The way his sheets smelled after a night of wicked dreams.

He realized she was looking at him, smiling. "What?"

"Do you know that when you get excited, those handsome brown eyes of yours light up till they shine like sunstruck whiskey?"

Mose didn't know about his eyes shining like whiskey, but he liked hearing she thought them handsome. It made his chest swell.

He reached for her, the silky scarlet wrapper shifting and whispering beneath his hands. Her own hands moved over his chest, as if seeking to mold the shape and feel of him. "You're built strong, Moses Weaver. I like that in a man."

He gathered her closer to him, but gently, as if he were trying to embrace a cloud. He was suddenly afraid of his own strength, afraid that he might hurt her. He lowered his head and brushed his lips over hers.

She turned her face aside. "No, don't. I don't kiss."

Mose had a hard time hiding his disappointment; he had wanted to rub his tongue over that crooked tooth. Still, he understood. "Kissing is sure enough a terrible sin," he said.

She giggled and poked him lightly on the chest. "Lord, the notions you all have."

Then her hands fell to his waist and somehow she got his buttons open, and his cock was cradled in her palm, and he heaved a chest-shuddering sigh. "My oh my," she crooned. "Will you look at that?"

Mose looked. It almost didn't feel like a part of him. It certainly didn't look like a part of him. He knew he ought to feel shame, for this lust that was a pain and a fire in him. But what he really felt like doing was crowing louder than a two-headed rooster.

Her fingers closed around him. "Judas!" he hissed through clenched teeth. He shuddered again, hard. "I've never . . . Oh, Judas, Judas . . ."

"I know, dearie." She pressed her face into the crook of

his neck, her hot breath bathing him, while her hand was busy gripping his cock, stroking it. "And it'll be real good, too," she said. "So good. Just you wait."

She fell back onto the bed, bringing him with her. The tick rustled like wind-stirred summer grass beneath them. He rubbed his face in her hair, burying his nose deep into the sweet honeysuckle softness of it. She tangled her fingers in his own hair, pulling his head up. "Hey, careful now. You'll mess me all up."

He almost tried to kiss her again, but then he remembered that she thought it a sin. So he touched her breast instead, pushing his fingers beneath the stiff jean of her corset. She moaned and squirmed beneath him. A funny strangling sound erupted from his throat. He ground into her, stabbing with his cock up between her legs, searching with his fingers for the slit in her drawers, searching, wanting desperately, desperately to push himself into the slit in her. She was saying something else now, something about slowing down, but all he could hear was the rush of his own panting breaths and the pulsing of the blood in his ears.

In the seconds that followed, he discovered two things: what the butter was for, and what the inside of a woman felt like. All hot and wet and grasping, and the closest thing there was to heaven on this earth.

HE COLLAPSED ON TOP of her, his skin wet and slippery beneath his clothes, all his muscles feeling heavy and battered.

She pushed against his chest with the butts of her hands. "That was wonderful, honey. But you're a big, heavy boy and you're crushin' me."

He flung himself off her onto his back, his chest pumping hard. He gasped, blinked his sweat-stung eyes, and gasped again. After a long while, the ceiling came into view.

"Those are bullet holes up there," he said.

She had rolled away from him to sit up. "Huh?" She tilted her head back to see what he was looking at. "Oh, some fool one night, he kept thinkin' he was hearin' a fly, and so he tried to kill it."

A great roll of laughter pushed up from Mose's chest. He opened his mouth and let the laughter shoot up to the bullet-pocked ceiling. He heard her snort and that made him laugh all the harder.

When their whoops had dwindled into giggles and their giggles into silence, he turned his head to stare at her. She looked surprised, as if she'd just caught herself out doing something she didn't usually do.

A sweet smile softened her face. "You're real nice, Moses." She leaned over and stroked his cheek. Then she shook her head. "A poor innocent babe who's so lost in the woods even the trees don't know what to do with him. But nice."

She got up and took the blue enameled pitcher out into the hall, where there was hot water in a covered tin container waiting on a trivet. She brought the filled pitcher back into the room and, turning her back on him, began to wash between her legs.

Mose lay on the bed and watched her, feeling a stirring again in that part of him he wasn't supposed to think about, but which seemed lately to have been occupying all his waking moments and most of his dreams. He had released his soul to a dark desire, sure enough. He had lain with a woman who was not his wife. The terror of the sin and its certain wages of hellfire haunted him already, but he knew he would be doing it again.

"Your time's about all used up," she said to him over her shoulder, "and I got Mr. Hunter a-waitin' downstairs for me to make nice to."

Mose sat up. He tucked his limp cock back inside his trousers and drawers, fumbling with the unfamiliar, worldly buttons. "Why can't he go with one of the other girls?"

" 'Cause it's me he always asks for in particular."

From out in the hall came the tinny clang of someone else replacing the cover on the water canister. He cleared a lump that felt the size of a crabapple from his throat. "I don't want you to be with him."

She whirled and bent over to thrust a stiff finger under his nose. "Now, you listen to me, boy. Don't you go gettin' your head all twisted around backwards. I'm a workin' girl, see. I open my legs for any man who's got the price of admission."

Mose stood up, his gaze falling to the pointed toes of his worldly boots. It occurred to him suddenly that he had forgotten to take them off. He hadn't taken anything off, except for his hat. "Will you . . ." He cleared his throat again. "I would sure consider it an honor, Miss Marilee, if you would go on a picnic with me sometime."

She slapped her hands on her hips, blowing out a big sigh. "Oh, God. Now he wants to go on a goddamned picnic—"

"Tomorrow?"

She sighed again. "Oh, God. Surely I got to wonder what's comin' over me. It must be the baby what's made me go all soft in the head." She sucked in her lower lip, and Mose thought that sin or not he was going to have to kiss her soon.

"Not tomorrow," she said, and for a moment Mose, who was still staring at her mouth, thought she was talking about kissing. "We'll go on that picnic real soon, though."

She pushed him toward the door. "Now you gotta git, 'cause like I been tellin' you over and over, I'm a workin' girl."

19

SHE RUBBED HER FINGERTIPS along the bare skin of his forearm, right below his rolled-up shirtsleeve. "You ain't exactly no flannel mouth, are you?"

Mose stared at her, enjoying the pink and pretty picture she made. She was dressed in some fluffy thing the color of primroses. Pinpricks of sunlight pierced her flat-brimmed straw bonnet, freckling her ear and jaw. The ringlets of hair that fell over her bare shoulders were the exact yellow of spring wheat.

"I don't know," he said. "What's a flannel mouth?"

She grinned at him. "Someone whose gums're always flappin'."

He could have explained that it was the Plain way to keep your thoughts and feelings to yourself. Words between friends were gifts to be shared and cherished, not spent profligately, or blurted in haste or anger. But she wouldn't have understood. Their ways were too different.

Marilee whipped a palmetto fan through the air with such exuberance the brim of her hat lifted a little. "Land, it's hot. I wonder if it's ever gonna rain again."

Mose squinted against the brassy sun as he looked out over the rolling miles of prairie. The hot dry days that had followed one after the other with no respite had already burned the grass a golden brown, although it was only June. The sky was the gray-yellow color of an old bruise.

His first thought had been to have their picnic at Blackie's Pond, where they'd met. But there wasn't enough shade cast by the stunted willows and wild plum trees there, so they'd moved up the hill a ways to this stand of cottonwoods and box elders. Although the leaves on the latticework of branches above their heads looked green, they rattled like bits of dry paper in the constant Montana wind.

They sat as deep into the shade as they could get, on one of his aunt Fannie's quilts, which he'd spread over ground that he'd cleared of stones and branches. When she'd promised to go on this picnic with him, he hadn't known whether to believe her. But here she was, and there was a delighted, almost childlike glow about her.

When he had driven up to the Red House earlier, in a flashy black shay he'd borrowed on credit from Trueblue's livery, she had come tripping out the door looking as fresh and promising as a sunrise, carrying a cloth-covered basket. "I ain't never been on a picnic with a man yet," she told him, "who didn't forget to bring along the victuals. So I decided to provide them for myself." She had laughed then, a bright quick laugh that made his belly tingle and his chest feel all soft and warm, and Mose had thought he must surely love her. All the way out here, driving the little black shay, he beamed like a full moon.

Now she lifted the cloth off the top of the basket, smiling sweetly at him. "It's only common doin's, I'm afraid. Pone and fried chicken and candied yam pie."

He leaned closer, pretending to admire the food, but admiring the softly rising swell of her breasts instead. "Did you cook this all up yourself?"

Her eyes widened slightly in surprise, then she gave him a coy look. "Well, I did want this day to be somethin' special."

He watched as she spread the food out on the quilt, and she kept casting quick little glances up at him from beneath her bonnet brim. The food smelled delicious. She smelled delicious.

He took a big deep swig of air and blew it out. "I liked what we did the other night, Marilee. I liked it a lot, and I want to come pay you another call soon. Soon as I can scrape up another three dollars."

She patted his arm with her little white palm. "I liked it, too, Mose. You make a girl feel special."

Mose breathed again, his chest swelling. A part of him knew she probably said such things to all her three-dollar gentleman callers, to get them to come back with another three dollars. But he liked hearing the words anyway.

She held out a chicken leg to him, wrapped up in a white cloth napkin. He was about to take it from her when he heard the sound of hooves drumming the ground. He rolled to his knees, shading his eyes against the sun glare. Three men were riding toward them on horses bearing the Circle H brand. Hunter men.

"Run," she said.

His head whipped around to her. "I'm not leaving you—"

She pushed him hard in the back. "Go on, you fool. Git!"

He stood up. Not to run, but because he wanted to meet whatever was coming on his feet. Fear clawed at his belly, though, and a knot of burning nausea rose in his throat. He fought it down. He couldn't bear to disgrace himself by being sick in front of her.

The man on the lead horse, a stranger to him, began uncoiling a rawhide lariat. The roiling fear in Mose's belly exploded with such force his knees buckled. They were going to do to him what they'd done to Ben Yoder. They would hang him here, from a limb of one of these cottonwoods.

He ran then, sprinting out across the prairie. He could hear hooves pounding the sun-baked ground behind him. He ran harder, the breath sobbing and catching in his throat.

He cast a look over his shoulder. The Hunter hired hand was thundering down on him, swinging the lariat in a wide floating loop over his head. Mose stretched out his legs, straining every muscle and sinew in one desperate forward lunge.

The lariat twirled and sailed and settled over him, roping him like a calf for the branding.

The rawhide sang taut, jerking Mose off his feet. He hit the ground hard, grunting as the air was slammed from his lungs. Through the ringing in his ears he heard laughter, and then the rope jerked again and he was suddenly being dragged over the ground, over rocks and brush and sticks that ripped at his clothes and flesh. He was hauled brutally back to the cottonwoods and Marilee and the ruins of their picnic.

The rope went slack and he slid to a stop in a shower of dirt and ripped bunchgrass. He lay there, gasping for breath, trying not to show his fear, while the three Hunter men dismounted and stood around him.

"Get up onto your knees," said the one who'd roped him.

Swaying and lurching, fighting down dizziness and nausea, Mose got all the way onto his feet. If he was going to be on his knees, it would be before his Lord. Not that he expected a whole lot of mercy from that quarter. He had sinned mightily, seeking the pleasures of the world to satisfy his own desires, and the wages of sin were hellfire. But he'd forgotten that before you passed through the gates of hell, you first had to die.

Mose tossed the dusty hair out of his eyes and looked up into the face of his murderer.

The man was short and slender, with a heavy upper lip, side-whiskers, and a small gray beard elegantly trimmed to a point. He was dressed fine, with a whiskey-colored velvet vest, a tall black hat, and a white silk tie. He looked like a cultured man, but he had a hog's eyes, small and dark and darting. He was smiling, gathering up his rope into a smooth, tight coil.

Mose's gaze shifted to the other two. One was Fergus Hunter's son, and he looked almost as ill as Mose felt. The other seemed to be just an ordinary cowboy, straw-haired, tall and rangy, dressed in chaps and a gray Stetson. He had Marilee in front of him, her arms gripped fast in his big hands. Mose thought she must have tried to run away while he was being roped, for her skirt was ripped and dusty, and she had a scratch on her cheek.

"What are you going to do to him?" she asked in a trembling voice.

"You should be worrying about what we're going to do with *you,* Miss Marilee of the Red House," said the man with the rope, who wasn't a hired hand at all, Mose decided. He was another stock inspector—a hired gun.

He met Mose's eyes, smiling still. "I said onto your knees, woolly puncher." And he backhanded Mose hard across the face, driving him down where he wanted him.

Mose's head swam. Blood from his lips dripped into the dirt. The hired gun loomed over him, but Mose didn't look up into the man's face this time. He looked at the man's polished fancy-stitched boots.

"I don't reckon you've ever been on a cattle drive, have

you, boy?" the man said. "Not with you being a woolly puncher and all. Well, there's a lesson we give out on the trail to wet-behind-the-ears youngsters like you, who don't know how to behave." He shot a look over at Marilee. "Horny-tailed boys who don't understand their place in the order of things. It's called a legging. What we do is we bend that boy over a wagon tongue or a downed log, and we whup his bare ass with a pair of chaps until he's too sore and raw to fork a horse . . . or a woman."

His hand snaked out, gripping Mose by the hair, and he began to drag him deeper into the cottonwoods. Mose fought back, but there were three of them and they beat him into submission with their fists until they had him tied over a downed log, like he'd been promised, with his trousers and drawers pulled down to his knees.

He lay staring at the sun-scorched grass. Fear pulsed sour in his belly, and sweat poured off him in rivulets, dripping into the parched earth. It was a rank stench, his own fear.

He heard the first blow coming before he felt it, a *whoosh* through the air, and he nearly screamed aloud at the fiery slash of pain. The chaps were heavy leather and studded with metal rivets. The leather blistered and welted his bare flesh, and the metal rivets bruised and tore at it. The whipping went on and on and on. He tried to hold himself still, to stop himself from writhing beneath the blows, but that was impossible. He bit through his lip to keep from hollering out loud, and still the pain went on and on and on, until he thought that maybe it wouldn't stop until after he was dead.

Long before that, though, the pain became a constant screaming agony and the blows blended one into the other. He didn't realize the whipping was over until he stopped hearing the noise of it.

He lay there, tied down over the log, gulping in hot air, his lacerated flesh shuddering and quivering, on fire. The pain still kept coming at him in waves, but through it he heard the hired gun say, "Spread her out over there on that quilt."

Marilee screamed. Mose jerked against the ropes that bound him, and nearly screamed himself as a fierce new wave of pain crested over him. "Leave her alone!" he cried, the last of it ending on a smothered sob.

The hired gun laughed.

Mose couldn't see what they were doing, but he could hear the scuffling, the ripping of her clothes, her small gasping cries—then silence, except for her frightened, panting breathing.

The Hunter boy spoke for the first time, his voice tight. "Why do you have to do this? If you want to poke her, she's there at the Red House every night."

The hired gun's legs came around into Mose's view. He slid a knife from his boot sheath, whetting it against his pant leg. Mose craned his head, looking up. The man was still smiling. "This is going to be more than a poke," he said. "It's gonna be a *lesson.*"

The cowboy snickered. "You heard your pa say how she had to be taught a lesson for selling her twat to a Plain boy."

The hired gun caught Mose's agonized expression, and his grin widened. He walked around the log, tossing the knife from hand to hand.

Marilee screamed once, a desperate wail, and then she began to cry and plead. "Oh God, don't do that to me, please, please. I'll be good. Oh God, please, don't."

Mose yelled, pulling against the ropes. Tears filled his eyes, only he thought it might be blood.

Marilee's sobs slowly faded into mewling sounds. Mose

heard a rip, like silk tearing, and the panting grunts of a man rutting. Then a sharp, breathless silence, followed by the same trumpeting bull-moose bellow he'd heard the other night at the Red House.

There was a rustle of clothing and a weak groan, and the hired gun laughed again. "Either of you boys want to take a turn? . . . No? Then there's one final lesson I'm going to teach this cunt."

Marilee screamed and went on screaming, and Mose was screaming as well, begging them to stop whatever it was they were doing to her, which he couldn't see, only hear, but he knew it had to be terrible from the horror locked in her screams.

After a long time, the hired gun came back around the log. Mose stared up at him through blurred eyes. Marilee wasn't screaming anymore.

The hired gun squatted down before Mose's face. He had his revolver in his hand and there was blood on the barrel. He pushed it under Mose's chin, forcing his head up. "I understand," he said, "that there's a man who lives with you Plain People, name of Johnny Cain."

He paused as if expecting an answer. Mose wanted to spit in the man's face, but he hadn't the guts. He nodded, swallowing, and tried to keep from sobbing out loud.

The man's hard smile grew even harder. "You tell him Jarvis Kennedy works for the Circle H now, and that Johnny Cain is a dead man. All he's got to do is pick his moment."

He pulled the gun barrel out from under Mose's chin with enough force to rip the flesh. "Come on, boys. Let's light out."

He walked off in a jangle of spurs, and Mose heard the squeak of leather as they mounted up and then the thud of hooves, fading, fading, fading into a stillness that hurt.

He called to Marilee. He could hear her whimpering now, but she wouldn't answer him. It took a long while to work his hands loose of the ropes. He could feel blood running down his legs. His buttocks were fiery raw, as if his skin had been peeled back with a scaling knife.

He crawled to her on his hands and knees. She was curled into a tight ball in the middle of the quilt, among scattered pieces of fried chicken and cornbread. And something that looked like sheaves of wheat, something he didn't quite understand until she uncurled enough to look up at him with anguished eyes so large and dark they looked bruised.

"My hair, Mose. They cut off all my hair."

Her hair, her pretty hair, looked like the stubble left in the field after the hay was cut. It had been sheared off so close to her scalp that in places she'd been nicked enough to bleed.

His hand hovered over her mutilated head, but he pulled it back when she flinched. "Aw, Marilee. I'm so sorry."

She whimpered and straightened her legs. There was a lot of blood on her skirt.

Suddenly her whole body jackknifed, and she clutched at her belly. Blood gushed out from between her legs, thick gouts of bright red blood, and Marilee screamed again, over and over again.

WHAT WAS LEFT OF the haystacks they'd built such a short while ago stood baking and tanning in the heat. Mose walked slowly toward them, his boots shuffling through the grass like an old man's. Each step was an effort and an agony. He kept shivering even though he was sweating.

A briny taste soured his mouth, the taste that came from tears of rage and pain and shame. He thought he'd taken some bad beatings from his father, but none had ever been like that. Still, the pain and humiliation of being whipped bare-assed with a pair of chaps was nothing to what they'd done to Marilee.

Lieber Gott, had she screamed! And bled. So much blood, on the quilt, on her dress, on the ground, on the cushioned seat of the shay—they had all become soaked with her blood. He had driven the shay wildly across the prairie back to town, with fear and rage punching his heart, punching, punching, punching, making it flat and hard.

He'd gone running with her in his arms, still bleeding and screaming, into Doc Henry's house. That was when the doc had told him she was losing her baby, a baby Mose hadn't even known she was going to *have.*

The hired gun had promised Mose he would be too raw and sore to ride a horse, but the rage in Mose's heart had made it possible for him to get on his mount and ride back across the valley to the Weaver farm and beyond. The rage made it possible now for him to be walking across the Yoder south pastures in search of Johnny Cain.

SHEEPHERDERS HAD A SAYING that trouble never traveled lonesome. And sure enough, Mose saw, trouble had come calling on the Yoder farm today as well.

Their ewes had managed to find a big thick patch of sweet clover and the silly animals were now proceeding to eat themselves into an epidemic of stomach bloat. Already a good dozen were on the ground foaming at the mouth, their bellies distended and swollen. Four others were on their backs, legs stiff in the air, stone dead.

Mose walked up to Johnny Cain, who was kneeling before one of the bloated ewes. "You got to lance 'em when they swell up," Mose said. "Let out all that bad air."

The outsider slanted an aggrieved look up at him. "I was fixing to do that," he said. And as the man leaned over the prostrate sheep, Mose saw that he did in fact have a bloating lance in his hand.

He stabbed the lance into the ewe's left flank. She let out a pathetic bleat and expired on the spot.

"Oh, shit. I've gone and killed her," the outsider said.

Mose squatted next to the dead sheep, setting his teeth on a moan as the movement pulled at all the cuts and welts and bruises on his backside. He took the bloating lance from the outsider's hands. "Here. Let me do the next one."

He walked on his knees over to another bloated ewe. He felt along the sheep's flank, searching for the proper point. "It's a bit tricky. An inch or two to the right or left, and suddenly all you've got is a wool pelt and mutton stew."

The bloating lance was actually a small tube with a blade passing through the hollow middle. He punctured the ewe's hide and rumen with the lance, pushing in the tube, then withdrawing the lance and leaving the tube in place. Hot, smelly air whooshed out of the tube with enough force to fan the hair off Mose's brow. And the ewe got a look on her face of sublime relief.

Such was the difference between life and death, Mose thought. The difference of an inch or two. He crawled over to the next sheep.

"Mrs. Yoder, she's the best at poking holes in bloated sheep of anyone I've seen. But young Benjo also knows what he's about."

"Yeah?" the outsider said. "Well, they all went off and left me alone with the goddamn woollies. The boy's taken

MacDuff over to his grandpa's to help with the shearing, and she's gone to help the twins pick over the beans for tomorrow's preaching service soup. So you got to figure with no one but me around something disastrous like this was bound to happen."

"That's sheep for you, all right. Even the Devil couldn't think up all the trouble a woolly can find to get into."

Mose looked at the quick-draw rig the man always wore on his hip, even here in such a place of peace as a pasture full of sheep. But it wasn't easy getting it out—his own trouble and what he meant to do about it, and the help that he would need from Johnny Cain. So he put the moment off until he'd punctured the last of the ballooning ewes, and they'd herded the band over to a field with less of the tempting clover.

They stood side by side among the grazing sheep, he and Cain, and still it wasn't easy getting it out. It was strange how he had been able to lance the sheep and talk to the outsider about it as if he, Moses Weaver, were his same old self, when all the while rage and fear and hate were gripping him so he felt brittle inside. It was as if he were two Moses Weavers. One a Plain boy and a sheep farmer, and the other this Mose who was far, far different, a stranger even to himself.

He cleared his throat. It felt as if he had ground glass in there. "Before now, before you came to be with us, did you do stuff for money? I mean, how much did someone have to pay you?"

Cain took off his hat and ran a finger around the inside leather, wiping off the sweat. "Pay me to do what?"

"Kill a man. Kill some shit-eating bastard."

The words had startled Mose coming out of his mouth. Not the words so much as the fresh rage that scorched them. The outsider turned his head slowly and gave Mose a long, steady stare. He couldn't have helped seeing all the blood before this, but now he looked at it deliberately—not with wild curiosity, more with a mild interest—and waited for Mose to go on.

"It's not my blood," Mose said. "Mostly not," he amended.

The outsider turned away as if even his mild interest had been used up. A silence fell over the pasture, a silence that blended with the buzz of the flies around the sheep dung, the caw of a magpie, the raucous breath of the wind.

"Who is he?"

Mose jumped as if he'd just been prodded. "What?"

"The shit-eating bastard you want killed."

"He said his name's Jarvis Kennedy." Mose paused, but the outsider's face showed no reaction. "He's the new Hunter stock inspector and he said to tell you Johnny Cain is a dead man, and that all you have to do is choose your moment."

This seemed to amuse the outsider, for his mouth pulled into a smile. But it was a hard, tight smile so reminiscent of the Hunter hired gun's that to see it again set Mose's belly to churning.

His raw buttocks burned and throbbed, and fresh tears of humiliation stung his eyes. He would never be able to speak to this man about the whipping, but there was Marilee, and she deserved vengeance. "Also, well, maybe you don't care, but he raped a woman. Miss Marilee from the Red House, who's a friend of mine. They said they were going to teach her a lesson for being with a Plain boy, and then they raped her. So bad she bled and lost her baby."

"Look at her, the gluttonous fool," Cain said. He was staring at one of the ewes they'd just punctured. "She's back to eating again as if nothing happened."

Mose had to swallow around the choking lump in his

throat. "Sheep have short memories," he said. Not like men. Mose didn't think he'd ever forget what had been done to him on this day.

But he was beginning to feel foolish, like a child trying to capture the attention of an adult who doesn't even know he's there. He had expected the outsider to be outraged, horrified, when he heard the story of what had happened, but he wasn't. In the Plain community, what was done to one was done to them all. But he'd forgotten that Johnny Cain was indeed an outsider, who would care only about himself.

"Of course, you probably just want to go ahead and kill the shit-eating bastard for yourself," Mose said. "For calling you a dead man."

Mose waited, but the outsider said nothing, and so he had to go on. "But since I want him dead as well, I'm willing to pay you."

The outsider brought his cold stare back to Mose. "You can't afford me."

Mose nodded, swallowed. He had figured such would be the case. It didn't matter. Once the gates of hell gaped open, there was no shutting them. "Will you teach me how to quick draw, then?"

Cain gave a bitter laugh. "I'm beginning to feel like the only whore in town and there's a line forming outside my door."

Mose wasn't sure what he meant by that, and he didn't care. He was suddenly tired, so tired, and he felt raw all over, not only the places where he'd been whipped. He could feel the rage, and with it his resolution, slipping away. He shut his eyes and made himself think of Marilee, of how she'd looked with her face white as death and all that red, red blood.

"He raped my friend and, with or without your help, I'm going to kill him for it."

The outsider moved so fast, Mose didn't see him coming until the man's hand was already gripping his neck, pushing his head up, and Mose was staring into eyes that were as lifeless and hard as blue glass.

"First," Johnny Cain said, "you are talking too stupid to live, boy. Second, I don't give a tinker's damn about you or your whore and her trouble. But Mrs. Yoder seems fond of you, and so for her sake I'm gonna give you one lesson with my Colt. One lesson, and what you choose to learn from it will be your own business."

Cain let him go, stepping back. "Are you ready?"

Mose nodded, stretching out his neck. He tried to hide his trembling. His legs suddenly felt so weak, he wondered how they were holding him up.

The outsider slipped his revolver from the holster and held it out to Mose butt first. Mose reached to take the gun, when it seemed suddenly to come alive. It spun around in the outsider's hand, a flash and blur of black metal. Mose heard a loud click, and he was suddenly looking at the black bore of the Colt's muzzle.

Slowly, slowly, the muzzle came up, until it was pointed between Mose's eyes. And Johnny Cain was smiling that smile, the smile of a man-killer. "What are your favorite flowers, boy?"

To Mose's bitter shame, he felt his whole body begin to shake. He squeezed his eyes shut and waited, waited. Then the sense of the man's words finally penetrated his fear, and he understood that Cain wasn't going to kill him, had never had any intention of killing him.

He jumped anyway, though, when Cain released the

hammer. He opened his eyes in time to watch the revolver slide back into its holster. Cain had already turned his back on him and was walking away.

"Wait!" Mose lurched forward, grabbing the outsider by the arm.

Cain wrenched out of his grasp and whipped around, his hand falling to the butt of his Colt in a movement that was as instinctive to him as breathing.

Mose raised his hands in the air and backed up a step, but he wasn't going to give up. "I'm not stupid, Mr. Cain. I know what you were trying to teach me with that lesson, and it doesn't matter. I want Jarvis Kennedy dead."

"No, you don't." Cain's eyes were wide and dark now, and he was breathing so hard he was almost panting. "You'd only be sorry for it afterwards, or dead yourself."

Mose shook his head. "I won't be sorry. I want that son of a bitch to pay for what he's done. You're making the same mistake everybody does, you think that because I'm Plain, I'm also ignorant. I want Jarvis Kennedy dead, and I know what it's going to take to make that happen."

The outsider lowered his head. When he raised it a moment later, his face looked gentle, almost sad. "It ain't about ignorance, Mose. It ain't even about innocence. There's plenty more lessons I could teach you. Like how to move quick and aim straight. And if you didn't prove out in the quick-draw department, I could teach you how to do it ruthless and dirty. How to get the drop on a man so's to shoot him in the back before he even knows you're there. I could teach you all that and everything else I know about killing, and you still wouldn't have what it takes to go up against a man like Jarvis Kennedy."

Mose's face felt wet, and he knew it was from tears. He

thought he'd been crying for a good while now. "What does it take, then, damn you?" The hot tears filled his eyes and splattered onto his cheeks. "Just tell me what it takes."

The outsider's gaze was focused on the distant mountains, stark and sun-haloed against the sky. Mose didn't expect an answer, but he got one.

"Nothing. It takes feeling nothing inside except it's either him or you. When you can empty your gun into a man's belly with the same amount of feeling it takes to step on a cockroach, then you'll have what it takes to survive."

He swung his eyes back to Mose, and they were empty, and so was his face.

"But something happens to you," said Johnny Cain. "Something happens and even surviving stops mattering so much anymore, and all you feel most of the time is nothing."

Johnny Cain walked away from him then, and Mose let him go. But after a few steps he stopped, stood still a moment, then slowly turned back around.

"I guess I am sorry a little bit about your friend," he said. He sounded surprised.

MARILEE OPENED HER EYES onto a paper trellis of ribbons and roses. There was many a day she had opened her eyes to such a sight, but she knew—even before she felt the aching, hollow emptiness in her belly—that this day was different.

She turned her head. Luc Henry was standing over her, frowning down at her and looking worried. This pleased her, for it meant he must care for her at least a little. But then he was a doctor, and there was that sensitive part of him that cared about the whole world.

He eased down onto the bed beside her, the tick rustling and sagging beneath his weight. He picked up her hand.

"Marilee . . ."

Her throat hurt, and she had to swallow. "The baby's gone, isn't it?"

"I'm sorry."

She pressed her head back into the pillow, squeezing her eyes shut. A sob exploded out of her and then another and another. "Oh, God," she cried, trying to push herself up. She wanted to be held, she wanted it so desperately, and his arms did come around her, holding her, and she clung to him, burying her face in his shoulder as the tears and sobs ripped out of her in shuddering heaves.

After a while she subsided into shudders and little hiccuping breaths. "It hurts, Luc. It hurts so bad."

"I know, I know." He held her tighter for a moment longer, then eased her back down onto the bed. "I'll give you one of my herbal infusions, in a moment." He summoned up one of his sweet, crooked smiles. "And maybe some patent medicine, too, just to be safe."

Her hand fluttered weakly up to her head. "They cut off all my pretty hair."

He wrapped his finger around a single curl that fell over her ear, giving it a gentle tug. "It'll grow."

She bit her lip as a fresh bout of tears, hot and salty, flooded her eyes. "He wasn't content just to put his cock up inside me, Luc. He had to go shovin' his six-shooter up in there as well. He ripped me up pretty bad, didn't he?"

"You'll be some time in healing, Marilee," Doc Henry said, but he averted his face, and she knew it was to hide his thoughts.

And so it was a long time before she was able to find the courage to ask him if she would ever be able to have another baby. And it was a longer time still before he spoke, and before he did, she saw the answer come first into his eyes, and that was when she began to cry again.

20

IT WAS HOT.

Blistering, sweat-cooking, drought-making hot. Hot winds shriveled the grass and licked at the water holes, drying them up. Clouds of dry alkali dust washed the blue out of the sky and turned the sluggish Miawa Creek the color of dirty soapsuds. Not a drop of rain fell to pock the ground. And it was still only the second week of June.

It was hot, and it was shearing time.

NOAH WEAVER WATCHED THE sheep come waddling, one by one, out of the bathing pool, water-laden and staggering with it. He thought if he heard someone say that it was hot as a cookstove one more time, his head might just explode.

It had been hard work this year, damming up the low-running creek and scooping out a puddle big enough to make a woolly bath. But a clean crop fetched higher prices, and at least in this hot weather the sheep would be dry enough to shear in no time.

Samuel Miller, who had the enviable job of standing

knee-deep in the pool and watching to make sure none of the sheep rolled over and drowned, tossed a smile at his brothers. He pretended to wring the sweat out of his beard. "Judas. It's hot enough to make the Devil feel t'home, *ja*?"

Abram laughed, but then his face sobered quick enough. "It's a drought we're in the making of. You tell me if we're not."

Sol nodded, his mouth so tight it all but disappeared into his beard. "It's as hot as a cookstove, it is."

Noah clamped his own lips together and forced himself to take a deep breath through his nose. He tugged on his hat, half afraid his head really would explode. He reminded himself to think of these days as a trial sent by the Lord to be endured with meekness and humility. God was testing him, saddling him with scorching days, a drought, and Johnny Cain, all in one summer.

He had been looking forward to this day, though. The day they sheared Rachel's sheep. He had made the outsider a promise—*ach vell,* you could call it a challenge, wicked though that might be—that the man wouldn't be able to last through a day of sheep shearing. Noah knew the outsider fancied himself tough, that he took pride in his toughness. Sure enough, the Bible was right when it said that pride goeth before destruction, and a haughty spirit before a fall.

Noah looked across the pool to where the outsider was trying to nudge a reluctant yearling into the water, and he smiled. *You'll not last the day, outsider. Might be you'll not even last an hour. And then we'll see. We'll see what my Rachel has to say to that.*

Noah knew these thoughts were prideful in themselves, that he damned his own soul with them, but he couldn't seem to stop.

Just then the excitement of being driven through the

pool brought on the bloat in one of the ewes, and Johnny Cain stepped right up with a bloating lance to take care of it. Noah couldn't find fault, although he watched and waited for a mistake, God help him, hoping the outsider's hand would slip and the lance would go in wrong, and then the outsider would look bad in front of Rachel.

When the ewe rolled back onto her feet with a hearty *baa,* Noah wondered at himself and his own spiteful thoughts. God help him, he had stood there and wished death on a poor innocent woolly, and all just to make the outsider look bad.

Noah shook his head, rubbing the sweat out of his eyes with his thumbs. Squinting, he looked out over Rachel's sun-seared pastures. There was not much grass there to fatten a sheep. This hot weather, it was toughening and leathering the land as the salt of hard-work sweat toughened and leathered a man. A little rain would certainly be welcome, but the good Lord must know that. His ways sometimes were hard to understand. It was better not to think too much about it, better just to accept His will.

Noah looked over to where his son Mose was wrangling the drying sheep into the shearing corral. For a moment their gazes met. Then his son's face took on that sour, flat-chinned look, and he turned around, giving Noah the stiff back, the cold shoulder.

Noah blamed the outsider for this, for the loss of his son. He couldn't have explained precisely how his mind had made the convoluted journey to lay this latest trouble, with the cattlemen and that strumpet from the Red House, at the outsider's door. It was a matter, Noah had decided, of being in the presence of evil. Johnny Cain had cast his corrupting influences over all who came near him, even the righteous.

Noah had told his boy that once his backside healed, he would take up the strap and give him a fresh set of welts. But when the day came he hadn't done it, he hadn't had the heart for it. Besides, he sensed the boy wasn't going to be taking any more whippings from anybody, ever again. He'd been changed sure enough by what had happened, altered deep, and in ways that Noah didn't understand. It frightened him, for his son seemed more lost than ever, lost to God and the church.

Lost to him.

THE BLADE MET THE whirring grindstone with a shriek and a shower of sparks.

Pumping hard, Noah Weaver grinned through his beard at the outsider. "A few more turns," he shouted above the noise, "and these shears'll be sharp enough to cut through wool like it was hot butter."

And then we'll see how you do, outsider. Then we'll see.

Once the sheep were bathed, the men had gathered inside the shearing shed for the ritual sharpening of the shears. Noah had offered to perform the task for the outsider, for there was a knack to it. Showing a humility that must be rare for him, certainly, Cain had accepted.

The shearing shed had been a lambing shed only a few weeks ago. The floor was covered now with two feet of fresh straw, over which a canvas had been stretched for the shearing area. Shearing was back-breaking work, and few sheep farmers did their own, so there were roving shearing crews who followed the market north from Mexico to the British provinces. But the Plain church discouraged the hiring of these crews, for they were known to be fighters and blasphemers and drinkers of the Devil's brew. The Plain preferred always to keep themselves separate and do their own work.

Samuel Miller took up a pair of shears, testing the edge with a callused thumb. "You might as well try to clip the woollies with a dull whittling knife," he said with a broad wink to Sol, "as to be using these pathetic things, our Abram."

"Ha!" Abram snatched the shears out of Samuel's hands, nearly clipping off the end of his brother's beard. "I'll have more naked sheep on my tally come the day's end than you ever will, see if I don't."

"It's a poor wool crop we'll all be getting this year," Sol said, the downward curve of his mouth matching the words. "What with that open winter we had, the sheep didn't grow as heavy coats as they should have. And now all this hot sun, day after day, the wind and the dust." He sighed, shaking his head.

"The fleeces have shrunk down to next to nothing, *ja*," Noah agreed.

He cast a glance at the outsider. They were all speaking in *Deitsch* now, excluding the man as they usually did. And as usual he was too proud to act as if it mattered to him.

Ja, gut, Noah thought. Let him stew in his pride.

Samuel said something that made his brothers laugh. Noah, watching the outsider, hadn't heard what was said, but he joined in the laughter. The outsider stood apart from them, his beardless face flat and empty. None of those charming, easy smiles to be found there now, and Noah was pleased.

The good thing about the shearing time, Noah thought, was the work, for it brought families and friends together. Everyone had something important to do. Fannie and the Miller wives were already in the kitchen preparing huge quantities of food, for shearing built up a prodigious appetite. Mose would be wrangling the sheep soon toward the end of the corral, funneling the bleating, frightened woollies into the cutting chute. Rachel would stand on top of the chute fence to open the gate, sending the sheep into the catch pen. Four at a time, one for each of the shearers.

Even the young ones would have work. Levi would tie up the fleeces and toss them up to Benjo, who would pack them into giant burlap sacks, the woolbags.

Samuel, who had the talent and the teeth for it, would do the castrating, biting off the testicles of the boy lambs, turning them into wethers, the poor things. Whereas himself, along with Sol and Abram, would do the fleecing. The outsider would take Ben's place with them on the shearing floor, and not an hour would he last. And then they would all see what Rachel had to say to that.

Noah passed the blades one last time over the grindstone, then handed the gleaming shears to the outsider. Cain wrapped his hand around the looped handle and squeezed the hafts. The long triangular blades, sharp as razors now, slid together with a sweet *zing.*

Johnny Cain didn't have a farmer's hand, Noah thought, not a big, blunt-fingered, rough farmer's hand. But still, those shears seemed to wed themselves to his fingers as if they belonged there.

Noah and the Miller brothers discussed among themselves in *Deitsch* what was to be done to put the outsider in his place. They decided that to be fair, they would have to show the man once how a sheep was properly sheared, and then he could be turned loose to make a fool of himself.

"You watch and see, and maybe you'll learn a little something, *ja*?" Noah said in *Englisch* to the outsider. Samuel and Abram hid grins in their beards. Sol shook his head, but there was a hint of a twinkle in his eyes.

"Give me a sheep!" Noah hollered to Rachel, who had already taken her place at the cutting chute.

A fat old ewe came waddling through the woolbag curtains that had been hung up between the catch pen and the shearing floor. Noah hooked her as she trotted by, grabbing her around her breast, under her front legs. She kept running, right up onto her hind legs, and Noah dumped her onto her rump easily. He gripped her tight to his body with his knees to keep her from wriggling free. The ewe, wise to the ways of a cruel world, saw the gleam of the shears and let out a loud bleat.

Noah worked quickly, his experienced fingers feeling where the fleece was fine, close to the skin. The shears flashed in mighty strokes, and the wool, soft and greasy to the touch, began to unfold smoothly in a spiraling ivory circle like the peel of an orange.

The ewe emerged from the pile of her wool, big eyed and naked. Noah relaxed the grip of his knees and gave her a gentle boost back onto her feet. She shook herself hard, no doubt feeling strange, and then trotted off with an embarrassed *blaugh!*

Noah looked up from his stooped position and showed his teeth in a hard smile. "Now, let's see how you do, outsider."

Noah could have called for another ewe, with udders and teats that Cain would have had to clip around. But he decided to make things easy on the poor man, outsider that he was, and asked for a big yearling wether instead. This time Rachel came into the shed along with the sheep to watch.

The outsider had trouble from the start. In trying to wrestle the animal onto its rump, he somehow wound up face to face and arm in arm with it. Rachel, watching him with her eyes shining bright and soft as spring sunshine, was trying hard not to laugh. Cain caught her eyes, and a look of boyish mischievousness flashed across his face.

He made as if to buss the wether on its bony nose. "Madam!" he declaimed. "May I have this dance?" And to Noah's astonishment, he actually managed to twirl the bleating sheep around on its tiny hooves.

"Oh, Mr. Cain," Rachel called out, her throat warbling with laughter. "Did you know that's a boy sheep you're dancing with?"

Cain stumbled to a stop and looked down in mock alarm. "Oh dear, so it is. Well, actually, something a bit less than a boy."

Rachel clapped her hands together like a young girl. Even the Miller brothers, caught up in the moment, were finding the outsider pretty funny.

Not Noah. He looked away, his teeth clamped together so hard his jaw ached. Not an hour, he reminded himself. The man wouldn't last through the first hour.

It wasn't as easy as it looked, to cut the wool off a living, panting, squirming sheep. The outsider's big mistake was not gripping the wether's body tightly enough with his knees. Cain had it only half shorn when the wether slithered free, gathered its legs underneath it, and ran off trailing fleece. The outsider had to chase after it, and Rachel laughed so hard she had to sit down on a stack of woolbags and hold her belly.

They all were laughing by then. Even Noah.

When the poor sheep was finally shorn entirely of its wool, it staggered off, blood-spotted and sporting ratty patches where Cain's shears had either missed completely or nicked the hide.

"I've cut him to pieces," the outsider said. He looked so

utterly miserable now that Noah had to turn his head to hide a smile. Rachel sat back down on the woolbags, her shoulders shaking, she was laughing so.

Levi, whose job it was to do the disinfecting, hurried off after the lacerated, bald, and scruffy wether with a rag dripping carbolic acid.

"I'm a butcher," Cain said.

"Actually, you've a deft hand," Noah told him grudgingly. "You'll pick up the rhythm of it in no time."

"I think, Mrs. Yoder, that you'd do better just to give me all the old ones with tough hides," the outsider called over to Rachel. And as Noah watched, feeling sick at heart, feeling like an outsider himself, their laughter blended in a music all their own.

THERE WERE SOUNDS, Noah thought, that belonged just to the shearing time.

The snick and click of the blades, as the shears were clasped and released, clasped and released, over and over, clasped and released.

The bleating and blatting and *baa*ing of the sheep as they were dumped onto their rumps and shorn naked of their buttery wool.

The thump-thump of Benjo stomping the spongy fleeces down into the woolbag.

A shearer calling, "Give me a sheep!" And Rachel coaxing one through the chute, *poorrrr-poorrrr-pooorrr*, sounding sometimes like a kitten and sometimes like a mourning dove. He loved the sound of Rachel singing to her sheep.

He had forgotten how quickly the work could wear on a man. The constant stooping, the clipping and clipping and clipping, rising just long enough to drag another sheep over and begin again with the clipping, clipping, clipping.

Ja, and the sound of his own panting breaths, of his sweat drip-drip-dripping like a rainspout onto the shearing floor—that, too, was part of this time.

And a new sound this year. Johnny Cain crooning softly to his sheep as he sheared them. The outsider seemed to have a genuine and gentle fondness for the woollies, which both astonished and bothered Noah. He found himself liking the outsider a little bit for it, and he didn't want to.

Noah finished with a ewe and looked up to see that Benjo was standing on top of a full woolbag. "Time to rest a spell," he called out to the others. Time to catch their breaths and stretch the kinks out of their backs, time to sharpen their shears.

Noah couldn't keep the grin off his face as he watched the outsider straighten up slow and stiff, like an old, old man. Cain rubbed one hand in the small of what was surely an aching back. His other hand, stiff as a claw, still gripped the shears. That hand had to be raw with bloody blisters by now. Even Noah's own palm, toughened and seasoned as it was, burned where he'd been gripping and working the haft of the shears for the last three hours.

Noah went to the water butt, stumbling a little; he was that tired himself. He brought a dipperful of water over to the outsider, and the two men stood staring at each other, rocking slightly on their feet, chests pumping with their sucking breaths, sweat pouring in streams down their drawn faces.

Noah said to the other man, softly so that only he could hear, "So, outsider? There would be no shame now, if you said you had enough."

A devil's smile flashed beneath winter hard eyes. "When hell freezes, Deacon."

As the two men continued to stare at each other, a hush fell over the shearing shed. It grew so quiet they could hear the fleeces, still live and warm, stirring in the woolbag—a faint sound, like soft breathing.

"What is this I see? You lazy men are taking a rest already, and here the morning not yet half gone." Rachel sailed through the woolbag curtains with her hands on her hips and a teasing light in her eyes. "Pee-uw!" She pretended to reel back in horror. Or perhaps it wasn't such a pretense, for the shed was steamy with sweat. "You men smell worse than any sheep ever did."

"It's a good smell," Noah said stiffly, as he turned to face her. "A smell that would please the Lord."

He flushed, wondering why everything he said to her lately didn't seem to come out right. They were good thoughts, yet when he put them into words they sounded vain and boastful. This time she smiled at him, but then her gaze went right to Johnny Cain, and they shared another one of those special smiles that came only into their eyes.

Noah watched her with helpless yearning as she went to the water butt. When she finished drinking, she headed toward him, and he felt a flutter of sweet anticipation. But she walked on past to Benjo, instead, and helped him finish sewing shut the woolbag. And then she went to *him*. To the outsider.

They stood close together but not too close, and they spoke not in whispers but plain, so anyone could hear. But Rachel's eyes shone like morning dew. And her mouth smiled quick and sweet. And her whole body seemed to be leaning, straining to span the distance between them, as if all of her was saying to the outsider *touch me, touch me, touch me, touch me.*

21

DUST DEVILS DANCED AHEAD of Lucas Henry's phaeton as he turned into the yard of the Yoder farm. The corrals were filled with bleating sheep, some still dressed in their coats of wool, others already shorn, their naked hides pale and quivering like an old man's paunch.

Lucas reined up and watched Rachel Yoder walk toward him through shimmering heat ripples. When she came abreast of the buggy he smiled and tipped his hat to her.

"Good day to you, Plain Rachel."

He didn't get a return greeting, but he was used to Plain ways and hadn't expected one. "I was just over at the Triple Bar," he said, "delivering a baby. Then on my way back to town I felt a wheel coming loose."

Rachel looked his wheels over. "It's your right front one, sure enough," she said. "I suppose Noah or Mr. Cain might help you repair it, but we're in the middle of shearing at the moment." She looked up at him and actually smiled. "You're also welcome to stay a spell and watch our poor woollies get scalped."

She turned and walked off, leaving him to decide on his own. He climbed out the phaeton and approached the low sheds next to the barn. A knot of Plain men stood, jabbering in their guttural tongue, long beards jerking, big felt hats flapping in the hot wind. They fell silent and turned in unison to give him a hard stare, and he immediately felt about as welcome as a whore in Sunday school.

Johnny Cain came out of the sheds just then, and Rachel went up to him and said something, lightly touching his arm. She seemed different to Lucas in that moment: more vivid, vital, more of a woman. It was as if he'd been seeing her in two dimensions, like a photograph, all light and gray shadows, and now suddenly she had come to full and breathing life.

He was seeing a woman in love, he thought, and he knew he should be pitying her for all the sorrows that were sure now to come her way. But instead it was himself he felt sorry for, because although love was often a misery, so could it be an ecstasy, distilled to its purest form and headier than any booze. Only it wasn't happening to him, and it never would again.

Rachel turned, pointing, and Cain came out into the middle of the yard to meet him. The man's Plain shirt was open at the neck, showing a throat slick with sweat and browned by days working in the fields beneath a hot sun. Bits of sheared wool clung to his hair and to his worn and patched broadfall trousers. But his Colt still hung from a bullet-studded belt on his hips, close by his right hand.

"Hey, Doc," he said. "Rachel figures you've a wheel about to come off."

Lucas pursed his lips in a silent whistle and made his eyes go round, as he looked the notorious desperado up and down. "The older I get, the more I see the importance of keeping one's sense of wonder. But what, I'm asking myself, are all your awed admirers and fearsome enemies supposed to think when they hear you've turned into a full-fledged mutton puncher?"

"The good Deacon Noah says such hard and humbling work is a fine thing for a man's soul."

"The good Deacon Noah wants to marry Rachel Yoder."

Cain's gaze went back to the lambing sheds. Rachel had an apronful of apples and she was tossing them one at a time to the men as she walked by, making a game of it. She lobbed one overhand like a baseball at Noah's head, and she laughed.

Cain smiled, though his eyes remained cold. "God doesn't always fix it so's the good man gets what he wants, though," he said. "Sometimes he lets the Devil have his day."

No, Lucas thought. If there is a God, He will have a care for a woman like Rachel Yoder. He will save her from the powers of darkness and a man like you. If there is a God . . . Ah, but if there were a God, He would have saved Lucas Henry's wife from Lucas Henry, wouldn't He?

The thought was so painful it was like a sliver of glass in the eye. The sun beat down fiercely, and he could feel the sweat running off him. He smelled himself, smelled the whiskey that had been flowing through his veins for almost thirty years, and almost choked on his own disgust. Yet still, he wanted a drink.

"So, isn't it too Christly hot a day to be clipping woollies?" he said.

Cain's gaze swept over the pastures and the sheep. "I'm beginning to think we are all out of our minds." He sounded almost happy, and he had said "we." He had counted himself as one of them. Lucas wondered if he knew he'd done it.

"How's the arm holding up?" Lucas said.

Cain stretched out his right arm, his hand curling into a loose fist. He had his shirtsleeves rolled up to the elbow.

The exertion of shearing had made his veins stand out like slender ropes and sheened his muscular flesh with sweat.

"You did a fine job of setting the bone, Doc. It feels no different than the other one. They're both about as weak as newborn lambs."

"Uh huh." Lucas took hold of Cain's wrist, turning it over. "And your hand's nothing but one big broken and bleeding blister. All in all you're in prime condition to perform your next killing."

Cain's smile was easy, but a painful light flared behind his eyes. "You wouldn't happen to have some witch hazel ointment in that doctor's bag of yours?"

Lucas went to his phaeton, not so much for the sake of Cain's blistered hand as for the opportunity to nip at the flask of Rose Bud he always carried in his medical bag. But as he lifted the flask to his mouth, his own words echoed in his head: *All in all you're in prime condition to perform your next killing.*

He'd heard the tale told so often, he might as well have been there. How Johnny Cain had got the drop on the Hunters' stock inspector, that day in the Gilded Cage saloon, through the judicious use of a sarsaparilla bottle. And how Cain had then been distracted by the Plain woman and almost let that hired gun get the drop on him.

Almost. Woodrow Wharton's body had lain on view in his coffin in the bay window of Tulle's Mercantile with a sign that said he was the twenty-ninth man shot and killed by the pistoleer Johnny Cain. Lucas had prepared the body. The man had been clutching tenaciously to his cocked revolver even in death—in the medical textbooks it was called a cadaveric spasm—and Lucas had left the gun there in the man's hand. He thought it was a nice touch of irony, not that anyone in town was likely to appreciate irony.

Woodrow Wharton had lain in state in the bay window of Tulle's Mercantile for only an hour or two, though. After a while the flies and the stink got to be too much, even by Montana standards.

And now they said Fergus Hunter had already hired himself a new "stock inspector."

As Lucas started back with his medical bag, he saw that Cain had moved into the narrow shade cast by the barn and taken off his hat to wipe the sweat from his face. The wind blew his hair into his eyes. It was as long and ragged as any Plain man's.

Lucas set his bag on an upturned nail keg, found the witch hazel cream, and rubbed it into Cain's blistered palm. As he gripped the man's wrist, he could feel that the pulse was fast, too fast.

Lucas looked up to find that Cain's eyes were riveted on Rachel. She and a handful of other Plain women were passing out sandwiches to the men, filling up tin coffee mugs from a big blue speckled pot. The wind lifted a stray lock of her dark red hair and laid it across her cheek. Absently she coiled it and tucked it back beneath her prayer cap.

As if he sensed that he was being watched, Cain replaced his hat, tilting it low. But his words startled Lucas, for they ran so close to his own thoughts. "I don't suppose you believe a man can find his God and himself through a woman?"

"Plenty have tried, but it's probably about as likely as finding God and yourself in the bottom of a bottle of Rose Bud," Lucas said. He looked up at the heat-hazed sky. "I was married once myself, for a time. She was like a butterfly, my wife. Flitting from flower to flower, drinking of life. Wild and fragile, and so beautiful. I thought . . ."

He had thought he would do anything, give everything

for his wife. But in the end he hadn't been able to do the one thing that would have saved her, saved them both. He hadn't been able to change what he was.

"I thought I loved her so much that she could be my heaven on earth. But then one day my beautiful little butterfly of a wife . . ." He stopped.

"She flew away?" Cain said.

Lucas's mouth twisted into a hard and painful smile. "Oh no, she loved me far too much to leave me. So I killed her instead."

If he had been either drunker or more sober, he would have laughed at the absurd high drama of it all. What was Cain supposed to do in the face of that little disclosure? Ask for all the lurid details? Offer condolences along the lines of: *I'm so sorry to hear about your wife, and to think you were the one to do her in.*

What he did do was look carefully away from Lucas's face and after a moment say, "I'll help you change that wheel now, if you like."

Lucas heard, as if from a long way away, the rattle of wheels over the log bridge that spanned the creek. He turned and saw a little black shay with green trim and fringed cushions approaching. A voice, trilling as a meadowlark, sang out over the wind. "Luc, oh Luc! Gwendolene's baby is a-comin', and she's fit to bust a gut!"

Lucas did laugh then, although even he could hear what a terrible sound it was. "Spare your poor blistered hand, Mr. Cain," he said. "I see *my* salvation coming in the form of a sweet little tart named Marilee."

THE SHAY LURCHED AND bucked over the ruts in the sunbaked road. The wind-whipped dust stuck to Marilee's cheeks and stung her eyes. She had to clamp her lips tight against the bitter taste of it.

She slid a glance over to the man sitting next to her. There was a tightness around Lucas Henry's mouth, too, and a bleakness in his eyes. But then he'd probably been no more welcome at that Plain farm than her.

She might not have even recognized Moses Weaver in the group of men with their drab clothes and big hats if he hadn't started toward her, for she'd never seen him dressed Plain before. But then an older man had said something sharp to him in that language they spoke. Mose's face had gone white, and he turned and walked away without a word of welcome—walked away and left her with a taste in her mouth as bitter as any dust the wind could whip up.

It wasn't as if she'd had any intention in the first place of going up to him and saying howdy, let alone of trying to cozy up to his family and make herself to home. He knew what she was, and so did she. But the *way* he'd looked at her, in that instant before he'd turned his back . . .

Of course the memory of the last time they were together was probably still as bitter for him as it was for her. Maybe he'd felt ashamed that he hadn't been able to stop what had happened, that he'd done nothing to make up for it since then. Well, she hardly expected a boy like him to go out and get himself shot defending her honor, especially when she hadn't any honor to defend in the first place. She didn't blame him for that, but he probably blamed himself, she guessed.

The wind slapped at the road, lifting another cloud of dust into the air. The shay's iron tires crunched over the hard ground. She slanted another look at the man sitting silent beside her. She didn't care about that Moses Weaver anyway. Luc was the one she was after.

She collected the reins some, slowing down so that she could talk to him over the rattle. "It's lucky, I guess, that I came after you when I did, what with your busted wheel and all, and Gwendolene's baby on the way. Imagine, Luc, two babies comin' on the same day. Next thing you know folk'll start complainin' about the Miawa gettin' crowded."

She was pleased to see his mouth curve a little beneath the thick droop of his mustache. "We do seem to be having an epidemic of squalling brats lately," he said. "But you shouldn't be gallivanting about. You'll pull your stitches."

"I'm only a little sore, Luc," she assured him. She was pleased, though, that he cared enough to mention it.

He fell silent again after that. Marilee thought up a dozen things to say that might start a conversation, but none of them made it past the end of her tongue. She was used to a mean Luc and a charming Luc, but this brooding Luc was a new one on her.

They climbed the last rise before town, where a big box elder reached for the sky and the fingerboard pointed the way down the road. She pulled off into the leafy shade, wrapped the reins around the brake handle, and folded her hands over her trembly, jumpy stomach.

Luc turned slightly on the shay's cushiony seat, making the leather squeak. When his eyes met hers, Marilee's stomach flipped right over.

"Am I to assume," he said, "since we suddenly seemed to be squatting here like a vulture on a fence post, that the arrival of Gwendolene's squalling brat is hardly imminent?"

Marilee flapped her hand like a palmetto fan. The man did have a way of talking fancy, using twenty notable words when three ordinary ones would have done the job. "Lord, that babe'll be hours yet in comin'. Gwendolene started yowlin' soon as she felt the first little pang, and Mother Jugs sent me to fetch you just to shut her up."

They sat in more silence after that, taking in the view. A hawk hung still like a snagged kite in the heat-flattened sky. Dust tarnished the rolling grassland. The sage was blooming itself dizzy, though, the yellow blooms giving their tangy turpentine scent up to the wind.

Luc reached inside his coat and pulled out a screw-top silver pocket flask. Showing off his fine Virginia manners, he offered it to her first. When she waved it away, he cocked a brow at her, and so she took it after all.

The whiskey burned a raw path down her throat. It didn't do much to settle her jumpy stomach. She gave the flask back over to him, smearing the wetness off her lips with the back of her hand.

"How did you know where to find me, anyway?" he said.

"Oh!" The word gusted out of her, lifting her breasts. "I went out to the Triple Bar to fetch you, but they said you'd already headed back to town. So I was following along after, when I saw your buggy parked in those Plain People's farmyard."

Back they fell into silence again. Marilee had splashed honeysuckle water all over herself before she left the house, but she could feel sweat pooling now between her breasts. Because she knew she would be seeing Luc, she had put on one of her prettiest dresses, a pale green linen cambric with lace flounces and a row of jade green ribbons down the front. In an effort to appear more modest, she'd pushed a white lace tucker into the bodice.

Jugs had meanly offered to lend her a big old poke bonnet to cover up her ruined hair, saying she looked like a dead rat the day after the cats had been at it. Instead, Marilee had chosen a delicate little white linen hat with a yellow primrose posy on its stiffened brim. She wasn't going to go around acting shamed just because she had been shorn like a sheep. Of course for all the notice Luc as usual had taken of her, she might as well have stepped out wearing a tow sack. She sighed.

Luc passed the flask over to her. "There sure was a world of sorrow in that sigh. Have some more whiskey, guaranteed to anesthetize the pain of heartbreak."

She didn't take the flask this time, but looked up at him instead. "I am indeed mighty blue, Luc."

"Poor sweet Marilee." He gave her knee a light squeeze. Luc being tender and sweet even when he was trying not to be. "The heart just takes longer to heal than the body sometimes."

She shook her head, jarring loose a single tear that ran down her cheek. "It's more than that. I don't think I can be an upstairs girl no more, and I'm scared. 'Cause what other life is there for me?"

She might have started out to work her beguiling ways on Luc, but suddenly the truth of what she'd said hit her. There was no other life for her. She was a strumpet, and she might as well have had a big S branded into her forehead, because to the world she was always going to be a strumpet.

"You could marry yourself a cowboy," Luc was saying. "I'm sure more than a few of your regular callers are already halfway in love with you."

"All men love their chippies a little bit. It ain't the same."

He seemed to think seriously about that a moment, then he said, "Yes, I suppose all men do love their chippies a little, and no, it isn't the same. But still, I should think if you put your mind to it . . ." He leaned back to regard her out of whiskey-brightened eyes. "Well, perhaps not your mind. One should, after all, lead with one's strong suit. With those bosom-lifting sighs and dewy eyes of yours, you could probably trap yourself a poor innocent like that Moses Weaver in no time."

"Hunh, a Plain boy! He won't ever, and you know it. And what do you always have to be talkin' so mean for anyway, Luc Henry? My heart might be the only part of me I ain't sold yet, but even a whore's got to draw the line somewheres. I don't want to be married to just any-old-body. I want to be in *love*."

That last word had come out on a wail of feeling, feelings she hadn't meant to give away yet. Lord, she had to be careful of letting her tongue get ahead of itself. Luc had already stiffened all up like wet leather left in the sun, as if he expected what was coming and was bracing himself for it.

"If you want love," he said, "get yourself a puppy."

She stared at him. He looked so fine in his gentleman's suit and clean white shirt with its starched linen collar. The other men she knew were simple in their natures, mostly just a collection of appetites. But there were complexities to Doctor Lucas Henry that she just couldn't seem to puzzle out. He had gentle hands, and a tongue on him that could slice a girl's heart into ribbons. He was wealthy and educated, but he drank too much sometimes and consorted with chippies. He seemed to despise most people, and that she could surely understand. But she wondered what he had ever done to make him despise himself so much.

"A cowboy did give me a puppy once," she said sadly. "Mother Jugs had her Chinaman drown it 'cause it woke her up come mornin's, yippin'."

Actually this had really happened to one of the other girls, but she'd counted on the tale to make him feel bad, and she could see that it did. Poor Luc. He worked so hard at being the tough, mean man, and underneath his heart was pure mush.

She decided to try another story on him, this one true. "You men don't like to think about it, but most of us upstairs girls don't start out our lives in a place like the Red House. I had a home, Luc, and a family. A mother and three baby sisters and two big brothers. And a daddy . . . Why, when I was little, my daddy used to love me up so. He'd give me pretty things like hair ribbons, and once he gave me a pair of pantalets that had crocheted lace around the ankles, and he never beat me like he did my mother. He'd have himself a snootful of his corn squeezin's sometimes, you see, and then he'd let go of his temper and it would wind up connectin' with my mother's face. She was a pretty woman, was my mother, when she was younger."

She hadn't meant to get into that particular territory, and for a moment the memories were so sharp they took her breath away. She had watched her mother's face be shaped into misery and ugliness over the years by her father's fists, yet it was her mother she'd ended up hating the most; for letting him do it, for *making* him do it. . . .

"But I'd barely started growin' tits," she went on in a rush, "when my daddy and my brothers started fightin' over which of them was goin' to use me which night. So you can bet I lit out of there as soon as I could, and the first bawdy house I come across I moved right in. I figured if I was gonna get poked every night I might as well be gettin' paid for it. It's just that since then I've had me more men than a chicken's got lice, and I'm feelin' tired, Luc, tired and old and ugly. Then I remember back to when I was a little girl and I think I might have had me some dreams once. Some dreams and some hope."

He had been leaning over, studying the hands he had clasped between his spread knees, but now he raised his eyes to hers. "I've noticed how old and ugly you're looking," he said with a teasing smile that held just a wisp of sadness at its edges. "I doubt even a horsefly would look at you twice." He reached up and rubbed his thumb under her chin. "Just look at this. Flapping like a turkey's wattle."

The laugh that came out of her didn't sound like herself at all. She'd done it again, started out to beguile him and wound up dealing herself a roundhouse punch with the truth. Sometimes she *did* feel old and ugly, and so deathly tired and full of misery that she wondered if there was any getting over it.

"Luc? Will you prove to me that I'm not old and ugly yet? Will you kiss me?"

He went utterly still, and she could have sworn he was going to tell her that he didn't kiss whores. She held herself ready for it, the way her mother had waited mute and dead-eyed for her daddy's fist.

But then his face softened, and a tenderness came into his eyes. He leaned into her, tilting his head, and his mouth came down onto hers. His lips were warm, his mustache gently tickling. He kissed her with such sweetness it was almost unbearable. She closed her eyes and trembled.

He touched her nowhere else, just with his mouth, lips pressing against lips. And when he pulled away he left her lips feeling naked, and lonely. She looked up at him through eyes blurred by real tears. She figured she probably wore an expression of pained love on her face, but she couldn't have held it back any more than she could have held back her next breath.

He looked away from her, out into the prairie. She wanted to touch him, but she didn't dare.

"Luc? What I was only goin' to say was that—"

"I won't ever marry you, girl, so you'd better put that thought right out of your head, right now."

She tried to breathe, but her throat hurt too much. "I never said . . . I was only . . . Is it because I'm a chippy?"

A ragged laugh tore out of him. "No, sweet Marilee. It's because I am a drunk."

Her breath gusted out of her with such force it left her feeling dizzy. "Well, sure you imbibe a bit too much on occasion, but—"

"Like your father *imbibed* a bit too much on the occasions he beat your mother?"

"You're not like him."

A trace of a smile twisted his mouth. "Sweetheart, I am more like him than you ever want to know."

"No, Luc, you're a real good man inside yourself. One day you'll see that."

She leaned into him and took off his hat. She ran her fingers through his hair that was like sun-warmed caramel. She cradled his face in her hands and brought her lips up to his again.

He held himself still, then his mouth opened beneath the pressure of her lips, and she slid her tongue inside. She felt the hunger shudder through him, felt him surrender to it, surrender to her.

He tore his mouth from hers, then he took a white linen handkerchief out of his pocket and wiped off his lips.

Marilee sat next to him on the fringed leather cushion with her eyes wide, her mouth partly open, and her chest near to bursting with bitter pain.

After a long while he twisted his head up and looked at her, then looked down again. His lip curled. "Ah, Christ. One would almost think I'd broken your heart."

"You are so mean sometimes, Luc Henry. You are just so mean."

He raised his hand as if to stroke her cheek, but then he

let it fall without touching her. "If I'm 'just so mean,' then that's all the more reason why you don't want me for a husband. And if you truly don't want to be a whore anymore, then best of luck to you but go find someone else to be your salvation, and let me continue on my merry way to hell all by my lonesome."

She lifted her head and drew her shoulders up proud. She unwrapped the reins from the brake handle and spanked them against the horse's rump. The shay lurched into motion, bouncing over the bunchgrass and back out onto the sun-basted road.

"Maybe I'll do just that, Lucas Henry. And maybe you'll be sorry someday."

He tilted back his head, upending the whiskey flask over his mouth and drinking until it was empty. "Maybe I already am," he said.

IT WAS STILL BLISTERING HOT a week later when Quinten Hunter and his father, and his father's wife, went to the stockyards at Deer Lodge to buy more beeves for their overstocked and overgrazed range.

"Overstocked" and "overgrazed" were the words that figured most prominently in Quinten's conversation throughout the long ride there, until the Baron told him to shut his yap and save his breath for breathing. Whereupon Quinten accused his father of being the kind of stubborn fool who wouldn't move camp to get out of the way of a prairie fire, and Ailsa almost smiled.

At least Quinten imagined that she almost smiled. She was wearing a black straw shade hat with a gauzy scarf that fell over her face. The prairie wind molded the scarf against her nose and mouth and cheekbones. She looked more distant than ever, a woman wrapped in a shroud. She drove her small purple shay in silence along the ribbons of wheel tracks that wound through the sere and wind-flattened grass. Quinten and his father rode alongside her, but she might as well have been alone in the wild and empty land beneath the brassy sky.

That night in Deer Lodge they ate antelope steak in the dining room of the new three-story brick hotel. The Baron, his face flushed with whiskey and desperation, talked about the old days when cattle could be fattened on the open range at no expense save for a few cowboys, some corrals, and a branding iron. The good old days, when a five-dollar steer could be run for a season or two and then sold for sixty dollars.

The good old days, Quinten thought, were like yesterday's dollars, used up and spent long ago. But try telling that to his father.

While they ate, Quinten watched the reflection of their table in the glass panes of the hotel's lantern-glazed window: a man and wife and their son, sharing a meal, the man talking and smiling, his wife seeming to hang on his every word. And beside them their son, raised in their image, the heir to their past and the hope of their future.

He smiled wryly to himself, his eyes slitting, and the reflection in the windowpanes wavered and fell away. Some truths were only illusions, he thought, and other truths were turned into lies, whether you thought you could bear it or not, and the accepting of that bit of life's knowledge was hard, hard.

And then there were those truths you shouldn't be thinking about at all. Like what had been done to that Plain boy and his poor chippy out by Blackie's Pond, what he had watched and *allowed* to be done to them. When he remembered what had happened on that day, he couldn't bear to look at his father's face.

You heard your pa say how she had to be taught a lesson....

God, she had screamed.

Quinten looked away from the window and caught the gaze of his father's wife. She stared back at him, and the deep emptiness, the utter indifference, of her violet eyes made something sink inside him.

"Christ and all his saints," his father suddenly said. "I've known a livelier time at a funeral." He yanked the napkin out of his collar, tossed it onto the table, then pushed heavily to his feet. "I'm going to see if I can find me a place where the company's more perky and congenial."

Quinten and his father's wife had not spoken before the Baron left, and they did not speak afterward. They finished their coffee and walked side by side in silence up the hotel's narrow Turkey-carpeted stairs. They had taken two rooms on the top floor: he and his father would batch it together in one, and Ailsa would have the other. In all the years Quinten had been with them, he'd never known them to share a bed.

He paused at her door and said, "Good night, Mrs. Hunter."

"Good night, Quinten," she answered. She glided inside and the door shut behind her with a soft click.

His own room was stuffy with the heat, and stank of the last occupant's chewing tobacco. Quinten threw open the window, hooked his gunbelt over the bedpost, took off his coat and shirt and boots, and lay down on top of the bed's nappy chenille spread. He stacked his hands behind his head and closed his eyes, but he felt too edgy to sleep.

A wagon with a squeaky axle rumbled by in the street below. Across the way a woman laughed and a piano struck up a tinny tune. A man came out of the saloon next door and pissed in the alley beneath Quinten's window.

He wondered what she was doing now—if she slept already, or if she lay there in the dusk like he was doing, counting the knotholes in the ceiling. He wondered if she cared at all that her husband had once again left her alone while he began the evening in some saloon and ended it in some whore's bed.

He must have drifted off, for he was suddenly jerked awake by the sound of crashing glass and gunfire. He snatched up his own gun and went to the window, but all the fuss was coming from a lone whiskified cowhand who was having a shootout with the street lamps.

Quinten put away his gun and stood a moment in the dark, in indecision. Then before he quite knew how he got there, he was standing outside her door and his curled knuckles were rapping softly on the wood. Too late he realized he was wearing only his trousers.

He had started to creep back across the hall when the door opened. She was still dressed in the dark purple silk dress she'd worn to dinner, except that three of the tiny jet buttons at her neck had been undone. She held a glass of whiskey in her hand. A faint blush stained her cheeks, like the first promise of sunrise in a pale dawn sky.

Her eyes registered on him and something happened deep inside them. It was as if a lamp that had been burning in a soft violet night was suddenly extinguished. He wondered if she had been hoping, expecting, to open her door and find his father on the other side of it.

"That gunplay," he said, his voice breaking a little over the words, "it wasn't anything for you to worry about. Only some cowboy with a bellyful trying to blow a week's worth of prairie dust out of his Colt."

She said nothing.

He swallowed, breathed. "Well, I just thought I'd see if you were all right."

She put her small white palm against the door and pushed it shut in his face.

THE SUN WAS COMING UP hot again on a new day when Quinten met his father at the stockyards. The Baron hadn't come back to the hotel the night before and he looked the worse for it. His eyes were bloodshot and his face raspy with beard stubble. He held his head as if it hurt even to breathe.

"Serves you right," Quinten said.

His father gave him a weary, bleary-eyed look. "Aw, bloody hell. Let's go buy us some cows."

It wasn't the best time of year to be buying stock. But the work of rounding up and branding and driving the herds to their home ranges could sometimes carry well into July, and a rancher looking to unload a bunch of mature cattle didn't always want to wait until the fall drives. So a man with the money to spend could often find beeves for sale in the summer months.

This morning, though, the pens and corrals that usually teemed with livestock were mostly empty. The wind blew dust devils down the open cattle chutes. Pole fences cast harsh shadow over barren lots. Only the middle pens held a couple of hundred ragged cows, which stood listlessly around the feeding and watering troughs, their heads hanging low in the heat.

"Jesus," the Baron said. "This place is as deserted as a church on Saturday night. Where is everybody?"

"Busted."

A tall man walked over to them from beneath the shade

of a water tank. He was so thin he looked put together out of sticks, and he was coated in red prairie dust from the crown of his black Stetson to the fringe on his worn chaps.

"Busted," he said again, smiling to show off teeth that were yellow as corn. "Nobody's selling, because nobody's buying." He pointed his long muzzle-shaped chin at the cows in the middle pens. "You're looking at all I got left of a ranch over in east Oregon. I been trying to hang on, but with the market glut and beef prices falling again this year, there ain't no way. I don't want to sell out—hell, not for the little I'm going to be getting. But I'm busted."

The Baron surveyed the quiet herd, his eyes squinting against the sun and wind-whipped dust. "They're a pretty ragged bunch," he said. "All horn and tail."

"They're trail weary, is all. Otherwise they're prime stock. All they need is a season or two of fattening up."

Quinten swallowed down a sigh and looked away. The sick feeling of the night before was back in full force, churning in his belly. He went over to a corral fence and leaned his arms on the top rail.

"I met up with a fellow last night who's willing to buy 'em for the hides," he heard the cowman say. "But I ain't said yes to his offer yet."

The sun, white as a flash of lightning, was searing the morning sky. Quinten closed his eyes.

In the Miawa country, not too far from the ranch, was a hogback ridge that shot straight up nearly three hundred feet into the sky and ended in a rocky, weed-choked coulee. In the years before the white man came, when his mother's people had been free to hunt the land of their birth, they had stampeded whole herds of buffalo over that cliff. As a boy, he had gone often to that place to walk among the piles of sun-bleached bones.

He had always wondered what those great dark hunch-backed creatures had felt when they took that last wild and frightening plunge off the edge of the world into oblivion.

He heard his father say, "I don't like taking advantage of a man when he's down."

And the cattleman answered, "I don't see myself as doing you a particular good turn, sir. In this market any man buying instead of selling is only chasing his own tail while he tries to catch up with himself."

The transaction was completed on a word and a handshake. His father had gotten a good deal, but Quinten didn't know where the money was going to come from. He didn't want to know. He told himself he ought to be concentrating instead on the logistics of how they would trail their newly acquired cows up to the Miawa, but it was too hot to think.

The cattleman said he had to go look up the hide buyer, to whom he'd promised an answer by this morning. He started to walk off, but then he turned around, pointing down the road, to a pair of wagons filled with huge jute sacks stuffed with wool and piled high as haystacks.

"Now there, sir, is the business you and I should be in. Sheep. Why, I bet them mutton punchers could buy us out twice over for what they're gonna get for just one of them wagons of wool clips." The cattleman hawked a short laugh and spat in the dirt, then walked off.

Quinten came up to stand alongside his father as they watched the heavily loaded wagons trundle toward them.

The man at the reins of the lead wagon had a thick ginger-colored beard that came to the middle of his chest. The wide brim of his hat flapped in the wind; his broad shoulders strained the seams of his old-fashioned sack coat. The driver of the second wagon was a beardless youth and he wasn't dressed Plain, but Quinten knew him. Remembering how he knew him stirred a shame that Quinten felt as a queasiness deep in his belly and a vile taste in his mouth.

The shame made Quinten angry with his father, who was the cause of it. "Looks like those Plain folk had themselves a good wool crop this year," he said. "I don't suppose they'll be wanting to sell out to us now or anytime soon."

The Baron said nothing, but Quinten could see the muscle working along the bone of his rigid jaw.

"And I don't expect a plague's going to come along and wipe them out for us either," Quinten pushed on. "Not with them being so godly and on the side of the righteous like they are. Pity that new stock inspector you hired isn't with us now. A man who can rape a woman with a gun barrel wouldn't have any trouble shooting down innocents in the street without provocation."

His father slowly turned to scowl at him. "What in hell are you yapping about?"

Quinten made his eyes go wide and innocent. "I thought I was just voicing aloud what you were thinking."

"What I'm thinking is that I'm hot and my head hurts."

"I don't know, Pa. You ought to be feeling good, what with the deal you just struck buying those mangy cows on the cheap. Why, with all the money you saved, maybe you should go talk to that Plain man on yonder wagon about acquiring some of his sheep. Since we're having so much trouble beating them head-on, maybe we ought to offer them a little roundabout competition by running some mutton of our own—"

He didn't see his father's fist coming until right before it connected with his jaw. The blow knocked his hat off his head and sent him sprawling in the dirt. But he scrambled back fast onto his feet, with his own hands clenched and raised.

The Baron lifted his head and jutted his jaw forward. "Well, lad o' mine, you with the smart mouth and cutting tongue? Let's see if you're as handy dealing out the hurt with your fists, eh?"

Quinten let his hands fall. "Naw. I don't fight with old men," he said. He bent over and picked up his hat, knocking the dust off against his thigh. The whole left side of his face felt like it had just had a set-to with a sledgehammer. "But I'll be damned if I apologize either."

His father gave him a hard smile. "I'm not so bloody old as you seem to think, and you can go choke on your bloody apologies."

He swung around and walked off, and it took Quinten a moment to realize that he was heading straight for the Plain folk and their wagons.

As Quinten started after him, his vision blurred beneath a wash of unexpected tears and his chest was suddenly choked with feelings—feelings of love and anger and dismay, and a growing disgust with himself. He couldn't change his father and he couldn't change what was going to happen. But neither could he walk away from it.

"Aw, Jesus, Pa," he said, and broke into a run to catch up. "What are you going to do now?"

IN THE PLAIN LIFE all was done according to tradition.

There were the old traditions, like the prayer cap and the hymnsongs, that went back so far no one could remember their origins. And then there were the new things, such as the sheep shearing and the summer pasturing. But even the new things were soon done in the same fashion year after year. It was the Plain way, this, to take the changes the world thrust upon them and make those changes into traditions that were woven into the pattern of their life. Into the straight and narrow way.

One of the new traditions was the selling of the season's wool crop.

Just as the Miller, Yoder, and Weaver farms all shared in the labor of their shearing, so too did they share in the selling of their fleeces. In good years the woolbags would be many and stuffed full, and it would take two big hay wagons, each pulled by a six-mule team, to carry them to market.

As the deacon, and thus less susceptible to temptation, Noah Weaver was always given the task of going out into the dangerous and corrupting world to find a buyer for their wool. Always before, he had chosen one of the Miller brothers to drive the second wagon, but on a morning three days ago he had looked up from his breakfast of fried mush and said to his son:

"You're a man grown enough, I should think, to come along with me to Deer Lodge this season and deal with the wool broker. To learn how it's done."

Mose had just taken a big drink from his coffee cup and he sputtered over the swallowing of it. "Are you saying you want me to drive one of the wool wagons to market with you?"

"I'm saying that, *ja*. Maybe you need to go wash out your ears."

So this season it was a changed Mose who had gone along with his father from farm to farm, loading the woolbags into the wagons. A Mose whose thoughts were dwelling on the traditions of the Plain life and his part in them. The bags, packed full with fleeces, were heavy to lift, but they were all big strapping men and it was good, hard, sweaty work. "The bad thoughts and feelings, they come out with the sweat," his father liked to say and Mose could see how this was so.

As he shared the work with the other men, he found himself looking at this life, the Plain life, in ways he hadn't done before. We are a good people, he thought. Strict and narrow in our ways, but our backs are wide and our hearts are giving.

They went last to the Yoder farm, and there a thing happened that was both hurtful and healing. A small thing it was, really, a small moment, and yet it made some broken part of Moses Weaver begin to feel whole again.

It happened after the last of the woolbags had been thrown high onto the growing piles in the wagons. They were standing in the farmyard, Mose and his father and the outsider, stretching the kinks out of their backs and wiping the sweat out of their eyes, talking about the fine crop they had sheared this season, when Mrs. Yoder came out of the house carrying a tin pan of cornmeal in her hands.

She began tossing the cornmeal to a flock of hens pecking in front of the barn. She flung her arm out wide, and the wind caught the meal and sent it swirling in a yellow cloud. The wind tugged at her cap strings and the loose strands of hair that curled out from beneath her prayer cap, and pressed her skirts to her legs.

Then she turned and looked their way, and her gaze locked with the outsider's.

Noah must have seen the look, too, for his face grew bleak with a hurt that cut deep. For once Mose saw his father not as the stern deacon full of righteous thoughts but only as a man who wanted desperately a woman who didn't want him back. And in that moment, Mose knew his father's pain as if it were his own.

Mrs. Yoder came up to him, dusting her hand off on her apron, smiling, and she said in that teasing way she had, "Well, young Moses, so it's you we'll be having to look to, this wool-selling season, to keep our Noah safe from trouble out in the wild and wicked world. Now, why do I think that's a bit like putting the coyote in with the chickens?"

Mose tried to smile, but he knew it must look all wrong. Since that terrible afternoon out by Blackie's Pond, he hadn't felt much like going out into the wild and wicked world.

"You got to quit thinking about that day, boy. Let it be like a bad dream you forget come morning."

The outsider's words nearly stopped Mose's breath, for the man rarely spoke to any of the Plain unless spoken to first. And it was disconcerting, besides, to have one's thoughts suddenly plucked out of the air and commented upon like that.

At least no one else had heard. Mrs. Yoder had turned to his father now, and she was laughing and picking tufts of wool out of his beard. Old Deacon Noah was trying to look stern, but Mose could tell he was pleased at the attention she was paying him.

The outsider's gaze lingered on her a moment and then shifted to the hill in back of the house, where young Benjo and his collie were herding a band of ewes through a gate and into a lower pasture. For just a moment a wistful look came over the man's face, a moment so quick Mose wondered afterward if he had only imagined it.

"It's days like this that are worth the remembering," the outsider said. "A day like this can stay with you, can settle down to live on in your soul forever."

"Yes, sir," Mose said, nodding, not sure if the man was really talking to him anymore or only to himself. And then he heard a startling thing. He heard his father laugh. Mrs. Yoder was threatening to cut off his father's beard to use for a broom, it was getting that long and thick, and his father was laughing.

Mose looked at his father. A big man, he was, with arms so strong they could toss a two-hundred-pound woolbag into a wagon bed and not even strain with the effort. A man so strong, so certain in his faith that angels probably found it hard to live up to his high expectations, let alone his only son.

Ja, a strong man was Noah Weaver, and a good man. Mose looked at his father's laughing face, and he felt the peace of the moment settle into his soul.

BUT THEN THE MORNING after the woolbags were all loaded, when the mule teams were hitched up and they were ready to set off for Deer Lodge, Mose had come out of the house wearing his flashy mail-order clothes. His father said nothing, only looked at him with the disappointment showing raw in his face. Mose set his jaw at a stubborn tilt, climbed onto the high seat of the hay wagon and picked up the reins.

And then as they were about to set the wagons to rolling out of the yard, Gracie came running down the road toward them, skirts flying, cap strings fluttering, and a cloth-covered basket bouncing on her arm. She ran right past him and stopped, out of breath and flushed, next to his father's wagon. She held the basket up and laughed.

"Oh, I'm so glad I caught you, Deacon Noah. I've brought some good Plain food for you, for your journey, so you won't have to do so much eating in those terrible *Englische* places."

"And a good morning to you, too, Gracie Zook," Mose called out to her, but she didn't answer him. The last time he had tried to talk to her, she'd told him she never wanted to look on his face again. *Ach vell,* she was a strong-willed girl, was his Gracie, and she surely wasn't looking at him now. But she had never before brought a food basket to Deacon Noah to take with him on his journey to the wool market.

Maybe it was a new tradition she was starting.

HE WAS THINKING OF GRACIE, of the way she had looked with her face all flushed so prettily and her bosom rising and falling with her panting breaths. He was thinking of Gracie and smiling, when he saw Fergus Hunter step into the path of his father's wagon.

They both had to pull up hard on their teams to avoid running over the cattleman. Their heavily laden wagons jolted to a stop, creaking and groaning. Mose's leader mules shied and bucked in the traces, and he had his hands full for a moment getting them back under control.

When he looked up again he saw that Fergus Hunter's son had come to stand by the man's side. Their gazes, Mose's and the other boy's, met for a moment and then jerked hard apart. A blush of shame burned hot in Mose's cheeks as he remembered how that boy had last seen him—bent over a cottonwood log, his bare ass getting whipped with a pair of chaps by the Hunters' hired gun.

They had pulled up across from the Deer Lodge stockyards. Mose's gaze searched the corrals and pens, looking for that hired gun now but finding only cows.

The cattleman's black eyes were studying Noah from beneath the brim of his hat. "I believe," he said, "that you are one of the preacher gentlemen I talked to last year. About you and your people selling your rangeland to the Circle H."

The wind came up, bringing with it the smell of cattle and sunbaked dust. And fear. Mose could smell the fear on himself, rank as rotting meat.

But if his father was afraid, he didn't show it. Noah sat in stillness on the wagon seat, his head up and his eyes on the road ahead, the reins loose in his hands. He sat in silence long enough for the cattleman to think he wouldn't be getting a response, and then he said, "*Ja*. You talked, outsider. And our minds, they have not changed."

Fergus Hunter's mouth thinned into a tight smile. "Now that is peculiar, it is. Because I was given to understand that you folk've been having a run of bad luck lately. Stampedes and hay fires and such."

Noah sat in his wagon, immovable and silent as a boulder.

The cattleman heaved an elaborate sigh. "And what with the way trouble always seems to run in bunches," he said, shaking his head and taking a cigar out of his vest pocket. "Well, I have to admit to you, sir . . ." He bit off the end of the cigar and spat the tobacco into the dirt at his feet. "I do have to admit that I don't know a whole hell of a lot about the business of sheep. Cattle being more in my line, you understand."

He put the cigar in his mouth and struck a long stove match on the wheel rim of Noah's wagon. "But a man picks up stray bits of facts here and there," he went on, speaking around the cigar now clamped in his teeth, and holding the burning match up to the end of it. "Like I been told, for instance . . ." He sucked hard on the cigar until its tip glowed red, then blew out smoke from between pursed lips. ". . . that there's nothing catches alight quicker than a bunch of oily fleeces."

Fergus Hunter held the burning match up in the air. Caught by the wind, the flame wavered and then brightened, and Mose's heart jolted with a new rush of fear. That single match tossed into a wagon bed full of woolbags, and they could all turn into one enormous pillar of fire.

The cattleman's son jerked a hand up as if he would snatch the match away, but then he let it fall back to his side. And the match went on burning, fanned by the wind.

"We will not sell to you, outsider," Noah said. "And you

can never defeat us. The Lord said to Abram: 'I am thy shield, and thy exceeding great reward.'"

For an eternity of a moment longer they all watched the flame eat away at the thin stick of wood. Then the cattleman shook his hand and the flame went out. He turned hard around on his heel and strode off, back toward the stockyards from where he had come.

"He wouldn't have done it," Fergus Hunter's son said. "He was only . . . He wouldn't have done it."

Noah said nothing to the boy, nor did he look at him. He gathered the reins, sitting up taller, although to Mose's eyes his father's broad back and shoulders already seemed to fill the world.

"Hie!" Noah shouted to his mules, and his wagon lurched into motion.

"Hie!" Mose shouted, his voice cracking.

He felt such a fierce pride in his father that his heart sang with it.

THE YELLOW LIGHT OF a full moon illuminated the farmhouse better than half a dozen lanterns. Mose had no trouble finding the window he wanted. He scooped up a handful of pebbles and flung them at the panes, rattling the glass.

"Gracie!" he croaked, trying to holler and whisper at the same time. *"Wo bist du?"*

The sash slid up with a loud screech. "You go away, Mose Weaver. I told you I never wanted to see your face again."

"It's night out, and you can shut your eyes. You don't need to look at my face, only let me—"

From deeper in the house came a man's sleepy, grumbling voice. *"Vas geht?"*

The window slammed shut with a screech and a bang.

Mose leaned back against the cottonwood logs of the house, feeling hard used. *What ever happened to mercy, Gracie Zook? What about love covering up all sins, and not being angry forever, and forgiving men their trespasses, huh?*

He bent over and searched through the bunchgrass for a rock, found a good-sized one, hefted it in his hand.

He swung around and threw the rock at the window just as the sash was flung up again. The rock sailed through black space and into the house. There was a thump, a clatter, and a loud moan.

"Gracie!" He scrambled over the windowsill, ripping his trousers on a loose nail and banging his forehead on the jamb. "Oh, God in heaven, Gracie. Did I kill you?"

Her white face framed by a white muslin night cap came at him from out of the dark. "You are a crazy person!"

"Let me come in. Please."

"You're already in."

She didn't tell him to get himself back out, so he took that as an invitation to stay. He stood where he was, letting his eyes get used to the dark. He heard the rustle of sheets as Gracie got back into bed.

He took off his coat and shirt, his boots and trousers. Still wearing his short-legged cotton union suit, he climbed into bed beside her. On a hot night like this the flannel sheets felt as scratchy as wet hay.

They lay in the dark, quiet but for their breathing. Nowhere did their bodies touch, nor would they ever touch until after they had spoken their wedding vows. Yet cloaked by the night, it was easy to talk, to share dreams and hopes and expectations. During a year of bed courtship, you grew to know well the heart and mind of the person you would share a marriage bed with for the rest of your life. You learned if you could take the terrible and the tender together.

The *Englische* thought it sinful, their tradition of bed courtship. Funny, but Mose had never seen how it could be sinful before now. Yet here he was imagining his hand sliding across the sheet and touching Gracie's arm, his palm covering Gracie's breast, his mouth kissing Gracie's mouth, his—

Judas, he was depraved! And heading straight for hell, with maybe a stop off at the nuthouse on the way.

He stretched out his legs to their fullest and linked his hands behind his head. "Gracie?"

She was silent for so long that he thought she was asleep, or pretending to be. Then she pushed herself up on her elbow. Moonlight limned her forehead and the soft curve of her cheek. "I don't think you fear God anymore, Mose—to do what you've done this spring and summer."

"I fear Him." He did fear God, and the pain of hellfire, but maybe he feared other things more. He feared losing her, and never being able to make things right again with his father. He feared the moment when he would finally have to choose between what he was and what he wanted to become.

He felt a stinging heat in his chest and eyes. No woman but her was ever going to help him to be his best self.

His hand trembled with the need to touch her.

"Gracie? Let's go for a walk."

He didn't wait for her answer but swung right out of the bed, fast. He stumbled around looking for his trousers and got dressed again, all but for his coat, which he slung over his shoulder.

He climbed first out the window, then turned to help her. As she swung her legs over the sill, she leaned into him and he saw that there were little yellow daisies embroidered on the yoke of her nightrail.

The grass rustled beneath their feet. The wind, still warm from the day's baking, lifted his hair and tugged at the loose strings of her night cap. They could see the wild roses that grew along the creek, the fat old moon was so bright.

They walked side by side, and she was the one to slip her hand into his.

"You're dressed *Englische* again," she said.

And you, my little secret rebel, have yellow daisies growing all over your nightrail. He didn't say it, though. Even he wasn't that big a fool. "I'm trying to figure it all out inside myself, Gracie, and I'm making progress on it. You got to believe that."

He wished he could talk to her about what had happened in Deer Lodge, about the way his father had faced down those outsiders in his own brave and quiet and Plain way. He didn't know the words to explain to her that he wanted to own the courage of his father's faith, but still wasn't ready to pay the price. To take to the Plain and narrow path and never stray from it again.

Someday he would talk to her about it all, but not just yet.

"I think you will always be something of a wild one," she was saying, "in your heart and in your head."

He tugged on her hand, turning her so that they were face to face. "Can you live with that?"

She gave him a decisive nod that was so much like her. His Gracie, whose thoughts plowed furrows that were straight and deep.

He swung his coat off his shoulder, feeling with his fingers for the breast pocket. "I almost forgot. I brought you something." He took out a photograph of himself that had been mounted on pasteboard. While in Deer Lodge he had crossed paths with an itinerant photographer and on a whim he'd decided to get his likeness taken. Moses Weaver in his worldly mail-order clothes. The photograph still smelled some of the chemicals that had permeated the man's wagon.

He held the photograph out to her and she took it, then

gave a funny little sucked-in breath when she saw what it was. "You are giving me this forbidden thing?"

"I was thinking that once I've taken my vows and am Plain forever, I might want a reminder of my wild and younger self, the crazy Mose who had to go and break all the rules." He huffed a little laugh, shrugging. "You can do with it whatever you like. Burn it if you want."

She curled her hands around the pasteboard and brought it up to her chest. "Maybe I'll keep it. I can always wave it in your face later, when you're acting the big know-it-all man around the house."

Her words warmed his heart. She'd spoken of later, of a time when they would be married and he would be the big know-it-all man around the house. He hadn't lost her, he wasn't going to lose her because she'd decided that she cared for him enough to wait until he was ready.

"Gracie?"

She leaned into him to brush her lips across his cheek. "What?"

"I think maybe tomorrow I will begin to grow a beard."

22

IT BEGAN WITH THE drumbeat of a redheaded woodpecker. There followed a glissando, the crystal chiming of the creek running along its stony bed. The rocking of the wagon wheels over the rough ground was a cradlesong.

And over, through, around it all was the whistle of the hot wind.

The music was with her—soft and sweet-flowing at first. The music quickened, became a runaway, roundelay tune. The music brightened to ebullient, joyful caroling, and Rachel's soul was stirring, Rachel's soul was flying.

The music left her.

It left her smiling as the spring wagon lurched over the track, although to call it a track was being kind. It was a sheep path cut through the humped, pine-studded mountains and leathered slopes of grassland where the Plain People summered their woollies.

The Yoder, Miller, and Weaver farms had always done their summer pasturing together. Each June they combined their sheep into a common herd, earmarking and docking the animals to tell them apart, then drove them up onto the mountain ranges. Then the men from each of the farms took turns at the sheepherding.

Ben had never liked the lonesome life of summer sheepherding. He couldn't stand living in his head so much, he'd said. But Rachel had always thought she would love it. Time moving slow and sweet through the long, pure days. Living in her head with the music.

She couldn't be a summer shepherd. It wasn't woman's work. But when it came the Yoder turn for the herding, Rachel did the camp tending. In her wagon bed now were white sacks of salt for the sheep and rawhide-covered boxes packed with coffee and beans and bacon for the shepherd. And on this day, when sunlight splashed through the pine boughs and ground larks flitted from under her horse's feet, she was bringing these supplies to Johnny Cain.

It was good that the outsider had gone up into the hills with the sheep, away from the farm now, away from her. Good for their immortal souls, and for her virtue.

It had only been a matter of days since she had danced in his arms on a new-mown hayfield, since she had kissed his man's mouth. Days she could count on fingers and toes, busy days of shearing and getting the sheep ready for summer pasturing. Yet for her, he alone had filled every moment of that time.

Even when they had all gathered for the sheep drive—when she was giving her brother Sol a letter-from-home to eat on the trail, and teasing Samuel, who hated to ride, about getting saddle sores, and laughing when the wind snatched away Levi's hat and a hungry ewe tried to eat it—even when she was safe within the loving family of her Plain life, always, always, she had been aware of Johnny Cain, and it was all she could do not to touch him, there before the eyes of Noah and her brothers.

Once, when they had a moment alone, he looked at her with one of those quiet smiles that touched only his eyes and he said, "You think that soon as me and the woollies are out of sight over yonder ridge, then you'll have whipped temptation. But aren't you forgetting how when your Jesus went out into the desert, Satan followed along after?"

"What I am thinking, what I am knowing, Mr. Cain, is that a month spent up on yonder mountain with our sheep should teach your soul much about the virtues of solitude and abstinence."

And he had laughed. "Lady, I don't need to go up on any mountain to be getting a lesson in abstinence."

It was then, in the midst of a thousand bawling, bleating woollies, that she had come the closest to telling him she loved him. Perhaps she had needed him to know, perhaps she had needed to tell him this: If it had been only her body that wanted him, then it would have been so much easier to let him go.

But his laughter had drawn looks from her brothers, and so she had turned away from him.

He sought her out, though, one last time before they left, and he said, "Come up with the supplies when the time comes. Don't send somebody else."

And she had said, "But you must understand that nothing will have changed. We will still be who we are."

"Promise me, Rachel, that you'll be the one to come."

"I promise."

THE SPRING WAGON LURCHED over a boulder, and the provision boxes banged and rattled. "Are you keeping a good hold on back there?" she called to Benjo, who was perched, legs swinging, on the open tailboard, with a fresh-baked shoofly pie under his tender loving care.

She got a muffled *umph* in response.

"You get your sticky fingers out of that pie," she said. She hadn't needed to turn around; she knew her boy.

They plunged out of the mellowed and muted shadows of the tree-shaded path and into the harsh sunlight of a clearing.

The dented tin stovepipe of the sheepwagon flashed a welcome from across the meadow. A few sheep were scattered over the sunlit grass but most were shaded down among the trees. MacDuff was there, ears pricked, tongue lolling, tail thumping. She didn't see the outsider.

They unharnessed and watered the horse, and tethered her loosely so she could graze. They unloaded the provisions, then took a walk among the herd. The sheep were much prettier now that their wool was coming in again.

The new growth had a soft knotty feel to Rachel when she rubbed a ewe's head.

"What have you done with your shepherd?" she asked the ewe, who looked back at her with eyes that were sweet, but empty.

She heard a sputtering, choking sound and saw that Benjo's forehead was puckered with worry, his eyes too wide and bright. His throat locked and clenched around the words he couldn't get out.

"Huh . . . huh . . . huh . . ."

"No, he hasn't," she said. She rubbed Benjo's head like she'd just done to the ewe. "He wouldn't abandon our sheep to the mercy of the coyotes and the bears."

But she understood her son's fear, for she shared it. One day they would look up and Johnny Cain would be gone, before it was his time to leave them.

"Perhaps he's off hunting a grouse or a rabbit for supper," she said.

Benjo headed deeper into the pines, his eyes searching. Rachel came along with him. They heard a panicked *baa!* first, followed by loud sucking noises, and a man's low, melodious cursing.

"You perfidious daughter of a promiscuous bitch. Any damned woolly as mutton-headed as you deserves to drown."

"Don't listen," she said to Benjo, her own ears burning. But she had to suck on her cheeks to keep from laughing at the sight that greeted her eyes.

A fat, bawling ewe stood mired shank deep in a bog that appeared to be caused by an underground spring. Either too mud-logged or too stupid to climb out, she stood shivering and complaining to the outsider, who was pushing on her rump, trying to shove her out.

Rachel didn't think he knew they were there, but then he said, "You going to stand there and cling to your high ground, Mrs. Yoder? Or get down here and wallow in the mud with the rest of us sinners."

"I believe I will cling, Mr. Cain."

Benjo, with a boy's love for anything wet and dirty, happily slogged into the mire to help. Benjo took the right loin, Cain took the left, and together they heaved. The ewe exploded out of the bog with a loud, sucking pop, like a cork out of a bottle. She turned around and around in a circle, huffing and bleating and shaking her head, and then trotted off to join the rest of the flock as if nothing had happened.

The man and the boy slogged out after her, bringing a good part of the bog with them.

Cain swiped the grit out of his mouth with his shirt cuff. "This has got to be the only mudhole left in all the Miawa," he said, "and that lady had to go and find it."

Rachel came to him. Using the hem of her apron she wiped the mud splatters off his face, and all the while she was doing it, she was looking into his eyes and smiling.

They walked back to the clearing together, the three of them, like a family. Rachel could feel a humming in her chest, as if her heart were warming up to sing. She thought how there was a certain purity to moments like this, moments all bright and shimmery, like the morning after a hard rain, when the whole world looked washed clean.

She slanted a glance up at him, wondering if he too felt the purity of the moment. He was looking so fine. The days spent beneath the summer sun had tanned his pale skin to the golden color of apple cider. His eyes had a bright, silvered look to them. She thought she could probably walk along beside him like this, looking at him, forever.

Their gazes met.

“So, Mr. Cain,” she said, “are you glad to see . . . us?” *Me.* She’d almost said *me* and he knew it.

“I’m glad to see someone who can make a decent cup of coffee. You could float a horseshoe in the sludge I make.”

“And besides the mud bath and your wretched coffee,” she said, “how have you survived your first days of summer herding?”

“Well,” he answered, drawling the word molasses-slow, “I started talkin’ to the woollies last Tuesday, and by Friday they were answerin’ back, but I didn’t really start to worry till this morning.” His eyes squinted at her, and his mouth deepened at the corners. “When what they said started makin’ sense.”

Laughing, she put a little skip into her step. She would have slipped her arm through his and leaned into him, drawn herself closer to him while they walked—if he were her man. But he wasn’t her man.

The flash of a red hide among the pines caught her eye. She thought it was a deer at first, but it was too big for a deer. Then she realized there were more of them, perhaps fifteen head, feeding on the few shriveled tufts of bunchgrass that grew up around the sparsely scattered trees.

“Huh—Hunter cattle!” Benjo shouted, pointing.

“A couple of days ago those cows decided to join our woolly frolic uninvited,” Cain said from beside her. “I keep chousing them outta here, and they keep coming back.”

“It’s such a hot dry summer, this year. The whole world seems to be running out of grass.” The poor cattle looked ragged and hungry, all bones and mangy hide. Rachel didn’t mind sharing the hills with them, but she doubted Fergus Hunter wanted to do any sharing with her.

The thought was like a fleeting cloud crossing the sun of her day. As if pulled there by a magnetic force, her gaze went to the gunbelt that hung heavy and deadly around the outsider's hips.

I'll kill them for you, if you want.

This time I'm killing them for you.

All of her life, she had never been afraid, for God had been with her always. All of her life, the Lord had been her shield, the Plain faith her comfort. But then Ben had been taken from her in an act of cruel and senseless violence, and a herd of stampeded cattle had nearly taken her son, and men had come out of the night with fiery brands to burn her hay. Fear had come into her life, corroding her faith, casting shadows over her soul. And sometime during this long hot summer, the lost part of her had slowly begun to embrace a new faith, the belief that Johnny Cain could be her shield and her comfort—Johnny Cain and his gun.

They passed through the flock grazing the parched bunchgrass, and all three of them, out of habit, began looking over the ewes and their babies. At any moment there were a million and one catastrophes that could befall a sheep. They required constant tending.

"We lost two lambs to coyotes last night," Cain said to her, as he lifted the tail of a yearling wether to check for maggots. "It looked to be the work of a single bitch with pups she's teaching to hunt. She's dragging a bum leg."

Benjo, who had stooped over to rub noses with a black-faced lamb, suddenly straightened up. His eyes fastened onto the outsider, wide and frightened and pleading.

"Nuh . . . nuh . . . nuh!" He ground the heel of his brogan into the grass as his jaw muscles bunched and clenched, chewing up the words before they could get out of his mouth. His lips pulled back from his teeth in a grimace. "Nuuuugh!" he shouted in one last agonized gasp, then lurched around and ran off in the direction of the creek.

"I don't know what's the matter with him," Rachel said. "He never used to be afraid of them before, but lately any mention of coyotes sets him off."

Cain was staring after the boy, his eyes narrowed slightly in the way of a man studying a mildly perturbing question. "Maybe he's witnessed a kill recently."

"Oh, I do hope not." She shuddered at her own memory of bellies ripped open, ribs thrusting through mangled wool, entrails spilled on the blood-soaked grass, and bones picked clean. "Benjo has such a soft spot in his heart when it comes to any animal, and it's such a gruesome thing, what the coyotes can do to a lamb."

"It's a part of life," Cain said, and the callousness of his words matched the look that came over his face.

She looked up into that face, into those eyes that were so relentless, so ruthless. She didn't want Benjo's eyes ever to look like his. Cain was a man hardened and tempered by life. By life in a world where sweet little lambs had their guts ripped out, where the sky forgot to rain and the grass dried up, where men came in the night with burning brands, and a woman's husband was hanged for no reason from the limb of a cottonwood tree.

Then even as she was watching him, she saw his face soften. And she saw the intent in his eyes before he raised his hand to touch her. He only brushed along her jaw, lightly, lightly, with the tips of his fingers, but it almost made her cry.

"Don't you and the boy be afraid of the coyotes," he said, in the gentlest voice she'd ever heard from any man.

THE OUTSIDER WENT LOOKING for Benjo so they could fish the creek for their supper.

Rachel was pleased to think of them doing this manly thing together. She hoped her son would open up to Cain about his fears. But he had such trouble getting his words out, and when the words were attached to strong feelings, it became nearly impossible. As for the outsider, who wouldn't crack open himself under a sledgehammer, he certainly wasn't going to probe and poke at Benjo's troubles. It wasn't his way, and it wasn't the way of people out here. For that matter, the Plain folk didn't do a lot of probing and poking either.

Rachel sighed. Probably all they would do was fish.

She decided that in the meantime she would do a bit of housekeeping in the sheepwagon. In her experience, a man living alone in a confined space tended to forget all about cleanliness being next to godliness.

The top half of the Dutch door was open to let in air. Rachel climbed the narrow steps and pushed in the latch to the bottom half, wincing at the squeal of unoiled hinges.

It always amazed her what an efficient thing was a sheepwagon. A narrow bunk was wedged across the back end, and a small square cookstove tucked into the front end. Along one side was a hinged table that could be folded up when you weren't using it. Along the other were storage bins that doubled as a place to sit. It should have felt cramped, but resting high on its narrow spoked wheels and with its round canvas top, the wagon held a feeling of spaciousness.

It was cleaner inside than she had expected, although there was a kettle of mulligan stew sitting on an iron spike that had sure seen better days. She took the coffeepot off the stove and gave it a shake. She popped the lid and wrinkled her nose at the tarry sludge stirring in the bottom. But she didn't set about brewing up a fresh pot right away. Instead, she unpacked the last of the provision boxes that she and

Benjo had carted up from the farm. At the bottom of the box, wrapped in butcher paper to protect it, was a gift she had made for Johnny Cain.

The yellow sateened muslin caught the light, shimmering, as she slid it from the brown paper.

She had done a wicked thing, buying the sateened muslin that terrible day in Miawa City. Then once she had it in her possession, she had done another wicked thing. Oh, not a terribly wicked thing, more a worldly thing. She had sewn up a set of ruffled curtains.

The sheepwagon had a single window on the side where the table was, framed by wood set into the thick canvas. It had oiled parchment in place of glass, but it was a fair size, big enough to let in the light, and the mountains and pines and acres of grass and the big Montana sky. Big enough for curtains made of yellow sateened muslin.

She would never have been able to make such a gift for a Plain man. But she didn't see what harm there would be in giving the outsider a little something just for pretty to brighten up the solitary, lonesome days of summer herding.

Kneeling on the table, she strung the curtains across the window with a piece of rope. She'd just folded the table back up when she heard the scrape of boots on the steps. She spun around, putting space between herself and the window, trying to look busy with the coffeepot. She was floating with sweet anticipation.

She wiped her hands on her apron, tucked a loose bit of hair beneath her prayer cap. "So," she said to him as he came through the door, "did you two catch any fish?"

"A whole mess of sockeye." His gaze was drifting around the wagon, alighting everywhere but on her. "I thought you and Benjo could take the bunk tonight," he said. He rocked a little on his heels and gave his hat brim a tug. "I've been bedding down outside most nights, anyway," he went on. "It's cooler. And I want to keep a watch out for them coyotes."

"I've a surprise," she blurted, smiling, floating, lighter than air. Loving him, loving him so much. "Actually, I've two surprises. One was a shoofly pie, only that boy of mine, he went and ate most of it on the way up here. But these I made up special just for you." She swung around, showing him the curtains, floating, smiling, loving him. "A little something just for pretty."

She was looking at the curtains, smiling still, and so she didn't notice the silence. She turned back to him, smiling, and she was still smiling even as she began to see that all the color had left his face and his eyes had gone stark and hard.

He turned on his heel and left the wagon, left her, without a word.

SHE MADE A CAMPFIRE out in the meadow and cooked the salmon he and Benjo had caught for supper, but he never came to eat it. Later that evening, lying snug up against her son in the narrow bunk, saying her prayers in silence, as was the Plain way, her gaze went to the window.

The curtains were gone.

THE WAIL OF A cougar woke her.

She sat up, fumbling for the tin matchbox holder in its place beneath the bunk. Benjo stirred in his sleep, but dreamt on. She used a struck match to find her half boots and her shawl to pull around her nightrail, but she waited until she was through the door of the sheepwagon before she lit the wick in the coal oil lantern.

MacDuff stood at the bottom of the steps, legs braced and growling. The hair on his neck had risen in a thick ruff. Some of the sheep were bleating and milling in alarm. The cry of a cougar was a terrible thing to hear deep in the night. It sounded like a woman's scream.

She listened, ears straining, but all she heard now was the wind making the treetops shake. MacDuff gave a muffled whine and lay back down.

Her lantern threw a pale glow against the pines, casting long shadows over the grass. She walked among the sheep, murmuring, soothing them. She prayed the cougar had passed them by.

When Ben did the summer herding, he would bring his old Sharps rifle along with him to take care of such things as coyotes and bears and cougars. But the Sharps rifle was in the barn back at the farm. And Johnny Cain, her shield and comfort, appeared to have deserted her.

If the outsider was still gone by morning, she would have to send Benjo back down into the valley to fetch Noah, for their sheep couldn't be left without a shepherd. She would have to look into Noah's eyes and admit to the mistake she had made.

The woollies settled down again, went back to their dreams of green meadow grass. But Rachel didn't go back to the bunk in the herder's wagon and her own troubled dreams. She extinguished the lantern and let herself be swallowed up by the deep blue night.

The moon, shining white and hard, balanced on the peak of the highest mountain. She tilted her head back, and it seemed she was falling into a big black bowl of a sky milky with stars.

But then she sensed a movement out the corner of her

eyes, over by the rock cairn that stood at the far edge of the clearing.

It had been built by the summer herders over the years, that cone-shaped heap. One by one, each rock had been added by the resident shepherd, one for each week spent up here alone. A tradition that had no meaning, except that the result of it had become a monument to loneliness.

HE WAS WEARING HIS black duster, so she could barely tell where he left off and the darkness of the night began. They stared at each other, and the air around them ached and trembled like the pause between lightning and thunder.

He came toward her suddenly, his duster flaring darkly, throwing shadows over her. He held a ripped and wadded-up ball of the yellow muslin in his hands.

She took a step back, and he stopped. He drew in a deep breath and then another. "I won't hurt you."

"I know, Johnny," she said, sparing him with a lie. For he could hurt her in so many ways.

The yellow muslin cloth fell from his fists, fluttering to the ground. "Don't leave me, then," he said.

She took a step toward him, and then another. She reached out her hand to him, and he met it halfway with his own, entwining their fingers.

They stayed that way awhile, touching in silence. Then he gave a little tug, pulling her closer, and she came. He sat at the base of the rock cairn, bringing her down with him, settling her between his thighs. She leaned her back against his chest and wrapped her arms around her drawn-up legs. They stayed that way a long time, silent, her sitting deep within the circle made by his body.

He rubbed his palm over her bent knee. His breath

stirred warm against her neck. "I always thought of sheep as being white, but they're gray," he said, bringing her into the middle of his thoughts. "They're the color of the gravy we had every Sunday for supper over soda biscuits. Gravy so watery it was the color of sheep."

"Your folks, they were poor, then?"

He fell silent again, but she didn't care. She would give him the silence and this night as a gift, for like the sheep and the seasons, he couldn't be rushed.

She heard a rustle, then a barking cry, and looked up to see the winged shadow of an owl flit across the moon.

His chest moved against her back as he eased out a held breath. "I'm no good at this, Rachel. It's like allowing a man to get the drop on you in a gunfight."

"Then let it go and just hold me instead," she said, for she had come to know that she could never understand the source of all the darkness that lived inside him. There could be no understanding of him, only acceptance.

His arms, which had been wrapped loosely around her, tightened a little. "There's this orphanage in east Texas, only they call it something more fanciful, the Blessed Are the Merciful Foundling Home for Boys. It has this big wrought iron fence and a gate in front of it. They told me that was where they found me, tied to the gate with a rope like an abandoned dog."

She picked up his hand, his scarred and beautiful and deadly hand, and wrapped her own hands around it as if she cradled a wounded bird. He tried to pull free, but she tightened her grip. She had to touch him, to comfort him, and he made it so hard.

"Every spring they'd have this day in church where they'd put us up for adoption, as they called it." His laugh caught on a tearing sound. "Aw, Rachel, we were so pathetic.

The way we'd scrub our faces and slick back our hair and put on begging little smiles, each of us hoping he'd be the one to be picked out from the others. Believing that if we minded our manners and worked real hard, then we wouldn't be brought back to the Home come winter.

"But we were always brought back, because there was never meant to be any 'adoption.' The Home was only renting us out to the local farmers for their planting and the harvest. Still, even after I got wise to that game, every damn spring I'd stand up in the front of the church and hope some family would pick me out for their son."

Rachel bit her lip so hard she tasted blood. She thought of the chair always there for her at her father's table. She'd never had to hope to be chosen because she had always belonged, cherished within the loving arms of her family and her Plain life.

"The summer I was ten I was rented out to a Mr. Silas Cowper, who was a hog farmer. He claimed to have owned slaves before the war, and I think he must not've put much stock in the Emancipation Proclamation, because he sure enough thought he owned my sorry ass, and I don't know if there was any slave ever worked as hard as he tried to work me.

"I ran away first chance I got, but he caught me easy enough. With dogs that he bred for bull fighting. He dragged me back to his place and he put shackles on my legs and arms and chained me to a post in the barn next to this big carcass hook."

He was talking in a raw, hoarse voice now, as if he were being strangled. She could feel a hard trembling going on deep inside him.

"Cowper took this hog and he hooked it through the neck and hoisted it up with pulling blocks, only the hog wasn't dead, and it hung up there for two days, squealing and bleeding and dying, with me chained underneath it."

She held herself still. She wanted to turn within the circle of his arms and press herself hard against him and tell him that she hadn't known, hadn't known. But she held herself still.

"Then when that hog *was* finally good and dead, Cowper gutted it and dropped it into a barrel of boiling hot water to make it easy, he said, to scrape the hair off its hide. He was talking to me, see, all the while he was doing it, telling me how he owned me and that if I ever ran off again he'd do to me exactly what he'd done to that hog. And I believed him."

He breathed, his chest pushing against her back, and she could feel his heart beating frantically like a trapped bird. "From then on he kept me chained to that post in the barn, when he wasn't working me, except for the nights when he hung me from that carcass hook and laid my back open with a shot-loaded hog whip. It took me nearly a whole year to weaken a link in that chain enough to bust it."

His throat locked up for a moment, the way Benjo's sometimes did. The darkness and the silence of the night lapped around them. Rachel's heart felt bruised and battered, as if it had been wrenched from her body and beaten against the rocks at their backs.

"I figured," he said, his voice gone flat and cold now, "I figured that if I wasn't going to wind up like a butchered hog, then I had to make sure Cowper couldn't come after me. So before I ran away that second time, I took up a pitchfork and went into his house and stabbed him in the gut with it. I did it three times to make sure he was good and dead."

Rachel brought his hand up to her mouth, pushing her

pursed lips hard on his knuckles against the pain burning in her throat. Just a boy. He'd been just a boy, hardly any older than Benjo, when those terrible things had been done to him. When he had done that terrible thing.

He turned her around to face him.

"Don't," he said. "Don't cry for me. It shames me to have you crying for me."

She looked down. More tears fell, splashing, wetting the wash-worn cloth of her nightrail. "I love you."

She heard his breath catch, and then she heard him let it out, slowly and carefully. She looked back up at his hard and beautiful mouth, up into his old-young eyes.

"Don't do that either," he said.

"It's too late."

He picked up the ruined yellow muslin from the ground and held it out to her as if offering it as a gift. "I killed a woman once," he said, and his voice was flat and hard and cold again.

"She was a dance hall girl in a town whose name I don't even remember. The night before I killed her I gave her a three-dollar token for a five-minute lay and I don't remember her name either, because I never knew it to begin with."

She watched as his hand that held the yellow muslin curled into a fist, and her heart was curling and fisting and aching for him, aching for herself. "Don't tell me any more, Johnny. I don't want to know any more."

He went on anyway. "The next morning, when I was coming out of the livery, I heard a man hollering my name. I didn't know the fellow. He was just another quick gun looking to take on my rep. We started shooting, and splinters from the livery door were flying every which way, and there was all this dust and smoke. And through it I saw her come running out of that saloon where she worked, I saw her, I know I saw her, but I couldn't stop firing, because it's something you learn, you see, not to stop until your gun is empty.

"And she took one of my bullets high in the chest. She was wearing a dress made out of shiny yellow stuff like this, and there was blood all over her pretty yellow dress."

He opened his fist and let the muslin flutter back to the ground.

"I went over and looked at her, looked down at her, and then I got on my horse and rode away. I kept thinking I ought to be feeling something. Horror or pity or shame, something, anything. I *tried* to feel bad for her, for what I had done, but there was nothing inside of me but this emptiness. And I was tired. I felt real tired, that's all. . . ."

He put a hand on her jaw, silencing her lips with his thumb, even though she hadn't yet spoken. "How I got from that pig farmer to shooting down a woman in the street like a stray dog was all my own doing, Rachel. I had some hard luck, but a better man than me would've faced up to life differently. Done it all differently."

Her lips moved against his fingers, the tip of her tongue touching them as she spoke. "If you come to the Lord with true repentance in your heart, then you will be forgiven all your sins. No matter how unforgivable they seem."

"I'm a man-killer, Rachel. I've killed and killed and killed, until now I'm like the coyotes and the wolves, a creature that kills because he must, without thought or feeling, but only because it's in his nature to kill." His mouth curved into a terrible smile. "I don't believe your God has that much forgiveness in Him."

She cupped his face with her hands, gripping him tightly, almost shaking him. "Then let me be your faith."

But in his eyes she saw the desolation of a man who believed there was no way off the dark path he had chosen to follow.

She couldn't bear it. She pulled his head to her breast, and she smoothed his hair as a mother would. But only for a moment, for then he was rubbing his open mouth against her throat, and she could feel the hunger surge through his body, the hunger a man felt for a woman.

He lifted his head, and she thought he would kiss her, but he said, "Will you do something for me? Will you take down your hair?"

She reached up and took off her night cap, letting it float to the ground, a flutter of white. One by one she took the pins from her hair and it fell over her shoulders in a thick, slinky mantle, fell until the curling tips of it brushed the ground where her cap lay.

He stared at her a long time. With trembling hands he cupped her hair and lifted it to his face as if he would drink of it.

"You'd better leave me now," he said, and he gently let her hair slip through his fingers.

IN THE MORNING she made them all a sheepherder's traditional breakfast of cheese mixed with canned milk and bread.

The sun came up hot again, casting a red patina over the thick bunchgrass and turning the sheep's woolly backs a rosy pink. The smell of dew-wet pine straw hung on the air, and the curlews sang their raucous song.

Her son seemed to have gotten over his fear of the coyotes and was again sputtering questions faster than she and the outsider could answer—or at least, faster than they cared to. The outsider sat with his hands wrapped around a cup of her coffee, his eyes looking edgy and wild. The air between them was so filled with feelings that there was hardly room for words.

He spoke to her only once, when the spring wagon was already hitched up for departure and Benjo had gone off for a farewell frolic with MacDuff.

"Send someone up to take over the care of your sheep and then let me go, Rachel. Let me go," he said.

"I love you," she said. "Soon I will show you how much I love you."

SHE DID NOT GO UP on the mountain again. Young Mose Weaver took over the camp tending chores, and one day in July Mose went up the mountain to stay for his turn at the herding, and Rachel knew the outsider would be coming home to her. Hoped he was coming home to her.

She sent Benjo to her father's farm, to help Sol whitewash the new fence they had built. She dragged out her galvanized tin tub and heated gallons of bathwater on the cookstove. She washed her hair. By late afternoon, when she expected him, her whole body was humming with sweet anticipation.

That was when Ezekiel, their prime ram, went crazy.

They kept the rams year-round in a fenced meadow, separate from the other sheep. Normally, these great woollies went about the business of eating and sleeping, storing up stamina and seed for their big progeny-producing days in the fall. But on that summer afternoon, for no apparent reason, the ram Ezekiel took it into his head that his day had arrived in the here and now.

He wanted to mount a ewe.

He brought Rachel running out of the house with his ferocious bawling—great bellowing *baa*s that sounded like a locomotive blowing its horn through a tunnel. He was pacing back and forth along the fence, butting his head against every post he came to.

Rachel was trying to distract him with a brown cracker, his favorite thing, when Johnny Cain appeared at her side. After waiting for him half a day, she hadn't heard him come.

Her hair was flying every which way out from under her prayer cap. She was panting so hard from all that running that she unconsciously splayed her hand over her chest. She hadn't quite decided what he would find her doing when he rode into the yard, but chasing a sex-crazed ram up and down a pasture had not been on her list of considerations.

"You came home," she said. "I wasn't sure you would."

"Is this my home, Rachel?"

"For as long as you want it to be."

He gave her a soft, slow smile. Her heart thundered against her hand.

Ezekiel bellowed and rammed his head so hard against a fence post that the wood cracked.

Rachel looked into the outsider's eyes and fell in love all over again.

Ezekiel bawled and plowed the ground with his thick, curved horns.

Cain slowly pulled his gaze from hers and looked at the ram. "Did he get into locoweed, or something?"

"Oh, he's just got lovemaking on his mind, the silly fool."

Cain dipped his head so his hat brim would hide his eyes, but she saw his mouth twitch. He muttered something that sounded like, "Who doesn't?"

At the far end of the pasture, another sheep began bleating and humping his rump into the air.

"The affliction appears to be highly contagious," Cain said.

"Well, that one can't actually . . ." A flush stained Rachel's cheeks, although she also wanted to laugh. "That is, he's our teaser. He's been, well, he can't actually *make* a lamb. We put him in with the ewes when they start their female cycles. The teaser mounts the ewes and that helps them to get in the mood for the rams."

Cain gave the teaser a horrified look. "That is the meanest, cruelest thing I've ever heard of. You ought to be calling him the teas*ee*. At least the ewes wind up getting satisfied eventually."

Rachel shook her head at Ezekiel, who was still pacing and bellowing and tossing his horns. "All this excitement isn't supposed to be happening for a couple of months yet."

Ezekiel's wildly rolling eyes settled on Cain. He let out another loud bawl and pushed his head through the fence, sniffing, and curling his upper lip.

"Oh, dear," Rachel said. "Now he thinks you're a ewe."

Cain looked from her to the ram, then back to her again. His eyes narrowed slightly. She could read his thoughts as if they were written on his forehead in printer's ink. He figured she was probably teasing, but on the other hand . . .

Ezekiel turned sideways and lifted his front leg, making his huge testicle sac sway. Deep gargles spewed up from his thick throat. His big black tongue flopped out of his mouth and hung there.

Laughter came gurgling up Rachel's own throat at the wide-eyed look of alarm on Cain's face. She wagged her finger at him. "Johnny, Johnny, you ought to be ashamed of yourself. You've got that poor ram positively love-struck."

He took a couple of judicious steps back. But she was laughing, and so he laughed himself, and she loved him so much in that moment she was nearly dizzy with it.

Their eyes caught and held, and held and held, and this

time they both knew that neither one was letting go. She reached out her hand, and he took it. She wove their fingers together.

His eyes focused behind her, going wide. "Rachel, should I be running for my virtue?" he said, just as the ram Ezekiel smashed through the fence with sex on his mind.

SHE RAN WITH HER hand tucked safe in his, all but flying above the ground, letting the laughter come in a wild rush of joy. On and on they ran, laughing, long after the danger was over—after Ezekiel became sidetracked by a mow of fresh hay and settled down to munch happily, all breeding urges forgotten.

They burst into the house, breathless, grasping each other to keep from falling.

He swung her up into his arms and carried her into the bedroom. The sun filtering through the cottonwoods outside the window cast a tea-green light over her plain white iron bed and star-patterned quilt.

He set her back onto her feet, letting her slide slowly down the length of him. She pulled out of his arms and stepped back, putting space between them. She took off her prayer cap. Carefully, she laid the cap in its place on the shelf beneath the window, and then she let down her hair.

He watched her—and then she watched him as he brought his hand to the gunbelt that rode low around his hips, and his fingers unbuckled the bullet-studded leather, and the gun gave up its embrace of him, falling, swinging through the air, hooking around the thin iron bedpost.

She came to him. She peeled off his suspenders, one at a time. She ran her hand over his chest, and his muscles clenched and seized under her touch. She took his hand

and brought it up to her breast, to the place where her shawl ends crossed in their modest, Plain way.

"Feel my heart," she said. "Feel it beating."

They fell onto the bed, onto a quilt of blue and white stars, pulling at each other's clothes. He rubbed his face in her hair, sucked on her nipples, stroked her belly and between her thighs, and she smiled and took him in her hand and put him inside her.

FANNIE WEAVER WALKED QUICKLY along the path that led through the woods separating their farm from the Yoder place. The yellow pines and tamaracks spread their thick-needled branches overhead, blocking out the sun. There had never been woods like these back in Ohio. She hated the woods. They were too much like the sky at night, dark and hulking. Smothering.

She hated it all, she hated the woods and everything else about this wild and barbarous country. Hated it, hated it, hated it. She didn't believe it a sin against God, her hate. For only the Devil could have created country like Montana.

A cloud passed over the sun, darkening the path ahead of her. Fannie gripped her shawl closer to her breast and shuddered. She told herself there were hours left in the day. Hours. But she couldn't stop the fear that was pinching her chest. She had a terrible dread of being caught out of her house after the night fell.

She lengthened her stride. Her whole body felt as if it were puffing with each heartbeat. Her breathing rushed like the wind in her ears. She tripped over an exposed root and staggered, nearly spilling the bucket of blackberries she carried swinging from one hand.

It had been Noah's idea that she bring the berries to Rachel. They grew in wild abandon on their side of the creek, way more than they could ever eat or preserve. It was only right, Noah had said, that they share God's abundance with others.

Hunh. Easy for him to say. Easy for him to promise blackberries to his precious Rachel, and then leave it up to his sister Fannie to be the actual bearer of his charity.

She emerged from the woods in back of the Yoder barn and immediately felt better out in the hot, bright sunshine. She felt disheveled, though, after rushing along the path like that, and so she paused at the bottom of the porch steps to put all of herself back in order. Rachel—now, she was the one to let herself go flying about without a thought for the hair escaping from her prayer cap.

The door creaked a little beneath Fannie's hand as she opened it. The Plain never knocked on each other's doors during the daylight hours, for no one ever did anything that was better left unwitnessed. Friends and neighbors were welcome at any time. The Plain always left their latch-strings out.

At the moment, though, the kitchen was empty, and Fannie was pleased to find it so. If Rachel were here she would have invited her to stay for some coffee *klatsch,* and Fannie did always love a good gossip. So she would have been tempted to linger and tarry and the next thing she knew she'd have been running home through the shadowy woods after the sun had already begun to sink behind the black hulking mountains.

This way, with Rachel off doing farm chores somewhere, she would be able to put the bucket of blackberries on the table and leave.

She did pause long enough on the threshold of the kitchen to glance around and inspect Rachel's housekeeping. All was in order, except for a bathing tub that leaned against the wall, tipped onto its end to dry out. And a damp towel was hanging from one of the wall hooks. Fannie wondered what had prompted Rachel to bathe on a day that wasn't Saturday. *Ach vell,* she thought, shrugging, Rachel had always been the one for breaking the rules.

She took a step toward the table, and the house moaned.

She thought it was the wind, until she heard it again. Deeper this time, more like a growl, like an animal in pain. Another moan, and a rough, harsh panting, coming from the bedroom.

With quiet steps she crossed the kitchen and walked right up to the door, for it was partway open.

Rachel lay sprawled naked on the bed, her legs flung wide, her hands gripping the white iron rails above her head. Her neck was stretched in a painful arc, her eyes flaring wide on the rafters, those terrible moans coming from her taut throat. And the outsider was kneeling between Rachel's spread thighs. He was naked all over and slick with sweat, and his eyes glowed wild and savage. And as Fannie watched, he gripped Rachel's bottom with his hands, lifting her, and he pushed his face into her woman's hair, and he—

Fannie choked and whirled, staggering with such force she banged against the wall. The bucket fell from her hand, clattering, spilling berries that she crushed beneath her half boots as she ran from the house.

She got as far as the barn before she collapsed onto her knees in the dirt and vomited up the pone and blackberries that she'd eaten before leaving home. Long after her stomach was empty, she retched and heaved, until she feared she would be spewing out her guts next.

Finally the heaves subsided to a few wrenching shudders. She pressed her fist into her open mouth, squeezing her eyes shut, but it did no good, for the horror of it was seared on her memory forever. The horror of what the outsider, that monster, had been doing to their poor Rachel.

He had been . . . Dear God in heaven, he had been *feeding* on her.

23

RACHEL WAS MAKING A slipped custard pie.

It was a foolish thing to be doing so late at night, and it was a tricky thing, too, which was why she was doing it. She needed something to occupy her head and hands, because when her hands were idle they started to shake, and she was too full of feelings to think. The mashed blackberries had left blue stains, like ink splashes, on her pine floor. Every time her eyes fell on those stains, her belly clenched with a sick dread.

She ran a spatula around the edge of the custard, separating it from the plate. *Da will be the one to come. No—it is the deacon's place to confront a Plain one who has been caught out in a sin. Noah I can face. It will be hard, hard, but I would sooner face Noah than Da.* She shook the plate gently, loosening the custard. *I'll have to face them all eventually, though, Da and my brothers, Mem, oh, poor Mem to be condemned even more for the daughter she has raised.* The custard wasn't loosening very well. She shook the plate harder. Judas, she was ruining it. *I'll have to kneel before them all and confess my shame and say I'm sorry. But what if I'm not, not sorry, no, I love him. I would do it again, I will do it again. . . . Rachel, Rachel, what are you saying? You are damning your soul, you have damned your soul, and I don't care, I don't care. Yes, I do care. I don't want to care, but I do.*

She held the plate of custard above the flaky pie crust shell. Slowly, slowly she tilted the plate and the custard began to slip. Her Benjo and Johnny Cain were out in the barn, getting a late start with the evening milking, getting a real late start when here it was barely an hour left before midnight.

So when she heard the barn door bang, her hand only jerked the littlest bit. The custard began slipping too fast, though. She tried to stop its slide by leveling the plate, and that was when she heard a stuttering shout that was unmistakably Benjo in a panic. The custard slid slickly off the plate to land on the floor with a soggy plop.

Rachel hurried to the window. Shielding the lamp glare on the glass with her hand, she looked out into the night-blackened yard. Lantern light spilled out the open barn doors, though, and she could see twisting, whirling shadows.

Shadows of men fighting.

She flung herself out the door so fast she bumped her hipbone on the jamb, and she cried out in pain. The wind had come up hard, whipping her skirts and cap strings as she ran. The barn doors swung wildly now with each gust, banging. The night was full of terrible noises: a horse's frightened neighing, men's harsh grunts and panting breaths, Benjo's inarticulate sputterings, the smack of fists against flesh.

They were all there, those Plain men who claimed to

love her—Noah Weaver and three of her brothers, Sol and Samuel and Abram—men with clenched fists and rage in their hearts, there to hurt the outsider she loved more than any other man in this world.

She had come hurtling through the door in time to see Sol, her big and gentle brother Sol, throw his full weight into a violent punch that snapped Johnny Cain's head back and sent him slamming into a stall door.

Rachel gasped to see her lover's face. That wasn't the first blow he had taken. Blood oozed from his mouth and from a cut on his cheekbone. One eye was swollen nearly shut. His shirt hung in ripped tatters, and bits of straw and hay dust clung to his hair. Yet he wasn't fighting back. Even with Samuel and Abram now taking turns to pummel him, he just stood there with his arms hanging loose at his sides while they beat him to a blood pudding.

"You stop it!" Rachel shouted in *Deitsch,* choking over her own breaths. "You stop it this instant!"

Sol didn't stop. He smashed his fist into Cain's face again, then followed with a savage blow to his belly. Cain grunted, doubled over, staggered, tripped on a sawhorse, and fell to his knees. Noah Weaver pulled back his brogan and kicked him in the kidneys.

The anger that flooded through Rachel turned the world red as hot, hot fire. She seized a hay rake off a wall hook and ran at them with it, shrieking, "You stop, stop it, stop it!"

But it was the outsider who stopped it, by shouting her name.

The quiet that followed was immediate and complete. The coal oil lamp guttered, casting grotesque shadows on the barn walls. The air was sickly sweet with the smell of spilled milk.

Benjo had his back pressed against a stall door. His face

looked leached of blood, his eyes were staring wild. His jaw and throat were clenching so, he looked to be strangling over his words. The sight of her son shuddering and choking with fear fired Rachel's rage again. That he should have had to witness this.

"Get off my farm." She waved the hay rake at them, jabbing the air with it. "Get away from me and mine."

Cain had pushed himself up as far as his knees. He brushed his forearm across his nose, staining his sleeve with slick red blood. Rachel's whole body leaned toward him, such was her yearning to go to him, to comfort him and ease his hurt. She couldn't bear it that he should suffer any more hurt.

The lantern flared as Noah took a step, holding out a clumsy hand toward her, his voice shaking. "Rachel, please—"

"Don't say my name! Don't you dare to say my name!"

Samuel walked right up to her, ignoring the stabbing hay rake. His breathing was strident, his beard bristling. He pointed a stiff finger at Cain, who still knelt in the milk-wet straw. "There's nothing left to your name, now that *he's* had you for his whore."

"You take back your filthy words, Samuel Miller—"

"No! I'll not!" He thrust his face into hers, so close she felt the hot breath propelling his words. "You've let him drag you through mud so deep even hogs wouldn't lie in your bedding." His lips twisted hard with his revulsion. He scrubbed at his mouth with his coat sleeve, then spat in the dirt. "And I've had me a hog's bellyful of him and you both."

He brushed past her and through the barn doors as if he couldn't get out fast enough. Abram followed, pausing only long enough to say to her, "'She that liveth in pleasure is dead while she liveth.'"

"And what of your deeds this night, our Abram, our Samuel?" she shouted after them. "You, too, will be answering for them on Judgment Day!"

She turned to her brother Sol, who stood as if his body felt too weighted to move. The knuckles on his right hand were scraped and swollen.

"Sol," she said, nearly choking over his name. Her cheeks felt stiff and cold, and she realized she was crying. "I know what you are. How could you have had a part in this?"

Sol lifted his big head and faced her squarely. "If we wish to destroy a weed we must pull it up by the roots," he said. But when he left the barn, he walked like an old, ill man.

Of those Plain men who claimed to love her, only Noah remained. It was too hurtful to look at him, so she focused her gaze on the hanging lantern above his shoulder. "You will take yourself away from here, Noah Weaver, and you will never set foot in my house again."

"He wanted you and so he took you," Noah said, his voice bleak with the knowledge of a thing he could hardly bear to accept. "He took you, and you let him."

"And that justifies what you've done?"

"If you couldn't have spared a thought for me, what about Ben?" His big farmer's hands were clenching and unclenching rhythmically, his powerful chest shook. "Did you imagine Ben up in heaven and watching the two of you doing . . . doing your lewd and disgusting perversions?"

She flinched a little, but she kept her head up. "Whatever perversion Ben saw on this day, was done by you and my brothers. To beat on a man with fists and boots, four against one, and with vengeance in your hearts—that has never been the Plain way."

He lifted his hands, palms out, and took a single stumbling step toward her. She saw the silver glint of tears on his cheeks, in his beard. "You remember that night, Rachel, the night of my Gertie's death? You said I was dear to you. Those were your words, Rachel. You said, 'You are so dear to me, my Noah.' You led me to believe that if it wasn't for Ben, you would have come to me that night, that you would have been mine. And now—"

"And now you have just torn my heart out at the roots. I never want to look into your face again."

His arms fell to his sides, and something seemed to collapse inside of him, like a rotted tree. He walked away, his brogans scuffing through the straw. But he stopped at the door and, bracing his hand hard against the frame as if he needed it to hold himself upright, he turned to face her.

"And him, Rachel? An outsider and a man-killer? What can he give you, besides misery and eternal damnation?"

HE WAS SITTING IN a chair in her kitchen. She knelt between his spread thighs, putting crowfoot salve on his cuts. When she had looked down on him kneeling in her barn, her thoughts had gone reeling back to that first day, when he'd come staggering across her hay meadow, bleeding unto death from a gunshot. There had been a wild terror in his eyes that day. There was no terror in his eyes tonight. They were flat and cold once again, like a pond reflecting a winter sky.

Together she and Benjo had helped him get back onto his feet. He'd had to lean on them a little walking back to the house. He'd said not a word to her, though, beyond shouting her name that once, to stop her from stabbing Noah in the back with a hay rake. She wondered if she would have actually done such a thing, to stab a man with a rake. The thought made her feel ill.

Yet she set about doctoring his hurts with calm efficiency. The crowfoot salve for his cuts. An elderflower infusion for his swollen eye. She chanted *Mutter* Anna Mary's *Brauche* prayers, even though she understood now that her faith would never be strong enough.

She tugged at his shirt.

He seized her hands. "Leave it be, Rachel."

She didn't say anything, only looked up at him, fierce in her anger with all men in that moment, with men and their violent ways, and he let go of her hands.

With tender care she eased the tails out of his broadfalls and pulled the ripped and blood-splattered shirt over his head. Her gaze fell to his belly, where a raw, purpling bruise spread like a blackberry stain over his flesh.

She sat back on her heels. "Benjo," she said, slowly and carefully.

The boy had been hovering over by the cookstove, as if he needed it for warmth, even though it was a hot July night. He hadn't once taken his eyes off Johnny Cain. He jumped when she said his name.

"Benjo, go rake out the barn."

"Buh . . . but it's n-night out."

She swung around at the waist, pointing to the door. "Go!"

Choking over words of protest, her son ran from the house, slamming the door hard behind him.

Rachel straightened up until once again she was kneeling before the outsider. She slid her arms around him and pressed her open mouth to his bruised flesh.

His hand closed over her head, crinkling her prayer cap. "Aw, Rachel, Rachel. Don't, darlin'. I've taken worse beatings—"

"I will not hear that!"

She couldn't bear him being hurt any more. She simply could not bear it. She moved her lips over the terrible bruise, kissing him again and again and again, as if she would imprint herself on him, deeper than the bruise and forever. The love she felt for him was so strong it burned with every breath.

She grew quiet after a while, although she didn't raise her head. She remained kneeling between his thighs, with her face pressed against the warm skin of his belly. I know him, she thought; I have taken his weight, he has pushed himself inside me.

"I know you, Johnny Cain," she said aloud, the words vibrating against the taut muscle of his stomach. "I know you, and so I love you."

His hand tightened on her cap. "Rachel, what happened to your brother Rome?"

She raised her head. He was looking down at her with those empty eyes, but a muscle ticked in his cheek and she could see the pulse beating in his neck, fast and hard. "Your particular friend and good neighbor Deacon Noah, he told me I was to ask you what happened to Rome."

She had a hard time talking around the knot in her throat, a knot made of tangled threads of fear, anger, and despair. "I told you what happened. He was banned from the church, shunned by his family, and he died."

"How did he die?"

She sat back on her heels again. Her gaze fell to her lap, where she was gripping and releasing, gripping and releasing, small handfuls of her apron.

"We wondered how he could do it, leave the church like he did, how he could just leave *us* like he did, just let his family go. We thought he was being so stubborn about it, but that he would relent someday. Relent and repent, because no one could actually *live* without the loving comfort of family. It's the same as what happens when a sheep leaves the fold."

Her throat had been getting tighter and tighter, as if a hand had wrapped around her neck, choking her.

"How did he die, Rachel?" Cain asked, relentless.

"He hanged himself in our father's barn with a halter rope."

He didn't move or make a sound, but she could feel something change in him. She looked up, into his eyes.

"What?" she cried. "What is it?"

He bent over and took her face in his hands, his thumbs lightly tracing the bones in her cheeks. "Before your brothers started in on walloping the bejesus out of me, I told them I would marry you."

"Oh," she said. She hadn't imagined he would do such a thing, never such a thing. They had both been driven by hunger, but she thought the caring had all been on her side. Tears welled in her eyes. She covered his hand with hers, holding it in place, so that she could turn her head and press her lips into his palm.

"Be my wife, Rachel."

She shook her head and the tears splattered. She squeezed her eyes tightly shut, trying to hold them back, hold them back. She hated tears, they made her feel weak and frightened, and she knew she had to be strong. Stronger than she'd ever had to be in her life.

"I love you, Johnny Cain. I will always love you. But a Plain woman must marry Plain, or she will be lost, shunned forever by her friends and family. Even the promise of life beyond death is denied to her. She will be lost."

He still had her face cupped in his hands. He leaned closer now and brushed his mouth across hers, almost with reverence. He started to pull away but she reached up and wrapped her arms around his neck, holding him, and she laid her head on his shoulder, and he rested his chin on her head. It was awkward this way, with her half kneeling and him almost out of the chair, but neither of them noticed it.

She didn't know how long they stayed that way. It was a commotion in the yard that pulled them apart. A commotion so late at night. Wagon wheels rattling over the corduroy bridge, MacDuff barking, and Benjo shouting a name—Mose.

Mose Weaver, who was supposed to be up on the mountain with their sheep.

She and Cain hurried out into the yard, snatching up lanterns on their way. Only something dire could have driven Mose to abandon the woollies.

Mose hauled sharply on the reins, and the light buckboard he was driving slewed to a stop, nearly running over Benjo and raising a whirlwind of dust. At first Rachel thought he was alone, but then she realized someone was lying hurt in the wagon bed. Even in the muted glint of the coal oil light she could see the red wash of blood on brown broadfalls. And a young, bony face beneath a thatch of leaf brown hair.

She hooked her lantern over the yard pump handle and ran toward the buckboard. "Levi! Oh, merciful heavens, Levi. What have you done?"

The boy struggled to sit up. "Aw, I'm all right, our Rachel. Don't fuss."

"He shot himself in the leg," Mose said. "It's not so bad anymore, now that he's quit bleeding. I made a tourniquet with some rope and a stick. It worked slick," he added, pride deepening his voice just a bit.

His face was pale and his grip on the reins shook a little, but his words as he told what had happened were calm enough. Levi, doing the camp tending, had driven up that afternoon. He'd come across that coyote with the bum leg, the one who'd been feeding regularly off their sheep, along with her pups. Levi had grabbed for his rifle and somehow the thing had gone off before he could aim it and he'd shot himself in the thigh instead.

"I'm driving him directly to Doc Henry, but someone's got to get back up there pronto to those sheep," Mose said. "As it is, we're going to have woollies scattered from hell to breakfast come morning. And then there's that murdering coyote." His gaze shifted over to Cain, his eyes widening slightly as he took in the man's appearance. "I was wondering if you could, I mean, it's going to take a dead shot to get that coyote. She's wily and man-wise."

Benjo jerked hard, and a harsh choking erupted from deep in his throat. He ran off, bumping against the outsider as he passed him. He ran so hard his hat flew off, but he left it lying there in the dust.

Rachel, shivering, gripped her elbows. Benjo's fear of coyotes might be strong, but it wasn't misplaced. Even leaving now, the soonest anyone could get there, riding under night conditions, would be dawn. In the murky light and purple shadows of dawn, coyotes were at their most dangerous to sheep. Whole herds had been known to be savaged by coyotes at dawn.

"Soon as I drop this clumsy *Schussel* off at Doc's," Mose said, with a nod and a wink for Levi, "this *Schussel* who hasn't figured out yet which end of a rifle the bullet comes out of, then I'll hurry on back to the woollies."

Rachel summoned up a smile for Levi's sake, who would surely blame himself for whatever disasters befell their sheep on this night. "In the meantime Mr. Cain'll be on his way," she said, "so don't you boys worry none."

Tugging at the reins, Mose began to turn the buckboard around. He tipped his hat at Rachel and flashed a sudden, cocky grin that reminded her strangely of Johnny Cain. "And don't you go worrying too much about your Levi. He missed the real vital parts by a good six inches."

Rachel stepped back and watched young Mose drive out of the yard. As they crossed back over the bridge she thought Levi might have raised his hand to her, and so she waved back. Maybe it was only the drama of the moment, but both boys had seemed different somehow. Especially Mose. There was a calm maturity about him that Rachel had never seen before. She thought how Noah would be proud of his son, and she was glad for him.

The wind whipped through the yard, tattering the cloud of dust stirred up by the wagon. Even without coyotes on the prowl, the sheep would be restless on a night like this. A night like this, they could stampede their woolly-headed selves over a cliff.

She felt the outsider come up close beside her. "When I first saw them," she said, "when I first saw Levi lying all bloody like that in the wagon, I thought it was the Hunters who had done it. Another persecution for us to endure."

"If you ask me, y'all could give the Hunter outfit lessons in persecution."

"Don't, Johnny," she said, but in sadness, not anger.

"Before I leave, I want you to tell me what they will do to you."

She turned and started back to the house, walking with fast sure strides. "I'll make you up some sardine sandwiches to eat on the trail. It's lucky there's a full moon rising. You'd never be able to ride all the way up there in the dead of night otherwise."

He gripped her arms and swung her around to face him.

"The coyotes can eat every damned sheep in Montana. I ain't leaving here until I know—"

She slipped gently out of his grasp. She didn't want him to feel how cold she was. She was shaking with it, she was feeling so cold. "To lie unwed with a man is a grave sin," she said, all calm and matter-of-fact, "but it can be forgiven."

"What are you going to have to do in order to be forgiven?"

"I will go on my knees before the church and confess my sin with you. I will beg to be absolved, and then I will vow never to sin in that way again and it will never more be spoken of by any of us."

"And?"

The cold, crushing sensation sharpened in her chest. "And you will leave here, never to return."

He stood there, saying nothing, his eyes and face a black void like the darkness beyond the lantern light. There wasn't anything about him to tell her he was hurting. But she knew him, she was bone of his bones now, flesh of his flesh. She wanted to hold him, hold him tight against the pain, but she didn't dare.

"Well, then, Mrs. Yoder," he said, the words clipped, hard. "Before I do leave, never to return, I suppose I could go kill that coyote for you. You can call it a parting gift."

THE WIND BLEW HARD through the treetops, rattling the leaves and branches. The wind shrilled so loud it sounded like a coyote's howl. Benjo shivered, wishing he had his coat and hat. Even though it was another hot night, the wind made it sound cold.

He was scared, was what he was, scared spitless and pissless. He'd already thrown up twice, so he supposed you could say he was scared gutless, too. He opened his mouth to laugh at the silly thought, but a sob squeaked out instead.

He had ridden their old draft mare a couple of miles down the road, concealing himself and the horse in the hedge of willows and cottonwoods along the creek. He was about a hundred yards from where the outsider would be turning off the road, taking the track that led into the foothills.

Benjo had a good-sized rock in the pocket of his sling, and the cords gripped tight in his hand. He'd never tried to bean a person before. The biggest thing he'd ever shot at was a beaver, and all he'd succeeded in doing was making that ol' beaver mad. She'd slapped her tail so hard in the creek, Benjo thought they'd probably felt the splash all the way over to Miawa City.

And there had been that horse he'd hit on the rump, the day of the stampede. That stock inspector's horse. 'Course the stock inspector was stone dead now, buried with his six-shooter still clutched in his hand. He'd thought himself pretty darn quick, but he hadn't been as quick as Johnny Cain.

"You can come on out, boy."

Benjo's heart thrust like a fist against his chest, so hard he was nearly knocked from the saddle. Judas Iscariot! How had he done that, how had Johnny Cain gotten down the road on horseback without making a sound? And how had he known Benjo would be lying here in ambush? The man was uncanny; he could see you coming even before the thought entered your own head to move.

He also acted like he had all night to wait for Benjo to emerge from his hiding place. Benjo let the rock drop out the pocket of his sling, and he tucked the sling out of sight before he nudged the mare out from behind the trees.

He was glad it was dark, but it probably wasn't dark enough to keep the outsider from seeing on his face exactly what he'd been up to. He would have given anything to be able to talk without stammering, although he doubted the words existed that would get him out of this trouble.

"I reckon," the outsider said, "you thought I could use some expert advice on how to chouse down a band of wandering woollies after they've been left alone to themselves for most of a day and a night."

The breath came whistling out of Benjo's tight throat in a mouselike squeak. "Yessir," he said. He wasn't sure what the outsider was about, but he wasn't behaving like he was angry. But then he had been smiling and talking all polite to that stock inspector right before he smashed a sarsaparilla bottle in the man's face.

"So, does your ma know about your good deed?" Cain said, still as casual as you please.

"I wr-wrote it d-d-down fuh . . . fuh . . . fuh . . ." *For her.* He'd sort of written it down. He'd scrawled GONE WITH CAIN in charcoal on the draft mare's stall door. And he'd shut poor MacDuff up in the lambing sheds to keep him from following.

The outsider laid his reins against his horse's neck, turning her head, and setting her back along the road, and Benjo realized with shock and a frisson of excitement that the man expected Benjo to follow him.

The outsider didn't say anything as they turned off the road and onto the sheep trail, climbing already, and there were hours left of climbing ahead. It was strange to ride this trail at night, Benjo thought, when you couldn't see much of where you were going, or where you'd been. They would never have been able to do it at all without the brilliant moon that was riding the sky. The moon was so big and white you could see the pocks and ridges in it.

The outsider was revealed to him in quick pulses as they

rode in and out of tree shadows and blue-shot moonlit patches. As his da would've said, Johnny Cain's face "looked like he'd crawled through a bob-wire fence to fight a bobcat in a briar patch."

Benjo would have thought picking a fight with a man like the outsider would have been like kicking at that bobcat. But he had just stood there and taken it. The memory of the fight had left Benjo with a shaky, betrayed feeling inside, as if Johnny Cain had somehow failed to deliver on a promise he had made.

And his uncles, who all of his life had taught Benjo to behave in one way, the Plain way—they had behaved worse than any outsiders he'd ever seen, except maybe for that stock inspector.

He sure enough had never seen his uncles that mad, not even his uncle Samuel, who had a temper on him. Benjo wasn't sure what had gotten them all so riled, except they thought the outsider had done something nasty to his mem. He knew what that nasty something was, only he didn't quite understand *why* it was nasty. It was only what Ezekiel the ram did to the ewes every fall when he covered them. As far as Benjo had always been able to tell, the ewes liked what Ezekiel did.

He didn't understand any of it, and just thinking about it had him feeling so full up inside that his eyes got all itchy. The words burst out of him before he even knew they were in his mouth. He didn't even stutter. "You just stood there. You just stood there and let them hit you."

Johnny Cain cocked his gaze around to him. "You would have had me shoot them?"

"You could've f-fought back. Only a cuh—cuh—coward wuh . . . wuh . . ." *Wouldn't fight back.*

"That don't sound much like a Plain boy talkin'."

"B-but you're not Plain."

He felt more than saw the outsider's shrug. "I would never hurt anyone she loved."

Benjo contemplated that for a while, and he found it eased those sick feelings of disappointment some.

They rode into a spell of silence after that. The wind still blew strong, thick with the summer smells of hot dirt and sun-ripened grass and yellow jack pines. With the way shreds of cloud were blowing across the moon, it looked as if the moon were skimming like a skipping stone across the sky.

"It's going to be a long night," the outsider said from out of the dark beside him, "and we got some hard riding ahead of us. Why don't we pass some of the time by you telling me how you came to be particular friends with a coyote?"

His words caught Benjo as if he'd flicked him with a whip. The boy jerked so hard on the reins, even the old draft mare shied. He wondered if he would have to answer; the outsider wasn't like Mem for making a fellow spill his guts. Yet he found he wanted those guts spilled. The dread and fear and guilt—most of all, the guilt—had been churning around inside his belly for so long, it would be a relief to spew it all out.

Even choking and stammering over almost every word, he was able to tell the outsider everything. He told about the Sharps rifle in the barn and how in the end he'd lacked the courage to use it. How instead he'd slid the ramp he'd made down into that pit and set her and her pups free. Free to feed off the poor helpless woollies.

All the while he was telling his story, he kept slanting looks at the outsider. He saw nothing beyond mild interest on the man's face, but he felt *something* was going on inside Johnny Cain. There was a tautness, a tension inside of him that was a vibrating hum in the air, like blowing on a piece of river grass.

"I g-guess I shouldn't've d-done it, huh?" Benjo said when he was finally done with his long tale. "I g-guess I should've left her to d-die. Or used the Sh-Sharps on her."

The breath eased out of the outsider in an odd sigh. He sounded almost sad. "You weren't ever going to change her nature, Benjo."

Something inside Benjo twisted hard. "I d-don't w-want you to kuh . . . kuh . . . kuh . . ." *Kill her.*

"Somebody's got to do it. If it can't be me, then it's got to be you. Or you can just let her and her pups go on killing your lambs until there's none left, and you and your mem go hungry yourselves next winter. I'll leave it up to you to decide which it will be."

Benjo slowly nodded his head. He thought he might have to cry, that he might have to start bawling like a big baby, but he swallowed hard a few times. Only a few tears trickled out the corners of his eyes, and he surreptitiously wiped those away with his sleeve.

He was surprised to realize the trail ahead of them had been getting lighter. They were nearly at the sheep camp, and no sooner did he have that thought than the wind obliged by quieting down enough for them to hear the silver tinkle of the wether's bell. Which meant at least some of the herd were still where Mose Weaver had left them.

The sky had bled to the color of birch bark when they rode into the clearing. Benjo let out a relieved breath to see sheep. They were nervous sheep, though, bleating and bunching and milling in the wind-riffled grass. His eye caught the flap of a buzzard's wing.

And then he saw the bodies of the lambs.

There were four of them. Mangled piles of blood-soaked wool and white bones. As they got closer to the carcasses, he heard a mewling sound, and he realized one of the lambs was still alive, just barely. Her throat had been chewed open.

Johnny Cain knelt beside her, took the knife out of his boot sheath, and finished her off.

Benjo made himself watch, he made himself look at every one of the slaughtered lambs. He felt shivery cold and strangely light-headed. His chest ached with a longing—no, a *need,* to make things right.

He ran his tongue over his cracked lips. "I wuh—wuh—wuh!" He sucked in a deep breath, swallowed. "I want you to kill her."

Johnny Cain said nothing, but then there was nothing to say. He'd left the choice up to Benjo, and Benjo had made it.

They made a bone pile some distance from the camp. Then they walked the sheep and found there were about two dozen missing. Mose had shut his collie up in the sheepwagon so that it wouldn't try to follow him down the mountain. They let the dog loose now, to help them search for the nomadic sheep.

They never found them, although they spent the whole day looking.

BENJO CAME AWAKE IN that quiet time just before dawn when the wind dies and the whole earth seems to be waiting breathless for the sun's arrival. He listened, ears straining, afraid it was a coyote's howl that had awakened him. He heard a bird rustling in the tree overhead, but nothing more. Neither he nor Cain had chosen to sleep inside the sheepwagon, but as his eyes got used to the night, he saw that the outsider's bedroll was empty.

Benjo found him sitting by the rock cairn, his rifle cradled in his arms. He didn't need to ask the man what he was doing. It would be dawn soon.

Benjo's legs suddenly seemed to turn to cornmeal mush. He sat down next to the outsider, Indian fashion. Now that the moment had come, he'd lost some of the day's assuredness. His heart felt like it was clubbing his chest, and he kept having to blink back tears.

He thought it was hard, real hard, sometimes to be a man.

The outsider had never said it aloud today, but it had been there between them, the understood and accepted knowledge of how a man was supposed to behave. His da had sure said it all to Benjo plenty often. A man had to be tough enough inside to own up to his mistakes. His da had called it "taking the consequences," and he'd usually said it right before he'd reached for the razor strop.

Benjo wondered if the outsider's refusal to raise his fists against Mem's brothers and Deacon Noah had been his way of taking the consequences. And maybe those Plain men had thought they would own up to their mistake by *using* their fists. The mistake of letting an outsider come among them in the first place.

Sometimes, Benjo thought, it was hard figuring it all out. He wondered if it was still hard when you got to be big, like the outsider and his uncles.

The sky was just becoming marbled with light when she came. Johnny Cain was as fast with his rifle as he was with his Colt. He fired twice, reloaded, and fired twice more. Then it was over, the coyote and her three pups were all dead.

They walked out into the meadow together, Rachel Yoder's son and the outsider. Blue veins of gunsmoke drifted past them. A magpie flew away with a flash of white-barred wings. The grass trembled beneath the silvery gold light of the rising sun. For a moment the wind ruffled the coyote's fur, giving her the illusion of life.

Benjo couldn't stop the tears and he didn't care if the outsider saw them. "I j-just wish shuh . . . she hadn't come after our sheep."

"It was in her nature," said Johnny Cain.

24

THE SUN WAS SETTING when Rachel Yoder's son came swaggering through her door, looking grimy and sweaty and all-around pleased with himself. Came swaggering through her door a full three days after he'd gone running out of it.

Rachel didn't even waste her breath on a howdy. She seized his arm and hauled him off to his bedroom so fast his feet barely skimmed along the floor. But when she sat on the bed, instead of putting him over her knees, she suddenly had him in her lap and she was crying and hugging him and rocking him like a babe.

"Mem!" he protested, struggling out of her embrace and pushing back onto his feet. He'd always hated her doing what he called "mushy girl stuff."

She gripped him by the shoulders and gave him a shake. "You are never again to go up to the sheep camp without first getting my permission."

The look Benjo gave back to her was one of genuine surprise, as if he expected the leaving of a message scrawled in charcoal on a barn stall to be permission enough. A message she hadn't even *seen* until she'd spent a whole frantic night searching for him.

She pushed her fingers through his ragged hair. It looked as if he hadn't combed it in three days. "Joseph Benjamin Yoder, you are filthy."

"Cain and me, we shuh—shot the c-coyotes," he said.

Rachel stared at her son. After a summer of jumping like a spooked cat at the very mention of coyotes, here he'd ridden off without hardly a by-your-leave to hunt down and slaughter the beasts as if it were all some grand adventure. He baffled her, this son of hers. She'd often wondered if it would be different with a daughter—at least she would have a hope of understanding a girl. And then she thought of herself and her own mem.

She fussed over him some more. She tucked in his shirt-tail. She wet a corner of her apron with spit and scrubbed the sticky dirt ring off his mouth. Finally she was able to get the words out. "Did Mr. Cain come back with you?"

"He's b-bedding down for the night in the b-barn. Are you going to whuh—whip me?"

She hugged him again, so tightly that this time he couldn't wriggle free. "I should, I should. But I won't."

She made Benjo take a bath—it was Saturday, after all. And she tidied her own self up while she was about it, putting on a fresh apron and prayer cap. She took extra care over supper that night, fixing what she had discovered over the summer to be Johnny Cain's favorite things: squaw corn on the cob and venison steak.

But he never came in to eat it.

SHE WENT TO HIM the next morning.

He had his saucy little mare's left rear hoof up on his

thigh and he was scraping caked dirt and dung out of it with a hoof pick. He straightened up, though, as soon as he saw her.

She could say nothing at all, only look at him, and it was so wonderful to look at him. But it hurt as well: to see his hard mouth that once she had kissed into softness, the long dark hair that had brushed across her naked belly, the hands that had touched her in all her woman's secret and hungry places.

It hurt so much that she was the one to look away.

The barn held a mixture of sweet and pungent smells, summer hay and manure, sour milk and the ripening sunlight pouring through the open doors. She sucked in a deep breath, feeling almost dizzy.

She came around to the mare's right side and petted the velvet nose. Her throat was hot and tight, full of the things she wanted to say.

Her gaze met his over the horse's head. At some time he had bought himself new flashy clothes, for he was no longer dressed Plain. He had on a white shirt with a crisp linen collar and a vest the color of rhubarb wine, decorated with shiny jet buttons. His trousers were black with a thin gray stripe running through it. He looked fine, not at all like a sheep farmer.

Even with his horse between them, he was close enough to touch. She wanted to reach out and pull his head down and press her mouth to his.

"I thought you'd left," she said. "That you'd leave without saying good-bye. Then Benjo said you'd come back with him, but you didn't come in to supper."

He had yet to take his eyes off her. He didn't seem to be breathing. "After the trouble I brought you," he said, "I thought our good-byes would be better said in the daylight, out in the open."

The moment stretched between them, a moment fraught with memories made and in the making, thoughts both sweet and bitter, and things better left unsaid. She saw him swallow hard.

"I had to see you one last time, though, Rachel. I couldn't go through the rest of my life without seeing you one more time."

Yes, they were words better left unsaid, for all the hurt they would bring later in remembrance. But they were such sweet words to be hearing now, such tender words. He had spoken carnal words to her in bed. But except for asking her to marry him, he hadn't said many tender words.

He made a hard, jerking movement, as if the memories and thoughts and words were now a rope binding them together, and he had to break it.

She watched him exchange the hoof pick for a dandy brush and begin to run it over the mare's neck and withers. He hadn't needed the horse for a quick getaway after all. Then it occurred to Rachel that he was preparing her now for a long journey.

"Where are you going? I mean, do you have any idea what you'll be doing . . . ?" She'd nearly said *with the rest of your life.*

His shoulders lifted in a shrug. "I'll get by. I've always been a fiddle-footed man."

She watched his hands move over the glossy cinnamon hide.

"Johnny—"

He reached up, the pearl buttons on his cuff catching at the mare's tawny mane, and he covered her mouth with his fingers. "I thought about us, Rachel, up on that mountain, I thought about whether I should stay and try to fight you for yourself." His hand fell away. "And I decided it was better just to end it now. Because someday someone was going to come riding down that road with a burning need to kill me. Someone who's just a bit quicker, who can shoot just a bit straighter, and if I'd stayed you'd only have had to watch that happen."

This time she was the one to reach across the horse's withers, to touch one of the smile lines that edged his mouth, although he wasn't smiling. "You still haven't learned, have you, outsider? You could have walked out into the yard and gotten struck by lightning, and I'd have had to watch that happen as well."

He shook his head, stepping back, moving out of reach of her touch. But now he did smile at her, with his eyes. "As much as I've gone out of my way to incur the wrath of the Almighty, He's yet to go throwing lightning bolts at me."

A panic gripped her chest so tightly that she thought her heart had stopped beating. "It's happening this morning at the preaching," she said, the words coming out of her on a searing shock of breath. "My confession and repentance." *My promise never to speak with you, never to see you, never to have thoughts of you again.*

His gaze fell away from hers, and he went back to currying his horse. "So young Mose told me when he came back to take over the herding."

"Will you bring me there, to the preaching this morning, and will you promise not to leave until after it's over?"

He made a raw, gasping sound, as if the breath had backed up in his lungs, hot and thick. "Jesus, Rachel. What do you think I'm made of?"

All that is fine and frightening, all that is sinful and beautiful, she thought. "Whang-leather," she said. It was what the old-timers out here said about a man or a thing that was tough. Tough as whang-leather.

She tried to smile, but she could feel it coming all wrong like a terrible grimace. "Please, Johnny. I need you with me because I'm not tough at all."

She backed up a step, and then another. She turned and walked toward the wet smear of gold light that she hoped was the open barn doors.

"Do you think it a sin, Rachel, the love we made?"

She didn't answer because she didn't know what the answer was.

THE SUN WAS A molten copper ball in a hard blue sky. The wind rippled the tawny grass. It luffed the wide black brim of Rachel Yoder's bonnet.

As she did on the way to every preaching, she turned around after they crossed the bridge and started up the rise, and looked back to the farm. For some reason she thought it would look different to her today, but of course it did not.

It was only herself and the outsider in the buckboard this time. Her brother Sol had come over with his wagon to bring her to the preaching, but she had patted his bearded cheek and sent him on his way with Benjo instead. It had seemed a terrible enough thing to Rachel, that her son would have to witness her shame as she confessed her sins of pride and fornication. She couldn't bear having him endure with her what would come before: that long walk past the silent rows of benches, through that sea of black and white prayer caps and black hats. Those long, long moments on her knees, of waiting, waiting, of time passing slow. Not sweet this time, but bitter. Bitter and hard.

The old horse shook her harness and plodded along. Johnny Cain's horse, saddled and groomed to a shine and tied to the back of the buckboard, was following along behind. Her hooves made a more lively sound. Not a plod-plod, but a clip-clop. Johnny Cain's getaway horse. The sun-baked road stretched before them, hard, but not long enough. Not nearly long enough.

I must do this, I must. For my son and family. For Ben, who is waiting for me to join him in the hereafter. I must do this, or there will be no place for me at the table.

Once, many years ago, she had made a vow. To renounce the world and the Devil. To live separate and walk with Christ and his church along the straight and narrow way, to remain faithful to God through her life until death.

Once, she had made and lived such a vow with joy in her heart. Soon she would make it again. Only now, she would be grieving for the rest of her life, for a love that had been lost to her forever. But neither could she make a promise twice and break it twice, and expect God to understand.

I must do this. For my soul's sake, I must.

She looked at him, but he kept his eyes on the road.

I can't become separate like you, Johnny. I can't live on the outside with you. She had always been joined, like a limb to a tree, to the church and to her family and to God. If she broke off she would die.

She thought this moment must have always been there, waiting in her future, like a prophecy. Beginning with that day he had come staggering across her wild hay meadow, and ending with this—when she must choose between her family and God, and her love for Johnny Cain.

I must do this. I must.

THIS SUNDAY THE PREACHING was in Noah Weaver's barn. To Rachel, his farm was so familiar to her, so much like her own, that she had a startling, frightening feeling of having ridden forever only to find herself back at home again.

But there were the rows of wagons and buckboards parked in Noah's pasture, and the rows of black bonnets hanging from the fence rail. The barn doors yawned open, and everyone was inside already, waiting for her.

There was a narrow track worn bald by wagon wheels that led from the road to Noah's farmyard. The outsider pulled the buckboard to a stop, rather than turn down that track. He was looking not at her but at his hands that loosely held the reins.

"When you hear the hymnsong," Rachel said. She was feeling feverish inside, all shaky and sweat-sticky and cold. And she kept forgetting to breathe. *I must do this, I must.* "When you hear the hymnsong, then you'll know it's been done. Then you will go."

She watched his fist clench around the reins, watched the beautiful, graceful sinews of his hand and wrist turn rigid. He raised his head, and she saw his heart in his eyes, all of his life in his eyes, a heart beating with hurt and hope, and a terrible, desperate need.

"Rachel, I . . . Damn this, and damn you for it. If this is what your God demands of you, then I don't ever want to come to know Him."

She breathed, and it was like swallowing fire. "Oh, no, no. You mustn't say that, you mustn't think it. Don't turn away from God because of me. Please."

He wrapped the reins around the brake handle and swung out of the buckboard. She started to climb down, but he was suddenly there to steady her, with his hands grasping both her arms, an excuse to touch. An excuse to touch one last time.

"Rachel."

This time, it was not he who spoke her name but her father. And at the sound of it, she turned and walked away from the outsider, and back into her Plain life.

Bishop Isaiah Miller stood before her in his freshly brushed Sunday coat. He wore the pain she had given him in his eyes.

Although she didn't look at him again, she was aware of the outsider standing in utter stillness by the buckboard. To her father, the outsider wasn't even there, was as invisible as glass, not worth seeing, not worth caring about anymore. For once his daughter confessed and repented and was taken back into the church again, once that was done and they all walked out of the preaching together, then Johnny Cain would be gone. Isaiah Miller's eyes were all for his daughter.

"You will make yourself right with the church, *ja,* our Rachel? You will make it right."

Her chest felt too full, her throat too tight to speak. She managed a nod, and it seemed to satisfy him, although the smile he gave back to her trembled at the edges.

They started to walk together toward the barn, but her legs wouldn't work right. She kept stumbling. She wanted to turn around, to look back at Johnny Cain, but she was afraid that if she did, then she wouldn't be able to take one more step toward a life without him.

You can never become lost if you walk the straight and narrow path.

"Da," she said, "this is so hard. It's too hard, I don't think I can bear it."

He wrapped his arm around her shoulders, bumping hips with her, clumsy and yet tender. "You'll feel better once you can walk again in righteousness. See if you don't."

He stood there for a moment, holding her, and it was

like the morning of her wedding when she had wanted it to last forever.

BISHOP ISAIAH MILLER STOOD with tears running over his cheekbones and into his beard. He read in a quavering voice from the Bible, about the prodigal son and about the faithful shepherd and his lost sheep.

Rachel Yoder knelt on the straw-strewn floor, facing the church, facing her family, her friends, her Plain life. She tried to make herself listen to the holy words, to endure this as she must, with humility, with a yielding joy and hope in her heart. But her mind kept wandering, and her heart echoed with hollowness.

She tried to make herself see individual faces beneath the rows of black and white prayer caps and black hats. Benjo—no, she couldn't bear to look at Benjo. But there was Mem, weeping quietly, with Velma and Alta propped on either side of her like matching bookends. Samuel and Abram with their mouths set stern. Levi with his bandaged leg resting on a pile of pillows and creases of worry across his forehead. Sol studying his clasped hands, hands that were gripped so tightly the knuckles had bled white. And Noah, his soft brown eyes staring back at her, bright with a desperate hope.

At no time in her life had she ever loved them more.

"'The Lord chastises me indeed but he hath not given me over unto death. . . .'"

The words were gentle, hopeful, but they hurt. Her Plain life spread before her. Beyond were the barn doors, wide open to the hot and dazzling sunshine. And beyond the doors an outsider stood waiting to hear the first hymnsong.

"Rachel Yoder, if you believe you can face the All-Highest

God with a penitent heart, then confess to your sins now in the name of God, and you shall be forgiven them."

The straw prickled her knees. The silence was heavy and solemn. And then a barn swallow fluttered through the open doors to disappear into its nest in the rafters, and it seemed for a moment like just another preaching.

This won't be so hard after all, she thought. I know the words, all I have to do is say them.

"I confess that I failed to keep myself separate. That I took the outsider Johnny Cain into my house and made him as part of my family, allowing myself and my son to be touched by his worldly ways and corrupting influences."

He'd been a hard worker around the farm, and so good with Benjo. And he wasn't as tough as he liked to pretend. He talked sweet to the sheep when he sheared them, and he did the milking for her cheerfully, even though it was woman's work. When Ezekiel the ram fell into lust with him, he had laughed.

"I confess to falling into the sin of fornication with the outsider Johnny Cain."

His mouth had always looked so hard. It had been such a sweet surprise when she kissed him, to feel how his lips were soft and warm.

"I confess to the sin of pride, of thinking I could bring salvation to the soul of the outsider Johnny Cain, when only God can grant to any of us the gift of eternal life."

He had killed in the coldest blood, with joy on his face. Then he had stood in a dark barn with torment in his eyes and said, "I am filthy." If she went back to her Plain life, he would go back to his old life. And eventually he would die bleeding into the sawdust on a saloon floor.

"I confess . . . I confess . . ."

The sunlight pouring through the open doors was blinding. Her vision blurred and whitened at the edges. She heard weeping, and a rustling of feet, and then all she heard was her own heartbeat.

I must do this.

"I confess," she said, her voice rising, firming, the words coming from her heart like a prayer, "I confess to having fallen into love with the outsider Johnny Cain. You say he is separate and so I cannot love him, but tell that to my heart. The love I bear for him, it's like the music, it just comes over me and over me, only unlike the music it doesn't stop, it goes on and on and on."

Her mind was wandering again. She blinked, swaying dizzily. Her prayer cap suddenly felt like a boulder crushing her head, and its strings were cutting into her neck. It had gotten so hot in the barn. She could feel patches of sweat on her forehead and cheeks. But, strangely, her hands were cold. She wrapped them in her apron.

"I think," she said, fumbling for the words a moment longer. Then she found them. "I think of time passing, of the sweet comfort of the seasons always being there in our lives, the lambing and the haying and the shearing. I think of how time passes and the days flow into one another, and I don't understand how I'm supposed to live without him."

She tried to draw in a breath, but it caught in her throat. "He is separate, you say. He is an outsider. But I think to myself: If God loves all of His creatures, even the unbelievers, why then would He demand of me that I deny the love I bear for this one man?"

At some time she had risen to her feet. Behind her, her father said something, a hard, desperate whisper. Sol had his head buried in his hands. Noah had his fist pressed hard to his mouth. Tears washed over her mem's face.

"I know what I must do," she said, lifting her gaze to that

dazzling, dizzying, frightening square of white sunlight beyond the doors. "I looked for the sorrow in my heart, for the shame I must feel for what I've done, but it isn't there. I'm sorry, so sorry . . . Mem, Da, my . . . my brothers and sisters in Christ, I am so sorry. But my heart is too full of my love for him."

The first step was the hardest, then she was running.

SHE DIDN'T SEE HIM at first, and the fear that he might already have left her was so strong her knees buckled with it. She sat in the dirt of the yard, hugging herself, rocking, buffeted by gusts of unbearable longing.

A lone box elder tree grew at the top of the lane. It was an old tree with a broad leafy canopy, a pale green parasol of shade on this blazing summer day. He sat beneath it, with his back pressed against its furrowed trunk, his arm resting on one drawn-up knee. He hadn't seen her yet, and then he did. He stood up slowly.

She cried out, a shout of joy, then she was on her feet and running again. And then she was in his arms.

His hands took hold of her face gently, made her eyes look up into his. "Come be my wife," he said.

From the open doors of the barn, low and slow, came the funeral-bell toll of the first hymnsong.

"Mem!"

Benjo burst into the sunlight, running hard, his hand holding down his hat, the legs of his broadfalls flapping. "Mem! Wuh . . . wait!"

He threw himself against her, stammering words she didn't understand. She held him tight, pulling his head into her belly.

She looked up at Johnny Cain. "I want to go home, please. Take us home."

They took the same road home, and when the Weaver farm was lost from sight and the sound of the hymnsong had long ago been swallowed up by the wind, Rachel took off her prayer cap. She held it up in the air a moment, and then she let it go. The wind snagged it and held it aloft a bit, sending it dipping and soaring, and then the cap fell to the ground and began to roll over and over the yellow grass like a tumbleweed.

THE CIRCUIT PREACHER WASN'T due in Miawa City for another month yet, so they journeyed up to the Blackfoot Indian Reservation to be married by the missionary there. Standing in the small logwood church with two silent Indians for witnesses, Rachel and Johnny Cain spoke the vows that made them man and wife in the eyes of the Montana Territory, at least, if not in the eyes of God.

She hadn't been able to stop herself from thinking how different this was from her wedding to Ben. It was the Plain tradition for the groom to help the bride prepare for the wedding feast by slaughtering the chickens for her. So that morning of their wedding, Ben had come to her door with a headless chicken in each hand, and wearing feathers on his head in place of his Plain hat and streaks of vermilion paint across his cheeks like a wild Indian. Oh, how they had laughed. Later, in the barn, after the preaching service, after the wedding hymn had been sung and their vows made, her father had put his hands over their clasped hands, and pronounced his blessing upon them.

She was given no such blessing now.

The vows were the same, though, then and now. To cherish each other, to care for each other rich or poor, ill or well, until death did them part. She and Ben had spent their wedding night at her father's house. She and Johnny Cain spent theirs in a borrowed tipi. And both times it was the same—then and now, there was love.

NOW, IT WAS THE middle of the day and here they were in their bedroom, Mr. and Mrs. Johnny Cain just back from being married, and they both knew for what, although neither of them had spoken of it.

Rachel watched while her new husband took off his flashy new hat—it had a rattlesnake skin band around the crown of it—and tossed it at a wall hook.

He lay down on the bed, stacked his hands behind his head, and crossed his legs at the ankles. He wriggled his hips, settling in. She loved the look of his hips, lean and hard, she loved their strength when they made love. Her gaze traveled down the long length of his legs, to his . . . to his dusty boots on her star-patterned quilt. *Ach vell,* he had some things to learn. And she would have some things to learn, as they fit into the harmony of living as man and wife.

He caught her eyeing his boots. "I suppose," he said, his voice sparked by his teasing smile, "we're gonna be having our arguments as man and wife. But I'm telling you this right here and now, I'm never sleeping out in any barn or sheepwagon anymore." His smile deepened, his eyes warmed. "Leastways, I won't be doing it without you to share the misery."

"Hunh. All this time I've been wondering why, and now I have the truth of it. You married me for my big wide bed."

The way he was watching her, she felt as if a hot wind were blowing through her, right through her. It was a wild kind of feeling, and she rather liked it.

He could move so quick. One moment he was lying

there on the bed, all lazy and relaxed and with his boots leaving dust smudges on the quilt, and the next instant he was up and swinging her around with an arm at her waist, sitting down in the rocking chair and pulling her onto his lap.

"I won't deny," he said, the whisper of his breath brushing her throat, "that when the preacher was prattling on about bodies worshipping each other, I thought about that big bed of yours and what we'll be doing in it most every night for the rest of our lives."

He spanned the back of her head with his hand, tangling his fingers in her hair and pulling her mouth down to his. There was a wildness in his kiss this time, a greed, a violence that staggered and excited her.

It staggered and excited the chair as well. The rocker tipped back onto the points of its curved slats, knocking against the wall.

"Johnny," she said into his open mouth, not quite able to let go of it. "Be careful. You're going to—"

The chair rocked back again, harder this time. The headrail and spindles smacked against the wall, and the momentum sent the chair reeling forward to dump them onto the floor in a tangle of arms and legs and rocker slats. He laughed, a full-throated, wonderful laugh. And she was laughing, too.

They grew quiet, content for the moment to lie close, side by side, face to face, to hold each other in sight.

He gave the rocker a nudge with the pointed toe of his boot. "I've never known a chair to turn rogue on me like that before."

She traced the shape of his mouth with her fingers. "You are the rogue."

"Yeah, that's me. I'm a naughty, naughty rogue, and you've always been hellbent on reformin' me." His breath swept against her hair, his soft laugh wavered on her cheek. "It's going to be a glory of a marriage."

NOAH STOOD ON THE PORCH, looking at the door and wondering what to do.

It might not be the Plain way to go knocking on doors, but he sure didn't want to walk in on a perversion like what poor Fannie had witnessed not so long back. His hands curled into fists. If he had been the one to see her . . . to see his Rachel doing . . . *ach,* dear God, even to think of it filled him with such a gut-wrenching rage. If he had been the one to see her, he might have killed her for it. The thought filled him with horror, with guilt and shame, so profound it shook the roots of his soul. But he knew it to be true. Such was the depth of the hate he now felt for her, such was the depth of his love.

He sucked in a deep breath and closed his eyes. *Rachel, our Rachel, how could you do this, how could you leave us? How could you leave me?*

He drew in another deep breath, sighing. He had his duty as deacon to perform now. *Ja,* he had his duty, he would speak to her one last time. And then her name would never pass his lips again.

As he raised his hand to knock, his gaze fell on his own knuckles, which were black and blue and scabbed still. Such a terrible thing, a Plain man with the marks of violence on his hands. Maybe we are all of us doomed and damned now, he thought. The outsider had brought his evil corruption to them all.

He had to knock twice, and the sight of her when she pulled open the door tore a choking gasp from his throat. She had on her Plain dress, but wore no apron, no shawl over her breasts. Her dress was unpinned at the neck. He could see the pulse beating at the base of her throat. Her hair fell over her shoulders and arms in a dark red silken quilt, caressing her hips with wanton curls and tangles.

He swallowed, hard. For a moment he thought of what it would be like for a man to bury his face and his hands in such hair. It put the sun to shame, her hair.

She stood there, blinking against the light that poured through the door at his back, and then she gasped.

"Noah." His name was a whisper on her lips, dark with sorrow.

For a moment he was blind to everything but her face. Her face was flushed, her mouth wet and swollen. But she looked agonized around the eyes. It both hurt and felt good to know that she was suffering.

He grabbed a breath, spoke through it. "Rachel Yoder . . ." He faltered, as he realized her name was Yoder no longer. But he would not give her an outsider's name. The Plain church didn't recognize her marriage anyway. She would die as Rachel Yoder. And she would die unforgiven as long as she cleaved to such a man. To an outsider.

He straightened his back and sought to put a spine into his words as well. "Rachel Yoder, you have been placed under the *Bann* by all members of the church of God. You will be shunned and avoided by us until the time of your repentance, according to the word of God. We will not share a table with you, or have discourse of any kind with you. Never will we speak your name. From this moment forth, until such time as you repent, or if you do not repent, then to us you are dead."

He watched as her eyes misted with unshed tears. She looked down at her hands, which were twisted up into a knot with her skirt. With a deliberate effort she unclenched her fingers, smoothing out the bunched material. When she raised her head again, looked at him again, her eyes were still tear-wet, but there was resolution there.

"You have done your duty, Deacon Weaver, and I have taken your words to my heart. But you should know . . . I'll not be repenting, ever."

Cloaked by dim shadows within the kitchen, the outsider had moved up behind Rachel. Noah saw that for once the man wasn't smiling that devil's smile. His hooded eyes, as always, were hard to read. He met Noah's eyes with a relentlessness that forced the Plain man's gaze to fall away.

"I don't know why you have done this," Noah said. "To seduce a Plain woman from her family, her life, her God—and for why? Weren't there women enough of your own kind that you could have taken to your bed? I don't believe it's because you care for her. If she matters to you at all, why then did you choose to become her damnation?"

The outsider stirred. He brought his hand up and laid it on Rachel's shoulder, pulling her back against him, as if claiming her, Noah thought, hating the man, hating the man with such force he shuddered with it and felt no shame for it.

"She isn't damned," the outsider said. "You know her. No God worth worshipping, no heaven worth striving for, would ever turn her away."

Noah shook his head. He knew God, he knew what was truth, what was light. There was only one path to salvation, the straight and narrow way.

He swung his gaze back to Rachel. His Rachel, with her hair falling wantonly down her back and with her mouth kiss-swollen in the middle of the day. His Rachel whom he didn't even know anymore, who was a stranger to him.

"Is he worth your soul, Rachel? Do you love him that much?"

She lifted her head. There was hurt in her eyes still, but there was that strength as well. "Yes. Yes, I do love him that much."

Noah's shoulders slumped. He turned, moving slowly, his legs and feet feeling as if they were dragging fifty-pound sacks of grain.

"Noah?"

He turned back.

She was crying now. Not a lot, just one or two tears that she probably hadn't been able to help. "Will you tell Da, tell my family, that I still love them all so very much, and that I'm sorry, so sorry."

Noah opened his mouth to speak, but his throat locked. He should have reminded her that he could no longer speak her name, that her family would be hearing no words purporting to come from the mouth of a daughter who was dead. He should have done that, it was his duty as Deacon to do that, but he still loved her too much.

So he only swallowed, nodded, and left her standing at the door of her house with the outsider at her back, claiming her with that hand on her shoulder. A hand that had killed and done all manner of foul deeds, and was now defiling his Rachel.

He dragged the weight of his feet and legs off the porch and toward the barn and the woods that separated her place from his. Unable to help himself, he paused once to look back. Rachel had stepped out onto the porch, the outsider with her. He stood with one wrist draped over her shoulders now, drawing her against his hip. And as Noah watched, the wind lifted her hair, whipping strands of it against Johnny Cain's face, in his eyes and mouth, and wrapping more of it around his neck, until he was bound by her hair.

25

FOR RACHEL, TIME PASSED both sweet and hard that summer.

It was sweet on the night she came awake to find him watching her. "Rachel," he would say, just her name, and his mouth would come down on hers, slow and hot, and she would feel his hunger burning through him into her. She knew a heady feeling of power that she could do this to him, make him want her so. And she felt helpless under his weight, the weight of the love she bore for him.

Once, in the middle of lovemaking, he had started singing at the top of his lungs: "Mine eyes have seen the glory of the coming of the Lord. . . ."

She tried to smother his mouth with her hand, thinking of Benjo sleeping in the next room. When that didn't work, she used her mouth to quiet him. "You are so wicked," she said into his open mouth, laughing.

It was like nothing she could ever have imagined, her life with him. She would look at him, sitting at the man's place at her table, eating a slab of fried cornmeal mush of a morning, and her heart would catch anew with awe and a shiver of excitement to think he was hers, her man.

Or she would suddenly be swept up into his arms in the middle of the yard, and he would be humming a tune and whirling her around and around and around in a dance, and she would think of the Bible words: *For ye have not passed this way heretofore.*

Or she would watch him shave, watch the razor scrape away the lather to reveal his arresting face to her eyes one more time, and an image would flash into her mind, sharper than a memory, of his hard body coming against hers. Of her body rising to welcome him, to take his weight and his thrusts and his need.

Often, though, she was reminded of how different he would always be from her. Like that day he came to her when she was carrying buckets of water out to her withering vegetable garden. He said that they ought to build themselves a windmill, and she'd answered, not thinking, with words a Plain woman would have used: "God provides us with water. We shouldn't ask Him to pump it, too."

He'd looked at her as if he thought a trip to the nuthouse might be in order. Then he'd laughed and kissed her hard on the mouth, and left her to her bucket watering.

By marrying an outsider she supposed she had gone *Englische,* but she didn't feel that way. She no longer wore her prayer cap, though. Not because he'd asked it of her but because, to her, the cap was a symbol of what she once was and could never be again.

Otherwise, she dressed as she always had, for much of what she was inside of herself was still Plain. Outside, though, she felt something vital was missing. She was less than herself, as if a leg or an arm had been cut off.

There was a saying in the Plain life. *Oh, das hahmelt mir ahn,* which was about calling to mind older times and pleasures with such vividness that the memories were akin to pain. She caught herself doing that often, remembering sweet moments: Setting a bowl of bean soup before her father at the fellowship. Hearing Ezra Fischer's voice push through the waiting silence with that first long and piercing note of the hymnsong. Sitting on a blue dahlia quilt, to *klatsch* with her mother and her sisters-in-law, and hold a fat-legged baby on her thighs. Placing that first cocoon of spring, trembling with new life, into her great-grandmother's hand. She would remember and know joy, and then the swift thrusting pain when she understood that it had all been lost to her forever.

And then there were those times she would look at Benjo, and the fear would burn hot in her breast, to know the future pain she had brought upon herself and her son. For although she was shunned, Benjo was not. His kin and his church were still there for him to have, and she would be sure he had them. She would raise him Plain and send him to the preaching and fellowship every other Sunday. He would go often to the farms of his grandparents, and all his uncles and aunts and cousins, to help with the haying and the shearing. He would eat at their tables. And then one day he would kneel in a Plain barn and he would say the traditional words: "It is my desire to be at peace with God and the church," and he would have to shun her then, his mother. She would become dead to him, and he would be lost to her. But if he didn't choose the Plain church, if he joined her in the world instead, then he would be lost to God.

As she was lost to God.

THAT FIRST WORSHIP SUNDAY after she was banned, she had decided she would drive Benjo to the preaching in the buckboard, rather than let him take himself there on their old draft horse.

Her *Englische* husband came to her as she was about to climb into the wagon. The look on his face was one she hadn't seen since their marriage.

"Don't do this to yourself," he said.

There wasn't a way she could make him understand, he who had never before had a home, a family. The spirit of the man that was Johnny Cain, the toughness inside of him, could sustain him alone forever. She wasn't like that, she needed others, she needed that place at the table. She loved her family so much, she would grieve for them for the rest of her life. Yet God had made their loss the price she had to pay for loving him. And she couldn't tell him any of this, for he wouldn't understand. Except for one thing, one thing he might understand.

She pulled his head down so that she could kiss him on the mouth, in broad daylight, on a worship Sunday, in the middle of the yard, and with her son watching. "I love you," she said.

But it was worse at the preaching than she would ever have thought it could be. She was not, of course, going to be allowed into the barn during the worship service. And she had known no one would speak to her. But she hadn't understood what it would be like to have people you love, family and friends you've known all your life, not even look at your face. To have them know you were there and behave as if you were not there at all—as if even their memory of you had long ago faded to nothing more than a dull ache.

The worst, the very worst, was when *Mutter* Anna Mary, sitting in her willow rocking chair beneath the shade of a weeping willow, "saw" Rachel coming with her blind eyes, and turned her face away.

That night, after it had grown dark, and supper had been cooked and eaten, and the dishes washed, and her son pried out of the kitchen and sent off to bed, Rachel went by herself out to the paddock fence. She stood there, listening to the saw of the crickets, to the gentle purl of the creek, to the soughing of the summer wind, opening her heart to the music, only the music wouldn't come. And suddenly she was doubled over the fence rail, burying her face in her arms and sobbing.

She didn't even know he had come until he'd already gathered her up in his arms and was walking back to the house, with her face buried in his chest and her sobs quieting now into hoarse whispers of breath.

He laid her on the bed, and then he lay down next to her. More than next to her, he lay almost on top of her, with one arm wrapped around her back, and one leg thrown across both of her legs, as if he would pin her there to the bed with his man's weight.

"Hold me, Johnny," she said. "Hold me tight."

He said nothing, but he held her tight.

LATER, HER *ENGLISCHE* HUSBAND was the one to come awake in the middle of the night, but not to find her watching. She was sitting in her spindle-backed rocker, staring into the darkness, into the nothingness of her soul. He got up and went to her. He knelt at her feet and took up her hands, which she had clenched in her lap, warming them with his own.

"The music is gone," she said to him.

"It'll come back."

A single tear streaked along the bone of her cheek and into her hair, where there was already a damp spot over her ear. He didn't understand. He hadn't the faith within him to understand.

She brought their clasped hands up to her mouth and kissed his knuckles. “No, it can’t come back. The music was God.”

SHE LOVED HIM DESPERATELY. And her love, her need, made her so afraid.

Since he didn’t believe in a better world after death, he lived wholly in this one, wholly in the moment. And up until the day he had come staggering across her wild hay meadow, he had lived the life of a skipping stone. She could imagine him waking up some morning and thinking that he didn’t want to be here, with a fallen Plain woman and a ten-year-old boy, on a sheep farm in the Miawa Country, and so he would just up and leave.

The first time this imagining came to her, it had sent her into such a panic that she knew she wouldn’t be able to take one more breath until she saw with her own eyes that he was still with her. He’d said something about going out to the barn to perform one of those eternal chores men found to do in a barn. But now suddenly she was convinced he’d gone out there to saddle his getaway horse.

She burst through the big open cross-hatched doors, shouting his name.

He spun around fast, his hand hovering above his gun. “What’s happened?”

She was breathing hard, and unconsciously she put the flat of her hand against her chest to still it. “Nothing.”

“What?”

“I thought you’d left me.”

The creases at the corners of his mouth deepened. She thought it was his heartfelt smile, until she heard the edge of his voice when he spoke. “We both of us promised till death do us part.”

And she understood. He was telling her he would hold her to her vows, and so he expected her to do the same with him.

He had been repairing a harness. He had one of the leather traces wrapped around his left hand. She looked at that hand, so long and fine-boned, so graceful in the way he moved it. She took his hand and peeled open his fingers to examine his palm. "Your hands are a farmer's now," she said. "You've calluses in different places."

AN HOUR LATER he came to her where she was hanging wash on the line and said, "I'm going into town." He paused, and when she said nothing, he added, "I thought I'd take our Benjo with me."

She could feel her heart in her smile. "You'd make that boy's whole week with that offer."

She watched him walk away from her, feeling so full up inside. Her heart sang with the way he had said *our Benjo,* in the Plain way.

It was just coming on to dusk when he came home. He had with him something big wrapped up in a canvas tarp in the wagon bed, and there was a paper-wrapped parcel in Benjo's lap, and he and Benjo both were wearing cat-in-the-cream smiles.

He made her go with him into the bedroom, just the two of them, and he had the paper-wrapped parcel with him.

"Open it," he said, and he had the kind of heated, lazy look in his eyes that made it hard for her to swallow.

She untied the string and laid back the brown paper to reveal a dress of soft velvet, the blue of forget-me-nots, frilled up with foaming waterfalls of ecru lace. "Oh, my." She had to sit on the bed, her legs were shaking so. Her hand hovered over the beautiful dress, but she did not touch it.

"But this costs a fortune!" she cried. She couldn't say the amount out loud, her head could barely think it. "I saw that sign in the mercantile window."

"Tulle was lookin' to unload it, and I drove a hard bargain."

She felt queasy inside to think of five hundred dollars. She would have felt queasy to think of one hundred dollars. "How much of a bargain?"

"It ain't polite to ask the cost of a gift. Weren't you ever taught that?"

"Oh, Jesus God!" she exclaimed, blaspheming for the first time in her life. She jumped to her feet, flinging out her arms. "What kind of crazy person are you?" She whirled to look again at the dress, hungry for it, frightened of it. "It's a watering hole dress. Where is there a single watering hole in all of Montana where one could wear such a dress?" She spun back around with her hands on her hips. "What ever in heaven's name were you thinking of?" Her legs started to shake again, and she had to stop to suck in a deep breath. "Oh, Johnny, bargain or not, we can't afford it."

His eyes were laughing at her. "You're pretty when you go all wrathy."

She sat back down, clutching the dress to her chest. Then she let go of it as if it had suddenly burst into flames in her hands. Judas, she was wrinkling it! Judas, it was beautiful. How could you marry a man and not know that he would up and go buy you a dress like this?

He was studying her now in that sharp, intent way of his. "I got a fair amount of money in a bank in San Francisco," he said. "With all my worldly goods I thee endow."

This shocked her more than the dress had. It shocked her breathless. "How did you come by this money? Did you rob banks?"

His eyes were definitely laughing at her. His mouth was nearly laughing, too. She could see him working to hold the laughter in. "Rachel, Rachel. Would a man who robbed banks for a living trust putting his money into one?"

"I don't know."

He bent over and brushed his lips across her forehead. "Now, you wait right here. I've another surprise for you."

Her gaze went back to the beautiful dress. Surely even the Devil at his most fiendish couldn't come up with such a temptation. She ran her hand over the soft velvet, and scared and excited feelings swelled in her chest. It was the kind of thing a man would do if he wanted to seduce a woman, buy her such a dress. But he already had her heart, body, and soul. She didn't know what was left to give him.

She heard banging as they came through the door from the yard, panting grunts, and Benjo's excited, stammered whispering. Her husband and her son came into the bedroom carrying the big tarp-covered thing that had been in the wagon bed. It was still covered with the tarp, although she could see wooden feet poking out from beneath the folds in the canvas.

They set the tarp-covered surprise on its feet in the corner nearest the wardrobe. He said something to Benjo too low for her to hear. Benjo backed out of the room, grinning at her all the way, and then she heard him leave the house, banging the door behind him. Her husband went to their bedroom door and shut it.

Rachel had gotten off the bed when they first came in with the surprise, and now she stood in the middle of the floor feeling suddenly shy with him, and a little anxious.

"Close your eyes," he said.

She closed her eyes, swallowing hard. She heard the sounds of the tarp being pulled off her surprise and rolled up. His hands fell on her shoulders, turning her around. "Look," he said.

She looked and saw herself. Saw a reflection of herself in a cheval glass with a mahogany frame. She didn't quite know what to make of what she saw. There was a woman, not very tall and rather skinny, in a Plain brown dress and apron and shawl, with auburn hair rolled up in braids on top of her head. There was a pink flush on her face and a sheen of sweat on her neck, for it was a hot day. Her eyes looked a little frightened, or perhaps only surprised. Like a rabbit caught in a sudden wash of lantern light.

He took one of her prayer caps from off the shelf beneath the window, where she kept them still, though she no longer wore them. She watched in the mirror as he came up behind her with the cap in his hands and he put it on her head.

"This is what I see when I look at you, Rachel. From the beginning this is what I saw."

"You see me Plain?"

"I see you."

It was a strange way of telling her he loved her, a man's way, she supposed. But it warmed her heart.

Their gazes met in the mirror, and they loved with their eyes. He leaned closer, his hair brushing her cheek, his breath warm and moist against her ear. Her heartbeat became hard and uneven.

"Are you going to take me to bed?" she said.

"Oh, lady, that I am."

After they made love, when she was alone in their bedroom, she put on the watering hole dress and looked at herself in the mirror. A cheval glass, she thought. Imagine! She could see why they were forbidden in the Plain life. You would certainly start thinking you were somebody pretty darn quick if you looked at your own self like this all the time. As for the woman she was looking in the mirror at now, the woman in a blue velvet dress with a cascading bustle of ecru lace—she was a stranger.

Rachel felt a little breathless and shaky as she took off the dress and put it away with loving care in the knotty pine wardrobe. She thought that someday she might wear it for him, but not just yet.

SHE WAS SITTING on the porch later that afternoon, with the butter churn between her knees, cranking on the handle, when she saw a Plain woman walking down the road.

Rachel's arm slowed its cranking. And long before the woman crossed the bridge and turned into the yard, Rachel knew it was her mother.

She couldn't imagine what terrible thing had happened in the lives of her family that would send her mem here. A death, surely—it could be nothing less for Sadie Miller to break the *Bann*. To put her own immortal soul at risk by acknowledging her wayward daughter.

Rachel stood, the churning forgotten, her thumping pulse filling her throat, as she watched her mother come.

Sadie Miller stopped at the bottom of the steps, as if she was afraid, or couldn't bear to come any further. Her prayer cap, starched and bleached, blazed white under the sun.

"Who is it?" Rachel said, her voice barely a whisper.

Confusion clouded her mother's face, then she expelled a loud breath. "No, no, we are fine, all of us. Well, your brother Levi, his leg is still paining him some."

Rachel's relief was so great, she felt dizzy with it. "Mem, what are you doing here?" She looked back down the road, squinting against the heat haze, as if she could find the answers walking there. "You shouldn't have come. If anyone's seen you, if they find out . . ." Then Sadie Miller also would be shunned by her church. Even by her own husband, she would be shunned. Bishop Isaiah would have to make his wife leave his bed, as well as his table.

Rachel's mother lifted her head and met her daughter's eyes. Hers were the only eyes in the Miller family that weren't some shade of gray. But then she wasn't really a Miller. "I won't come again," she said. "Only just this once. But I had to see with my own eyes how you are."

Sol had been the one to discover Rome's body hanging from the barn rafters. But Mem had been the one to bathe and dress her boy child for the last time. Not in a white suit, though, for he had not died Plain.

Rachel's heart ached, and the feeling was both sad and sweet. Sad for her mem, whose fate it was to suffer the loss of two children to the world. Sweet for herself, because her mother cared enough to come see with her own eyes how she was faring.

"It's hard for me some days, some moments, but I'm happy," she said to her mother, and the truth felt good to say, good to acknowledge inside herself. She was happy. But then suddenly a vast longing filled her to have her mother see, have her understand, why their lives had taken the turn they had. Why she had brought such hurt to them all, including herself.

"I love him so very, very much, Mem. He is everything to me."

She couldn't tell if her mother understood. It wasn't the Plain way to flaunt one's love with open displays of passion, or even affection. Indeed, it was never spoken of. Isaiah and Sadie's marriage had been a quiet and somber one, but their children all knew the bond went deep.

Then her mother said, "It's a wonderful and hurtful love

you must have for this outsider. Hurtful because you've given up everything to possess him. And wonderful because you believe him to be worth it all."

He was worth it, of that Rachel had always been sure.

Her mother was looking at her in a way she'd often done when Rachel was a girl, with a mixture of exasperation and confusion and surprise. "I don't know if God's always so smart," she said, "in the way He matches us all up, the one to the other. Sure enough, I wasn't the right mother for you."

Something caught at Rachel's chest. "Oh, Mem—"

"There you see, always you're the one to be jumping right in, worse even than our Samuel, and you don't let me finish. I used to look at you growing up, *ja,* and even after you married and had a boy of your own, I used to look at you and I would think to myself: This is my daughter? And I'd feel such a wonderment, how this had happened, that you had come from me, Sadie Miller. For sure, I could never see how that could be. You've always been so strong, so complete inside yourself. Like a hymnsong, always sung in the same, sure way, you always knew right where you wanted to go, how you wanted to be."

"I don't feel so much that way now," Rachel said.

"You will make yourself that way again. You are so strong, my daughter."

My daughter. Rachel hadn't known how badly she'd been needing to hear those words, and they were doubly sweet and doubly painful because she knew she would never hear them again after this.

Tears filled her eyes. As she walked down the steps and into her mother's arms, she moved as if blinded. It was an awkward embrace, for they weren't used to it, and it left them both feeling a little shy and foolish, so that when they pulled apart, neither could look at the other.

Rachel's mother dabbed at her eyes with the corner of her apron. "I never said it to Rome. I never said it to him and I've had to swallow back many a bitter regret since. So I'll not leave here without saying it to you."

She dropped her apron and stared up into her daughter's face, as if she were etching it into a memory that she would be able to take out and look at again and again. "You aren't dead to us, our Rachel. Not to your da or to your brothers or to me, no matter how we must behave to you. You are with us always, in our hearts."

Rachel watched her mother turn and walk away from her, and she knew Sadie Miller would be strong enough after this to keep to the straight and narrow way, and so they would never speak again.

The afternoon sun blazed hot at their backs. It cast Sadie Miller's shadow long and dark before her on the road.

QUINTEN HUNTER STOOD ON the gallery of the big house. You could see a long way from anywhere in Montana, he thought, the sky was so big, the horizon so far. And what he saw on this day hurt. The prairie grass was so brown, the sage foothills gray with dust. Tag ends of clouds clung to the mountains, but they were empty of rain.

The dour slapping push of the hot afternoon wind made him feel a bit crazy. On the renegade side, as they said up on the reservation. His mouth tightened into a bitter smile. Maybe he should go take some paleface scalps, or chase down a herd of stampeding buffalo, if he could find any, or get wild-assed drunk on firewater. Get the Indian out of his system.

He went on into the house instead, in search of his father. As he walked down the hall toward the Baron's study, he could hear that tobacco-fed voice growling to someone about "this Christly drought."

The door was open only a crack. Quinten had raised his hand to knock when he heard his father's wife say something about having to find another way, and he paused, his fist suspended in the air.

"There is no other way!" the Baron bellowed. "Everything's already been mortgaged twice over, including the bloody air we're breathing."

"That money's mine," Ailsa said, steel beneath the soft snow of her voice. "I'll not be giving you any more of my family's paltry legacy to pour down the dried-up waterholes of a dying ranch. There's precious little of it left, as it is. I shall need it for myself, for when I leave here."

The Baron made a howling noise, as if he were in pain. "You're never leaving here, you're never leaving me, more's the bloody pity of it. You enjoy tormenting me too much, you perverse bitch."

Quinten knocked and went through the door in one motion, without waiting to be invited.

The Baron was sitting in his maroon leather swivel chair behind his massive black walnut desk. He had put his dusty boots, with cowshit caked on the soles, on the green leather top of that desk because he knew how it would irritate his pure-bred wife.

Ailsa, elegant in brown silk, was sitting in a Boston rocker stenciled in gilt that caught the sunlight pouring through the lace panels on the windows. She didn't look irritated, only beautiful. And untouchable.

"Ah, there you are, Quin, m'boy," his father said, waving his cigar in an expansive gesture of welcome. "I was just telling your mother that we've been having buzzard's luck lately, eh? Can't kill anything and won't nothing die."

Their fighting had gotten savage, if the Baron was referring to his wife as his bastard's mother. Quinten thought she probably hated that above all things, although you would never know it to look at that cool, remote face. But then his father's snarling courage had never been any match for her cunning cruelty.

"If cattle prices don't start coming back up, it won't pay us to ship them to market this year," his father was saying. "It'll be a fine skinning season come fall. And yet did you hear what those damned holy-howler mutton punchers got for their bloody wool? The range is getting sheeped out, and they're getting rich off of it, the cocksucking bastards."

Ailsa Hunter's lips might have thinned a little at her husband's crude language, but her violet eyes remained deep and unassailable.

"The sheep men aren't having things totally their way this year," Quinten said, weary already of the argument that they had been playing out all summer. "I heard they've been forced to throw their herds back onto the slopes of buttes they'd already eaten across once. This drought is affecting us all."

The Baron gave him the snake-killing look Quinten always got whenever he tried to calm the troubled waters his father was always stirring up between himself and the mutton punchers. "If things don't turn around here soon, we'll be so broke we'll have to sell our saddles," the Baron said, naming the worst fate that could befall a cattleman.

"What does it matter?"

The words, spoken in Ailsa's snowbank voice, silenced the room. Quinten could hear the wind blowing through the cottonwoods outside, and the tick of the brass pendulum in the polished oak hanging clock.

"Matter? Bloody Christ on His cross, it matters!" The Baron swung his boots off the desk, pushing to his feet with a creak and groan of leather. "Do you think I've sweated blood only to watch this place die before me? I want Hunters to be ranching this valley a hundred years from now. The boy—"

"The boy!" To Quinten's shock, she actually laughed. "None of it has ever been for the boy, and the only fool who believes that is him."

Slowly she turned her head on its long thin neck to look at him, and Quinten felt the breath back up in his throat. He knew he was about to find out, at last, how the Baron's half-breed bastard had come to be brought to this house fourteen years ago. He would discover the Devil's bargain his father had made with this woman.

"You've always thought you were something special to him," she said in that cold, cold voice, "because you think your mother was special. Well, he had himself a new squaw every winter. A new squaw and a new buffalo robe to keep a man warm during the long, cold Montana winters, isn't that what you used to say, Fergus?"

The skin around the Baron's mouth had grown taut. "She's lying," he said.

Something caught at Quinten's chest, hurting. He had this strange liquid feeling, as if his heart had been ripped open and was bleeding inside his chest. "He brought me here," he said. "My . . . the Baron brought me here to the ranch."

"I made him do that. You were my price for staying."

"Goddamn it, she's lying!" his father roared, as if shouting her down could make his own words truer.

"Why?" Quinten said, looking only at her. A little malicious smile flickered on her mouth, and a trace of color had risen under her skin.

"He promised me he would give up his red-skinned tarts once we were married, and he did for a time. Until that winter I grew heavy with his child, then he took your mother back to his bed. He'd already experienced her charms during an earlier winter, which is how you came to be." She lifted her slender shoulders in an elegant shrug. "I don't know why he chose to have a second go at her. Perhaps he'd been through them all at least once, and he was starting over at the bottom again."

She had her face turned up to him, and she was looking at him, really looking at him, and he felt as always that bittersweet yearning, the raw longing, even while he was listening to her speak words that hurt worse than the thousand slights, worse than all those years of benign indifference that she had ever given to him.

"But I had my revenge on your father," she was saying. "I willed our baby to be born dead. I *willed* it. And I never let him touch me after that. Instead I made him bring you here, to his precious ranch where he was going to build his dynasty—you, his get by an Indian squaw. I made certain he would never have a legitimate son, a white son, and every time he looked at you he was going to remember why and what it had cost him."

She stood up, sleek and cold and deadly as a sword. She came to him where he was, rigid in the middle of the plush floral carpet of his father's study. She dug long painful fingers into his arm. It was now the second time she had touched him. The second time in a lifetime.

"Why don't you ask him who will get all this worthless and beloved land of his after he dies?"

Quinten watched her glide from the room. She left behind her an arctic silence. The sun burned through the windows, making the gold paper and tin wainscoting on the walls glow and glitter. But it might have been winter outside.

"Don't you go putting any stock in what she said, Quin. She's crazy. She's been crazy for years."

He turned to look at his father. The Baron had taken a fresh cigar out of the cedar humidor on his desk and he was peeling off the silk band. "Who gets this ranch after you die?" Quinten said.

His father pointed the unlit cigar at his face. "What a bloody thing to ask your old man. Do I look ready for the bone orchard yet?" His eyes were haggard, his color high. But his jaw was set strong, and his brogue thick. "Ye're my son, damn yer bloody hide. Ye're my son."

Quinten looked at his father. He wanted to believe. He *yearned* to believe, and the emotion was so powerful it left him feeling weak. But he was a breed. In the eyes of the white world, that made him inferior. And in some hard and bitter corner of his heart, he'd always known his Indian blood had made him inferior in his father's eyes as well.

His father turned away with a snarl. "Bugger it all, then. What did you blow in here for if it was only to glower at me?"

Quinten had to swallow twice before he could speak. "I was out riding line and I came across a dead steer. But I don't think this one died of thirst. It had swollen legs."

"Are you telling me you think we got blackleg now on top of everything else? Shit, boy. Sometimes I think you wish the bad luck on us."

"The dead beef was one of those you bought off that Oregon man in Deer Lodge a couple months back. Beeves we didn't have any range for in the first place."

The Baron's jaw bunched, then he pushed out a hard sigh. "When it comes to this subject, conversing with you is like discussing the meaning of life with a stump. We had the range once, and we would have it still if those bedamned, holy-howling, Bible-banging mutton punchers hadn't settled the north end of the valley. And if our cows have got the blackleg, then it probably came from their damned bloody sheep."

"You don't know that—"

"I'll tell you what I know, and for once in your life you're going to shut your yap and listen. We had the range once and we'll have it again." He held a match to the end of his cigar, sucking and puffing to get it going. Then he pointed with the smoking end of it at a pile of gunnysacks on one corner of his desk. It was the first Quinten had noticed of them.

"Tonight," his father said, picking up one of the sacks, handling it almost lovingly, "we're going to booger those mutton punchers so bad they'll be run out of this valley for good, every last woolly one of them."

Quinten looked at the gunnysack in his father's hand, feeling weary and sick and scared. This was wrong, what his father was planning to do, wrong and ultimately pointless, because all the grass in all the valleys in all the world wasn't going to make their troubles go away. But the Baron in this mood could make himself believe that fire wasn't hot.

"Getting rid of the Plain folk isn't going to drive cattle prices back up or put rain in the clouds," he said, knowing it would do little good.

His father gripped the brown burlap in his fist, shaking it before Quinten's face. "Life isn't owed to you, boy. You got to earn it. You are my son—I've said as much to the whole valley, to the whole bloody world, and I mean it. But if you want this ranch, then it's time you learned how to fight for it."

"Johnny Cain married that Plain widow he was working for. That sheep farm of hers now belongs to him, and there's a man who's always lived by the gun. He won't run."

"Johnny Cain might be more feared in these parts than the Almighty, but he's only one man."

Quinten closed his eyes for a moment, afraid suddenly

that he was going to weep. "You used to tell me a story when I was a little tacker, when we'd go out on hunting trips up to the res. About some fellow back in Scotland, years ago, who single-handedly rallied his people to drive the English off their lands. No man in the wrong can stand up against a fellow that's in the right and keeps on coming, you used to say that to me, remember, Pa? One man who won't run can stop an army."

"Hell, those were only stories, boy. In real life, your one man just gets himself killed. He gets trampled in the dust, until there's nothing left of him or his bloody gun."

"I want no part of this," Quinten said to his father's weather-toughened face. But the words came out of his mouth mangled, as if he were chewing leather.

"You'll have a part of it," the Baron said, his voice hard now, as hard as his eyes. "Or you'll have none of it."

Quinten nodded, hearing his father's threat, accepting it. A moment ago he'd been fighting back tears. Now his eyes were so dry they burned. And he felt empty inside. As if one of those spirit thieves his mother's people believed in had come and whisked away his soul up into the sky, and he was looking down on this room now, down on this moment, from far away, lost in the blueness of the vast Montana sky. There stood his father stiff-backed with pride and stubbornness. And there stood himself, hearing the echo of his father's words in his heart: *You are my son.* Tasting the certainty, bitter like alkali dust, not only that what they were about to do was wrong, but that the consequences were going to be bad. Maybe deadly.

He said nothing, though. There was no reason to say what could be more plainly shown. He picked up a gunnysack from his father's desk. He left the study with it in his hands, left the house with it.

Outside, the hot wind was blowing so hard that he had to put the strings of his hat through the toggle and pull them tight to his chin. The wind was blowing up the dust in a fine spray that stung his eyes and dried his throat. He could feel the heat and the wind toughening his skin, leathering it, seasoning Quinten Hunter into what he would be for the rest of his life.

His mother's people believed that a man couldn't own the land, only his own life. But he felt a possessive love for the Circle H that ran gut deep. If he couldn't own the land, then he would allow it to own him. In that at least he was every bit his father's son.

26

A COYOTE HOWLED A LAST sad lament to the deepening night.

Benjo Yoder shivered, and then looked to see if the other boy had noticed. But Mose was busy turning the grouse that was sizzling on a stick over the campfire, while at the same time trying to wave the billowing smoke away with his hat. The wind was blowing wild tonight, swirling and gusting, and they kept having to shift around the fire.

The sheep were bunching, the ewes calling to their lambs and the young ones answering. The woollies liked to huddle during the night, protecting themselves from the darkness, Benjo supposed. But then people were much the same, in that they liked to sit around a campfire, putting its warmth and light between them and the dark.

He felt proud that he'd been sent up alone to do the camp tending for Mose this week. This wasn't the first summer he'd been given the responsibility, he'd done it once or twice before, and he thought he was probably getting big enough to handle a few weeks of shepherding, too. But his mem would have none of that yet. Criminy, she got nervous enough when all he had to do was drive the wagon back and forth between the sheep camp and the farm.

Benjo watched while Mose opened a couple of cans of deviled ham with a knife and emptied them into a pair of battered metal dishes for their dogs. MacDuff dug right in, but Mose's dog, being female, approached her food with a bit more daintiness, even sniffing it at first. Mose's dog, Lady, had a sorrel hide that was going gray in patches so that she looked like she had a bad case of the mange. She was getting real old, was Lady. Too stiff-legged to do the herding much longer. Benjo had overheard Deacon Noah threatening to have her put down come the end of summer.

That thought led to thoughts about coyotes being put down, and gave him a tight feeling in his belly. He told himself for maybe the thousandth time that he had done the right thing, the manly thing. She was a sheep killer. She had been teaching her pups how to be sheep killers. He had done the right thing.

"Duh—did that b-bear ever come back for its kuh—kill?" Benjo asked the other boy, wanting mostly to get his mind off that coyote. Yesterday, at the preaching, he'd heard Mose's father tell how a bear had killed one of the yearling wethers. Bears liked meat better after it had spoiled some, so they would often bring down a sheep and leave it lying for a while.

"Nope, she hasn't yet," Mose answered. He patted the

stock of the Winchester rifle he kept handy by his side. "But when she does, you can bet I'm ready for her." He cocked a grin at the wide waistband of Benjo's broadfalls. "So, how about you, David the giant killer? You got that sling of yours all loaded up and ready to fire?"

Benjo grinned right back at him, saying nothing. The fact was, he did have the socket of his sling filled with a stone. His sling was the reason why they were having a big fat juicy grouse for supper.

The grouse had turned a nice golden color, dripping fat that flared in the flames and made a delicious sizzling. Benjo leaned over to punch at the fire with a stick, sending red sparks spiraling into the blue of the night.

He thought at first it was the sparks that set the sheep off. Even in their calmer moments, the woollies went through life in a near panic. They could look at something they'd seen a hundred times and suddenly spook. So when they spooked this time, he thought it must have been the sparks that set them off.

Until the men with no heads came riding at them from out of the black night.

MACDUFF LET OUT A night-splitting woof, but it was Lady who charged, snarling and growling, at the galloping phantoms. There was a shot, then Lady howled and went down in a spray of blood and red-gray fur.

"Bastards!" Mose cried, reaching for his Winchester.

But it was Benjo who screamed as the other boy's arm exploded into a spurt of blood and bony splinters.

The men on horseback spread out over the clearing, going after the frenzied sheep. Mose lay on the ground, writhing and crying in pain, cradling his shattered arm. The most Benjo had been able to do was stand up. All of him, his muscles and bones, had locked up with fear.

He understood why he'd thought the men were headless. He hadn't seen their faces because they had gunnysacks pulled over their heads, with holes cut in them for their eyes. But although their faces were hidden, the Circle H brands were plain on their horses.

And they had clubs in their hands.

They rode among the bleating, milling sheep, smashing those clubs into woolly skulls. MacDuff, instinctively protecting the herd, went after a blaze-faced sorrel, leaping up at the rider's leg with his snarling teeth.

The man on the sorrel twisted in the saddle and swung his club, catching MacDuff with a terrible *thwack*. The dog went flying backward, yelping and smacking hard into the ground. He lay whimpering, with his hind leg twisted crooked, splintered bone ends sticking up through blood-wet fur.

Bastards! Benjo screamed inside his head. He pulled out his loaded sling. He gripped the two ends of the rawhide cords in his left hand and whipped it hard above his head. He let go of one cord sharply, and the rock whizzed through the night air.

He'd aimed for the red glint of reflected firelight he saw in the slit of the mask, the man's eye, and the rock struck true. The man shrieked, throwing up his hands, grabbing for his face, blood spilling out from between his fingers.

Eye for an eye! Eye for an eye! Benjo screamed in his head.

Another man came galloping up to the campfire. He had a torch in his hand, which he set alight. He held the torch high as he spurred his horse, jerking its head around by the reins.

"No, Pa! Don't!" cried the man on the blaze-faced sorrel. He tried to follow after the man with the torch, but he reeled dizzily in his saddle, nearly falling. Where the eye slit in the gunnysack mask had been, there was only blood.

The man with the torch was laughing. He leaned over and set the blazing wood to the back of a fat ewe. The ewe turned into a bawling wild-eyed torch herself and ran, frenzied, into the middle of the flock, touching off the entire herd in one blazing lanolin-fed fireball.

The masked men rode around the clearing, clubbing all the bawling, woolly heads they could find, sending others with their fleece in flames off into the pines. And then they seemed suddenly to ride back into the black night, from where they had come.

Only one man stayed behind. He hadn't been doing any sheep killing. He'd just sat there on his horse and watched, his cocked shotgun in his hand.

Now he sent his horse in a slow walk toward the campfire and Benjo watched him come, the sling hanging empty from his own hand.

The burning sheep had set the pines and the buffalo grass on fire. Benjo could feel the heat of it blazing at his back. The fire had lit up the whole clearing with an eerie red glow. And the world was full of terrible noise: the crackle of flames, Mose's cries, MacDuff's whimpers, the screaming bleats of the sheep, the roar of the wind.

The man brought his horse right up to Benjo. He had his shotgun lying across his lap, his finger on the trigger. He leaned over, and the mask made him seem as if he were looking at Benjo with a blinkless stare. "You know a Johnny Cain, boy?"

Benjo's chest was crushed with fear. He was sure he'd never get the words out, that all of his words were dammed forever in his throat. But they surprised him by coming out with barely a hitch. "H-he's my father."

Benjo couldn't see the man's smile, but he could feel it, like a cold draft from behind the gunnysack. "You tell him that Jarvis Kennedy don't give a shit whether he's gotten religion or not. You tell him that I'm getting plumb wore out waiting for him to rediscover his guts. He can find me in the Gilded Cage. Anytime tomorrow, I'll be there."

He turned his horse's head around and started off, but then he came back. "You tell him, too, that if he don't show, then I'll be coming to wherever he's at." The man laughed. "You tell him I am his Armageddon."

MOSE'S BLOOD SEEMED TO BE everywhere, lying in puddles on the grass, smeared over the pine straw, splattered in black wet streaks all over his clothes.

Benjo knelt beside him, and Mose looked up, wild-eyed with pain and fear. "Benjo . . . I need to get to a doctor, bad."

Benjo nodded his head extra hard so that Mose would be sure to see. There was no way he was ever getting any more words out of his throat. His throat felt like it had a noose tightened around it. A hangman's noose.

He didn't realize he was crying until he brushed the hair out of his face and his hand came away wet. He took off his coat and wrapped Mose's arm up with it, wrapped it up tight. He didn't want to think of what that arm was like.

He went to check on MacDuff next. The dog's leg was broken in two places and the bone had cut through his hide. He was whimpering, soft little yelps of pain. His eyes showed white around the edges.

They had to get off the mountain. Not only because they

needed to get to a doctor, but because the whole mountain was going up in flames. The fire was blazing wildly through the drought-struck pines, licking hungrily through the dry grass. And the wind that came roaring out of the night was whipping at it, feeding it.

Somehow he got both Mose and MacDuff into the wagon bed, although he couldn't have explained afterward where he found the strength. The sky rained cinders, blistering their skin. Thick roiling clouds of black smoke rolled overhead, burning their throats raw. Benjo drove the wagon, lurching, over the trail, with the fire crackling and clawing at their backs.

He looked back once. It was as if all of heaven had gone up in flames.

RACHEL STOOD IN THE yard watching as her son drove their wagon across the corduroy bridge and turned into the yard, hours before she expected him.

Behind her, she heard the door bang shut, heard her *Englische* husband come out of the house. She didn't have to turn around and look to know he was already wearing his gun. He slept with it looped over the bedpost at night. He put it on first thing in the morning, along with his trousers.

She was running alongside the wagon before Benjo could pull it to a complete stop. Like something out of a terrible dream that kept coming back night after night, she saw that a boy was lying in the wagon bed, only it was Mose Weaver this time, and his leg wasn't bloody, it was his arm. His arm was wrapped up in Benjo's coat. MacDuff was back there, too. She thought the dog was dead until she saw his head move.

Her boy's face looked bloodless beneath a covering of soot and ash. Rachel's gaze jerked off her son for an instant and lifted up to the mountain where their sheep summered. She hadn't noticed it before, probably thinking the red glow was part of the rising sun, but she could see it plain now. The mountain was on fire.

Benjo's lips pulled back from his teeth, his throat worked hard, his eyes bulged with the effort to force the words out, but they weren't coming. Young Mose Weaver, though, was conscious enough to tell them most all of what had happened.

Her *Englische* husband didn't offer to kill them for her this time; he didn't even bother to tell her he *was* going to kill them. He just went about the business of getting himself ready to do it.

Their old draft mare's head was dragging the ground, and her legs were splayed with exhaustion. He unhitched her from the harness and brought out his own horse. There was no thought, no feeling, nothing showing on his face. Nothing.

"I'm going with you," Rachel said.

He gave her a curt nod. "I want you and Benjo both with me, where I can keep you safe. You heard what the boy said about that man-killer threatening to come after me here. But you do what I tell you once we get into town, Rachel. You stay put where I tell you to stay put."

"Johnny." She touched his arm. The flesh beneath his shirt was rigid. He stepped back away from her, out of her reach. "Please think about Jesus. About how, although His person was always yielding, His heart was never weak."

"Better to say here's where he ran, than here's where he died, huh?"

"Don't—"

He looked up from buckling the harness parts, and his hard blue gaze met hers like a blow.

"You remember what I told you up on the mountain, about killing that hog farmer? I told you how I killed him, but I never said how I felt about it. After I'd done it, when I looked down on him, on what I could see of his face through the blood, I knew he'd broken me because I was still scared of him. Even with him dead, I was scared of him. And I hated him worse than ever then, because I knew I was never going to be free. I was always going to be his slave."

She heard his words, but it was his eyes that broke her heart. It was like watching a blizzard blow in from the north to seal up the land in a cold sheet of ice. He can never change, she thought. Never.

"But not ever again, Rachel. I'll not be a slave to another man ever again. I won't yield, I won't run, I won't turn the other cheek." His voice was as hard and cold as his eyes.

"I will pray for you, Johnny Cain," she said.

"I HAD TO TAKE the Weaver boy's arm off," Doctor Lucas Henry said.

He spoke to the woman who sat on his black horsehair sofa. She had one arm wrapped around her son, and she was holding him pressed close to her thighs. At Lucas's words, she put her curled fingers to her mouth and bowed her head to pray.

Except for no longer wearing the starched white cap on her head, she looked the same as she always had. It was hard for the mind to accept that she was wife to the man standing at the window.

Johnny Cain was looking through the dusty panes at the deserted street beyond, waiting. He was apart from everyone in the room, drawn into a taut alertness deep inside himself. A true outsider.

Lucas was worried about the boy, that he might be going into shock. He went to him for a closer look, squatting to put himself at eye level. He saw that while the pale skin beneath the gray eyes looked bruised, the eyes themselves were clear and bright. He was tougher than he looked. He took the boy's wrist, feeling for his pulse.

"I set your dog's leg," Lucas said, his voice gentle, yet firm. The boy's pulse was normal. "What was his name again?"

The boy's head jerked, his throat clenching. His lips pulled back from his teeth. "Muh!"

"MacDuff, isn't it?" Lucas dropped the boy's wrist, straightening up. "Well, he's going to be just fine. Though he might not run as fast as he used to."

"The jackrabbits out at our place will be grateful to hear that," Rachel said. She tried to smile, but she couldn't. She put her trembling mouth to her son's head and held him tighter.

The boy's left hand hovered near his sling, much the way Johnny Cain's stayed close to his gun. A couple of hours ago, Lucas had cleaned out and sewn up the right orbit of young Quinten Hunter, who had lost an eye for forever after to a rock hurled from that sling.

But then, young Quinten and his father had set fire to a whole herd of sheep and had shot off a boy's arm. So who was to say he didn't get what he deserved? Lucas thought. Maybe God liked to balance things out after all.

Rachel stirred, holding her boy closer. She was praying again: she had her eyes closed and her lips were moving. Lucas marveled at the depth of her faith, envying her.

How can you look at what your own son has done, at what has been done to you and yours, and not know what we are in our hearts, Plain Rachel? How can you not see the self's dark potential that exists in us all?

A boot heel scraped on the walk outside, and boards creaked. Lucas's gaze jerked to the man at the window, but Johnny Cain stood in stillness. His hand didn't go for his gun.

The door banged open without a knock. Noah Weaver stood at the threshold, his eyes searching.

Lucas started toward him, but the big man pushed him aside and headed for the back room. "I had to amputate his arm," Lucas said. "He's had a severe shock to his nervous system and he's lost a lot of blood. He shouldn't be moved."

Lucas might as well have been talking to a stone wall. The Plain man's broad back disappeared through the door.

He came out with the boy in his arms, carrying him like a babe, his cheeks, his beard, gleaming wetly with tears. The boy groaned, his eyelids fluttering, but he didn't awaken.

"He is my son," Noah Weaver said. "I am taking him home."

Rachel stood up, holding out her hand to him. "Noah . . ."

The Plain man looked at her, then through her.

He walked straight and sure out the open door, with his son in his arms, taking him home.

They all stood unmoving and Lucas could hear no sound in the room but his own breathing. Then Johnny Cain left the window and walked to the door. He didn't look at anyone, he didn't move quickly, he just walked to the door and went through it.

His wife watched him go. "He didn't even tell me goodbye," she said.

"I reckon," Doctor Lucas Henry said, going to the door and pushing it closed, "that's because he figures he's coming back."

JOHNNY CAIN WALKED OUT into the middle of the sunbaked road. He walked slowly, letting his eyes adjust to the brighter light, letting his ears open up to hear even the slightest of sounds. His hat was pulled low, shading his eyes, so he could see better. He flexed his fingers, unconsciously limbering the muscles for the draw.

He saw the town barber dart into the Gilded Cage saloon, and he smiled. He felt a single, quick pulse of fear, and then nothing.

He stopped across the street from the saloon, directly in line with the swinging summer doors. He leaned against the post of a hitching rail, next to a horse trough, and waited.

Jarvis Kennedy burst out of the doors, firing, a Colt in each hand. But Cain had seen the toe of his boot coming a full second before the rest of him.

Cain's revolver was in his hand in a motion so quick and smooth and natural that it was like the act of breathing.

His first bullet ripped Jarvis Kennedy's throat open. Blood spilled in a scarlet wash down the front of his white vest and shirt. The second bullet got Jarvis in the back as he spun around. He fell through the saloon's doors. He was dead before his face came to rest in the sawdust on the floor.

Cain was already swinging the barrel of his Colt to the right, aiming, firing at the man who was coming at him from an alley with a shotgun.

Shotgun pellets smacked into the trough behind Cain with a splintering crackle, but he ignored it. The first of his bullets went through the man's coattails, the second went where it was supposed to, right where a gold watch chain hung with seals stretched across his belly. The man screamed, doubling over, his arm clutching at his middle. He started to crawl, bleeding, back toward the mouth of the alley, and Cain fired again. The man jerked and went still.

The sound of the last shot fell, echoing, into a breath-held silence. Skeins of gunsmoke drifted past on the wind. Cain opened the gate of his Colt, ejected the empty cartridges and reloaded, his fingers moving sure and fast. He could taste the bitterness of gunpowder on his lips.

The man lying in the road, at the mouth of the alley, was dressed rich and had a fine head of white hair. Cain thought he could be Fergus Hunter, probably was, but he really didn't care a damn. If he didn't get Hunter today, he'd get him later. He often didn't know the names of the men he had killed, and didn't suppose it mattered one bit, to them or to him.

He knew there was someone else in the alley, but whoever it was had apparently quit on the notion of dying today. Cain kept his gun cocked, his finger a hair's breadth from squeezing the trigger, and waited.

A young man with long dark hair and a bandage wrapped around his head to cover one eye inched out of the shadows into the light, his hands raised high in the air. "I threw down my gun!" he called out, his voice breaking. "That's my father, please . . ."

Cain didn't move, not even his eyelids stirred. The young man fell to his knees and crawled through the dust to the man who lay in a spreading pool of blood. He pulled the dead man into his lap, and the man's arm flopped over, revealing a gaping hole in his belly. But a man didn't die from a gunshot, not right away. The killing wound, Cain knew, was the bullet he had put right in the middle of the man's forehead, like a third eye.

The quiet that came after death was different than any other silence, Cain thought. There was almost a terrible beauty about it. All he could hear was the beat of his own heart.

Cain waited. He waited a long while, gun in hand, because you could never be too careful. Many a man had died from holstering his pistol too soon.

Something banged behind him.

He whirled . . .

When he saw Rachel come running out Doc Henry's front door, crying his name, he had already fired.

"JOHNNY!" SHE SHOUTED, and felt something slam into her chest, knocking the breath out of her, and she fell.

She couldn't breathe. She could smell the bitter stench of gunpowder, but she couldn't hear or see anything. And she still couldn't breathe. She opened her mouth and then the breath was there, filling her lungs, as sweet and biting as spring water, and just as cold.

In some calm part of her mind there came not a thought but a certainty: *I am dying.*

She fought to open her eyes. And suddenly they were open, and she saw the face of her *Englische* husband. His sweaty face was streaked with dust, his eyes were glittering brightly, and she tried to smile at him, to say his name.

But there was a terrible pain now inside her chest, and she thought her eyes must be filling up with blood, because the world was turning red.

Johnny.

JOHNNY CAIN SAT IN the dust with his wife's head in his lap, and he watched her die.

The bullet hole in her chest bubbled blood. Her

eyes widened, focusing on his, then slowly drifted closed. Her lips formed his name.

"No, please," he tried to say. He curled his body over her and pressed his face hard into her chest. He opened and closed his mouth as if drowning, and tasted her blood.

He felt hands pulling him off her, he heard Doc Henry saying they ought to get her inside. The boy was there, too.

He couldn't look at the boy.

He stood up and backed out of the way, letting them have her, because she was dead now and it didn't matter, nothing mattered.

He kept hearing in his head, over and over again, the crack of a gun firing. He kept feeling the recoil of the Colt against his hand. He kept killing her, over and over again, he saw himself killing her.

He looked down at his hand. It was red and wet with her blood, and his gun was still there. In his hand. He'd held her and watched her die, and all the while his gun had still been in his hand.

SHE WAS BREATHING STILL, but barely, and it was a sucking chest wound. He had never seen anyone live with a sucking chest wound.

Lucas Henry had laid her on the couch in the examining room. There was nothing he could do but stand here and drink, and watch her die.

Her boy sat on the floor in the corner, his knees drawn up beneath his chin. Every so often his head would jerk and his mouth would open, but no words would come out. Lucas thought Rachel's son was probably trying to beg him to save her, and so he was glad the words were stuck in the boy's craw.

He brought the bottle of Rose Bud up to his mouth and drank deep. He heard footsteps crossing the parlor. He turned, unsteady on his feet. "Cain?" he said.

But it wasn't Johnny Cain, come to weep over the body of the wife he had slain. It was Miss Marilee of the Red House. She had herself all decked out in black taffeta, her idea of the respectable, respectful matron out to do a good deed, he supposed.

"I've come to help you lay her out," she said, her mouth solemn. She even had tears in her eyes, although Lucas couldn't imagine what they were for. As far as he was aware, she didn't know the woman.

"She isn't dead yet," he said.

She stared at him, her eyes wide, her forehead wrinkling a little. "Then why aren't you doing something to help her?" she asked.

He sighed. "Because she has a forty-four-caliber bullet lodged next to her left pulmonary artery, the bullet having first ruptured the lung, which has brought about pneumothorax, or air in the pleural cavity, complicated by valvular emphysema. Does that answer your question, Miss Marilee?"

He brought the bottle of Rose Bud up to his mouth with one hand, while the other lowered the sheet, exposing the wound. It pulsed blood and air with her weakening heartbeat, and Doctor Lucas Henry went on, deliberately cruel, wanting to punish her since he couldn't punish himself enough, "Or maybe you'll understand this better: she's dying, and I haven't the skill or the knowledge to prevent it from happening."

Marilee leaned over for a look, her black taffeta skirts rustling. "Can't you get the bullet out?"

"No." He pushed out a breath thick with the reek of

whiskey. "It would take a miracle. And she'd likely die in the end anyway."

Her eyes met his, and a hard, calculating look came over her face. "I think you're scared to try, Lucas Henry. You're scared because you know you'd have to put down that bottle to do it."

"Ah, Miss Marilee, sweet Marilee." He curled his lip and tried to put a cutting edge on his tongue, but he could hear the quaver in his voice. "I'm beginning to think your sweetness is more like spun sugar—all air."

Her chin went up a notch. "I can be real nice when I want to be, and mean when I have to be. But one thing I ain't ever been is a coward."

He stared at her. He started to bring the bottle back up to his mouth, then let it fall. His hand, his whole arm, trembled badly. He could feel each separate breath as a shock to his chest.

He knew he couldn't do it. He thought maybe if he hadn't pickled his brain and palsied his hands with the booze for so many years, he might have done it. But now, it was too late—years too late.

And, besides, a man couldn't really be redeemed for all that he had done by a single act, could he?

"All right, damn you," he said. He looked around the room, terrified to begin. He had never set out to perform a miracle before. Miracles were for fools who believed.

His gaze fell on Rachel's son, who sat huddled in the corner, a look of hope on his face. "Get the boy out of here," Lucas snapped.

He tilted back his head and drank from the bottle of Rose Bud, drank long and deep, searching for that whiskey-induced edge between belief in his own worth, his own capabilities, and the knowledge, deep in his guts, that there was nothing there to believe in.

Marilee coaxed the boy to his feet and gently led him to the door. Lucas stopped her with a hand on her arm. "Take this with you, too," he said, and held out what was left of the Rose Bud. But then he couldn't let it go.

The sweat was running cold on his trembling flesh. He could smell himself and the whiskey. He gripped the bottle so tightly his whole body shook with the effort. "Maybe we should pray for that miracle," he said, his voice breaking over the last word. "Well, Miss Marilee of the Red House, do you think God'll listen to the prayers of a drunk and a chippy?"

She gave him the sweetest smile he'd ever seen. "I always figured God listens to the prayers of sinners first, Luc. We're the ones who need His help the most."

She pried the bottle out of his rigid fingers, and he let her have it.

GREAT COLUMNS OF BLACK SMOKE rolled over the burning prairie grass. Flames leapt along the buttes and ridges, flinging sheets of lurid red light, flinging cinders, sparks, and ashes up against the bruised sky. The wind was blowing from the north. It had driven the fire down the mountain and across the cattle rangelands of the Circle H.

The big house was a pile of black, smoldering ruins when Quinten Hunter rode up to it. Even the bullet-riddled signboard had burned to the ground. Strangely, the long line of stately cottonwoods still stood.

It was beneath the cottonwoods that he found his father's wife.

She must have saved the horses, at least she had saved one for herself. Quinten got off his own horse and went to stand beside her. She didn't look at him. She looked at the ruins of the house where she had lived with her cattleman husband for sixteen years, and she said nothing.

Quinten's eye, where his eye used to be, throbbed with a fierce pain, as if he were being stabbed there over and over with an awl. He seemed to be unbalanced by it, by only seeing half, so that he couldn't walk very straight, and as he came up to her, he stumbled, bumping into her. For the length of a heartbeat he caught his arm around her waist to steady himself. She smelled of smoke, and soot dusted her pale face.

She pulled away from him and took a step back.

"He's dead," Quinten said to her, to his father's wife. "Johnny Cain killed him."

She stood still, facing him, for a very long time, and then he saw tears well in her eyes and spill over onto her cheeks, leaving streaks in the soot.

"Why?" Quinten said.

Her mouth curled just a little. "Oh, you foolish, foolish boy. I loved him. Do you think I would have done it, done any of it, if I hadn't loved him?"

She turned abruptly away from him and mounted her horse. Her skirt rode up around her knees, revealing black lisle stockings and button shoes. She didn't look at all like herself, straddling that horse like a boy. He thought how he had never really known the first thing about her, and now he was never going to.

He looked up into her face, so beautiful, so cold, and shining wet with an incomprehensible grief. "Where are you going?" he said.

He didn't think she would answer, but she did. "I don't know."

"Are you ever coming back?"

"Perhaps."

Quinten watched her ride away. He watched until she disappeared from his sight, and a body could see for a long time in Montana, even a one-eyed body. He knew she would never return, but he thought that it would be many years before he stopped waiting.

RACHEL'S SON WALKED THROUGH Miawa City, searching for Johnny Cain.

A sooty black cloud had swallowed up the sun. It made Benjo think of the story his grandfather often told during the preaching, about a time of earthquakes and famines and fearful sights and great signs from heaven, and then Jesus with His fiery angels would come again, and no one would ever die after that.

A part of him knew the black cloud came from the fire on the sheep mountain, but another part of him, the part that was a heavy ache in his chest where his heart was, wanted to believe the darkness was one of those great signs from heaven, that Jesus was coming to help Doc Henry make the miracle.

Benjo's brogans stirred up puffs of dust as he walked toward the livery. The road was deserted and it made him feel scared, scared of being alone forever. He found Johnny Cain beside the barn, sitting in the dirt with his back pressed up hard against the wall that was papered with wanted posters.

Benjo wanted to shout, but he couldn't. His tongue was tangled up so bad, he didn't think it was ever coming loose again. Words, a torrent of words blocked his throat, choking him.

He made a lot of noise, walking, because Cain had his Colt in his hand and he was jumpy. But Cain didn't seem to hear or see him.

As Benjo watched, he brought the gun up to his mouth,

he rubbed the barrel back and forth, back and forth, over his mouth. He put the muzzle in his mouth and closed his teeth around it.

And he smiled.

Benjo opened his own mouth, but nothing would come out. He couldn't even scream. He thought he would strangle over his own breath.

He took the last few stumbling steps at a hard run and threw himself at Cain's arm, his fingers wrapping tight around the wrist of the man's gun hand. The blow jarred the gun out of Cain's mouth, but he still held the barrel pointed at his face.

The man's eyes stared back at Benjo, and the strong muscles of his wrist flexed and tightened beneath Benjo's fingers, as he brought the gun barrel slowly, slowly back into his mouth.

"I killed her, partner," Cain said, and his voice was gentle, almost sweet. "I killed her."

Benjo shook his head hard, and tears splattered from his eyes. The words were piling and swelling in his chest, pushing against his skin and rib bones, crushing his heart.

"Fuuuuhhh!" he shouted. "Fuh—fuh—fuh . . . father!"

He let go of Cain's wrist and grabbed for the gun, knocking the barrel up into the sky. The gun fired, and the crack of the shot echoed in the hot, thick air.

Benjo wrenched the gun free from Cain's hand, and he flung it away from them with the same hard, violent motion he used to hurl his sling. They watched together as the gun flew, end over end, far, impossibly far, in a wide, high arc across the dark, ash-filled sky, over the willow brakes and chokecherry trees, to land with a splash and a silver spray of water in Miawa Creek.

And Johnny Cain screamed.

He stopped the ragged noise of it with his hands, pressing his hands hard against the bones of his face, his breath coming in tearing sobs. Benjo wrapped his arms around the man's shuddering back, and he held him. He closed his eyes and imagined opening his mouth, he imagined the words pouring out of his mouth, slowly, easily, like water from the spout of a pitcher.

"D-Doc Henry . . . He's g-going to muh—muh—make a muh—muh—muh . . ."

Miracle.

DOCTOR LUCAS HENRY WALKED into his parlor, wiping his hands on a huck towel, and looked up to find Johnny Cain standing at his open door with Rachel's son at his side.

The man's and the boy's hands were gripped together in a single fist. It was hard to tell who was holding on to whom. The boy's face was pale, his eyes wide and dark. But the man looked as though he'd passed through to the other side of hell, to a place where the sun had burned to ash, and he had been left screaming in the darkness.

Cain said, "The boy told me she's not dead yet. That you were trying to save her."

Lucas shrugged. "I've managed to remove the bullet, and to repair some of the damage. But I can't lay claim to saving her yet. She has to survive the surgery. And the risk of pneumonia later is considerable."

Lucas knew his words were callous, but he was too tired to care. When he lifted the bullet out of Rachel's lung and saw the faint tremor of a pulse in her neck, he had felt more powerful than God. Now, though, all he wanted was another slug of whiskey.

And here was Johnny Cain, man-killer, wife-killer, standing in the doorway, holding himself still, as though he feared if he so much as breathed he would shatter.

"I've put her in my own bed for now," Lucas said. "You can go on in to her . . . and if you have it in you somewhere, you might try praying."

"I don't know how."

"You could always begin by getting down on your knees."

It was the boy, though, who moved, pulling the man after him.

They walked hand in hand up to the bed. Cain stood, looking down on her. "Rachel," he said, her name a torn whisper.

He dropped abruptly onto his knees beside the bed. He wrapped one arm around the waist of Rachel's son. The other hand stretched out and gripped the sheet that lay across her breast. His back bowed and his head came down, pressing into her dark red hair that lay like a spill of wine over the pillow.

LUCAS LEANED AGAINST THE jamb of his open front door, a half-empty bottle of Rose Bud dangling from his hand, and looked down the deserted road. An acrid haze smeared the horizon and the sky above was murky. Toward the south, where the Circle H spread lay, a big boil of a black cloud was rising and spreading.

He heard the rustle of black taffeta, smelled honeysuckle toilet water. Miss Marilee of the Red House.

She came up to stand beside him. "That Johnny Cain, he sure does love his woman. It's gonna go real hard on him if she dies, after what he done."

"'Two loves I have, of comfort and despair,'" Lucas

drawled. He slanted a look at her, lifting his eyebrows in deliberate mockery. "That's Shakespeare, Miss Marilee."

She lifted her shoulders in a pretty little shrug that set her crop of short curls to bouncing. He saw that she had Rachel's blood on her cuffs, and a streak of it on her neck, like the mark of a kiss.

"I don't know about that, Luc. But I know there's all sorts of love. Deep and shallow, pure and naughty. Blessed and cursed. But the best love, I reckon, is the kind that comes back at you from the person you give it to, bright and blindin' like the sun bouncin' off a mirror."

"I had a love like that once, and I wound up killing her for it." The words shocked him coming out as they did, without thought or premeditation. They burned his throat as if they were fire, and they hurt him in the guts, tearing at all the old wounds that had been suppurating and putrefying for years.

He turned full around to face her, so that she could look into his eyes and know him for what he was. "And I do mean that literally, my dear. I am as much a wife-killer as Johnny Cain in there."

He watched her eyes go wide with hurt and shock, and he almost smiled, for he had at last gotten what he wanted. Or thought he wanted. But then, the years of drinking had taught him not to trust himself or his motives. He was always his own worst enemy.

He turned away from her and settled back against the door frame. His eyes focused on the flame-glazed clouds of smoke billowing on the horizon. "Now, I don't want you to get things all backwards in that pretty and empty little head of yours, Miss Marilee. I didn't become a drunk because I killed my wife, you understand. I killed my wife because I'm a drunk."

He lifted the bottle of Rose Bud and looked at the world through green glass and amber liquid, and then he drank from it, proving to her and to himself that he was as he claimed.

"She begged me to quit," he said, "and I told her I would, but I never really meant it, because a drunk can think of no worse fate than being deprived of his whiskey bottle. One night I came home—inebriated, of course—and found her packing her clothes in a trunk, leaving me just like she promised. We argued and I hit her and she fell down a flight of stairs and broke her neck. She wanted to save me and I knew it, and so I destroyed her before she could. Don't you think that must have been the way of it, sweet Marilee?"

She backed up a step and crossed her arms over her chest. A bright, painful light glittered in her eyes.

"I was cashiered from the cavalry and spent seven years in Leavenworth for what I'd done, and you would probably say that wasn't punishment enough, but you would be wrong." He smiled and he could feel the horror of that smile as it twisted over his face. He held the whiskey bottle up to her, tilting it so that it caught and refracted the sunlight in prisms of amber flame. "Because I have found a way to go to hell without dying."

She shook her head, hard enough to send a single teardrop splashing onto her cheek. "It don't change things, me knowin' what you did. Probably it ought to, but it don't. I love you, Luc Henry, and it won't ever change things either if you can never find it in you to love me back."

Lucas closed his eyes, swallowing back a sigh. He didn't know how he could make her understand that his craving for whiskey was stronger than his need for someone's love. "You think you know what you're saying, but you don't. You think you'll be able to change me, but you can't. I might never break your lovely neck, but I will still end up hurting you."

She struck her breast with her fist, so hard he heard it. "Oh, don't you understand, Luc? *Life* is going to end up hurtin' me, so why not you?"

He stared at her. Her bosom lifted and swelled with her panting breaths, and a blush bloomed like hothouse roses in her cheeks. Her eyes, wet and wide, could shame the blue right out of heaven. She was sweet and pretty, and he thought she probably really did love him, in her way.

She opened her hand and let it fall, looking away from him. "I thought I'd go on up to the Red House and have myself a bath," she said, after the silence had stretched out too long. "But I'll come back later, if you want a little company."

"It's not Saturday."

She gave him a punch on the arm. "Oh, you! I never said nothin' about engagin' in any bed sport. There's always conversation. You ever done that with a woman, Doctor Henry—engage in a little conversation?"

He laughed, and felt his heart warm. But whiskey sometimes had the same effect on him, and he was past telling the difference.

She gave the place on his arm where she had just hit him a little rub. "I'll come back. I ain't nothin' if not persistent."

He watched her walk away, those modest skirts swaying with the chippy's swivel of her hips. Today, for the first time, he had noticed that beneath her dirt-poor ignorance and voluptuous body was an admirable amount of grit. It frightened him that she just went on loving him in spite of everything.

Lucas watched her until she turned down the road toward the Red House, then his attention was caught by the churning dust of a Plain man's wagon. The man pulled the wagon up on the edge of town and climbed out. He walked slowly toward Lucas, but he didn't come all the way up to the house.

He stood in the middle of the road, his long black beard lifting and falling with the hot, gusting wind. He just stood there, silent, and waiting. Lucas had the feeling the man had within him the resources to wait forever.

Lucas didn't have such resources himself. He set his bottle down on the boardwalk and went out to talk to the man. He dispensed with any polite greeting, because a Plain man wouldn't expect it and wouldn't want it.

"If you're here for Rachel, I can tell you she lives for the moment, although I can't promise anything more, and you're not taking her anywhere without first going over my own dead body. But you can come in and see her if you want."

He didn't think he would get a response from the man. There was no expression on that bearded face, or in the pale gray eyes.

But then the man said, "No," and the word came out on a gust of hard breath. "My daughter is dead to me, but you come tell me if she dies, *ja*?"

"Yes. I'll tell you," Lucas said, not understanding. And yet he had the feeling that just by being here this big, gruff Plain man had been forced to surrender some of his rare and precious innocence.

RACHEL OPENED HER EYES, and the first thing she saw was her *Englische* husband kneeling at her bedside. Standing beside him was her son, so she smiled.

Benjo's face was wet, and she thought it must be raining and she was glad, because it had been such a long, dry, hot summer up till now. And then she breathed and it hurt so, she thought the air had caught fire in her lungs.

The rush of pain brought with it the memory of what

had happened, and the hurt from this, from remembering this, was as terrible as the hurt in her chest.

Rachel breathed, gasping; the room darkened and faded. She was cold all over but for the fire in her chest, and she knew that she was dying. *Benjo.* She was dying and leaving her son to grow up without her.

She opened her eyes wide, trying to see her Benjo, but it was so dark, and she was so cold.

Her husband took her hand and brought it up to his mouth. "Rachel," he whispered.

She breathed and the air washed into her lungs on a gust of nearly unbearable pain. "You've killed me, Johnny Cain. You and your gun."

She wasn't sure whether she'd said the words or only thought them. But he must have heard them somehow, for he pressed his face into the side of her neck and she felt his tears. "If I could go in your place . . . Rachel, oh God, Rachel. Let me die for you."

He didn't understand; he'd always had such trouble understanding her and her faith. She didn't fear death, for she would be in the loving arms of her Father in heaven. But it was the thought of the loving arms of those she was leaving behind that broke her heart, the thought of all those joyful moments now lost to them forever.

She could hear her son stammering over his imprisoned words, and she groped for his hand. She had so much to say, to give to him, so much for her son and her man both. But it was so hard to talk when each breath was like swallowing fire.

Her boy's hand felt small and fragile in hers, and she couldn't bear it. "Benjo . . . be strong, be good . . . love God."

She turned her head, her lips brushing her man's cheek. "Johnny . . . never forget how I love you."

A cry of anguish broke deep in his throat. "Rachel. Forgive me."

No, he didn't understand. It wasn't a matter of forgiveness. She loved him with the kind of love that could forgive anything. But even if she had never loved him, she would have had to forgive him.

"I am Plain," she said, with one last surge of strength before the darkness enshrouded her. *In my heart I am Plain.*

THE NIGHT LAY SILENT over Miawa City, but inside Doc Henry's house a lamp was lit at the bedside of the sleeping woman. A man sat nearby, in a winged leather chair, his head nodding as he reluctantly succumbed to a fitful slumber.

It was the music of the wind that woke her: whining in the kitchen stovepipe, whistling under the tin roof, clanging the signboard of the saloon next door.

Rachel breathed, pleased to discover that she could, and that it didn't hurt quite so much anymore. She felt all fuzzy-headed, as if all her senses were wrapped up in wool. Wisps and veils of strange memories clung to her mind.

The man in the chair stirred and leaned over her. His face was dark with a rough growth of beard. His eyes were haggard and red-rimmed, but even in the murky light of the coal oil lamp she could see that they were happy.

"I'm not gonna outlive this love, lady," said Johnny Cain. "So I'd take it kindly if you wouldn't die on me."

She smiled at him, for she knew now she wasn't going to die, and because he had said in his roundabout *Englische* way that he loved her.

Her gaze searched the night-shadowed room for her son. "Benjo?" she said, but it came out as a frog's croak.

"He's sleeping. I'll go get him."

"No, not yet . . . in a moment . . ." Those strong wisps of memory were claiming her again, soft and sweet and filled with such a wondrous and dazzling light. She closed her eyes, trying to recapture them, but they were elusive, fading . . . gone.

"Johnny, I dreamed. And in the dream I heard the most beautiful music. I wanted to stay there, with the music, but I couldn't. I had to come back, to you and our Benjo."

"You've had pneumonia. You almost died so many times we all lost count, and Doc Henry said he was going to write you up in some medical journal as scientific evidence that miracles do happen."

"Do you think it was a miracle?"

His gaze broke from hers and fell to the hands he had clasped between his knees. When he raised his head again, she saw the old wariness in his eyes, but a fragile hope was there as well. He *needed* to believe, and maybe that was all faith really was, she thought. Simply a need to believe.

"I love you, my *Englische* husband," she said.

A stain of color spread across his sharp cheekbones. "Yeah. Me too," he said. "I mean, I feel the same as you do. For you."

She laughed, even though it hurt to do so. She had thought they were forever parted and now they had it all again, their lives, their love. Her gaze traveled lovingly over him, and stopped at his hips.

No gunbelt. No gun.

"It's somewhere at the bottom of Miawa Creek," he said, although she hadn't spoken.

"And is it there to stay, Johnny? Or will you only go and buy another?"

His eyes met hers and they were no longer empty, no

longer cold. "I love you, Rachel. So much it scares me, and I have a hard time even saying the word. But I can't become Plain for you. And I can't change what I've done or the man I've been."

She wanted to reach up and touch him, touch his face, his mouth. But when she tried, all she could manage was a flutter of her fingers. She was so weak still, yet inside she felt strong. Strong and alive.

"I know what you are, Johnny Cain," she said. "I've always known this. But the past is done, and God with his miracle has given us a future."

"My past can always find me," he said. "And I won't run, you know I won't run."

She knew. She had accepted from the start that loving him would be hard and dangerous.

She had to touch him. She lifted her hand, at the same time that he reached for it. He kissed her palm, and then her wrist, where her pulse beat.

"Rachel, I want . . ."

"What is it you want, Johnny Cain?"

They shared a smile, as deep and intimate as a kiss. "Only to go home and raise sheep and watch our Benjo grow into a man, and spend the rest of my life loving you. Just that."

"You ask for a lot, outsider."

He laid the back of her hand against his cheek. His smile was so tender and fragile, it hurt to look at it. "What I've learned of love, I've learned from you. I don't believe in anything, but I believe in you."

He brought her hand to his mouth, and rubbed her knuckles over his lips, his man's lips that looked so hard, but were soft and gentle and loving.

"There was a song," he said. "A hymn we sang in church

when I was a boy." And he said the words in a voice that was deep and roughened with all the feelings he was showing her, offering to her as a gift with his love. "'Amazing grace! how sweet the sound . . . ' And more I don't remember, except for this:

"'I once was lost but now am found.'"